The Pulse Effex Series:
Book Three

DEFIANCE

L.R. Burkard

Lilliput Press

Cover by Design Xpressions, Dayton, OH
Contact TheDesignXpressions@gmail.com

DEFIANCE
Copyright © 2017 by Linore Rose Burkard
Published by Lilliput Press, Ohio

Library of Congress Cataloging-in-Publication Data
Burkard, L.R.

ISBN 978-0-9989663-0-4
ISBN 978-0-9792154-6-9 (ebook)
1.Apocalyptic—Fiction   2. Post-Apocalyptic—Fiction   3.YA Futuristic—
Fiction 4. Christian—Fiction

Printed in the United States of America

All Scripture quotations are from THE HOLY BIBLE, NEW
INTERNATIONAL VERSION®, NIV® Copyright © 1973, 1978, 1984, 2011
by Biblica, Inc.® Used by permission. All rights reserved worldwide.

Catch the gripping start of the *PULSE EFFEX SERIES* in Book One, **PULSE.** *Free download, below.*

"GRABBED MY HEART AND NEVER LET GO"
Had me spellbound! You won't want to miss this gritty and powerful series."
NORA ST. LAURENT, CEO, Book Club Network

No one forgets the day the world stopped.

Andrea, Lexie and Sarah are just ordinary teens until a mysterious event shuts down all technology. In this suspenseful Christian tale, most of the population doesn't survive. Pitting faith and grit against a world without power, the girls and their families must beat the odds.

Told in journal-style prose by three 16 year old girls, PULSE takes readers into a heart-pounding future for America while affirming the power of faith in the darkest of times.

DOWNLOAD FREE CHAPTERS OF *PULSE*:

http://www.LinoreBurkard.com/READER_EXCERPT_PULSE.pdf

(Enter the address into the *browser* for best results)

PULSE is available in print, ebook, and audio editions.

RESILIENCE, Book Two in the *PULSE EFFEX SERIES,* picks up the thrill-ride where *PULSE* left off!

"BAR OF EXCELLENCE RAISED TO NEW HEIGHTS!"
L.R. Burkard is back with the next tale in her dystopian series, and the bar of excellence is raised to new heights with this top quality literary offering!
DEENA PETERSON, Blogger, Book Reviewer

Now that an EMP has sent the U.S. into a dark age, Andrea, Lexie and Sarah struggle to survive against ever-increasing dangers. The appearance of refugee camps could be reassuring—but why is the military forcing people into them?

In this action-packed sequel to *PULSE*, author L.R. Burkard takes readers on a spine-tingling journey into a landscape where teens shoulder rifles instead of school books, and where survival might mean becoming your own worst enemy.

DOWNLOAD FREE CHAPTERS OF *RESILIENCE*:

http://www.LinoreBurkard.com/READER_EXCERPT_RESILIENCE.pdf

(Enter the address into the browser for best results)

RESILIENCE is available in print and ebook editions. Audio coming!

READERS PRAISE *DEFIANCE*

"L.R. Burkard has proven that it's not profanity and sex that makes an intriguing read. With her *Pulse Effex Series*, she delivers action, adventure, and suspense that will captivate readers of all ages!"
MARK GOODWIN, Author of *The Days of Noah Series*

"The riveting story continues with even greater urgency! Ms. Burkard is to be commended for her amazing storytelling - and for portraying how God strengthens his people and gives hope in the darkest hour."
ANGELA L. WALSH, Publisher, Editor, *Christian Library Journal*

"Hooks you from the very first scene and keeps you turning pages. Crackles with tension as you get to know three ordinary teens thrown into a terrifying reality. Strap in and experience the Pulse!"
TERESA SLACK, Author of *Joy Redefined*

"You HAVE to read this series! I finished *DEFIANCE* after re-reading the first two again. ALL within a couple of days! It was awesome!.. I hope you have more coming!"
DAVID PERHAM, Pastor, Former Marine

"You won't want to put it down! You will be challenged in your faith as you read this series."
JODIE WOLFE, Author, Reviewer

"Burkard does her usual great job telling each girl's story, thereby enabling us to keep them straight as we move from one point of view to another. A writer who can keep the reins of various plots in hand without overemphasis on any one is truly to be admired."
PEGGY ELLIS, Writer, Freelance Editor

"What a climactic ending! If that bit with Sarah & Richard doesn't get your heart pounding, you need to check your Pulse! (see what I did there?) ;)"
NICOLE SAGER, Author of Inspirational Fantasy

"A beautiful story that I highly recommend!"
LEE BROOM, Book Reviewer

"When you start one of L.R. Burkard's books, you get sucked in quickly and the outside world fades away. You feel like you could recognize each of her characters if you ever saw them on the street... Although there are many different voices, she does such a wonderful job making each unique, telling them apart is no problem!"
CHRISTINA LI, Author, Journalist

"Another Great Read! Don't Miss It! My 13 year-old son and I are both L.R. Burkard fans! Dystopian Fiction is my favorite genre, but there isn't much that I can allow my son to read due to the language or situations presented. L.R. has filled this void with her 3 novels."
CALE NELSON, Podcaster, Amazon Reviewer

"I finished *DEFIANCE* in the wee hours this morning - a riveting read and a fitting finish to the series!"
DAVID VAN VELDHUIZEN, Amazon Reviewer

"WOW! I've waited for months for *DEFIANCE* and I wasn't disappointed. The author has masterfully woven the lives of 3 young girls and their families into a story that not only draws you into their world...but provides valuable insight into how to survive in a crisis."
SANDI CHRISTIAN, Amazon Reviewer

"Awesome! Great series with characters that do not lose their faith during a very trying time in this country."
DARYL STANDRICH, Amazon Reviewer

"Gripping. Heart-Stopping. Excellent storytelling and highly recommended!"
DONNA SHEPHERD, Author, Pastor's Wife

"This book is a roller coaster ride. I recommend scheduling yourself the time to read it in one go!"
JAIMEE DINNISON, Amazon Reviewer

"Irresistible page turner! L.R. Burkard is a gifted writer and storyteller! DEFIANCE is as fast-paced and exciting as the first two books!"
DIANE ARCHIBALD, Amazon Reviewer

"Yet another fast-paced book in this series where the reader is anxious to see how everything will turn out, yet at the same time doesn't want the book to end!!"
LISA BOGAN, Amazon Reviewer

"I found I could not read this book before going to sleep because I couldn't put it down. Then, when I did finally force myself to go to sleep, I would dream about the story -- it really pulled me in!"
AMAZON REVIEWER

"My teenage daughters and I (father of 55 years old) have very much enjoyed all of these books. They have not only caused us to spend time together reading but we have had lots of meaningful conversations about topics in the books."
DALE STRONG, Amazon Reviewer

"Gripping, Suspenseful Adventure! Warning: this book is hazardous to chores and sleep - once you start, you won't want to put it down!"
AMAZON REVIEWER

"Great for teenagers. I feel as if there isn't a lot of good literature for teenagers and I love it when I come across books for them. I highly recommend this book."
WENDY MARPLE, Amazon Reviewer

"The excitement continues! The action and suspense are intense."
EDWARD ARRINGTON, Amazon Reviewer

"L. R. Burkard has achieved the Tri-fecta of a great read with her Survival series for the family. We dare say we are blown away!"
AMAZON REVIEWER

"Gripping suspense, good character development. I was mesmerized by the writing!"
M. FITZGERALD, Amazon Reviewer

"A Page Turner! I stayed up all night reading! You can't go wrong delving into this book or the other two!"
KASSY PARIS, Book Reviewer

"Incredible, Action-Packed Finale! I feel like I've been on a journey with each one of these characters and now 'normal' is something that means no electricity, no running water, and no letting your guard down. *Ever.*"
AMAZON REVIEWER

A PEEK INSIDE

Angel took a handgun out of a side holster and handed it to me. "We're gonna need you, Sarah."

"I—I've only had a few lessons," I said, weakly.

"Just aim and shoot when you need to," she said, quietly. "It's already chambered. Remember what we taught you—when a bullet's chambered, it's ready. Don't aim it until you're gonna use it and *don't* put your finger on the trigger until you're gonna shoot."

"Here they are!" Richard cried.

The gang of marauders appeared, descending upon the cabin with hoots and shouts that made my blood curdle. I took the gun with a sense of unreality. How could this be happening? It couldn't be, because I, Sarah Weaver, did not take part in real battles! Sarah Weaver was an anxious, fear-filled teenager with enough insecurities for ten girls. I was the one to have panic attacks when alone; the one who'd been taking anti-depressants for two years—until the pulse stopped that.

I held the pistol up with shaky hands. And I knew: This was reality now. This was life, and there was no room for the old Sarah. I could not allow myself to crumple in weakness or fear.

Table of Contents

Who's Who

Andrea Patterson – Former rich kid, best friend of Lexie, rescued with her family and brought to the compound by the Martins (In Book One, *PULSE*).

Lexie Martin – Farm girl whose homestead is now the compound.

Sarah Weaver – Friend of both Andrea and Lexie; town girl, on the run with her brother since the pulse until reaching the McAllister's homestead (in Book Two, *RESILIENCE*).

Richard Weaver – Sarah's brother. College kid, home on a winter break when the pulse hit.

Mr. and Mrs. Martin – Lexie's parents, farm owners whose land is now the compound.

Blake Buchanan – "Boy wonder," science geek, Lexie's boyfriend.

Roper – (Full name, Jerusha Roper). Handsome, trumpet-playing former youth minister intern and worship band leader.

Jared Grice – Stoic ex-military man; came to the compound with his widowed mother, Jolene.

Tex and Angel McAllister – The homesteading couple who took in Sarah and Richard.

Lainie and Laura Martin – Lexie's young twin sisters

Justin Martin – Lexie's toddler brother.

Mr. and Mrs. Buchanan – Blake's parents, good friends of the Martins', the earliest people to move onto the compound.

The Little Buchanans – Blake's younger siblings.

Aiden and Quentin Patterson – Andrea's young twin brothers.

The Wassermans – Young family, church friends, who joined the compound shortly after the Buchanans.

Mr. Simmons – Ex-cop.

Mrs. Schuman – The compound's seamstress.

Mr. and Mrs. Philpot – Latecomers to the compound; Mrs. Philpot is a registered nurse.

Mr. Clepps – D.O. (Licensed physician; a doctor of osteopathic medicine).

Marcus and Bryce – Brothers who lived together before the pulse; Bryce served in Iraq and suffers from PTSD.

Jolene Grice – Jared's mother, former neighbor of the Martins'.

Mr. Prendergast – Large man from the neighborhood, never married; a former teacher.

Cecily Richards – Tall, beautiful black woman of strong faith.

Evangeline Washington – 11 year old daughter of *Mr. Washington*, left at the compound when her father disappeared on horseback with Mrs. Patterson, Andrea's mother (in Book Two, *RESILIENCE*).

Tiffany Patterson – Andrea's mother, not seen since leaving the compound on horseback with Mr. Washington.

(Other compound members are unnamed characters)

Unless the Lord Almighty had left us some survivors, we would have become like Sodom, we would have been like Gomorrah.

He (the LORD) sent darkness, and made the land dark.

Isaiah 1:9, Psalm 105:28a

And the Light shines on in the darkness, for the darkness has never overpowered it. *John 1:5*

CHAPTER ONE

SARAH

I saw him through the morning fog, appearing like a phantom out of the haze. You'd think the sight of a man approaching through the field would send me scurrying to the house in alarm. You'd think it would have me shouting for Angel and Tex to come with rifles at the ready. But I knew who it was. I recognized the wearied determination. That deliberate walk.

But not at first. I'd been out at dawn fetching the morning's water at the pump, and I froze when he came into sight, my heart thumping with fear. People were about the scariest thing you could encounter these days. Then I saw: *It was Richard!* He'd left me here at Tex and Angel McAllister's homestead three weeks ago. When he left without a word to any of us, the McAllisters let me move from the barn loft to their living-room so I wouldn't be alone at night.

See, the McAllisters took us in, letting us sleep in the barn. After the EMP knocked out the electric grid in the dead of winter seven months ago, we were forced from our apartment by a building fire. At first we'd taken shelter in the town library—everyone from our building did. But the library was dirty and crowded, and we were slowly starving. I lost my mother and baby cousin Jesse to starvation.

As soon as the weather allowed, we took off to make our way to Aunt Susan's farm. It was a treacherous journey and we never got there—instead, we ended up here with Tex and Angel. They were wonderful to me and extra kind since Richard took off. But I missed my brother.

A huge lump filled my throat when I saw how defeated and beaten he looked. But I swallowed it and slammed down my half-filled bucket, and ran. I barreled into him, crying on his shirt.

"Hi, sis." He wrapped a weak arm around me. Poor Richard! He must have endured a lot out there. I couldn't talk. I'd been afraid I'd never see him again, that he'd disappear like Dad, and Jessie, and Mom. I didn't realize until seeing him how convinced I'd been of that.

Finally, I pulled my head back to study him. My normally handsome brother was disguised beneath a coat of mud and grime, out of which dull eyes returned my gaze.

"Are you okay?" I asked.

He stared, saying nothing, filling me with alarm. *What had happened to him?* I knew we'd get the details eventually, so I forced myself not to ask. From the house, the dogs barked with excitement—they knew it was Richard, too. I heard the door open and, turning to look, saw Tex and Angel emerge while the dogs spilled out at their heels. Tex carried a rifle in one hand. I came apart from my brother and smiled as the couple approached. They searched Richard's face, unsmiling. Weren't they glad he was back?

Richard hadn't welcomed their Christian evangelizing, true, but he was a good hand on the homestead. He chopped and stacked wood, and had been learning to hunt and process meat. He fished, caught frogs, and set traps for small game. He plucked a newly-slaughtered chicken faster than Angel; and he dug holes for garbage—the stuff that wasn't biodegradable and had to be disposed of somehow. He'd even been the one who always checked the pit (the one I'd fallen into) and the snare that sent him hanging upside down when we first got here. He made sure the traps were set properly, and checked to see if anything was in them.

"Hello, Richard," Tex said, in his heavy voice. Tex had the build and look of a motorcycle gang member, but he was a lot less scary than he appeared. Angel, petite but stocky, nodded her greeting at Richard, her green eyes softer than her husband's.

While Richard tried to deflect the eager attention of all three dogs as they greeted him, she said, "You must be hungry. We're just getting breakfast. Come on in."

Tex, however, hesitated. He studied my brother. "Why'd you come back?"

I didn't think he was sorry to see Richard; I think he wanted to know what made him return when he'd run off like a scared rabbit only weeks ago. Richard sniffed and swallowed. He looked down for a moment. "I had to."

We turned towards the house. "I'll get the bucket, you go ahead," Tex offered, bending down to grab it when we reached the pump. But suddenly the dogs barked differently. They'd come alert, ears perked, and were staring hard across the field to the woods—the direction Richard had come from.

Half-hearted yaps could be ignored, or even a couple of barks by one of the animals. And sometimes the dogs barked at nothing—maybe a bird taking flight, or an animal they could sense or smell that we couldn't see. But before we could stop him, Kole was off, barking furiously, running towards the wood line. Angel grabbed Kool's collar and I got Kane's—just in time.

Tex shouted after Kole, but the dog was off like a thoroughbred at the races. Nervously, I fingered my pepper spray—danger was never far these days. Besides looters and marauders, there were foreign guerrillas on our soil to worry about. Even with Kane at my side I never went out without it. It was the only weapon the McAllister's would trust me with until I submitted to more shooting lessons. For my own safety, they said.

I wanted to learn gun safety and how to shoot; I just couldn't find a good time to do it. Whenever Tex or Angel were ready to spend time on it with me, I had something else to do or was in the middle of something I didn't want to quit. Deep inside, I guess I didn't want to learn. If I knew how to shoot I might have to use that knowledge. *I might have to kill someone.* I'm glad Angel and Tex have guns but I don't think I could live with myself if I had to use one on a human being. I still avoided the memory of the time I put a knife in a man's back to save Richard's life—I could hardly bear to think about it. I couldn't imagine having to deal with more such gruesome memories. So, I just kept putting off lessons.

Tex stared hard after Kole, who had disappeared into the tree line. And then we heard a shot.

"Oh, no!" Angel's voice broke with emotion. "Someone's shot Kole! I just know it!"

"Everyone to the house," Tex ordered, "Until we know what's coming!" He dropped the bucket to pull his rifle, which he often wore slung across his back, into both hands. He cocked the barrel, giving me goosebumps on my arms.

Dragging an unwilling Kane by the collar, I said, "Maybe it's just somebody hunting." I hoped this was the case. "Someone who got frightened by Kole."

"Hunting on our land!" Angel said, her face hard with grief and anger. She doubled her grip on Kool's collar. He was the smallest of the three dogs, a muscular Husky.

"We'll see," said Tex. "We don't know for sure yet that Kole's been shot. We don't know anything but let's not take chances."

As we hurried towards the house, I remembered the bucket—we'd left it there, half-filled with the morning's water. But I was spooked by that shot and no way was I going back for the bucket. Before coming to live with Tex and Angel, Richard and I had encountered ruthless marauders and worse, foreign guerrillas—I didn't want to come face to face with either.

4

"Sarah, you have GOT to learn to handle a firearm!" Angel scolded, as we neared the house. I felt a stab of conviction—she was right, of course. Life wasn't about doing what felt comfortable, it was about staying alive. Surviving. And learning to shoot might be the most important survival skill of all if we got overrun by a gang. Or by a truck-load of those foreign soldiers.

Watching my brother ahead of me, I realized we were lucky to have Richard back—just in time—if this was going to be a battle! At least, I thought it was lucky. Until we got in the house and Tex turned suspicious eyes to my brother.

"Did you come alone?"

Richard scowled. "Of course." Tex stared at him a moment as if trying to read his thoughts.

Angel was at the side of the window, carefully poking aside the curtain with the barrel of her rifle. "I just want to see Kole come out of those woods," she said, and bit her lip. Kane and Kool hadn't ceased their barking, and ran to the windows eagerly the moment we released them in the house. Both dogs had their paws on the sill. They stopped barking only to emit mean, snarling growls, while their eyes searched the outdoor scene.

If we'd let them, they'd run out there like Kole. They were real guard dogs. But we always brought them in if we feared intruders were about lest they'd get killed or taken for food. I tried to silence thoughts that this may have been Kole's fate. We needed our pets. In my heart, I knew it was more than just needing them. We loved them.

Suddenly Angel gasped. "It's a group! They're coming! And I don't see Kole! I'm sure they shot him!"

Tex joined her at the window, his eyes narrowed. I hurried over too. We looked out past the field to the woods where Kole had disappeared. Sure enough, in the distance a group of people had emerged from the tree-line into the field. They were coming from the same direction Richard had come from. Tex turned accusing eyes to my brother.

5

DEFIANCE

"We've got company," he said, heavily. "And something tells me you've been expecting them."

Heart thumping, I realized Tex thought my brother had brought this gang! I started counting them. With the fog almost gone, it looked like maybe fifteen people. They carried things—weapons!—and were definitely coming towards our cabin.

Richard came up next to me and looked out. Turning to Tex, he cried, "I didn't know they were coming! I don't know who they are! I didn't bring them here!"

Tex eyed him grimly. "You're a traitor, Richard."

For a moment I thought Tex would send my brother out there, banish him. I mean, what else could he do, right? But his next words not only ruined that hope but sent a wave of horror down my spine.

"You're a traitor. And traitors deserve death."

CHAPTER TWO

SARAH

I wanted to scream at Tex. *Are you crazy? Richard is not the enemy!* But no words would move from my throat.

"I'm *not* a traitor!" Richard growled.

"He would never do that!" I added, choking out the words. Bile rose in my throat.

The dogs ran from the window to the door and jumped against it, barking savagely. I tried to hush them but it was no use. I felt heart-stricken by Kole's disappearance but having Tex suspect my brother of treachery was worse.

Tex studied the approaching gang with a grim look. He turned to Angel. "We need to lock up. This ain't a social call." Glancing toward my brother, he told her, "Stay with Richard while I shut things down." To me, he said, "C'mon, Sarah! Secure that back door! Get it bolted! We've got no time to spare." Richard looked poised, ready to help, but Tex told him, "You just stay put with Angel here. While I decide what to do with you."

"I could be helping!" he cried. Biting her lip, Angel watched my brother but her face and eyes were sympathetic. It was just how I felt. I shot him a look that I hoped told him so as I passed. Richard's face glowered angrily. He was slumped in the chair as if he'd given up trying to reason with Tex. But as I hurried towards the back I heard him say, "You're just gonna sit here and wait for them to reach us?"

Then, Angel's voice: "We can lock this place up really good. What would you have us do?"

"Fight!" my brother said. "Start on 'em, now, before they get here! Let them know we're not just sitting here waiting to go down!"

I heard Tex closing shutters in the master bedroom as I reached the door. They weren't shutters at all really, but special steel sheets which could be manually lowered by a crank to cover the window completely in a steel shell.

The cranks were folded inside small recesses in the walls so I hadn't noticed them right away when Richard and I first got to the cabin. But like other preparations Tex and Angel had in place, the window coverings were sheer genius.

In fact I now knew about all the defenses they'd built into the cabin; things that made it extra secure against threats like this approaching band. Things that weren't visible to the eye at first but which I'd discovered over time or been shown by Angel. So instead of the normal log cabin I thought it was (albeit one with a great deal of nifty survival gear) now I knew there was nothing normal about it. It was a specially crafted survival home—and we were about to find out if the extra defenses were going to keep us alive!

I found the back door locked as it was supposed to be. We kept it that way so we didn't have to worry about anyone entering without an invitation. So all I had to do was slide the bars across it and lock them into place to secure it further. From the outside it looked like a regular wooden door but it was reinforced with rebar in the wood, extra-large steel screws in the frame, and with seven steel bars across it, there was no way it would be breached.

The cabin had other built-in defenses, too. The logs of the walls were also reinforced with steel bars and metal wiring. As I said, brilliant. But I'd never seen the cabin in full lock-down before and with each steel shade that Tex lowered, the interior grew darker. It felt like getting sealed up in a tin of sardines. Yet, despite a mild sense of claustrophobia, I felt reassured—especially when Angel lit a battery-powered lamp so we could see better.

I was struggling to lower the shade over the storage room window when Tex joined me and finished the job. I started to apologize for needing his help but he said, with a wink, "The crank is meant to work without electricity—not without muscle."

As we returned to the main living area, Richard asked, "If you close up every window, how are you gonna know what they're doing out there?"

Tex, ignoring him, proceeded to lower the last metal shade over the window that faced the on-comers but stopped when it was halfway down. Daylight—our last connection to the outside world—filtered through. He turned to my brother. "If they want to talk, I'm listening. If they shoot, I'll lower that shade and we'll be like snug bugs in a rug."

"But blind as bats!" Richard said.

Angel and I stood by tensely.

"Are you worried about your friends out there?" Tex asked.

Richard, sighing, shook his head. "I don't know those people! I don't know anybody out there!

Tex, standing to one side of the window, peered out carefully. "Maybe we should send you out there and find out."

"No!" I shouted.

Tex eyed me with regret. "I'm sorry, Sarah, but you know yourself these people came on his heels." He stared outside for a moment. "Looks like about twenty of them." To Angel, he added, "This may be too many for us, even with our precautions in place. Get ready for Plan B. But first—" He looked at Richard. "You betrayed us."

Angel, wide-eyed, scurried to the kitchen. "Plan B—already?" she asked, as if not wanting to believe it. She grabbed an insulated cooler that we used when gathering garden produce, and shoved it at me. "Empty whatever you can from the ice box into this, quickly."

Richard, frowning, said, "If you were smart, you'd be taking shots at them by now! *Why* are you letting them get close?" But Angel and Tex ignored him.

Angel asked, "You really think we need Plan B? They can't get in, hon! That was the idea to begin with, wasn't it? Being able to stay up here as long as possible, even through an attack?" Her face twisted as she pleaded.

My eyes met Richard's. I knew he was wondering about this mysterious "Plan B." Neither of us had been trusted with that information but I was highly curious. I began doing as Angel said, filling the insulated tote, but I found myself moving slowly. It didn't make sense to me to stop and pack a bag; it felt useless. Sure, food was precious, but how could we carry it? And where did Angel think we could run to? It seemed stupidly time-consuming if what we needed to do was run. Tex, meanwhile, was looking back and forth from the oncoming mob to my brother, his eyes creased with concern.

"I didn't betray you, I swear! I'm telling you to start picking them off! Would I do that if I was their friend?" Richard cried.

Tex answered slowly. "I don't know what you do to your friends, Richard. That's the problem right now, isn't it?"

"THEY are the problem!" Richard said, nodding his head towards the outdoors. "You need to start shooting! Now, before they get close!"

I took a quick peek to see how far they were, and saw—no one! "They're gone!" I cried, in relief.

"They're not gone, they've dropped down. They're crouching and crawling towards us," Angel said, sardonically. She'd been periodically watching their progress while stuffing kitchen supplies in a huge duffel bag. At the window, the dogs whimpered because the gang had gone out of sight. They ran to the door, sniffing intently along the bottom and side, desperate to keep the scent. Low, guttural growls came from their throats. Tex set his rifle down, letting it rest against his leg, and pulled out a smaller gun from a waist holster. I watched in mute horror as he pointed it at Richard!

"I didn't betray you!" Richard growled.

"I think you did, Richard. But that's not why I'm doing this. I'd settle for banishing you for treachery—but I don't dare open the door now. And I can't let you see what we do next. Our backup plan has got to stay secret—from that crowd." He nodded back towards the approaching gang.

"I didn't bring them!" Richard cried. "I came back alone! I even checked to make sure no one was on me!"

10

"How do you explain that?" Tex asked angrily, jerking his head towards the intruders. "They came right on your tail."

"I didn't bring them!" he insisted. "I was running FROM them!"

Tex sighed heavily. "You ran them right to us."

Richard looked bewildered. His face fell. "I didn't mean to," he said, quietly.

My heart went out for my brother. He'd tried to be careful, but unwittingly had led them to our homestead! Surely Tex would understand he hadn't meant to!

"Fine. Go on; do it," Richard said, grimly, eying Tex's handgun. I gasped. My heart flew to my throat.

"I didn't mean to bring them," he continued. "But I guess I did."

"No!" I shouted. "He didn't bring them! It was just"—I groped for words. "Bad luck!"

"I don't believe in luck, good or bad," Tex said. He was staring at my brother, never taking his eyes from his face.

"You may as well let him shoot me," Richard said to me. "We're dead anyway, by the looks of it. Because we should be picking them off right now but we're all sitting here like zombies doing nothing."

"No!" I cried again, looking from my brother to Tex, while all the agony I felt sent hot blood to my face. My heart pounded in my ears and suddenly I was the old Sarah, the one who fainted when things got horrible. I sat quickly and put my head down, taking deep breaths. How could Tex be willing to shoot my brother? I knew it wasn't something he wanted to do, but if push came to shove, Tex did what needed doing. I prayed he would realize this was *not* one of those things.

Angel touched my arm gently. She said to Tex, in a coaxing tone, "C'mon, hon, leave him be. Richard didn't mean to lead anyone here." My brother looked into her face and I saw something in his eyes waver, as though a sliver of hardness fell away. Sudden hope filled my heart—Angel believed Richard!

I raised my head and stared imploringly at Tex. "He would never lead a mob to you—or to me," I said. Hardly realizing it, I was clenching my fists.

Tex stared at Richard—I found out later he was praying silently, asking God to tell him what to do!

Suddenly from outside the eerie sounds of hoots and hollers and whoops descended on us. They were bone-chilling sounds, battle cries! We were like pioneers facing savage Indians on the warpath. I was grateful for the extra defenses of the cabin, but it spooked me that Tex didn't seem to put much stock in them. He was ready to move to his mysterious Plan B.

"Sarah, you're wasting time!"Angel scolded, turning on me. "You should have emptied that ice box by now!"

"I need to know he's not going to shoot my brother!"

"Instead of worrying about me, you could have been taking down *that* crowd," Richard, said, nodding towards the howling intruders. "We could have wiped them out by now!"

And then, while Angel and I looked imploringly at Tex, he nodded at Richard, while returning his pistol to its holster. "Okay," he said. He turned his gaze to Angel as if his next words were for her benefit. "We'll take your word for it, Richard."

His slow, heavy voice never sounded sweeter! I had an urge to run over and hug him. Instead, I took a shuddering breath deep with relief, and went back to stuffing supplies into the insulated tote bag. Richard sprang into action. He fell to his knees and pulled out one of the AR-15s Tex and Angel kept beneath the furniture, and then, scrambling to his feet, rushed toward the window.

"What're you doing?" Tex asked him, his face creased in concern.

Richard gritted his teeth. "Defending this place!" And in the next second, he'd sent a shot out, and then another and another. My ears ached, my heart raced, but I kept grabbing supplies. I filled the insulated tote and grabbed a box, filling it with blankets, an axe, oil lamps, anything that I deemed useful, though I had no clue how we'd actually manage to bring it all if we did end up following a back-up plan.

Angel dropped to her knees in front of the bookshelf and pulled out another AR. "I'll get all the guns." She pulled a few more rifles from hiding places, as I half-watched and half-worked, hardly knowing what-all I threw into the tote.

The dogs threw themselves at the door, barking viciously. And then a burst of gunfire blasted through the half-opened window, sending shards splintering into the room. Tex rushed over to the right of the window as the barrage continued. Angel and I fell to the floor. As I lay there helplessly covering my ears with my hands, I knew what it meant to have your heart in your throat. I literally could not swallow.

Richard fired until he'd emptied the magazine of his rifle. Looking around, he threw it aside and grabbed one that Angel had dragged out, checked that it was loaded, and sent more shots out the window. He'd become well versed in using guns—unlike me—since he had practiced often.

I was unable to do anything now except lay there in frozen terror and misery, my head exploding from the noise. My few shooting lessons had been with a small caliber pistol—outdoors. Here inside, the AR was deafening, going through my whole being.

Angel nudged me and put something in my hands. "Put them on," she said. "It'll help." I looked down and saw two small orange foamy things. Earplugs! I stuffed them into my ears.

Tex had been trying, between dodging bullets and returning fire, to lower the metal shade. Outside, the awful cries and whoops continued, seeming to circle the house now, though I couldn't be sure. My throat tightened again. It seemed certain than ever that we'd never be able to escape the cabin and go to any backup plan! They had us surrounded! Why hadn't Tex and Angel realized this would happen? How had they expected to escape?

Richard said, "If you close that up, we can't fight back."

13

"I don't want to fight back if I don't have to," said Tex. "I just want to keep us safe." But even as he spoke more gunfire sounded, hitting the walls of the cabin and the door.

"Tex!" screamed Angel. "Move away from there!" He moved aside slightly, still determined to lower the metal. I saw a splotch of red appear on his side. He'd been shot!

As he struggled with the crank, we realized the sheet was not going down.

"Look, it's damaged!" Richard cried, pointing with the barrel of his rifle to a bubble in the metal right near the side groove. It was a warp caused by a single bullet but it was enough to prevent the sheet from going down. Meanwhile, their shooting continued. A picture on the wall behind me lurched and fell with a crash.

"That settles it!" Tex said. "Time for Plan B."

"This window is only one opening!" cried Richard. "We can use it against them."

"I say we run," said Tex. "We were supposed to be safe here— heck, invulnerable, with every opening fortified. This is a break in our defenses and that's all an enemy needs—one opening, one weakness."

"But it's also a strategic advantage for us—it gives us a way to fight back instead of just sitting in here and doing nothing!" Richard cried. "We shouldn't run without a fight!"

I thought my brother heroic at that moment considering he was already battle weary and exhausted even before this attack. He'd come home grimy and tired, and yet here he was, his eyes blazing with conviction, championing a fight. I felt proud of him—even though I liked Tex's idea, too—of sealing up the cabin and hunkering down in safety while chaos raged out there. But much as I detested the noise and cringed at the danger, I too believed fighting was our best hope. After all, Plan B was doomed. It had to be. I couldn't understand how Tex and Angel could be foolish enough to think we could possibly escape— they were so smart about everything else!

Tex eyed Richard. "My plan was to rely on our defenses when the time came to do so. But when I see what's out there—and this weak spot—this opening—I can't do it. I need Angel safe." Tex's eyes were usually either sparkling with humor or absolutely unreadable. But as he spoke now he swallowed, and his eyes revealed a turmoil I'd not seen in him before. When Angel's life was on the line, it brought out his heart, loud and clear.

"We've got *great* defenses everywhere else!" Richard cried. "The four of us can defend this one window! No one is gonna get over that windowsill alive!"

"You think we have a chance against a horde like that? They've got axes and hammers—they're gonna tear this place apart!"

"We've got cover. They don't," Richard said. "Are there any hidden traps around the property?"

"They got past the traps—thanks to you," Tex answered, heavily.

"No, not the ones out there, I mean closer traps—ones I don't know about. Don't you have any close to the cabin?"

"No, they'd endanger the dogs! But look—all that crowd needs to do is throw in a few burning torches—or tear gas—and we're sunk. We'll be overrun in minutes."

"If they had tear gas, they would've used it already," said Richard. "But what have you got besides rifles? We need something like...grenades."

Tex shook his head. "We're not like them out there," he nodded towards the outside. "We didn't plan on ways to hurt people. Just ways to stay safe. If you notice, we caught you and Sarah by trapping you— not harming you." He looked at his wife. "What do you say, darlin'? Do we run—or keep fighting?"

Angel frowned. She glanced from Richard to Tex and back again. "I agree with Richard," she said. "I think we should fight. Then if we *have* to, we'll go to Plan B."

That settled it for Tex, who started issuing orders. "Drag all that stuff down the hallway," he told Richard, motioning at the duffel bags and other totes that Angel and I had filled.

"Just leave them in the hall?" Richard asked, surprised.

"Yes!" Tex's voice was sharp. "And hurry! If we're gonna do this—defy this invasion—we need to get at it!"

I watched Richard hurry the bags down the hallway. Now and then I'd seen Angel pile things up there, things that later disappeared but didn't end up in the storage room. I figured it all went to the *mystery* storage area—the one Angel hadn't let me see yet. But how could we take that stuff anywhere now? With marauders circling the place! And why bother bringing it to the hallway at all? If we did eventually have to make a run for it, any baggage would only slow us down.

Angel had leashed the dogs after the window shattered, circling the leashes around a wooden post away from the broken glass. They submitted with surprising docility to being leashed. I sensed they were tired from all the excitement since their fierce barks had degenerated into occasional shrill yaps, though they kept up a stream of suspicious snarls, eyes glued to whichever direction the outside noises came from.

Tex and Richard overturned the coffee table and lined the sofa cushions against it. The four of us crouched behind this like soldiers in a trench, guns at the ready—except for me, since I don't shoot.

Angel spotted the blood on Tex's shirt and gasped. "You've been shot!" She dropped her rifle to take a better look, but Tex gently removed her hand.

"It's just a flesh wound," he said. "Glass got me, not a bullet." Then he turned to me. "Sarah, you need to be armed, dumpling."

I stared at him uncomprehendingly. Angel took a handgun out of a side holster and handed it to me. "We're gonna need you, Sarah."

"I—I've only had a few lessons," I said, weakly.

She placed the heavy pistol in my hand. "Just aim and shoot when you need to," she said, quietly. "It's already chambered. Remember what we taught you—when a bullet's chambered, it's ready. Don't aim it until you're gonna use it and *don't* put your finger on the trigger until you're gonna shoot."

"Here they are!" Richard cried.

The gang of marauders appeared, descending upon the cabin with hoots and shouts that made my blood curdle. I held up the gun with

16

a sense of unreality. How could this be happening? It couldn't be, because I, Sarah Weaver, did not take part in real battles. Sarah Weaver was an anxious, fear-filled teenager with enough insecurities for ten girls. I was the one to have panic attacks when alone; the one who'd been taking anti-depressants for two years—until the pulse stopped that. But I took the pistol, heart pounding in my throat.

I saw a dark figure approaching through the jagged window. Brief blurs rushed past as the hoots and shouts picked up. Tex and Richard were taking shots, deafening blasts that made me wince despite the ear plugs. Then we heard whacks at the doors—axes hitting the wood from both the front and back of the cabin! Tex said, "That ain't gonna work; they'll hit rebar. And we got three inch screws in those joints. Nothing's gonna break those doors in."

His words did not remove my fear or the pounding of my heart. But as I raised the cold metal gun with shaking hands, I knew: This was reality now. This was life, and there was no room for the old Sarah. I could not allow myself to crumple in weakness or fear.

"Can we pray?" I gasped.

"I *am* praying," breathed Angel.

Richard looked at me. I felt myself blush, knowing how he scoffed at God and prayer. He'd left because of his aversion to God. Would he mock me? Show his disgust, as he had before? To my surprise, he nodded. And then said words that amazed me.

"I'm praying, too."

CHAPTER THREE

SARAH

The four of us remained hunkered down behind our makeshift protection while Angel prayed aloud.

"Amen," I said, afterward, followed by Tex, and then—to my delight—by Richard! My heart glowed with the thought that for some reason, though he'd had to return to us beaten, admitting defeat—his attitude to the Lord had somehow softened. I couldn't wait to hear his story but right now the unnerving sounds of axes and hammers—or whatever they were using—pounding the walls and doors made it hard to think of anything except what was happening outside. My whole body seemed to throb with each whack.

Suddenly we heard more metallic thuds instead of the sharp whacks or sounds of wood splintering, which had been common at first.

"They're hitting the rebar," said Tex.

Around the windows we also heard whacks and thuds—they were trying every possible opening to get inside. At least the gunfire had ceased. When I asked why they weren't shooting, Tex said, "I don't think they have bullets to spare—that's good news for us." Then, after another minute of waiting, he said, "I've got an idea." He rose cautiously and disappeared down the hallway.

I peeked above the top edge of the table and saw, from time to time, an intruder rush past. Each one looked fierce, holding some kind of weapon such as an axe or shovel, and with faces painted in camo or black. They held things I didn't recognize too, but which looked like tools. Whenever a blur rushed past, Richard sent shots out after it.

"They've got men down," he said. He quickly drew the mag from his rifle and pulled another from a side pocket and shoved it into place. "Maybe they'll start to have second thoughts." There were whacks still coming against the wall between the window and door.

Peering outside carefully from beside the window, Richard suddenly stuck out his head and let loose with the gun, aiming right towards whoever was out there against the house.

He took three shots and then hurried to pull himself in again. To my horror, I saw he had just dodged being hit by a heavy axe which whammed down on the windowsill where it became lodged. I'd been frozen in position, still holding the gun. It never even occurred to me to pull the trigger when I saw that figure. My head and my hands were miles apart. But Angel was also in firing position, and no sooner had Richard pulled himself out of the way than she took her shot, dropping the would-be assassin with a thud.

The axe remained eerily stuck in the wood. I heard shouting and recognized the sound of women's voices, which surprised me. Somehow, the idea of murderous marauders had always been of men. But it wasn't just men—there were women in this raiding party, too! A sickening feeling grew in the pit of my stomach.

While I stood there reflecting, Richard called to Angel for another mag. Suddenly the axe in the window moved—someone had grabbed it! Angel rushed forward, her face grim and determined. When she took her shot, I wasn't surprised to see the axe handle sway unsteadily for a moment—and then fall.

"Good shot," Richard said, nodding at Angel. But she looked deeply disturbed. I could tell she hated having to shoot anyone.

Tex finally returned holding a bullhorn in one hand. He stopped by Angel. "Maybe I can talk some sense into these people," he said.

Richard shook his head. "They're losing men and they're still coming at us. Your bullhorn isn't going to stop them."

Ignoring him, Tex went beside the window, peering out as best he could. Richard went over to the door, listening intently to the sounds of hacking that were still coming from outside. He raised his gun and aimed—at the door.

"You could hit rebar," said Tex, "and have that bullet bounce right back at you."

19

Richard said, "No. Look." He nodded at the door, where the head of an axe was just beginning to splinter through. When it was pulled out for the next whack, Richard aimed right at that small opening and sent two bullets out in quick succession. The axe didn't reappear.

Tex nodded, but he said, "Cease fire for now. I'm going to try and reason with them."

Richard sniffed and drew back. Tex turned to us. "Stay behind the table there in case they start firing again." Turning back to the window but keeping to the side, he pointed the bullhorn out.

Attention! Stop your assault! You have lost men and will continue to lose more. This structure is reinforced with steel—you will not be able to take it down.

I liked how his voice took on extra authority through the bullhorn. Tex had a powerful voice to begin with. It may have been hiding a big heart but most people would never know it. Through the bullhorn, he sounded formidable.

Be aware, Tex continued, *we are prepared to use chemical weapons that will wipe you out. If you do not cease and desist, we WILL use these weapons!* He paused. We heard nothing in response, so he added, *Turn around and go back the way you came, NOW.* He waited two beats and added, *You will have NO survivors!*

Turning to us he said, "If this don't work, we're bailing out of here."

"You mean give up?" Richard asked. "I thought we agreed not to give up—we can fight!" He paused. "And there's no way we can get away from here—they've got us surrounded by now or they're idiots."

"If they keep hacking at these walls, rebar or not, they will get through," said Tex. "We are not impregnable."

"If they hack at the walls, we shoot them through the walls."

"That sounds good, Richard, but if they breach a wall, get inside, we are bound to get hurt—or killed. I can't have that."

I had a horrible thought. "What if they burn us down?" I'd never forget the somber memory of how Richard and I had been burned out of a wonderful, food-rich home. Before that, we'd been burned out of our

20

apartment—right after the pulse happened—and then out of that well-supplied house, which was like a sanctuary. The burning of homes and businesses seemed to be the new order of the day. That last house had been filled with stored food and other supplies—things marauders would want—but foreign soldiers had heartlessly burned it. This band wasn't military but what if they resorted to the same tactic? No amount of steel-reinforced walls could save us, then. We were so packaged up inside this place that we'd burn right down with the house. We were trapped like rats.

Angel had been watching through the window. "Wait a minute, I think they're leaving!" she hissed.

I glanced outside. "They are!" I counted ten people walking quickly away from the cabin, back the way they'd come. Only a small circle of them remained, two men and a woman wearing a green knit hat. They stood, glancing back and forth at us, conferring. I wondered why anyone would wear a hat in late June, but had no time to think about it further because Tex's voice boomed out again.

You have been warned! You have ten seconds to retreat! This chemical agent will rapidly cause death! He started a countdown. *Ten! Nine! Eight!...*

The circle of marauders glanced at us but continued their little pow-wow. One man seemed to be the leader, as he was doing the talking. I felt breathless with anxiety as we waited to see if Tex's bluff would work. What if they didn't buy it? What if they set fire to us? Could we really fall back on their Plan B? What sort of plan could possibly help us out of such a jam?

Five! Four!

The leader gave a mock salute. And then, right before our eyes, they started away, back towards the woods, the way they'd come. Angel peeped, "Praise God!"

But I froze in a stupor of confusion and sorrow. That man's salute—it was exactly the gesture my dad used to give me when I argued a point with him successfully. Most of the time I didn't win an argument with either of my parents, but if I had a really good point—

such as why the family should make a certain purchase or not go on a particular vacation—my dad would concede defeat with a mock salute. In the past, it made me or Richard smile—it conveyed a measure of respect, even if only a small measure. Now, the gesture filled me with a stab of grief. If only that stupid man hadn't done that! It made me think of my father and remember, with a hollow ache, that I missed him terribly.

Richard touched my arm. He'd seen the salute, too. "It's okay," he said, as I blinked tearfully at him. "Don't let it get to you. It's just a coincidence."

"Don't worry, Sarah, they're *leaving!*" Angel repeated, not understanding what upset me. I heard Tex give out a big sigh—he was as relieved as any of us. But then, while we watched, three men appeared from around back.

Three! Two! Tex resumed his count. I noticed then I was covered in cold sweat. Was I about to have a panic attack? After months without one—the worst months of my life and with more reason to panic than ever—I'd stopped having attacks. But right now I felt one coming on. I wasn't really surprised. Even though I was no longer that old Sarah, the new me couldn't handle this! *A real battle, with real guns and people dying—and an eerie reminder of my father!*

As the men argued, Tex barked out, *ONE! Your time is up!* I held my breath as we watched. And then, oh, the relief, as the stragglers, the last of them, turned tail and took off running. The leader and the woman in the hat had lingered, waiting for these last few men, motioning for them to follow the others. They now joined the line of retreat, the woman in the rear.

"Thank God!" I said. My hands and head were clammy, and my stomach, queasy. But they turned back! And they hadn't burned us down. And we hadn't had to resort to the mysterious Plan B. We were alive and well.

Except, perhaps, for Kole.

I pulled out my earplugs and glanced at Richard. I tried to give him a smile but knew it wavered. I wanted to curl up and cry tears of relief, really. But suddenly a shot, so close and loud and unexpected that I gasped and fell, shattered that small window of relief. It was Angel! For a moment I could only gape, scowling at her in shock, while my ears rang. She, in turn, was frozen in shooting position, her rifle still pointed out, poised as if to shoot again. She had a look on her face such as I'd never seen before. And then she seemed shaken, blinking back tears.

Tex stared at her in consternation, and then back out the window. "Hon! They were retreating! And you hit a woman!"

"Why'd you shoot?" I cried.

While we watched, the leader and another man turned back, holding their hands up in a gesture of surrender. They bent over the fallen figure. In a moment they lifted her to a sitting position and then the second man hauled her up and over his shoulder. The leader stared back at us scowling, it seemed to me. I didn't blame him—Angel had gone against Tex's word. Even though they were retreating, she'd shot one of them.

Angel wiped away a tear. "That woman was wearing Doris's hat! That means they've killed Doris! She would never give up that hat willingly!" I'd met Doris and her husband Tim, old friends of the McAllisters. They were the nearest neighbors to the right, after a quarter mile of woods. They were not as prepared as the McAllisters with defenses but had stored a great deal of beans and rice and other food stuffs. They knew how to bypass the traps and reach the cabin safely but hadn't been by lately. Angel had expressed concern about them, since we hadn't seen them for a couple of weeks.

"I'll bet they cleaned them out and that's why they came to us, now!" she cried, still wiping a tear from her face.

"No, hon; they followed Richard here."

"That was Doris's hat!" Angel insisted. "I just know she's been killed!" Her voice broke, and Tex put an arm around her. The four of us continued to stare out, watching as the last of the marauders disappeared into the woods.

Tex pulled Angel into an embrace. "We'll check on Doris and Tim when it's safe." He paused. "Let's just hope this band suffered enough here not to come back."

Richard stared silently out at the now empty field. "They didn't suffer enough." He shook his head. "We should have wiped them out before they even got close."

———————◆———————

Angel came to us tearfully that night, holding her Bible against her chest. "I'm sorry I killed that woman," she said. "It's God's job to get revenge, not mine. I shouldn't have done it—that hat just made me sure they'd killed Doris!" She shook her head, and a few tears ran silently down her face.

"How do you know it was Doris's hat?" I asked.

Angel looked at me with somber, tortured eyes. "Why would anyone be wearing a hat now, in June, unless they just got it?" She paused. "Besides, I can tell it's Doris's." She shut her eyes, holding back tears. "I made her that hat."

"Well, you didn't kill her," I said, trying to help. "I saw her moving when they picked her up."

Angel shook her head. "Injuring her might be even worse. They can't exactly take her to the nearest hospital! I've made them mad."

After a heavy pause, she added, "Now they'll want revenge—and it's all my fault!"

CHAPTER FOUR

SARAH

We took turns keeping watch, and stayed in the house for the rest of the day except for a tense hour while Tex and Richard checked to see if we had any chickens left. The barn had been locked but was broken into. It worried Tex that the marauders had seen Daisy the mule.

"She was loose," he said, "which means they tried to take her. I scratched behind her ears and sweet talked her; got her tied up again." He looked at us. "Thank God she's 'stubborn as a mule,' and won't go with a stranger—or we'd have lost her."

We were all glad Daisy was still with us. But Tex figures that gang wasn't starving—or they'd have killed her for meat. Maybe they still planned on returning to do that.

Out of all our chickens, only three were found. Two were missed by the marauders because they'd been foraging in dense shrubs behind the cabin, and one was on top of the coop. Angel was downcast about losing the rest. Eggs were an important part of our diets and, unless we found a rooster somewhere, the three hens would eventually stop laying and we'd be out of luck.

It was hard to see Angel, who was mostly a happy person, walking around with a frown. She'd come through the EMP—which meant the loss of so much like electricity, transportation, communication, and technology—without losing her customary optimism. But somehow the attack on the cabin had chipped it away. Kole hadn't returned and the loss of the chickens, the damage to the house and the close call we'd had with marauders—plus that Doris and Tim were likely dead—were all taking their toll. I told her how sorry I was. She looked surprised for a moment and then searched my face.

"It's O.K., Sarah. I'll bounce back." Her smile was sad. "I always do. I just need to get alone with God for awhile. The Lord has a way of changing my perspective about things." She took a deep breath. "And I'm thankful, really, that we're alive."

Towards evening we spotted a new black plume in the sky in the north. Tex estimated the fire was within a mile or two of us. That made me nervous because I had to wonder if those foreign soldiers were in the area. Like the ones that burned up the last house Richard and I stayed in for awhile. But Tex thinks the fire is a sign of that gang who attacked us, still in the vicinity.

Anyway, Tex and Richard moved the three last chickens and their nesting boxes into the back storage room of the cabin. Tex said they'd build a shed right up against the house for the animals so it would be easy to take them inside in the future.

"Bring the mule in the *house*?" I asked.

"Only when we have to." He chuckled at my astonishment. "You know, in Jesus's day, the residents of a house slept in the upper floor and the roof—while the ground level was for animals, to keep 'em safe from thieves at night. Looks like we need to go back to first century practices to keep our animals safe. But see, it ain't that unusual."

"It will be, for you," I said. "You don't have a second floor. I'm used to barn smells from sleeping in the loft—so is Richard. But I think you'll have some adjusting to do."

Angel smiled. "I can do that. It'll be worth it to keep our last livestock."

"In the meantime," said Tex, "we'll only let them out where it's fenced." We had a large fenced-in area behind and to one side of the cabin that was primarily "dog domain," a place for them to be outdoors without us worrying about them taking off. That reminded us of Kole, who had not returned.

Tex looked at Angel. "I'll take a look for Kole tomorrow."

She shook her head. "No, you won't. If he's alive, he'll come back. If he's not—there's no sense risking your neck."

"We're going out to lay new traps so I'll just keep a look for him while we're out there."

I hope Kole is alive! Even though the cabin is more crowded than ever with chickens in the storage room, and the hallway crammed with boxes and totes we moved to make space for them. I'd been sleeping on the sofa at night since Richard left—and now I was gladder than ever about that. The cabin withstood the attack, but the barn hadn't. The industrial, heavy-duty lock on the barn door had held despite being tampered with, but they'd got in anyway, by hacking a big hole right through a wall. I wouldn't feel safe out there anymore.

Now I'd be sharing the front room with Richard, I supposed, because he wouldn't be safe in the barn, either. I'd always found it strange that the cabin had only one bedroom. I once asked Angel why they didn't have at least two and she said the cabin was built as a "getaway" house, not a place to entertain friends or family. Angel and Tex had lived elsewhere before the pulse. I tried to get her to talk about it, their home, and where they'd come from, but all I got was an impression. The impression was that they'd had plenty of money, more than one home, and had built this safe house "just in case."

When the EMP took down the grid, that "just in case" became home.

The totes from the storage room remained in the hallway, which looked like a loading dock. It still defied reason to me, because I saw no means of ever getting all that stuff away from the house if we had to make a run for it. But I did get a chance to read labels I'd never seen before such as, "Work Gloves, Cleaning Supplies, Extra Socks." Others were full of things I did know about, like tissues and toilet paper and napkins—precious as gold now that stores weren't around. The totes were wonderfully reassuring because their contents made the difference between feeling like primitive campers or comfortable ones. But what if we had to leave the cabin? We'd be on the run again! I dreaded the thought.

We'd had to survive, Richard and I, for months without paper goods or any new supplies, without decent food or enough water. It was blissful not to live like that anymore. I admired the McAllisters for their foresight—but I wished I knew how their "Plan B" could help us keep it all.

While Richard and the dogs kept watch, Tex hauled in some water—using a plastic bucket because our steel one had vanished, and Angel began to prepare a simple supper of beans and rice. I set the table. We were all trying to pretend things were normal but nothing felt normal.

As if reading my mind, Tex said, "We'll get the critters into a new shed as soon as possible and move you and Richard into that room." He paused. "For tonight, you'll both have to make do in the front room here."

Richard had grabbed everything remaining of our meager belongings from the loft but I'd already moved my important stuff into my backpack, which I always kept near me. Even before the attack I was still in an "apocalypse mentality" you might say, and I wore my backpack if I went anywhere on the property. In addition to its holding my two-way, I just felt like every little thing was precious. I didn't want to risk losing anything.

It had grown heavy and Angel admonished me more than once that I wasted energy carrying it all around when I already had so much work to do. But I wanted all of it—my water bottles, granola bars, tissues, flashlight, extra batteries, pepper spray, needle and thread, scissors, band-aids, antibiotic lotion, my journal, a pen and a pencil, a ponytail holder, nail clipper, matches, and floss. The floss was for fishing line but now and then I couldn't resist the urge to clean my teeth. I have a toothbrush which I keep in the cabin (thanks to Angel) but on those rare occasions when I floss—ah!

Richard did still have things in the barn that he hadn't taken with him when he left us—an extra shirt and socks, and I don't know what else but it was all there. The marauders hadn't bothered with the loft, probably because most held nothing but hay.

Tex spent more than an hour trying to flatten the bubble in the metal shade that hadn't worked during the attack. He couldn't seem to get it flat enough, or something else was preventing it from working.

Finally, he nailed some boards across the opening. "Tomorrow," he said to Richard, "we brick up this window."

"Oh, hon, that'll make it so dark in here!" cried Angel. "We'll have to use up more candles and batteries just to see what we're doing."

"Dark and safe," he said. But he nodded towards Richard and we saw that my brother had fallen asleep at the table. He hadn't even made it over to the corner of the room where we laid his sleeping bag. His head was on his arms, his face to one side, and he was sleeping like a baby.

"He's exhausted," said Angel, softly. "Think about it—he got home this morning in bad shape and then he fought with us and went out with you to the barn—my goodness, he probably needs a week of sleep to catch up."

"Well, he can't sleep for a week," said Tex. "He can't sleep more than a night. I'll need his help tomorrow. We've got repairs to make, and that shed to build—." He paused, took a sip of water and added, "Besides rigging up a whole lot of new traps. I don't trust that bunch to stay gone for long. Not when they got all those chickens here and saw the mule."

◆

By next morning I felt less imperiled—daylight does wonderful things for even the worst problems—but we stayed on "red alert," watching and listening for signs of intruders. After breakfast, we finally got to hear Richard's tale of woe. I wanted to know everything.

"So what happened out there to make you come back to *us*?" Tex said, as though he understood it could not have been Richard's ideal course of action. We all knew he'd high-tailed it out of here as if he couldn't wait to get away.

Angel and I were clearing dishes to soak them in the sink but we went to the table to listen. Tex had tried to get the story before we ate but Angel had clucked her tongue and said, "I want to hear, too, but Richard needs to eat, first, hon."

Richard nodded at her. "Thanks."

"You're still not lookin' too good," she told him cheerfully. She served us fried eggs and corn cakes in a cast iron griddle still smoking from the woodstove—making the room "hot as Hades," as Tex said; but we all ate like people starving, Richard especially.

Afterwards, he told his story. He'd gone away to get to our aunt's farm—that much we knew already. He said he not only wanted to see if Aunt Susan was still alive but to find out if by some chance our father had made his way there. He needed to know—he admitted a little sheepishly—if there was another place where he and I could live.

Angel surveyed him sadly. "You didn't even say goodbye." I realized I wasn't the only one who felt abandoned. Richard and I needed the McAllisters a heck of a lot more than they needed us but I was glad to see that Angel had come to care for my brother.

Richard was silent a moment, eying her with surprise. "I'm sorry," he said.

"He didn't say goodbye to me, either," I piped in, hoping to make her feel better. I gave Richard a brief scowl to show I resented that.

Tex said, "Go on."

Richard took a deep breath. "Going was slow. Gangs just popped up out of the blue. One minute I'd think I was alone and then in the next, I'd be running for my life. I didn't take much food with me and I ran out fast. That wouldn't have stopped me but I knew the trek was getting longer each time I had to detour to avoid a gang—or once, even a couple of army trucks."

"United States Army?" Angel asked, hopefully.

Richard shook his head. "I don't think so. I had to duck out of sight so I couldn't really watch. But Sarah and I saw lots of those trucks in the past and I don't think they're good news."

We'd already told the McAllisters about the refugee camps, so they nodded, but Angel said, "Oh," with disappointment in her voice.

"So, anyway, I had to keep leaving the roads in order not to be seen, and walking at night wasn't helping—seems like there's a lot of activity now at night. People are using torches as well as flashlights and

30

I kept finding myself in the middle of scratchy bushes or marshy ground to get away from them. And the bugs! They were eating me alive."

It was true. He had red bumps everywhere. "I'm good at dodging," Richard continued. "Most of the time no one ever knew when I was near." He sounded proud of that fact even though he'd come back with a gang at his heels.

"Evidently this last time I was wrong—I guess they were on me. But I swear I didn't know, I thought I'd lost them. Usually, they stick together and aren't stealthy so I would have heard them following. I don't know how they did it without my hearing them."

"Probably had a tracker. So most of them would have hung back far enough for you not to hear," Tex said. He took a gulp of coffee. I shuddered for Richard, recalling not only the gangs of marauders we'd seen before coming to the McAllisters', but also at the memory of the garish painted faces yesterday. I was glad they hadn't caught my brother—even if he had led them here while they tried.

"Why would they follow him?" I asked. "They didn't know he'd lead them to a homestead with supplies."

No one had an answer to that.

"What else are people up to?" Tex asked.

Richard took a deep breath and shook his head. "The ones in the camps just mill around a lot or stay in their tents. The ones on the road seem to be on the move like I was. Moving in camps, heading south from what I could tell." He paused, thinking. "I wanted to join one." His voice fell as he remembered. "They were heading west; mostly men. I only saw a few kids and women." He glanced pointedly at me and Angel. "I don't know if the women stay put while the men look for food and supplies—or if fewer of them survived." He looked at Angel as if she might solve the riddle. "But since there were a lot more men than women, I figured they wouldn't want any more." He ran a hand through his hair.

"So anyway, I was skirting around this one camp when someone saw me and started shooting." He looked ahead, lost in the memory and said, "I've got two bullet holes in my backpack from that."

DEFIANCE

His eyes darted to survey us. "Two bullet holes—they went clean through my pack and didn't even graze me!"

"Praise the Lord for that," said Angel.

"I don't know why they didn't hit me." He shook his head. "I must have been moving in such a way that my pack fell to one side and that's when the bullets went through."

"I know why they didn't hit you," Angel countered, with eyes softly shining. "God was watching out for you."

Richard met her gaze evenly but said nothing. He swallowed and then continued the story. "I thought they just wanted to scare me off because no one chased me that I could tell. I ran for a long time just in case. After about a mile I had to slow down." He was pensive for a moment. "I guess you could say I collapsed. I thought it was good Sarah wasn't with me." He looked from Tex to Angel, and with a very uncharacteristic sheen in his eyes, added softly, "I was thinking it was a good thing she had you."

They nodded. I wondered if they knew those words hadn't come easily for my brother. He was not especially strong in the praise or thanks department.

"I was hungry and thirsty and getting nowhere fast, so I decided to head back." In a gruff tone, he said, "I realized out there how amazing it is that you took us in." Lowering his eyes, he said, "Thank you for that." He raised his gaze. "Thank you for everything."

Those words seemed to break the ice and suddenly everything felt cozier, as if Richard had never left, almost like we were going to be a happy family. I must have been grinning from ear to ear, because Richard glanced at me and broke into a sheepish grin of his own.

"You're smiling!" I cried, reaching my arm across the table to pat his arm. Even as unkempt and rough as he was, he looked sweet and cute when he smiled. "I like to see you smile." Everybody was smiling now, if you could call Tex's sparkling eyes a smile. He isn't a smiley sort of person. But his eyes were happy.

"Well, Richard," Tex said. "We're glad to have you back. I know you need to catch up on your rest so you can turn in early again, but first, we've got a lot to do."

I figured Tex was referring to the usual amount of cumbersome work it took to run the homestead but he wasn't. Richard had carefully bypassed all the booby traps on the property—the ones Angel and Tex had set against wandering marauders—showing the gang how to do it, too. Now they were probably useless, at least against this group. Some could be moved. Others, such as the deep pit I'd fallen into, had to be duplicated.

When Richard told Tex they also needed to find barbed wire and dig a trench around the cabin, I knew one thing for sure. They expected more attacks.

CHAPTER FIVE

SARAH

Tex's new motto is: STOP THE YAHOOS. I only knew Yahoo as a search engine on the internet—our long lost internet!—so I had to ask what he meant. Turns out, he means the marauders. But he stared at me when I asked, and said, "Haven't you ever read *Gulliver's Travels?*"

"No."

"Everybody used to have to read *Gulliver's Travels*—it was part of a well-rounded education."

"Not in my school."

Tex snorted. "No wonder there's so many yahoos out there—our education system raised them up, didn't it? Why don't they teach kids the classics anymore?" He didn't expect an answer, so I didn't give one. Besides, I had no idea why they'd stopped teaching *Gulliver's Travels*. Maybe if Tex has a copy, I'll read it.

Anyway, Richard and Tex are gone for hours every day in order to STOP THE YAHOOS—they're rigging new traps, digging pits, and putting up fencing. They take weapons, a two-way radio, and, just as important as anything else—Kool. He'd smell and hear anyone coming long before the men would. Angel and I get to keep Kane, my wolf-dog buddy, which is a big comfort.

Kane and I have been on peaceful terms since the first time I fed him but we enjoy far more than mutual toleration. I love him! He's a protective guard dog and a good companion. One time he growled at the grass and barked at me, warning me away. It turned out to be a big old corn snake, according to Angel who killed the thing by slamming a shovel on its head. (Angel is a small woman and still surprises me with her muscle—and her pluck.) Tex skinned it and we actually ate snake meat! But I hadn't seen or heard it when it was right next to me, and if it had been poisonous, I might have gotten bit without Kane's warning.

Another time he scared away a coyote—Angel was sorry about that though, because she'd rather shoot the things than scare them off. "Any meat is meat," she said, shaking her head after I told her what happened.

It reminded me how, back at the library right after the pulse, the rumor circulated that we'd been eating dog-meat. Even now, so long after the fact my stomach turns at the thought. But we'd been starving then. I guess if we got desperate enough coyote meat would be as good as any. But Richard and I are blessed by getting to eat lots of food that most people don't have and wouldn't be able to prepare without modern conveniences if they did. Tex and Angel are geniuses when it comes to that.

Cooking, for instance. Angel has the top of our wood-stove for indoor cooking, a sun-oven, and a compact rocket stove—which, in case you don't have one, is pretty cool. Tex calls it "a marvel of efficiency" because it only needs the smallest fodder for fuel, like kindling and rolled newspaper, but burns hot.

They lived "off grid" for quite some time before the pulse and it really paid off. Losing power didn't ruin their lives the way it did the rest of us. Were it not for the danger of other people and foreign soldiers, Tex and Angel would get along just fine. Back when I first arrived, I noticed right off they were well supplied. But soon I realized they had more supplies than I could see—hidden storage. The storage room holds mostly non-food items; but now and then Angel appeared with packaged goods like cookies and granola bars, or instant oatmeal and jelly—things unopened, as if she'd just gone shopping.

Once, when she appeared with a 25-pound sack of flour, my jaw about dropped.

"Where did *that* come from?" I knew it wasn't from the small pantry off the kitchen, and I hadn't seen any totes labeled "flour" in the storage room. This is when I first learned they had an additional, hidden area with food.

She just smiled. "Oh—we have a few things on hand."

I have to confess that I went searching for this secret place once, looking for a loose floorboard or that sort of thing. But I'm stumped. I wish they'd trust me enough to show it to me but it doesn't bother me too much. It's like when you know your parents have Christmas presents hiding somewhere. It would be fun to find them but you don't have to. Angel and Tex were storing food. I didn't have to know where.

Anyway, aside from his protection as a guard dog, Kane is just good company. He seems to prefer me over Angel, which is a mystery to me. Angel is nothing but good to the dogs. But Kane will come trotting after me instead of her. My only competition for his affection is Tex. The dogs consider Tex their true love (Kole did, too) and transform from growling, snarling menaces to meek and eager love-things where Tex is concerned. With Kole gone, the remaining two have kept up this love-sick contest for his affection. Kane rushes from my side the moment he hears Tex approaching the cabin, long before we can tell he's coming.

This week I am extra grateful to have Kane with me whenever I have to leave the cabin. I try to stay alert but I listen more for Kane's low, guttural warning growl than anything else. He comes with me to the water-pump, the barn, and the garden. I'm spooked by that gang, no doubt about it. Now and then I'll stop what I'm doing just to take a quick survey of the surrounding fields and pastures, clear to the tree line, half-expecting to see them returning. Even if they don't, there are countless others out there to watch for.

LATER

While we ate supper that night, Angel put her fork down and looked earnestly at Tex. "Tex, hon, I want to check on Doris and Tim— maybe they're okay. I need to know. I still feel badly about shooting that woman as they left."

Tex swallowed and cleared his throat. Troubled, he said, in his heavy voice, "I'm ahead of you, darlin'." He sighed. "I been there and

36

back. They're gone, sweetheart. House was pillaged and everything taken or used."

Angel stared at him sadly. "Did you see any sign of Doris or Tim? You think they might have gotten away?"

Tex looked uncomfortable. "They did not survive, sweetheart. Don't ask me for more details." He paused, looking at his wife with sad eyes. "I think it was that gang who got to our neighbors. I think you were right—it was Doris's hat."

Angel's face sank. I thought she was about to dissolve into tears.

Richard's eyes flamed. "You see? We had every right to shoot! We should have shot them all! Then we wouldn't be worrying about them coming back. They came here to kill and steal—they tried to hack down the cabin!" He shook his head. "I don't see how you could feel bad about it. We didn't do ENOUGH damage."

Tex said, "Now that I've thought about it, I agree with Richard. We were too passive. If we started shooting them when they were still in the field, we'd have our chickens and berries and a lot less damage to the cabin and barn."

I don't think I mentioned our visible garden plots got trampled, all of the seedlings squashed. And the raspberry bushes on one side of the property were stripped, as well as some herbs and peas, leaving the area a sad mess.

Angel was crying silently. "I wish they had made a safe room like we told them!"

"What do you mean? What's a safe room?" I asked.

Tex and Angel exchanged looks. After a few seconds during which he looked like he was trying to decide how to answer, Tex said, "A safe room? That's Plan B."

And that's all they would say about it.

◆

The next day Angel and I went out to double-check our crops while the men went further afield to lay traps and such. If ever I've been thankful for Angel's foresight in planting "survival gardens," the ones that aren't neat and delineated but hidden in plain sight, it is now. Angel and Tex had planted squash among oak and maple trees, tomatoes among brush and weeds, blueberries alongside conifers, and strawberries mingled among marigolds. Most people would walk right by and never realize they'd passed food.

Thanks to other such plantings we still had grape vines, beets, acorn and spaghetti squash (the butternut squash were mostly destroyed) and beans, blueberries, pumpkin, watermelon, Jerusalem artichokes, and peppers. There's probably more I'm forgetting to mention—but this gang would have decimated all of it if it had been in a neat garden. They'd missed the survival plantings, thank God, because they were well camouflaged.

Before the raid, I'd been bringing in slim, dark, early zucchini each day. It was odd—one day I wouldn't see any—then suddenly, the next day I'd spot a group of the shiny vegetables, begging to be picked. But I wasn't complaining. Zucchini was the only plant that wasn't calorie dense, besides fruit and tomatoes, that Angel would bother growing. She says it isn't worth the manpower to grow green beans or cucumbers—not when we can use that space and energy to grow things we could store for winter and count on for much-needed nutritional support during the dark months. Things with calories and carbs, like potatoes and beans and winter squash.

Why no corn? Angel says it's too visible to marauders.

CHAPTER SIX

SARAH

So it's been two weeks since the marauders were here. We figure they've moved on. Tex has studied past famines and disasters from all over the world, and he said, "Marauders will swarm like locusts to an area until its resources are depleted, and then move on to greener pastures."

"You mean easier targets," Richard said, his voice heavy.

Tex nodded. "Yup."

We were at the table after dinner while Angel made out the following day's chore chart. We'd accomplished much since the attack. The house now had a lean-to in back, inside the fenced-in area. The three chickens and Daisy the mule share it with the dogs, who seem perfectly happy with their new companions. The front window with the faulty metal shade has been bricked over—except for a slit of glass to the side; Tex left it there so we can see out, hopefully on the sly. And last, the totes—those that hadn't vanished to the mystery storage area—have been returned to the storage room. We stacked them differently, leaving space so one corner of the room now holds my sleeping bag and a plastic bin of my belongings; another corner holds Richard's.

Speaking of few belongings—I desperately need clothing. I've got rips in my jeans and I'm ashamed to say what my underwear looked like before Angel gave me two pairs of panties in her size. She's smaller than me but I'm skinny, so they'll do.

On a grim note, Richard and Tex stripped the dead that were left from the gang, searching their clothing for anything usable like pocket knives, and cigarette lighters. But it was a dismal business. The look on their faces when they came back to the house made me glad I hadn't had to help. They looked haunted.

But we gained one pistol—no bullets—and one sledgehammer, in addition to the other few belongings. Only one of the dead was a woman and, though I may have a pair of jeans from her, I hate the thought of it. At the very least they have to be cleaned, and we haven't had a chance to wash clothing since before the attack. I won't wear them until we do. (And then I'll have to forget that it came from someone who died attacking us like in some horror movie!)

Problem is, washing laundry takes a lot of water and a lot of energy to heat the water. Maybe now that we're beginning to feel safe, we can trek down to the stream and do a cold-water wash. But it's not the kind of thing you want to be in the middle of while you're watching for marauders!

"We need to find barbed wire," Richard said, not for the first time. "Build a perimeter they can't pass." He told Tex about the Steadmans' house and how Mr. Steadman had planted homemade mines around his home. They were far enough not to damage the house and spread out so that an unsuspecting person wouldn't get to the house in one piece.

"Well, that's just nasty, ain't it?" Tex said, leaning back in his chair. He rifled a hand through his hair.

"It's effective." Richard also sat back, stretching his neck to the side and rubbing it with one hand. "They were two old people getting by just fine because of their nasty mines."

"Did this Mr. Steadman happen to teach you how he made them?" Tex asked.

Richard shook his head ruefully. "There wasn't time."

"How did you avoid the mines?" Angel asked. I pitched into our story with the Steadmans. I'd told Angel about them in the past so she only needed a few more details to get the whole picture, but I explained that Mr. Steadman had carefully steered us around the explosives.

"I'll do some research," Tex said. "See what we might be able to devise—but I'd put warning signs around. I don't want to blow anyone to pieces."

"Research how?" I asked. For me, research meant getting online. Without that possibility I had no clue how to find out anything.

Tex smirked at me. "Ever hear of such a thing as an encyclopedia?"

Angel smiled gently. "We've got a survival library—I'm sure there's something in there that will guide us."

"Whatever we build has to be kept far from the house," Tex said. "I can't chance having the dogs getting hurt."

"It'll mean they can't run free," said Angel, with a worried frown.

"But it'll make us safer," said Richard. "And that means they're safer, too." He opened his hands expansively. "Look, we'll put our explosives—mines, whatever they are—outside a certain perimeter. Closer to the house, we dig a trench--."

"Son, a trench is only good if you can ensure that they'll only come at us from one direction."

"That's the idea," Richard said. "It's a military strategy. You force the enemy to come at you on your terms, on your ground, where you can control the fight. If we can get our hands on barbed wire, and put a perimeter of mine fields around the house—."

"Oh, Richard," said Angel. "I don't want to live that way! We love our property. If we surround us with a mine field to keep people out, we are also making our own prison. We'll be stuck inside that perimeter."

"It beats being stuck in just the cabin," he returned, his eyes somber. "And if they come back, right now our only recourse is to retreat inside like last time. And what if the next bunch doesn't buy the chemical weapon story?"

Everyone fell silent thinking about it. I liked the idea of having a safety zone.

"Don't forget we'll keep a safe passage out," my brother continued. "A narrow passage. You'll be able to access the woods and whatever else you want."

"But an enemy can find that," Tex interjected. "And once they break through —and it could be anywhere in the line—they'll have an entry point, and those mines become meaningless. Except they'll pose a danger in the future for some unsuspecting people."

"They won't find it!" Richard insisted. "And we'll keep a diagram of where we plant every mine." He was being really patient, for Richard.

He paused, searching Tex's face. "Look, you've done so much to prepare for something like this. You've already set the wheels in motion but you didn't turn them all the way. Setting mines out there and getting barbed wire and trenches—that's turning the wheels all the way. That's doing everything in our power. Otherwise," and he shook his head. "We're just sitting ducks, waiting for the worst and hoping when it comes they'll play nice. We can't be that easy."

"I appreciate your ideas," Tex said. "But here's a few things you need to remember. One: I don't have barbed wire. Two, we may not have the materials to build more than a few explosive traps. And three, digging trenches takes a lot of work—and time. But that is the one thing you've mentioned that we can do with stuff we've got. If there's time. We should start immediately." His eyes turned to me.

"I'll help!"

Richard said, "But we need the mines, too. A trench will only work as you said, if we can keep them from coming at us from behind."

"How does a trench help?" I asked. My idea of a trench was a place to collect water like a moat. But I didn't think that was Richard's idea.

"It's a line of defense," Richard explained. "A place to fight from where we can hold them back."

"What if there's too many to hold back?" asked Angel. "We could get overrun."

"If there's too many, we double back to the cabin. That's why you want the trench close." He sniffed. "Ideally, I'd like to have a minefield and barbed wire for them to cross before they get that close but if we don't have it, we don't have it."

42

Tex eyed my brother with a gleam of admiration. "Did you do time in the military?" he asked.

Richard shook his head. "No. I read a lot."

"Too bad you didn't read where to get barbed wire and land mines."

"Too bad you didn't." For a second I wondered if Tex and Richard were about to have an argument but both men took the criticism jovially, almost smiling.

"I'll find the encyclopedias and a few other books," Angel offered, rising from her seat.

"Can I help?" I asked. And then I realized that the library must have been part of the secret storage area because Angel hesitated, looking at me.

"No thanks," she said. "But you can start supper."

So I did. I dug out some salt pork we keep in a barrel and started beans and rice. It was a common, boring meal. *Thank God for common, boring meals!*

The next day all of us except Tex got started on digging a trench. Tex was holed up in the barn with an assortment of supplies like fertilizer and stump remover in order to make an explosive. Looking back, I think if we'd had time to complete the plans, everything might have been so different. So different!

But just as dusk was falling the dogs started barking and we had no choice but to seal up the cabin again—just in case. Angel and I brought the chickens in, clucking and squawking. They were already in their nesting boxes so we carted them in, boxes and all! But Daisy was stubborn and was put in the lean-to. We tied her up to a post, hoping Tex would have time to coax her into the house.

Had they been ready, our new defenses might have prevented what happened next. But suddenly we heard the dreaded sounds of that war cry, the hoots and hollers we'd heard last time. The gang was back.

Tex and Richard grabbed rifles and crouched beneath the front window, the side that wasn't bricked up. Smashing out the slit of glass that remained, they took turns rising and shooting into the gloom. The other metal shades had been lowered so that aside from that half of the front window, we were once again encapsulated in the cabin like a watertight ship.

Angel sniffed loudly. "Do you smell that?"

Something was burning and it wasn't the woodstove. While the dogs barked madly, Tex turned to re-load his rifle, his back against the wall. Richard was still at the window. The look on his face made me rush over so that I could see what he was seeing. The horrible truth was all too evident. Shooting up into the settling dusk of the sky, coming from the single high opening in the barn—which Richard and I had painstakingly boarded over while we slept up there—were orange and blue flames and dark smoke, darting in and out.

I let out an anguished cry. "The barn's on fire!"

CHAPTER SEVEN

ANDREA

Life on the compound is perfectly normal lately—and that should be a good thing, right? No new attacks, no illness or injuries. But Roper and Jared have been gone for almost three weeks now and no one seems very concerned but me! Even Lexie acts like I'm worrying over nothing. (If it was Blake that went with Jared instead of Roper I think I'd be hearing a different tune!)

I try to go on like everyone else as though nothing is wrong. I *try.* But at night when I pray for them, I cry. All I have to do is remember how my dad died—it is a crazy, dark world out there! And I think of my mother—I asked Roper and Jared to try to find her, check our house—but I just know she's dead by now. How could she not be? She'd have come back if she was alive. And now *they're* both probably dead, too!

Except no one else seems ready to believe it. Are they forgetting what it's like out there? If Roper doesn't come back, I'm going to be one very depressed girl. But if Jared doesn't? We're one very vulnerable compound. Everyone else should at least be worried about that!

But everything gets me down lately, like having to use newspaper in the outhouse, or not having new clothing, and eating oatmeal for lunch. And every morning, no sooner do my feet hit the floor when I remember that my sweet guy is gone. It fills me with a nameless, vague dread that I can't get rid of. It's a weight. Nothing feels right without him.

Is it weird? I haven't even known him that long—but it feels so important to have him back!

I guess that's what happens when you love someone.

LATER

It's getting hotter by the day and I hate it. My jeans had rips so I cut them into shorts. Lexie has real shorts. She offered to lend me a pair but I like my jean cut-offs. Anyway, as I went to get my baby sister Lily this morning, I was deep in my usual worries, wishing Roper hadn't gone out there with *Jared,* of all people. (Even Lexie agrees with me on that.) I saw Mrs. Martin as I was coming back down with Lily on my hip and she gave me a smile.

"How's the arm feeling these days?" She asked, in her mild southern drawl.

Mr. Clepps, our D.O., and Mrs. Philpot our nurse, had done a fine job of stitching my arm up after I'd been shot. It was healing well. There were hours and hours when I almost forgot I was hurt. But it still ached where the bullet passed through, especially if I did too much work. "Pretty good."

"So why the long face?" she said, and chucked my chin with her hand. She stroked Lily's fine blond hair and gave her a big smile.

"They've been gone so long…" My voice trailed off.

"Oh, Jared and Jerusha."

I had to smile. "You're the only one who calls him that. He hates his first name."

She smiled back. "Well, I like it! Much better than Roper." She leveled her gaze at me and the humor left her face. "They're big boys. They can take care of themselves."

I stared at her. "So was my dad."

She looked thoughtful. "Just keep praying, sweetheart. That's the most powerful thing we can do. Remember—we serve a mighty God."

"Even if they haven't run into trouble, they must be starving by now! It's been *three weeks!*"

I saw a glimmer of something flash in Mrs. Martin's eyes— worry, perhaps? But she only said, "I gave them hardtack and jerky;

enough to last this long. And they've got water filters. And neither one of those men is a dummy. Stop worrying." In a softer tone, she added, while stroking the side of my face, "Pray for them, but stop worrying."

I suddenly wanted to cry. Mrs. Martin always brings out the child in me. She was just so darn...motherly. In order not to cry, I spoke sternly instead. "We've lost our father and mother." I was speaking for both myself and Lily. "Don't tell me not to worry!"

Mrs. Martin gave me an understanding, sorrowful look. "I know," she said, nodding sympathetically. "I know. This is hard." She went to put an arm around me but I shrugged her off and hurried away. If I had stayed, let her hug me, I would've cried. I didn't want to do that while Lily was with me. I didn't want to cry in front of anyone but especially not Lily. I want her to think everything is fine.

Maybe I wouldn't think of Mom so much except Lily is her baby, and she's reaching milestones, and Mom's missing it. Yesterday Lily started to crawl! And she's picking up new words, like "ball," and "bye-bye." She says "na-na" for banana. (Freeze dried banana, that is, after I've soaked it in water to soften it. The Martins treat freeze-dried food like gold, but because Lily's a baby, she's allowed a daily ration.) She loves to play with Bach and Mozart, our German Shepherd and Great Dane, even though they are soooo big. And she adores Justin, Lexie's little brother—My mom would so enjoy seeing all this.

But her milestones aren't all good—as she gets bigger, she wants more attention. I've had to switch some of my chores to spend extra time with her because she just cries and carries on unless I'm with her. Lexie and Evangeline do most of the barn chores, now.

Evangeline and I avoid each other. My mother went off with *her father* and when I see her, it makes me think about it. It gets me angry that they ever came to this compound! Mom would still be here if that idiot—Mr. Washington—hadn't agreed to go off with her. She probably feels about my mom the way I feel about her father. I guess they're both to blame. But I'm still not getting friendly with Evangeline. She's too young, anyway.

But when I'm not worrying about Mom, I'm wishing she were here to take care of her own baby. I love Lily—but I'm *not* her mother. I hate having to wash diapers. I'll be seventeen in September. I shouldn't have to be a surrogate mother!

The only way I would want to be a mother is if Roper were the father. And I've got precious little chance of that happening if he doesn't come back!

———————◆———————

During breakfast, Lexie and Blake were sitting close together and talking. Seeing them filled me with fresh worries about my beautiful guy. I feel like I'm going to explode sometimes from all the worries in my head.

I hate that the world is like this—a war zone. It's worse than the wild west or the frontiers the pioneers faced. Our own countrymen are as much a threat as foreign invaders.

CHAPTER EIGHT

LEXIE

I was outside hanging laundry today with Mrs. Wasserman when suddenly I heard a soft nickering which hadn't come from the pasture. My first thought was of Rhema, my missing horse. But she'd been gone since Andrea's mother and Mr. Washington foolishly left the compound, taking her and one other horse, nearly a month ago.

Even though I knew it couldn't be Rhema—I didn't dare hope—I almost dropped the shirt in my hands to peek around a sheet on the line to get a glimpse, my heart pounding in my throat. And then—I couldn't believe my eyes! It *was* my horse! She came from the woods, near the trail I'd always ridden her on, saddled but with no rider, broken reins flapping.

"Rhema!" Hearing my voice she picked up speed and I had to run to keep her from swiping our clean clothing. *Oh, my gosh!* Tears sprang into my eyes as I grabbed the reins and hugged her. I couldn't believe how great it felt to have her back! I praised her and stroked her head and face and mane, laughing at how she nuzzled me, almost knocking me over with her large head. Mrs. Wasserman watched us with a smile.

"Did anyone come with her?" I asked. My heart surged with the hope that Andrea's mother might be back!

"I don't see anyone," Mrs. Wasserman said. "I'll get someone and we'll go look." Meanwhile, I started checking my beloved horse for signs of trouble or injuries. She'd definitely lost weight and was breathing hard. I wondered how long she'd been traveling in this heat, and led her to a water trough. As she noisily began to drink, I stroked her neck. She needed a good brushing–and I couldn't wait to give it to her. Andrea came into sight. Running towards me, she called, "Is my mom back?"

"We don't know yet," I yelled back, but I was worried. Surely if Mrs. Patterson had been with Rhema, she'd have ridden her. It was possible that she and Mr. Washington were trailing behind; maybe they'd come stepping out of the trail just like my horse—but I had a sinking feeling it wasn't going to happen.

Andrea ran up to me with wide, hopeful eyes and drank in the sight of Rhema.

"What happened?"she asked, breathlessly.

"I don't know. Rhema just came walking out of the woods!"

"Alone?"

"Yes."

Her eyes turned to gaze at the tree line. "Where?"

"From the horse trail."

She took off running towards the trail. I shouted after her, "Don't, Andrea! Don't go in there alone!"

"I'm fine!" she yelled, not even turning.

I wanted to run after her but I didn't want to leave Rhema—I'd just got her back! She was still drinking but since I couldn't let her drink her fill anyway (she might get sick if she drank too much at once after being without water) I led her to the barn, hurrying her along. I hoped that one of our lookouts was watching and would report that Andrea had gone into the woods alone. But if not, I would grab the two-way from the barn and get help from the house.

I got Rhema settled, grabbed the radio and turned it on as I hurried back outside. I almost ran into Mrs. Wasserman with my dad, who was speaking into his unit.

"How long ago?" he asked. "Right... No, stay up there... Okay, thanks."

As soon as he switched off, I cried, "Dad, Andrea ran into the woods alone! She thinks her mom might be on her way here!"

"I know, I know, I just heard," he said, and then glanced at the barn. "I'm glad you got Rhema back, honey."

I nodded. "Yeah!"

He eyed me worriedly. "She came alone, huh?"

"She did." I paused. "Do you think—do you think they might be following?" I didn't need to say who "they" were—my dad knew I meant Andrea's mother and Mr. Washington.

He turned to leave, his expression veiled. "We'll see," he said. "Get back to work, ladies. We'll take care of this."

As he left, Mrs. Wasserman met my eyes. Hers were sympathetic.

"I need to feed and brush down my horse," I said.

"That's fine. I'll finish the laundry." Neither of us said a word about whether the two missing adults might be coming back to us.

I got busy taking care of Rhema, removing the bridle, saddle and saddle-bags, and noting that her blanket was still there—that was something. Roper once said when people found anything worth anything, they'd take it or destroy it whether they needed it or not. It was a small miracle that Rhema was back at all, much less with her saddle and blanket.

I didn't give the mare a big meal, though she hungrily ate up the hay and dried oats I offered. If she'd been without food—and her leanness told me she had—it could cause her to colic if she ate a lot at once. Horses are powerful creatures but also delicate. I checked her hooves and cleaned a few pebbles with a hoof pick, glad to see that nothing was stuck in the "frogs," the part of the hooves most likely to pick up a stone and cause trouble.

As I worked I prayed for Andrea. If Mrs. Patterson and Mr. Washington weren't on that trail, she'd be heart-broken. I almost felt guilty that my horse had returned to me whole when her mother might not.

About an hour later I heard voices outside and thought I recognized my dad's among them. I gave Rhema a final parting hug, telling her what a special girl she was, and then tore myself from her to catch my father outside.

I halted at the barn door. They were heading to the house, my dad and Mr. Buchanan, with Andrea between them, crying. The men had rifles slung on their shoulders and my dad held one of Andrea's arms. I knew he cared about her but I couldn't help thinking they looked like M.P.s bringing in an AWOL soldier. Poor Andrea! At that moment she looked up and saw me.

I nodded, and she said something to the men and then veered in my direction. I felt so badly for her. If only her mother had returned along with my horse!

She said, without preamble, "I want to look at Rhema," and she walked right past me.

At the horse's stall, she stood there glowering, staring at her. "What are you looking for?" I asked.

"Did she come with anything on her?"

"You mean like a saddle? Yeah, she had her blanket and saddle."

"Saddle bags?"

"Yeah."

"Can I see them?"

"Sure." I led her to where I'd hung up the bags. She took them down and started rummaging in one, searching.

"They're empty," I said, wondering what she was up to.

"You checked them both?"

I hesitated. "I think so. What are you looking for?"

"I'm just looking and being thorough." She spoke with difficulty—I saw then a silent tear running down her cheek. She sniffed and wiped a hand across her face. She dug her hand in the second bag and ran it along the bottom inside seam.

I thought the second one was empty like the first but suddenly Andrea gasped and withdrew her hand. She held it out, brandishing a small, sparkly hair tie.

"This is mine!" she exclaimed. "I have a bunch of hair-ties like this, in lots of colors! My mom must have made it to the house!"

The fact that nothing else was in the bags and even worse, that her mother was nowhere to be found, did not bode well, so I made no reply. Even if her mother had made it to the Patterson's home and grabbed tons of stuff, she hadn't made it back. And neither had the stuff. Except for the hair tie.

I looked sadly at Andrea. "It could be anyone's."

"Anyone's? This is your horse! Is it yours?" She handed me the little band. I took it and stared down at it. I knew without a doubt it was not mine—I never wore sparkly hair bands even though I often tied my hair back, especially in summer. But if Andrea thought it was mine, she might feel less upset. She would have no reason to believe her mom and Mr. Washington had made it to her house—but not back.

"Oh, it might be mine," I said. "I used to put my hair in a ponytail when riding."

"I've never seen you do that," she shot back.

"Because my hair's shorter than it used to be." She couldn't argue with that one. We'd both let my mom cut our hair once the heat of summer set in. It was just too hot to keep it long, and much easier to manage, not to mention it took less water to wash.

"I still think this is mine," she said, taking back the little band and turning it over in her hands. Finally, she shoved it in a pocket. She pressed her lips together, trying not to cry. We stood there in awkward silence for a moment. I wanted to give her a hug but for some reason was afraid to, sensing she might push me away.

"I'm sorry, Andi"—I began, using her family nickname, but she turned on her heel and stalked towards the door.

"Don't," she said. "Don't even say it!"

I went back to pet Rhema one more time. My happiness at her return was dampened by Andrea's loss but still it seemed a miracle to have her again. Most anyone out there would grab a horse if they could. Might Rhema have been too skittish to let anyone near her? What were the odds of her making it all the way back to us without someone nabbing her? And what had happened to the other horse? It had belonged to one of our newer families; I couldn't remember its name. But why hadn't that horse returned with mine? We'll probably never know.

My mind went from one scenario to another and I got more and more worked up. What if our missing adults had ridden the animals but got ambushed somewhere close by? Or were injured? Or got trapped somewhere with hostiles surrounding them? What if we could help them? If there was even a chance of getting Andrea's mother back, we had to take it! We had to try!

Back outside, I saw the clothes drying on the lines but no Mrs. Wasserman. I headed to the house, intent on finding my dad to see if we could look further for Andrea's mom and Mr. Washington.

———————◆———————

I found Dad talking to my mother in the kitchen where she and Mrs. Wasserman were making dinner. Mom was happy for me about Rhema but I could see there weren't any plans to search further for Andrea's mom.

"What about Andrea's mom and Mr. Washington?" I asked. "If Rhema made it back, they may have been with her for part of the trip."

My dad looked at me blankly. Putting his hands on his hips, he said, "What if they were? That still gives us NO IDEA where they might be now." He looked around and lowered his voice. "Or even if they're alive."

"Maybe they got waylaid when they were close! How far did you check? Don't you think we should go looking?"

"Oh, here we go," said my mother, frowning. "You're back to wanting us to save the world."

"Thanks a lot, Mom!" I felt my face grow hot. "Wouldn't you want us to go looking for you if you were the one whose horse came back without you?"

She gave me a long look. "You are not sending your father out there to search for a woman who should have known better!" She paused, her eyes wide. "Y'all know that if she and Mr. Washington were able to come back to us, they would! I am not about to see your

54

father put himself in harm's way for two people who chose to do that to themselves!"

My dad put an arm around my mother. She turned to face him and they went into a full embrace. I stood there glowering, still trying to decide if I should argue my point any further. But my dad glanced over and said, "Don't you have chores to do?"

"You didn't answer my question," I insisted. "If mom's horse came back without her, wouldn't you go looking for her?"

"Lexie, I will not discuss this with you right now," my dad said. "Mr. Washington had a horse too, and that animal did not come back. Rhema found her way but we have no idea how far she had to come, or how long ago Mrs. Patterson gave her up."

"She wouldn't give her up! She was forced to!"

"Which is why we'd be on a fool's errand to go looking. Looking for trouble, is what I'd call it, as your mother said." A sound from the doorway just then made us turn to look. I saw Andrea's distraught face just long enough to know she'd heard some of that conversation before she turned and hurried off. I felt awful for her. I gave my dad an accusing look.

"I'm truly sorry we can't help Andrea or get her mother back—I know she's lost both her parents—."

"And now she might have lost Roper, too! The least you could have done is told Roper not to go with Jared! Andrea has no one!"

"Andrea has us!" my mother said, in a scolding tone. "She has you, and she has her brothers and Lily, and she has us! *And* she has the rest of the compound, just like we do. She is not alone."

"Yeah. That's a big comfort," I said, turning to leave.

"One moment, Lexie." My dad's voice made me stop but I didn't turn to face him. "You seem determined to see everything that's happened to Andrea's family as being our fault. May I remind you that you were the one who insisted we go get the Pattersons to begin with?"

My mouth hardened into a tight line and I spun around to face my father. "You're right, Dad, I know that! Why do you think I want us to do something to help?"

He took a breath and let it out. "We did help. We brought them here. Her mother is an adult and didn't consult us before leaving. She'd be alive and well if she'd stayed. There is no reason for you to blame yourself for what's happened—but we aren't to blame, either."

Someone touched my arm and I looked up to see Blake, his expression one of sympathy. "C'mon, Lex, I have something to show you."

Taking my hand, he led us out of the room. "I thought you might need a distraction."

"Thanks. I do."

Bach and Mozart had been dozing peacefully on the floor but they immediately scrambled to their feet as if they knew we were headed outdoors. We let them trail along.

"You okay?" he asked, once we got outside. "At least you've got Rhema back. That's great!"

"Yeah," I said. "I can hardly believe it! But I still think we should keep looking for Andrea's mom."

He was silent a moment. "That's what Roper and Jared are doing."

"We *hope*." He didn't answer and for a few minutes we walked in silence. I felt self-conscious knowing our lookouts were probably watching.

"Where are we going?" I asked, though my heart and mind were still on Andrea and her mother.

"You'll see." Blake took us around the riding ring, past the cabins towards the hill. When we reached the bottom he veered and headed towards the tree line.

"Are we heading to the stream?" I asked.

Blake nodded. "Uh huh." Beyond a narrow stretch of trees, a lazy stream meandered along the property, rocky and shallow and shaded. It was so quiet you'd never even know it was there until you're right on it. In the hottest summers it sometimes dried up. We hadn't reached it yet but memories bubbled up.

56

"There used to be more water in it," I said. "When I was little I used to wade to my knees trying to catch frogs or crayfish. I also loved to pull out rocks. They always looked so pretty and colorful in the water. I once asked my mother if she'd traded all my pretty rocks for ugly ones. That's how boring and gray they looked when they dried. I still don't understand how water can make a drab rock look pretty, but it does."

Smiling, Blake nodded. "You may find the stream worth wading in again now." I looked at him with surprise—and admiration—trusting that he'd done something wonderful.

"You did it, didn't you? You got more water to flow?" I was grinning in delight and hurried my steps towards the stream. Even before reaching the embankment, I knew there was a change. "I can hear it!"

Blake watched me with a hopeful little boy look about him. We were both smiling as we hurried through the brush and came out by the stream. The dogs, as if they couldn't wait to get wet, splashed happily into the water, staring into its shallow depths. Bach seemed especially curious about what was beneath the surface and dipped his head low to find out. But as soon as his snout got wet he snatched his head out again, shaking the water from his whiskers. Mozart seemed transfixed by the water rushing past his legs and stood looking around and around as if to solve a mystery.

"How'd you get it deeper?" I asked. "It hasn't been raining a lot."

Blake shrugged as though it were nothing. "I detoured water from a cross-stream higher up on the property. We just dug out a trench for about fifty feet and then we made a dam in the other stream, so now it's all coming this way."

I laughed. "Wow! Why didn't we think of that sooner?"

"Because no one else thought about utilizing water power except me."

"So we're going to get some power from this?"

He nodded. "That's my next step. I think it will work. It won't be much, but enough to—."

"We have an old Frigidaire from, like, the sixties. Could we power it?" I asked, as excitement rose within me. "Wouldn't that be heavenly to have cold drinks again?"

But Blake's expression sobered. "My dad thinks we'd need to put any power we can harness into re-charging car batteries—which could theoretically work, but probably won't. Anyway, the council will have to decide what the power can be used for."

I frowned. "Oh. Yeah, I guess." Nevertheless, having any power was a blissful thought. I looked up at him admiringly. "You're a genius, you know that, right?"

He laughed. "Water power's been around for millennia."

"Maybe, but not on our compound."

"Well, it's not here yet, either." He leaned over and kissed my cheek. "Keep your fingers crossed."

I wrapped my arms around his middle and nuzzled my head into his chest. "I will."

For a few sweet seconds we shared a good hug, which morphed seamlessly into a good, long, kiss. Then Blake gently drew me apart from him. "We gotta be careful."

"What do you mean?" He took my hand and started leading me up the ravine on to where the new trench had been dug.

"I mean, your dad gave me a talk the other day about the 'danger of temptation.'"

I stopped cold. "*What?*" I felt my face burning.

Blake grinned sheepishly. "It's okay. I know where he's coming from. If I had a teenage daughter..."

"No, it's not okay! If he wanted to talk about something like that he should have talked to me, not you."

Blake nodded, still smiling faintly. "I guess he figured I'd be having more trouble handling it than you."

I practically snorted. "I think he got that backwards!"

Blake chuckled. "Yeah, maybe—but that's okay."

"What's okay? That I'm more attracted to you than you are to me?"

We'd resumed walking, but now Blake stopped. "That's not it, Lex. I just don't let myself think about it." He paused, searching my face. "That's. Not. It."

"Fine." I said, but I didn't feel reassured.

We came to the new trench but I was starting to feel uneasy about it. We'd passed a boundary of the property and had kept going. It was a beautiful trench, already lined for twenty feet with stone and rock to prevent erosion.

"Pretty cool, huh?" Blake asked.

I hesitated. "Um. There's one problem."

"What?"

"The trench…it isn't actually on our property."

"What? You own a hundred acres!"

"A hundred and twenty-six. In that direction." I pointed to the right.

"But back there," he said, pointing beyond the stream, "is your land, too. We have lookouts over that way!"

"I know. I know," I said, shaking my head. "But this area isn't ours, I'm just telling you. Property boundaries are weird."

"So who does it belong to?"

I shrugged. "I don't remember their name."

In a softer tone, he asked, "Are they still alive?"

"I don't know. We never got to know them."

He sighed. "Well, if they miss the water, I guess we'll find out about it." He looked back up. "If they're alive."

"I'll ask my dad. Maybe he knows."

Bach and Mozart had stayed with us but zig-zagged around with their natural curiosity. They came up, tongues lolling, from the heat.

Blake took my hand again. "We need this water, Lex. Having a little power will be a major encouragement to everyone on this compound. We could run a clothes washer one day a week, maybe!"

"Oh, man, I'd love that!" He'd found my sore spot with that suggestion. Like most every other woman, I detested hand-washing heavy clothing. It took hauling water and then the actual washing, and the use of manual wringers just wasn't fun. Clothes stayed plenty wet without a washing machine to spin them before drying. I missed a washing machine more than I missed air conditioning. On wash days, anyways.

As we went back down the hill with the dogs at our heels, Blake talked about his plan to get actual power from the stream. He had to build a waterwheel but it wouldn't be very difficult, he assured me. As we walked and talked, I almost forgot that our biggest worries weren't about having no electric gadgets, or about the manual labor required to get life done. Our biggest worry was about the next attack on our compound. We had no way of knowing when or if it would come although past incidents assured us that it would.

We just didn't know when.

CHAPTER NINE

LEXIE

I woke up not feeling well. After thinking about it, I realized I haven't been feeling quite myself for a few days. But today was worse—I felt totally zonked. I complained to my mother and she gave me the day off—yay!

Of course I still had to go lay eyes on Rhema and feed and water her. Then I put her in a separate pasture that Dad sectioned off with chicken-wire and metal poles so she can get used to the other horses again and so they can get used to her. Horses can be funny that way, and I didn't want to take any chances of Rhema getting bullied.

Now I'm back in my room and I have time to write more than usual but all I can think about is the latest scoop Dad got from the ham radio. There's something new we have to worry about: suicide bombers! The compound has successfully fought off attacks since the grid went down; and the last time we were up against foreign soldiers it was hardly something to sneeze at—but they didn't use bombs against us. The only grenades in play were ours.

But Dad says there are now VBIEDs—"vehicle borne improvised explosive devices," to be precise, causing a lot of death and destruction in nearby states. Manned vehicles. Supposedly run by extremist Muslim invaders.

They drive into places where they think people are congregated—like our compound! If they find us, I'm so afraid they'll find a way to get past all the obstacles we've put out front and do the same thing to us.

Jared pushed really hard for us to build a fence along the front. Not out by the street but closer to the house. We've already got heaps of obstacles along the front, including the two trucks that were destroyed during the last attack—thanks to Jared's home-made grenades. Plus, there's other debris and garbage and tree trunks and anything big we can find that isn't needed. But the fence never got built—now all the men are scrambling to get one up. We've got the hill behind us which is a natural defense, and acres of woods on one side. The fields are less of a barrier, but there are ravines here and there that should keep anyone from being able to come at us by vehicle through them.

Anyway, putting up a fence—a strong fence—is now top priority. The idea was to gather fencing from other places in the area that were abandoned since the pulse and cart it here using our wagon. But after scouting out some fences, the men decided it would be too arduous—even with a hydraulic jack it was a lot of labor, and would require being off the compound and in harm's way. So today a new open shed went up that is solely for the purpose of making cement blocks. Well, it's sort of cement—it's a homemade mortar, which we pour into scavenged, cleaned-out boxes and cartons—then let dry. We're hoping these blocks dry quickly. (The summer heat is awful without air conditioning, but at least it will help the blocks dry.) When they're fully dried, the men will use them to put up the wall across the front of the house and yard.

My dad had the idea of leaving some holes here and there in the wall—places to rest the barrel of a rifle and shoot from. "Better than a trench," he said. "And a heck of a lot safer."

Eventually we hope to surround the houses and cabins with this wall. Then we'll really be what we call ourselves: A compound! I asked my mother if we could possibly enclose most of our land—like China's great wall. But she said, "That would be impossible. We don't have the materials."

Even so, if we get the wall built around the house and cabins before one of those suicide VBIEDs finds us—I'll give a great big *Hallelujah*!

———————◆———————

I prayed with Andrea last night. I heard her crying from below me. She sounded so sad it made me miserable. She's worried about

Roper and I don't blame her. She's lost so much this year! I mean, not even counting the stuff we've all lost like technology and normal life. She's lost her dad and mom, and Roper and Jared have been gone far longer than we anticipated they would be. But I couldn't tell her *I'm* worried. My mom cautioned me against expressing any negative thoughts about Roper because Andrea's already been through so much.

We're all doing our utmost to stay positive around her. Except Cecily, who doesn't have to work up a positive attitude. She's just naturally positive. Or maybe I should say she's supernaturally positive because she says she gets her hope and faith from God. She feels strongly that both Roper and Jared will return to us. I wish I had her faith to believe it!

Cecily is an amazing prayer warrior and she gets lots of good words to share with us during her closeted prayer times with the Lord. I pray she's right about the men! Because I feel guilty around Andrea. Compared to her, I've had it so good. I live in my house, I have both my parents. We've had to accommodate a lot more people on our land, but we're on OUR land. It's still home. Andrea's home is like a distant memory. All of life before the pulse is like a dream. I wish we could go back to that dream and sleep forever—but we can't. We can't do so many things. So I can't tell her that I think the men have been gone too long.

I can't add to her worries.

And we don't know for sure they won't return, and we do have Cecily praying for them EVERY. SINGLE. DAY.

EVENING

We hold church services at night because there's so much work to do while there's daylight. It's nice, because every service is a candle-light service! Even though we're used to candle-light now, when it's a church meeting the feeling is different.

Anyways, Cecily must have heard about Andrea's mom not returning with Rhema and how worried Andrea is about Roper. She stood to share some encouragement with us—not an unusual thing for her to do—but her remarks were aimed at Andrea more often than not.

She reminded us (ostensibly all of us, but she kept looking at Andrea) that we must never give in to despair. She said, "Whatever the worry, whatever the fear, give it to God. He's the only one who can give you peace when everything in the world points to unrest." She quoted Isaiah 26:3, reminding us that God gives perfect peace to those who keep their minds on him and trust him. And she encouraged all of us to memorize I Cor.10:13.

When we were in our room later I asked Andrea if she felt encouraged.

"Honestly? No. My heart is bleak and dark. I know I need to believe what God says in the Word. But sometimes I feel like I can't endure this—this worrying. Or maybe it's the thought of losing someone else I love." Tears filled her eyes. "If he—if he doesn't come back—."

"He will!" I wanted her to feel better. I can't stand it when Andrea cries.

She nodded, sniffed, and even tried to smile a little. "I need to believe that." After a second she added, "The only good thing about having to watch Lily so much and having all our other chores, is that it keeps me too busy to wallow in self-pity like this all day long!"

"Yeah," I said, feeling stupid because I hadn't been wallowing in self-pity—but I wanted her to feel I understood.

"I have moments when I'm convinced I'll never see my mother again, or Roper." She looked at me with her large brown eyes, filled with pain. "I can't stand those moments!"

I nodded.

"Lily still asks for my mom. She looks at me with her blue 'Lars' eyes, and asks, *Ma-ma? Ma-ma?*"

I resisted the urge to smirk at her reference to Lars—he was her mother's gym trainer, and Lily's father. It wasn't a high note in Andrea's life when her mother admitted to the affair, so I kept listening as though she hadn't said it.

"I just stroke her hair and distract her with books or a toy. I need the distraction as much as she does."

Again she stared at me with agonized eyes. "I've lost too many people, Lex! I couldn't stand to lose Roper, too!"

Frankly, I was concerned that Andrea was growing more in love with Roper by the day. *In her mind.* They hadn't known each other very long unlike Blake and I who have been friends for years. But I nodded understandingly. "I know," I said. "I know." Her distress had brought me to tears. We hugged.

I can now say I feel just like Andrea.

Bleak and dark.

CHAPTER TEN

ANDREA

When I came awake today the first thing I noticed was heat, the insufferable July heat. I hadn't got out of bed yet and I already felt sticky. Mrs. Martin kept saying we'd get used to it, but I didn't feel used to it. How long did it take to "get used to it?" I miss air conditioning! Summer will probably be ending by the time I get used to it.

Lexie entered the room and brushed hay off her shorts. I realized she'd been to the barn while I was still in bed dreading the day.

"We've got a bunch of new rabbits," she said, "New Zealands." Then she looked at me. With concern in her eyes, she asked, "You okay?"

Last night she'd prayed with me about Roper, and I'd told her Lily had called me mama, and didn't know whether I should let her call me that, and how I was convinced it meant my mother had died.

Lexie pointed out that baby Lily is only a baby and can't know that my mother died. I can see that she's right, but I can't shake the feeling that it was some kind of omen.

"Don't live by omens," Lexie had said. "Live by the Word." She'd held her Bible down over the side of the bed, and I'd reached for it, but she didn't let me have it.

"I'm reading. Use your own Bible."

So I did.

I guess it's superstitious to believe that Lily calling me mama meant anything. And yet the fact that she's forgotten I'm NOT her mother says a lot in itself. It isn't superstitious to know that my mother being gone this long probably means she won't come back.

So anyway, when she asked me if I was okay, I said, "I'm tired. And my arm aches."

"That's it?"

I hesitated. I knew she was waiting to see if I was still upset about my mother and Lily. I was. But I was upset about a lot of things. And suddenly it spilled out.

"I hate life and I want to go back to my old life. I want to be in air conditioning. I even want to go to school! I could see friends. I want to get my hair cut and buy new clothes and make-up; I miss my mother and I know I'll never see her again, and I miss my father and I may not ever see Roper again, either!" I got more upset as I spoke, and by the time I'd finished I was wiping away tears.

Lexie had certainly gotten more than she expected, but all she said was, "Oh," looking at me with worried eyes. She came and sat down on my bed, frowning. "I can cut your hair."

"I know. Thanks." Blinking, I studied her. She hadn't felt well yesterday. "You don't look so good either." Her face was pale, and she had circles beneath her eyes. Lexie never had circles beneath her eyes. She slept remarkably well and usually had a look of country peace and wholesomeness about her, even now when most of us seemed chronically stressed out. Today she looked like one of us.

She said, "I'm okay. Why don't you get a day off? Tell them you don't feel good. I got the day off yesterday, remember?"

By "them," she meant her mom and other women who would be overseeing the day's chores.

"You should take today off, too. You look tired."

"I'm better," she said. "Anyway, I'll watch Lily today so you can chill out and rest."

"Chill out? Not in this heat!" But I had an idea. "Why don't we *both* try to get the day? Imagine having a whole day just to hang out like teenagers? Wouldn't that be cool?"

She got a far off look in her eyes, as though she was reaching back, back before the pulse, back to what it had felt like to be an ordinary teen. For both of us, it felt like a previous life. I could hardly fathom how I used to get upset over such meaningless stuff—a friend giving me the cold shoulder, or an assignment I'd handed in late. It was

67

all meaningless, now. And I thought I had worries. *Really? They were nothing!*

Next to what's on our plates now, I'd take the worst day of my former life in a heartbeat. A small voice inside reminded me that if I went back I wouldn't know Roper; I wouldn't live with Lexie; wouldn't know how to cook pancakes and stew and corn bread and other things from scratch. I wouldn't ride horseback, or be a sharp shooter.

I wouldn't have a bullet hole scar in my left upper arm, either— but that was life. Anyway, Lexie's expression changed. She looked doubtful.

"They'd never let us both off; there's too much work to do." She sniffed. "But you look like you really need it. So get the day off."

"To do what?" I asked. "Read a book?" I'd seen Lexie the day before with her nose so deep in a book that she hadn't even noticed me when I came up to the room to change into clean clothes. I'd been helping in the garden and needed something not drenched in sweat.

She smiled. "Yes! Or help in the kitchen. Today's baking day; that beats working in the sun."

"Alright. I have to put some clothes away and then I'll go ask. Thanks." I forced myself out of bed. As I put away a pile of line-dried clothing stiff to the touch that someone had brought in from outside and left, I decided Lexie was right. Why shouldn't I get a day off? My bullet arm ached; I had no energy; and I couldn't stop worrying about that incredibly handsome, sweet guy who I knew now that I wanted to marry. I kept seeing his blue-grey eyes, sparkling like a lake in sunshine. If only I'd gone with him! If he'd been killed, then I'd be killed, too. I wanted out! I wished I could get off this rotten compound!

At the very least, I would insist on a day off from my usual chores. Maybe I'd even escape in a book like Lexie.

As I rounded the door into the former women's bedroom which now Lexie and I call sick bay (in honor of *Star Trek,* which we both miss) I felt relieved; at least I wasn't confined here any longer, as I had been after I was shot. Hearing a sound, I stopped to listen. Someone was getting sick. What used to be a closet was cleared out for a dry sink and a portable toilet. This made the room more like a real sick bay and right now it seemed someone was really sick.

I backed out to the hallway because the sound was getting to me. I didn't want to get sick, too. And then to my surprise the person who walked out a minute or two later still not looking like her usual healthy self, was Lexie. She seemed startled to see me.

"Lex! You're sick!" I cried.

"I'm okay."

"I heard you—you're sick. You need today off more than I do."

"I'm not sick," she said. "It's just something I ate." She looked at me. "Did you get the day off?"

"I came here to ask. I—."

"My mom can give you a day off. You don't need Mrs. Philpot to sanction it just because she's a nurse."

"OK; but she'd know if I really need it."

"You need it. My dad had a friend who used to take days off and come out to the farm to play at being rustic; he called them 'mental health days.' So if nothing else, I think you deserve a mental health day." I held my stomach just then, as a strong cramp overcame me.

"Ohhh, it's that time of the month," she said.

I stared at Lex. How annoying of her to know right away. She was right, of course. I sniffed. "Maybe."

She patted my arm, looked around and then back at me, and whispered. "Look. I still have some sanitary pads. I'll give you a few so you don't have to use rags on the heaviest days."

"You still have some? And you didn't tell me?"

She looked taken aback. "I don't have to share EVERYTHING with you. I'm allowed to keep some of my stuff, you know."

I frowned. "But you listened to me griping last month about not having pads and you didn't offer me any then."

She rolled her eyes. "I'm offering you some now. Do you, or do you not want them?"

"I do." I forced myself to add, "Thank you." I was miffed that she'd been holding out on me, though.

"Okay," she said, and started to walk off.

"Can I have them now?"

She turned and smiled. "So it IS that time. I thought so. You're weepier than usual. I'll get them." She walked off, grinning.

I felt freshly annoyed. There was nothing funny about me getting weepy because it was my time of the month. If anyone had anything to be weepy about in fact, it was me. And she got weepy too—sometimes. And it's not like I can actually help it. My mother was the same way.

I decided the real reason Lex knew was because once we were rooming together, our periods got more and more in alignment. I suppose if we'd asked Blake about it, he'd know some scientific reason why that happens when women are in close quarters. That's what Mrs. Martin told us last month—that it happens. She didn't know why, something about hormones. But isn't it weird that an internal thing like a menstrual clock can be affected by somebody else's menstrual clock?

And then it struck me. Why didn't Lexie have HER period? Had she offered me her pads because she DIDN'T NEED THEM? And I'd heard her getting sick! Suddenly it seemed startlingly clear: Lexie was pregnant! She was carrying Blake's baby!

The thought stunned me. I almost wanted to run after her but I didn't feel like running. When she returned and handed me a full package of pads, I guess I was staring at her because she asked, "What?" Then, misunderstanding my look, she added, "You can have them all."

"I guess you're not going to need them, huh?" I spoke slowly. She looked at me strangely, but her mom called her, and she said, "Gotta go! See you later!"

We'd had talks about whether to get physical with guys. We'd talked about her and Blake, mostly. She always insisted she'd wait until marriage and that Blake was on board with that, but now I wonder. I think all of her protests about it being wrong and sinful were just to throw me off track.

I can't imagine what Mr. and Mrs. Martin will say! Of course I'll try to keep her secret but I have to admit I'm disappointed with Lex and Blake. Lexie has always seemed like the model Christian—aside from when she wouldn't forgive me for flirting with Blake. At least now I know she's human.

LATER

I love having regular pads again! Not quite as good as the brand I used to like but it's wonderful next to the rags and paper I've been using.

Anyway, I found Mrs. Martin and got the day off from chores except I still have to watch Lily. So really it's not a day off. That baby is work! But she's precious and I enjoy her. Although my arm is extra sore because she was getting goofy and rammed her little fist into my arm, right where the wound was. *Ouch!*

Some days I actually forget I've been shot. Other days I'm sure I can feel a bullet in there but Roper assured me he'd found "my bullet," as he calls it. Jared asked to see it the day I was shot—I was unconscious, but Lexie told me Roper gave it to him. And he's never given it back.

If Jared returns, I hope he still has it—though I won't have the nerve to ask him for it. And he'd better have Roper with him, too.

◆

After two hours Lily finally took a nap. When she did, I got to do—nothing!

.

Chapter Eleven

ROPER

When they started out from the Martin compound, Jared had confidently asserted that he and Roper should only be gone a few days. Jared needed certain items to build more weapons and Roper had come along to be of help. They'd each taken a horse with saddle bags, not only for provisions, but in hopes of needing the animals to help bring back the booty.

Both men knew it was risky business. Numerous times they'd had to leave the road to take cover when they heard vehicles approaching. Each time it was an army truck or a group of them, just like the ones that had attacked the compound.

On other occasions they'd led the horses through brushy woods or swampy ravines to get out of sight from bands of men. They were often forced off the road this way or stuck waiting for it to clear—and meanwhile the days passed, and they still lacked what was needed.

It was now going on three weeks and they'd gathered precious little in the way of supplies—not enough to fill a saddle bag.

From the outset, it had become clear to Roper that he and his companion were cut from two very different cloths. They disagreed on just about everything. Their mission, for instance. Way back on day one, Roper wanted to check Andrea's house first, fulfill their promise and get it over with. But Jared said, "We'll check her house eventually, but first we concentrate on weapons."

Roper said, "We should check the house first, in case her mother is holed up there."

Jared shook his head. "Look, you know as well as I do that Andrea's mom is a goner. She was dead the moment she stepped foot off the compound. Her and what's his name—Washington—they were both dead the minute they left."

Roper frowned. "We don't know that for sure."

Jared snorted. "They were stupid enough to leave, they weren't trained in the use of firearms or any survival skills I know of—what do you really think their chances were? They're gone, I'm telling you."

"We gave Andrea our word that we'd check her house—."

"And we will. If we can. Weapons, first. The whole compound is depending upon us. I'm not gonna risk this mission for a fool's errand."

From then on, it seemed like one thing after another raised disagreements between the two. When Roper agreed to put off searching for Mrs. Patterson, he said, "Okay, so how do we find weapons?" They were on the road, alert for the presence of other people or other threats.

Jared glanced at him, caustically. "We don't." After a long pause, during which Roper tried to decide whether to ask another question of his ornery companion, Jared added, "I told you—I told everyone at the last meeting—we build them. What we need to find are the ingredients."

Roper's brow was raised, as he wondered where they'd find material to make guns or bullets. Jared's next words revealed he had other things in mind, however.

"The Martins have sugar and fertilizer we can use, if I can keep them convinced it's more important for defense purposes than for growing crops."

Fertilizer and sugar? Oh, right. Jared's idea of adding to the compound's arsenal meant making a stash of homemade bombs and grenades.

"That means we only need to find fuel," Jared continued. "And aluminum or some other metal that can be flaked or ground up."

"Where do we get that?"

Jared shrugged. "Garbage dumps. Garbage piles. Abandoned homes."

Roper's face scrunched in thought. "I read once that you could use just fertilizer to build bombs."

Jared didn't turn, but nodded. "Yup."

"So if the Martins have a lot of fertilizer, I mean, they're farmers and should have a lot, right? Why not make bombs that use just fertilizer?"

"I might do that—in winter. Fertilizer—that's ammonium nitrate—those bombs need to stay cold. They're not stable. Right now I'm looking for stuff that's gonna work without ice, because we don't have ice." He looked scornfully at Roper. "Unless you happen to know where we could get us some."

Roper didn't bother to answer. No one had ice, now.

They scoured the countryside for buildings or storefronts that might house useful items but so far everything had been a wash; either already emptied out or burned down.

Even the roads which had been sprinkled with dead cars after the pulse, were now cleared in the center for as long as they could see in either direction. They figured the guerrillas, who needed to get about in army trucks, had cleared them. The cars had been pushed roughly out of the way. Many sat at odd angles, their rear tires upended, or on their sides; some were even completely upturned or pushed off-road.

They slowed their horses when they came upon a complex of huge storage buildings. According to the sign, it had been a giant indoor flea market before the pulse. The large warehouse doors were busted and hanging open but otherwise intact. There was no evidence of arson. Jared slowed, surveying the place.

"You think there's anything left in there?" Roper asked.

Jared nodded, looking thoughtful. "Looters look for food. Could be they've left behind things we need. Like fireworks. There's lots of black powder in fireworks. Maybe we'll find us some nails, tacks, BBs, or ball bearings…Keep an eye open for anything that can cause damage after an explosion."

74

"It would be easier to check out Andrea's house first while we're not carrying a lot. We can come back on the return trip and get whatever's here."

Jared's brows furrowed. "If there are supplies here, they can be taken by anyone. We need to determine what's here, take what we can while we can, and then get to the house."

Roper's face went bland. He hadn't expected Jared to budge but figured he'd give a last-ditch effort for Andrea's sake. Surely the more time that passed, the less chance there was of finding her mother alive. He'd do it alone if he could, but he didn't dare split up—they were supposed to have each other's back.

"If you see anyone, don't stop to ask questions," Jared said, as they approached the building.

Now Roper's brows creased. "If I see people, I usually talk to them. Unless they are clearly a threat—."

"All people are a clear threat."

"Not *all*." He gave Jared a look of alarm.

"Okay. 99.9% of people are a threat. Don't stop to ask questions. Shoot first, talk later." He gave a sardonic smile.

"Shoot first?" Roper's tone mirrored his shock. "I thought you meant ignore them, not shoot them!"

Jared sighed as if he was trying to be patient with a recalcitrant child. "The only way to handle a threat is to REMOVE it," he said, pointedly. "If you don't remove the threat, it'll turn and remove you."

They'd almost reached the gaping entrance so they dismounted and approached the first of the wide doors, half-open, swinging on its hinges. But Roper halted. He had to iron this out, now.

"Look, I won't shoot on sight, unless someone's shooting at me."

Jared glared at him. "Keep your voice down!" he hissed. Then, answering him in a whisper, "That's foolish. Anyone can be a hostile. A child can be a hostile." He surveyed Roper coldly.

Roper gave a little smile. "They could also be lost. I'd give them the gospel."

Jared snorted, unable to hide his disgust. "That is the stupidest thing I ever heard! Even if it wasn't taking your life in your hands, we don't have time for that! If we see anyone, we take care of them and we move on. That is the ONLY way to ensure the safety and success of this mission."

"Take care of them?"

Jared motioned with his head towards Roper's rifle. "That's why we're armed," he said, as if it should have been obvious to a fool.

"There's no way I'm gonna shoot on sight," Roper repeated.

Jared shook his head. "Why did they send YOU with me? Of all the—."

"Most people aren't dangerous," Roper insisted. "And some could be an asset. I met a guy in Pennsylvania who was a scholar and medieval architect. He could have been helpful to the compound, showing us the best way to build defenses, old-style, like things castles used in the Middle Ages. I wish he'd stayed with me."

Jared poked his head cautiously past the first swinging door, looked around and then back at Roper. "So what happened to him?" he asked, still keeping his voice low.

Roper was silent a moment. "He didn't want to leave the city. Felt it would be safer in the long run."

Jared motioned them forward, and they went in, straining eyes and ears for anything that seemed suspicious. "Most professionals," he said, and paused, listening. "Even the smart ones;" Another pause. "Weren't smart about survival." His eyes roamed the dim interior, alert as a predator. "They're gone, man." Continuing to stop and search between remarks, he added, "It's people like you and me. Who are still here. Ex-military, survivalists. Homesteaders, preppers... We're the only ones who knew how...to stay alive this long. And in my view, we're also the most—dangerous." He turned and looked full at Roper. "That's why if we see anyone, I say, shoot on sight. Ask questions later."

Roper eyed his companion gravely. He sure hoped they would not run into anyone. Jared was seriously reckless, a danger to society—

even post-apocalyptic society, which was already seriously dangerous. He'd noticed that Jared fell into dark moods, and seemed especially dangerous then. Once, he'd emptied a full magazine at a line of hedges after hearing a noise from behind it. Turned out to be a bird.

"I don't fit any of the categories you mentioned. I'm not ex-military, I'm not a homesteader or survivalist."

"You are now," Jared shot in.

"But I wasn't before. I wasn't ready for the grid to go down, but I'm still here. You're not giving people enough credit."

Jared eyed him sideways. "You got lucky. Other people—those who DO fit the above categories, took you in. Or you'd be gone, too. Anyway, we have the compound depending on us to get back with supplies. And this is war. We shoot on sight."

Roper's mouth hardened. "We're not at war with fellow Americans!"

Again Jared motioned them forward a few steps but shook his head, smiling humorlessly. "Where have you *been* since the pulse? How can you say that? Most of our conflicts have been with fellow Americans." Sneering, he continued, "The foreign hostiles may be the most dangerous, better armed, but we've been fighting our wonderful compatriots since the grid went down. And that isn't going to change. It only gets worse as more people starve to death."

Roper mused silently for a moment. "Sometimes," he finally offered, "the secret to unexpected things—even great things—lies in welcoming strangers into your life. You shoot the stranger—heck, don't even kill him, just fail to welcome him, and you kill the great thing, the thing that might have been."

Jared made no response. He was digging into his saddle bag for something.

Roper continued, "Sometimes you have to move from your head to your heart before knowing what to do." He swallowed. "God speaks to the heart before the head."

"You're always spouting the Bible! What are you, a priest?" He pulled out a battery-operated lantern and held it in one hand while he closed up the saddle bag.

Roper gave a gentle smile. "Not a Catholic priest, if that's what you mean. But the Bible says all God's chosen are a royal priesthood, a holy nation. So that includes me." He smiled suddenly and even Jared could not be wholly impervious to Roper's wildly charming grin. There was something winsome, inviting, and warm in Roper's smile. It was an attribute totally foreign to Jared's features and perhaps explained why he didn't reply with a stinging bit of sarcasm as was his usual wont—but simply fell silent.

"We're moving in," was all he said, once again motioning with his head for Roper to follow. But he paused and said pointedly, "Stay behind me and keep your mouth shut."

They proceeded slowly, leading their horses by the reins. The interior quickly grew dark. After ten feet or so it was inky black. The horses stamped and snorted uneasily. Roper stroked his mare's head, speaking soothingly, while Jared switched on the lantern. A wide middle aisle appeared before them, the air thick with stagnant dust. Jared directed the beam into each stall or storefront to their right and left, revealing the remnants of ransacked, ravaged goods.

Everything was damaged. Perfectly good chairs and sofas were ripped across their middles as if someone in a rage had destroyed them for no discernible reason.

Roper silently shook his head. He'd seen such sights before. It was as though something evil didn't want anything to survive and be useful. It was needless destruction. Ripping up furniture, tearing apart clothing and linens—what good did it do anyone? It didn't put food in their bellies or warm their homes.

In addition to the mess, the place had the foul smell of a urinal.

"People must have holed up here during the cold," Jared whispered. "Still stinks."

"I think we're wasting our time in here," Roper said. He'd never been on a reconnaissance mission before, certainly not to find material to build weapons, but he'd been through plenty of abandoned buildings since the pulse—places he'd stopped for shelter at night or to escape the worst of a storm. He had a feeling about places, whether they'd contain anything useful. Nothing about the reeking remnants of this once bustling flea market held promise.

And then they passed a counter of dried flowers, many still intact—Roper grabbed a garland of red roses with greenery and white pearl accents. He strung it across Scarlett's saddle so that it hung down on either side. "Give me a flag and a lance, and my steed and I are ready for the joust," he joked.

Jared glared at him. "We're gonna need every inch of that saddle and the space in your bags for important stuff."

Roper returned his look with one of innocent surprise. "It's for the girls." Besides, he added to himself, they hadn't found any supplies thus far. He had plenty of space.

He thought momentarily of Andrea. She'd like the garland. He caught Jared's steely gaze upon him at that moment and somehow felt the other man knew he meant to give it to her.

"What?" Roper asked.

Jared shook his head. His look was one of contempt but he said nothing.

They moved on, passing stalls festooned with cobwebs and with empty, broken shelves and shattered boards and bricks. A former toy-store, eerily dark and still, held some toys and dust-covered stuffed animals. Jared said, "Wait," and handed Roper the reins of his horse while he quickly scanned the aisles. He stopped and grabbed a boxful of something, and then another, tucking them beneath one arm. He moved on and grabbed a box of something else and finally returned to Roper in the main aisle.

"What'd you find?" Roper asked.

Jared was stuffing the boxes into his saddle bag. "BBs and firecrackers. Not enough to make me happy but it's a start."

They kept going up and down the eerie aisles strewn with garbage, shining the lamp into stalls long enough to ascertain if there was anything left of interest. Turning at the end of one aisle, the foul scent suddenly grew stronger. Roper froze.

"That is sick!" he exclaimed. Scarlett snuffled as if in agreement.

Jared looked at him, annoyed. "We gotta keep going."

"The other way, man," Roper said, coughing. "Something is—something's gotta be *dead* in that direction!"

Jared nodded. "Yeah, so what? We won't have to worry about hostiles—they won't stay with that odor. There could be good stuff. C'mon."

Roper shook his head, frowning. "Fine. Wait a sec." He grabbed a bandana from around his neck and tied it over his mouth and nose. Jared watched, whether amused or annoyed, Roper couldn't tell—or much care. Again it was evident the two were certainly not soul mates. Jared with his shaved hair and face beside Roper with his curly locks and beard—both of which had grown straggly at the ends. Jared had the discipline of a cadet, shaved with a disposable razor each morning (he seemed to have an endless supply of those) and somehow maintained a neat overall appearance that was totally impossible for Roper.

Jared still dressed like an Army guy too, in fatigues and combat boots—even now at the start of summer when it was oppressively hot in direct sunlight. Only his head was bare. Roper sported well-worn jeans, a light cotton plaid shirt, and newer sneakers—a pair he'd found in an abandoned car shortly before coming upon the Martins' compound. They'd come in handy since he'd long ago discarded his shoes in favor of winter boots donated by a Good Samaritan right after the pulse. He'd done a great deal of walking in those boots...from Pittsburgh to south-western Ohio.

As they moved forward coaxing the horses along, their thoughts were as far different as their appearance. Roper understood what they were looking for but he couldn't help searching for practical items like homestead equipment or clothing. He'd have been equally happy to come across sheet music or a new music stand though he wouldn't have mentioned that to Jared for anything. Occasionally he got to play his trumpet at the compound but it wasn't like the old days before the pulse, when he played in the worship band.

That had been his old life. It had surprisingly ensured him entrance into the Martins' compound since they recognized the trumpet as an instrument to sound the alarm if an attack was imminent. Good thing he'd held onto it...and there had been plenty of opportunities for him to ditch it. Trying to keep his mind on their mission, Roper couldn't help the sudden memories that accosted him...

CHAPTER TWELVE

ROPER

(January 14^{th,}
Three days after the pulse)

They were stranded. It was undeniable now. Roper and his fellow worship team members were stuck in Pennsylvania, thousands of miles from their home in Southern California. At first they'd hoped like everyone else that the outage and the failure of electronics was temporary. But now everyone agreed something irreversible had happened though the theories differed as to what it was.

The fact remained, no matter what had caused their predicament, that Roper and his friends were unacceptably far from home. Still thinking that surely there'd be a fix, that things would start working again or somehow the government would mitigate the circumstances, he and his friends waited—weighing their options—and watched chaos descend upon Pittsburgh. Gangs, looting, violence—life was getting more and more dangerous but the weather was mortally cold. If it warmed a little, it snowed. Then the pastor with whom they were staying admitted he couldn't keep feeding them. They had no choice but to begin the journey home.

From the moment he and his band realized the grid was down indefinitely and they'd have to walk back to California, food, water, and heat—perhaps heat most of all—were the constant things on their minds. Still, if they could *stay together* Roper felt sure they would somehow make it across the country.

Then, one by one, he'd lost his team. The drummer re-injured an old wound on the first day's walk; Roper didn't like doing it but they left him at the house of a church member. The family kindly took him in but they were already wondering how they'd keep feeding their own children now that the stores were empty. He hoped they wouldn't force his friend to leave when things got really desperate.

Then his bass guitar player who was overweight and not keen on making the journey decided home in California was too far. He bailed out when they came across a huge mega-church that said they had water for anyone who wanted it.

"You can't live on water," Roper said. "We'll fill our bottles and keep going. Together."

"I'll only slow you down, man. I'm okay. Leave me here."

So now it was only Roper and Aaron, the second guitar player, and the female singers. They were Aurelia, who sang lead, and a duo of backup singers, Jocelyn and Jackie. Aaron was the youngest member of the team, a slim teen on his first mission trip. He was lean and lanky and seemed to be doing okay although he suffered from the cold more than the rest of them and required stops so his hands and feet could thaw out. The women walked faster than he did but Roper figured he'd spent too many hours playing video games instead of developing muscles.

Eventually, even though they'd all managed to bundle up with donated clothing from the church before leaving, the kid was unable to get warm at all. No amount of layers did it for him. Unless he was plopped down right in front of a fire, he shivered. The whole team considered waiting out winter somewhere but Aaron wouldn't hear of it. He badly wanted to get back to his family in California and insisted he could do it.

Being Californians, the cold and snow was a shock to all of them. Every night was a struggle for warmth but there seemed to always be a business or store they could find a corner to hole up in. At daylight, they'd start out again. For awhile Aaron seemed to be getting hardened to the freezing weather.

Roper's presence was surely one of the reasons they managed to get as far as they did. He had a saintly attitude about their journey. Like a Franciscan monk, he trusted God for each day's needs. Not just hoped, but really trusted!

He'd tell the others, "Hey, God has made us dependent on him in ways we would never have been dependent before. Remember St. Francis? He embraced poverty, saw in it God's gracious hand, the opportunity to rely completely on him for food and shelter. We can do the same."

And it had to be divine provision that kept them alive, considering that everywhere they went they encountered death. But at each business or empty home they chose to stop in, they'd find something—packaged crackers, cookies, even beef sticks. Some of the places had been thoroughly looted before they arrived, but even there they'd come across small things that hadn't been found by their predecessors.

Progress was slow due to the snow. They carried two donated sleeping bags and shared them at night—the girls using one and the guys in another. This helped them survive many a cold night with no fire. But days passed while they were forced to wait out a new snowfall. When they did move, they took advantage of roadside barrel fires or small bonfires other travelers were using to thaw frozen limbs and fingers—Roper's belief that they could make it all the way home grew even stronger. At the outset, he'd hoped they could. Now he was believing it.

Until one morning when they went to wake up the kid—and he didn't wake up. Roper was shaken. He felt responsible. Sure, they'd all been living on too little but aside from his sensitivity to the cold, Aaron hadn't seemed sick.

Aurelia said, "He was feeling worse every day."

"Why didn't I know that?"

She frowned. "He was a low-level diabetic." When Roper turned indignant eyes upon her for he'd known nothing about it, she added, "He begged me not to say anything! He was afraid you'd make us stop somewhere; he just wanted to get back home." Her eyes filled with tears. Roper nodded. He was aggravated that Aurelia had kept Aaron's condition from him, but there was no point in chewing her out for it now.

It was impossible to bury the boy due to the frozen ground. They waited a whole day in an empty small house in the middle of nowhere trying to decide what to do with his body. How could they dignify this young person's death when the ground was frozen solid, covered in two feet of snow? Finally, they agreed it was best to cremate the remains. Afterward, Roper found an empty spice bottle in a pile of rubbish and they put some of the ashes in it. He had that bottle, still. One day, if he got back to California, he'd give it to Aaron's family—if they were alive.

So then it was just Roper and the three women. He felt a responsibility he'd never known before, being the only man in the group. It wasn't easy for a single young man to have three women curled up around him, snuggling against him every night in the sleeping bags—which they zippered to form one large bag. But it was the only way to stay warm.

As soon as the weather permitted they left the site of that misfortune. Roper tried to encourage the women, to bolster their faith and hope—and thereby their energy. "This is a pilgrimage, a pilgrimage of trust," he said. "God will get us where we need to go, but we gotta hang in there. We gotta be willing to keep on keeping on."

"Trust God for what?" Jocelyn asked. "To stop the snow? To bring back electricity?"

Aurelia added, "To die like Aaron?"

Roper said, gently, "To care for us through the generosity and kindness of his people, and through his Creation."

"His Creation is killing us," said Jackie.

"I don't see provision happening," said Jocelyn.

"It's been happening all along! We're still here, right? We're almost in Ohio—we're almost a state closer to home! We can do this."

He reminded them how Jesus on one occasion had sent His disciples out with *orders* not to bring anything with them. He read the Scripture from Mark chapter six, "Take nothing for your journey except a staff: no bread, no bag, no money in your belts."

He also reminded them that God's very name, Jehovah Jireh, means, *The God Who Provides*. He pointed out that thus far they'd never gone so much as one full day without some nutrition, even if it was only crusty bread (such as what they'd been given that very day by a homeowner whose house they'd passed and inquired at—a full loaf!). Another day a woman offered a small plastic bag of little black seeds—"chia seeds" she called them, saying that in Colonial days a teaspoonful was regarded as sufficient nutrition to sustain an Indian brave for a day's forced march.

It didn't make their stomachs happy but they did indeed keep going on the strength of those seeds for days. At night they'd slept in the pews or basement of churches, in garages or in barns. Even the occasional empty house such as the one where Aaron had died afforded shelter for days at a time while outdoors the snow and sleet made travel unthinkable. Somehow, some way, provision was happening. They always found a place to lay their heads, a bite of something to nourish the body, and Roper recited scripture to feed their souls. Roper was always good for reciting things—he had a near photographic memory.

But despite all that, when they saw they were in Amish country, the girls refused to keep traveling. Aaron's death was still keenly felt. They were demoralized.

"A pilgrimage is always filled with uncertainty," Roper said. "If it was easy it wouldn't be a pilgrimage. Our faith is being tested; our souls are being tested." His look became imploring. "The only way I can do this is if I do it for God," he said. "That's the only way this has meaning. Right now this is our calling! Don't give that up."

"This is too much testing," Aurelia said. The others nodded. "We need a break. We're stopping at the next farm."

"What will you do? How can I leave you there?" he'd asked.

"We'll find an Amish family to take us in."

"Why would they do that?"

"We'll offer manual labor in exchange for upkeep," Jocelyn, one of the back-up singers, said.

"A million other people probably done that by now," Roper said. "They can't take in endless people. We ought to keep going."

"We've talked it out, Roper; come with us."

"Look, if the Amish are going to help people, it'll be their neighbors, not strangers." That fell on deaf ears. He tried another tactic. "Think of your people back home. They are wondering if you're still alive. Don't do this to them, don't keep them wondering. We can get back. We can go *home*."

"Come with us," was their response. "We'll travel in the spring when it's warm. You ought to do what we're doing."

Roper sighed. "Look" he said, "I didn't want to say this but think about it. It's only a matter of time and the Amish are going to be forced to give up whatever supplies they have. MIGHT will win over RIGHT. It's what happens, if you look at history. When a society collapses, whether it's caused by war or a natural disaster, the strong thrive at the expense of the weak."

"So you're saying the Amish are weak?" asked Aurelia.

"They're pacifists," Roper said, shrugging. "They don't believe in weapons. Not even for self-defense. And you saw what was going on in Pittsburgh. That's bound to spread here as well."

The girls however, persisted in their desire to seek out a compassionate Amish homestead. He shook his head. "Then I'll go with you. I need to know you're getting help before I move on."

But after being turned down at a couple of homes, they told Roper, "Go on without us. We've noticed how they're looking at you. We think we'd have a better chance of getting help without you."

At the next farmhouse he hung back but stayed waiting nearby until he knew for sure the women had secured lodging for at least the night. They had assured him they could make themselves useful enough to earn their keep and stay on. Roper wasn't so sure, but he committed them to the Lord. What else could he do?

So then he'd been on his own. And things on the road had gotten so ugly that he stopped moving during the day. Dead bodies and mean looking men were common sights. Roper prayed, walked, prayed, and walked.

And kept heading west.

In cold, lonely moments he began to suspect that perhaps he'd been misguided to trust God for safety in such circumstances, that he would never make it—there were too many dangers in a world without rule of law. His stamina was bound to run out. His survival skills were practically nonexistent—all he remembered, vaguely, was from reading *Hatchet* as a boy. And, *My Side of the Mountain.* Something about you could make flour out of acorns. That was it. Sure, living off the land was possible. If you happened to be Davy Crockett.

As it turned out, you could live off the goodness of God, too, if you happened to have the faith of St. Francis. Or of a Roper. He repeated verses to himself as he walked, such as, "You are my hiding place; you will protect me from trouble and surround me with songs of deliverance, Psalm 32:7." Or, "Our God is a God who saves; from the Sovereign LORD comes escape from death, Psalm 68:28."

The days passed, and he reluctantly discarded his cell phone and any supplies that weren't necessary for survival like a notebook, sheet music, and a foldable music stand. He kept only his trumpet and a small Bible he'd picked up at one of the churches where they'd found shelter; it was half the size of the old leather Bible he'd been carrying, which had belonged originally to his grandfather.

The trumpet was heavy and common sense told him he ought to ditch it. But he found he could not. Instead he tied a bungee cord around the case and attached it to his backpack. It was extra weight, but it was part of him. He'd been playing the instrument since the age of four. Somehow hanging onto it gave him a feeling of normalcy. Even now when the world seemed to be ending, he still had his trumpet.

He kept lighters, matches, socks, gloves, flashlights—anything he came across that aided him on his journey. Nevertheless, with so little possessions, he did seem to personify St. Francis, the famous mendicant. He even had the hair and beard to look the part, and lacked only a brown cowl robe with a rope belt to do justice to the Catholic saint.

He made a mysterious-looking figure, shrouded in a large anorak that he was given at the very outset of the pulse by the pastor whose church they'd been ministering in. The hood was fur-lined and surrounded his face so that when it got encrusted by snow, the frozen outline of fur framed him, making a wide border. It dwarfed what could be seen of his head, which wasn't much to begin with thanks to the beard and mustache. These also got snow-encrusted and formidable. He looked like a walking, snow-covered Yeti.

A stark difference between him and the gentle 12th century monk became evident when he was able to acquire a rifle and handgun: Roper accepted them as part of the divine provisions. He had wearily entered a run-down, abandoned building to get out of a sudden snowfall. He hadn't eaten that day and was famished. But he spoke to a stranger who was sitting face-down, his head upon his knees, recognizing, he thought, the look of the downtrodden. He was instantly ready to minister to him as a Christian, pray with him, when he discovered—to his chagrin—that he was dead!

The cold had preserved him beautifully. Roper thought at first that he had to be alive. Closer inspection proved otherwise; and revealed a rifle, still partially slung over one shoulder, which Roper retrieved. He wasn't happy about the man's fate, but he couldn't be sorry to get his hands on the firearm, not after witnessing so much violence out there.

Why the man died, he did not know. There was a crumpled Mylar blanket beside him, as if he'd thrown it off. Roper gently retrieved it, sighing. The world was full of death. But this one death provided more than a rifle; he marveled how, like the cycle of life in nature, this man's passing instantly bequeathed his belongings to whatever soul found them—and Roper was that soul. And, because he had a backpack that contained real treasure, his death gave Roper life.

He'd almost missed the backpack because the man was sitting on it, but it contained a pistol, two mags of bullets, a sharp knife, a

water filter, ice pick, a bundle of kindling, matches, a nail clipper—
Roper grabbed that as if it were gold—and, most amazing of all—ten
MREs.

MREs—Meals Ready to Eat—were military rations, as the
labels clearly explained. He'd never handled one before. But it was
food—with such supplies the man hadn't starved to death. Why had he
allowed himself to freeze? He even had kindling and matches—Roper
surmised that he'd probably not intended to die; had likely stopped to
rest and succumbed to hypothermia. It was a fresh reminder that
hypothermia was a constant threat. Falling into it *would* remove a man's
judgment, cause him to simply sit and freeze to death.

He debated whether to make a fire and cremate him, for burial
was out of the question; but in the end, after removing the man's coat—
an effort that turned out to be more difficult than he anticipated since
the body was stiff—and closing his eyes, he left him.

He managed to fit the coat beneath his anorak, knowing every
layer was added safety from the cold. He moved to another part of the
building and eagerly tore into the first MRE. It delighted him that it
came with not only an entree, but crackers, a candy bar, matches, salt
and pepper, instant coffee and powdered creamer, a wet wipe and a
tissue! It didn't even require building a fire to heat, as the entrees came
in a self-heating pouch. Sweet!

Soon he was munching with unbelievable appreciation for every
bite and giving thanks as he ate. It wasn't his ideal manner of finding
nourishment—to take it from a dead man—but it was food and it was
Providence that had led him to it.

He forced himself not to gorge on that first meal. His body
wasn't accustomed to calorie-rich food. He collected snow in an old tin
can, melted it over a small fire, and drank the coffee. Even instant
coffee with powdered creamer tasted wonderful. With rising excitement
Roper realized that if he rationed these meals they would last him for
perhaps ten days. If he ate only one a day—and he could do that,
because each meal promised a minimum calorie-count of 1,250—he'd
still be eating more per day than he'd had since the pulse.

In the morning he was ready to be off. There was fresh snow, glittering in the cold, but a clear sky. Beautiful walking weather—or so it seemed to a guy who'd been trudging through gray days and ice storms for weeks. With the candy bar from last night's MRE as the day's portion, he started off on a long stretch of lonely road, framed on either side by woods. It went on for miles like that.

Judging by signs he passed periodically, Roper figured he was covering about eight miles a day—not too bad for winter walking. Dark moments made him figure it was just a matter of time until he'd be the one to freeze to death but each night found him in some kind of shelter, just as it had happened for him all along. God was still providing.

Older people, much to his surprise, were usually less helpless than younger folks. They had memories of life before electricity or knew stories from their parents about how to get by without it. Some, to his utter shock, even had outhouses on their properties. In the United States! He'd no idea that outhouses were still in use in some places. But he was discovering that these remote outposts were better prepared for the grid being down than their wealthy, techno-loaded counterparts. They had wood stoves, small rooms that kept the heat in, stores of firewood near the house, dried meat and beans—things the wealthy often lacked.

In late February when the weather seemed at its worst, one man gave him shelter for several weeks in exchange for labor. Roper chopped wood, gutted, skinned and cleaned small game, tended the fire, even cooked for this guy, Jeff. When he finally left in late March, he had snowshoes and two packages of jerky for the journey, which Jeff insisted he take—things he credited his survival with. He made it through a long stretch of forested roads between Pennsylvania and Ohio, thanks to those provisions.

Many weeks later, by the time he reached the perimeter of the Martins' property and came across two lookouts—one of whom was Blake—he carried little else but his weapons, trumpet, and now a guitar as well. He'd found it in the last house he'd stayed in, an abandoned older home that had the usual broken windows and ransacked disorder.

Pure stubbornness had kept him from ditching the instruments, but even that turned out to be providential.

Blake later said when he saw the trumpet and guitar, he figured Roper couldn't be all bad.

It was another God-thing, just like his survival, he told Andrea later. At the compound, Roper's journey would become almost legendary.

Legendary, that is, to everyone except Jared.

Chapter Thirteen

JARED

To Jared, the abandoned flea market was a wind-fall of potentially weapon-able items, things necessary for building the bombs he could make to help protect the compound. But every foot forward was dangerous. Each forsaken stall, store, or counter had places anyone could be hiding behind. If someone had made this warehouse home, he and Roper could be killed quickly and easily as they made their way down the wide aisles.

He said nothing to Roper about it since the man was incapable of caution to begin with. Anyone who would hesitate to take quick action when faced with a threat was unlikely to be alert to them in the first place.

As they led the horses along, he mentally rehearsed the recipe he'd learned in the military for making IEDs, "Improvised Explosive Devices." All terrorists were well-versed in how to build them and he'd learned what they were made of and how to mix them, too. He hadn't actually built anything except homemade grenades before, but was sure he could reproduce the methods to make the bigger stuff.

If.

If he could find what he needed to make them.

Well, there was more than one way to build Rome. Different recipes meant that if he failed to find the exact ingredients for one, they might luck out with what was needed for another.

"So what else are we looking for?" Roper suddenly asked, his voice muffled behind the bandana. It was as though he'd read Jared's mind, and he glanced quickly at the man. But Roper's eyes were scanning the walls, counters, and stalls they were passing, not even looking at Jared.

"Lead pipes—or any thick metal pipes," he answered. "Jerry cans would be handy. Magnesium powder; and some potassium chlorate and potassium perchlorate."

"Whoa! What?"

"Well, if I knew how to remove an airbag initiator, we could get the perchlorate from dead cars. Unfortunately, I haven't ever done that, so—"

"Oh, there I can help you," said Roper. "I used to work as an auto mechanic—while I was waiting to get a job in the ministry."

Jared stared at him. "Why didn't you say so? We've passed about a hundred cars already!"

Roper stared back. "Why didn't *you* say so? I didn't know you could use airbag initiators!"

Frowning, Jared moved on. Secretly he was impressed. He did not work on cars himself and it was the first thing he'd seen in Roper that garnered respect—mechanical ability. It sure beat his claim to fame as a trumpet player!

"I can get initiators out easy enough," Roper continued. "But you gotta be careful with those things, man. They'll explode on you in a heartbeat if you don't—."

"I can handle the explosives—." Jared interjected. "Just get me the parts."

———————— ♦ ————————

Roper nodded. But he remembered the warning he'd seen on numerous airbags, especially newer model ones. *DANGER—POISON. Contains sodium azide and potassium nitrate. Contents are poisonous and extremely flammable.* Due to his photographic memory he could recall the full warning: *Do not dismantle or incinerate this unit. Do not probe with electrical test devices. Dispose as instructed in the airbag shop manual.*

Most of the airbags he'd removed had been deployed in a car accident. They no longer posed a danger. Jared wanted to remove ones that hadn't deployed in order to access the chemical cocktails inside them. As he thought about the careful steps he'd take to do this, Jared said, "We could get potassium chlorate from firecrackers, maybe sodium chlorate, too. And magnesium powder is an industrial lubricant, but lots of farmers use it." He glanced at Roper. "Not the Martins, unfortunately. We'll look in abandoned factories." He paused. "A little petroleum jelly and red phosphorous will help, too."

"Is that all?" Roper asked, drily. He had no idea where or how to find such ingredients.

"If we can find us a whole bunch of pyrotechnics, we'll have it all," Jared said. "Keep an eye out for fireworks."

"What'll you use to hold the mixture, when you make these bombs?"

Jared shrugged. "I can use a few jerry cans, or empty fire extinguishers. If push comes to shove I can make do with empty 2 liter soda bottles. But I'd rather have the heavier stuff."

Roper was silent for a moment, thinking. "What about empty oxygen containers? I saw some at the compound."

"You sure?" Jared looked doubtful.

"They were for an old lady who died. A friend of the family."

"How many?"

"I don't know; at least a dozen, maybe more."

"They'd be perfect," Jared grunted. He added, "You look for stuff like work gloves, dust masks and safety glasses—I'll look for the other stuff."

Roper's horse nickered and pulled back, then came to a halt. Roper was puzzled for only a second, for suddenly the stench was worse and even his bandana could not mask its strength. Calming the animal with one hand, he coaxed her along. Jared's horse didn't seem bothered but they each kept a tight hold on the reins.

They had reached a former pet shop which previously sold live animals along with other pet supplies. It still had cages and feed and hay and animal toys. And the source of the stench. Inside some of the cages were the rotting remains of dead animals.

"Why didn't anyone just let them out after the pulse?" Roper asked, softly. His eyes were full of glinting sorrow.

Jared said, "It happened in the dead of winter. Probably no one got here for days afterward. The animals would have frozen to death or been dehydrated by then." Muttering beneath his breath he added, "I'm surprised no one ate them."

He again handed Roper the reins and quickly went through the place, grabbing leather leashes, dog chews, treats, and even flea medicine. When he'd stashed it all in a pack, they moved on.

"We'll pick up a few cages on the return trip," Jared said. "They can be used for traps, or scrapped for metal."

Roper was trying not to puke behind the bandana. Jared sure had a strong stomach. He gave a dry heave and Jared sent appraising eyes at him. "Dead animals getting to ya? Save it. You'll need it for worse than this."

"I've seen worse," Roper said, quietly. "I hope not to again."

Jared gave a low whistle. "Until this ends, there's no guarantee of that."

"I know."

They continued down one aisle and another, each turning at the end and opening onto the next. Eventually the stench lessened. Jared said, "So how come you still believe in God? After seeing what happened? So many people dying?"

Roper was silent for a minute. "You've been to war," he said, "right?"

Jared said. "Yup. Iraq and Afghanistan."

"Did you see a lot of death?"

"Enough."

"Did it make you stop believing in God?"

Jared didn't answer immediately, but raised his head, thinking. "I'm not sure I ever believed in God."

"Do you believe in evil?"

Jared snorted. "I guess so."

"How can there be evil, how could you recognize evil, if you didn't also know and recognize good? God is good—and all good things come from him."

And then a loud crack and an impact behind them sent the men scurrying for cover. The sound echoed off the walls, making it difficult—even for Jared—to tell what caliber shot it was, or how far the shooter might be. A second shot sent Roper's horse Scarlett crashing to the ground, whinnying in pain, while Roper scurried out of the way. Jared turned off his lamp and stowed it. Both men drew their rifles and cocked them, preparing to shoot.

CHAPTER FOURTEEN

ROPER

Roper waited, his rifle at the ready. The mare had taken the bullet in a wither and was bleeding heavily, not trying to rise. He patted her helplessly, wishing he could do something for her but first they needed to know where the shots had come from—and if more were forthcoming.

Only silence ensued.

Looking at Scarlett's wound, a flare of anger went through him. Horses were valuable and needed for riding and work. Shooting one was just plain mean—or foolish. Some people were desperate enough to see a horse as their next meal, though. He wondered if that was the case now.

After listening and watching for tense minutes and hearing nothing, Jared murmured, "We need to move; we're gonna stay low, take it nice and slow, and see what we're up against."

"What about Scarlett?" asked Roper. "We can't just leave her like this!" He had no experience with big animal husbandry, but it appeared the mare wasn't going to get to her feet—and he didn't want to leave her to suffer on.

Jared took a look at the wound which was bleeding profusely. "I can't help her and neither can you. We have to put her down or leave her this way."

Roper stroked the mare's long, smooth nose, and then her neck, whispering soothingly. Frowning, he gently laid aside the rifle and drew his Glock. Putting the gun against her head, wincing, he was about to shoot, when Jared hissed, "No!"

"You said we have to!" Roper shot back in a whisper of equal caliber. "She's in pain!"

"Not yet." Jared was staring ahead, in the direction the shot had come from. "You shot our horse, moron!" he suddenly yelled out.

Roper stared at Jared, surprised he would try to "engage the enemy." A few seconds passed, and what came to their ears next was a complete surprise.

"I'm—I'm sorry!" It was the agonized voice of a woman. The men exchanged surprised glances. What should they do? Roper made a movement as if to rise, but Jared motioned him back.

"It's a *woman*!" Roper said.

"I doubt she's alone," Jared replied, his lips tight.

"Tell her we have to put down the horse; that we're not firing at her."

Jared eyed him steadily, as if considering whether to agree. He glanced at Scarlett, then shouted, "We have to put down the horse. We're not shooting at you!"

"Okay!"

Roper, meanwhile, had plugged his ears and with a sigh, after re-positioning the handgun, closed his eyes and made the shot.

"Whoa!" Jared had to keep his horse from taking off at the noise. After the echo had reverberated around them in a deafening cacophony, another sound came faintly to their ears: running feet. Listening hard, Jared murmured, "She's running away, not towards us."

Roper said, "Maybe she *was* alone."

"I'm gonna go after her."

"What for?"

"To take her down, what else?"

"Let 'er go! C'mon."

"She could be running for help," Jared said.

"Look, let's get through this place and get out of here. If you go after her, I could lose you." In truth, Roper wasn't worried about losing Jared. But he'd say anything in order to save that woman's life.

Finally, Jared shrugged. "Whatever. If she brings back company, don't say I didn't warn you. C'mon, let's move."

Roper leaned over Scarlett, giving her lifeless head one last stroke. "I'm sorry," he whispered. When she'd fallen from the shot, it was right onto one of the saddle bags. Both men had to work to get it free. Afterward, Roper hoisted them onto his shoulders, while Jared switched the lantern back on.

Roper grabbed the festoon of flowers and draped it across Jared's horse. Jared grabbed it and threw it roughly to the side. "Get that off my horse!"

Roper eyed him silently. "The girls would've liked that."

"Weapons first. When we got that covered, you can stock up on pantyhose for all I care. But weapons first." Jared moved on, but behind him Roper quickly grabbed the garland and swept it into his pack, except that a foot-long stretch of it remained dangling out. He ignored it, quickening his steps to keep up with Jared.

"Hold onto my horse," Jared said suddenly, handing him the reins. "While I check out this aisle. In case there's some other moron in here. Hang tight." He took off surreptitiously, making as quick a reconnaissance of the aisle as possible. Roper, meanwhile, noticed that the booth he stood in front of held antique prints, posters, books and newspapers. In the past, he'd have happily perused the boxes of printed matter. He had a great collection of old song sheets back in California.

Why not? He entered the stall, leading the horse. As he held the lantern over the boxes of prints, his eyes lit with a sudden gleam and he headed to the back of the booth. He was rummaging through dusty boxes of stuff when Jared said from the aisle. "What are you doing? C'mon. It's clear."

"Hold on," said Roper, who continued to pore through a large box. Jared watched him, silent and frowning.

"I was right!" Roper exclaimed. "These are Ohio Yellow Pages, not too old, either."

"And what, pray, do we need Yellow Pages for?" Jared's dry question merely brought a smile to Roper's face.

"To find the nearest pyrotechnics factory," he stated, calmly. Jared's expression changed.

"Bring it out here," he said.

In seconds they were scanning the pages by the light of the lantern. But shortly Jared threw the book down in disgust. "The nearest one's twenty-five, thirty miles away. We can't risk going that far."

"I walked more than two hundred miles before I came to the compound," Roper said. "We can do thirty."

Jared eyed him with his usual steely look. "Where'd you walk from?"

"Pittsburgh."

Jared shook his head. "Was that place a mess?"

Roper nodded, his eyes darkening. "Crazy, man. Crazy." They resumed walking, their eyes roaming the garbage-strewn stalls as they passed.

"So how long did it take you to get here?" Jared asked.

"About five months. We headed out four days after the pulse hit. I made a few lengthy stops, and still got to the compound by June, so—."

"We?"

"Me and my worship band."

"So where's your band?"

The men faced each other. For the first time a glimmer in Jared's eyes hinted at softening.

"One of 'em died; the rest? I don't know," he said. "But I got here, and I was alone most of the way. Together, we can—."

"We don't have five months," Jared said.

"We don't need to walk two hundred miles."

"But thirty there—and thirty back—plus the danger. Plus, no guarantee that someone else hasn't already raided the place for the same reason we want to."

"Fine. Let's look for stores that might have sold fireworks," Roper said.

"I have a better idea. We're in farm country. Let's find a farm or farm supply store."

"They'll be emptied out," Roper said.

101

"Most people aren't looking for stump remover or saltpeter. If we get some of that and add it to fertilizer I can make us a nice little package for the next foreign army trucks that come at us. Even foil if we can grind it up, can help."

At that moment Jared glanced at the garland dangling from Roper's bag. His look of disgust was quickly followed by a grab for it—he pulled it out and dashed it to the floor, giving Roper a contemptuous sneer as he did so.

Roper, undaunted, bent down to retrieve the garland—and at that precise moment a loud shot came ringing at them, landing with a *thwack* in the wall behind them, missing Roper only because he'd made that swipe. Jared shut off the lantern and slapped his horse in the rear, sending it into the stall to their right. "Stay down!" he said, curtly.

Roper had no intention of doing otherwise. Crouching low, he slowly moved so that he was in the doorway of the stall with Jared beside him. "We gotta get outta here, man," Roper breathed. "We're just sitting ducks."

"Lots of these stalls have back doors," Jared said. "The proprietors use them to load and unload their goods." He headed to the back of the booth, stopping only to take the reins of the horse. There was no door.

"The bigger ones have the doors," Jared said. "C'mon."

At the threshold of the main aisle they hesitated, listening. Jared guided the animal ahead of them, out into the aisle. He motioned Roper to follow, but he refused.

"We need that horse. Don't put him out there in harm's way."

"Better the horse than one of us," Jared said.

"If we do find the right stuff, we'll need him to cart it back."

Jared hesitated. Meanwhile sounds started up, coming their way.

"Which one of you fired that shot?" A man's voice demanded.

"It was Timmy!" Another voice said.

"Take his gun," the man replied. A scuffle ensued and they heard a young man's voice. "It was an accident! I'm sorry! I won't let it happen again!"

"You sure won't because you won't have a gun," said the first voice.

Jared whispered, "You'd think this place is Grand Central Station! But they don't know we're here. C'mon, quietly."

They slunk out into the main aisle, going in the opposite direction of the voices, back the way they'd come. When they turned the aisle into a cross lane, they quickened their pace, putting more distance between them and the others.

They continued straight, passing aisle after aisle until they reached the last one and there found an exit door at the back of the first stall. Outside they moved quickly down the road, getting off it to cross a field as soon as the terrain was suitable.

"This is crazy," Roper said, now that they were safely out of earshot. "We just lost a valuable animal and we had two close calls in there… The stuff you need…it's not just sitting around waiting to be found!"

Jared turned a twisted smile to Roper. "That's the beauty of IEDs; the stuff IS just waiting around."

"Maybe before the pulse—but not now."

"I'm telling you, it's out here. We'll check barns and storage sheds."

"You think people are just going to let you mosey on into their barns or storage buildings? The ones with these supplies…they're farmers, man. They had food, dried grain, they're still here. It's the city people who didn't make it…I know, I've seen it." Roper shuddered. "But these people have survived and they will want to keep what they've got."

"Most barns aren't right next to the house. We'll go in at night."

Roper shook his head. "These bombs—."

"IEDs."

"IEDs—Fine. You said you needed special chemicals to make those mean things, right?"

"Give me a bunch of stuff you could have bought at your nearest drug store and I'll make you an IED."

"Barns aren't drug stores."

Jared sniffed. "You'd be surprised."

"Why don't we just go for the cars, the airbags, like you said? We can head back and hit every vehicle on the way."

Jared was silent a moment. "We came this far and I can use this other stuff, too." He paused. "Besides, we're getting closer to Andrea's house." Roper had forgotten about that! He didn't argue further.

They crossed a ravine, went up the other side and came upon a farm. At first sight it looked abandoned; the tall grass that characterized property now that lawn mowers didn't work made it seem so, but they soon noticed wisps of smoke, just visible against the sunny sky, coming from around the back.

Jared pointed to the right. There was a barn about two hundred feet from the house. Painted the quintessential barn red and bearing a quilt square design on one side, it sat looking bucolic and downright pretty. Beside it was a large fenced pasture where the grass was uneven but short. That meant cattle. Without farm animals the grass would have been above knee-high by now, like it was most everywhere else. The formerly neat homes and yards of suburbs and countryside looked very much like post-apocalyptic America.

They remained in the ravine for cover. Jared led them towards dense brush which had Roper leading the horse around thick branches and twiny vines until Jared stopped and took a deep breath. "We're out of sight. We'll wait here until dark, watch for movement, and then check out the barn."

"Wait for dark!" exclaimed Roper. "That's hours away, yet."

"You got a better idea?" Jared asked, lazily.

Roper surveyed the farmhouse. "Yeah; we ask them if they have the stuff we need. Maybe they'll give it to us."

Jared snorted. "Look, even if they've got no earthly use for what I want, as soon as you tell them we want it, they're gonna want it, too."

"Let's trade something."

"Like what?"

"Labor. Let's do some work and earn the stuff."

Jared shook his head, spitting out a piece of grass that had found its way to his mouth. "You're kidding, right? That won't change anything. If we say what we want they're gonna want to know why we want it. If we tell them, they'll want it too."

"They won't know what to do with it, or how to do it."

"They'll try anyway. Wouldn't you?"

Roper sighed. "No. I guess. I don't know."

Jared said, "I'll take a quick look around for wild edibles; stay here and watch the horse."

Roper sighed heavily. He'd hoped their mission might be accomplished a lot faster. But he thought back to how far he'd come, his "legendary" trek from Pittsburgh to south-western Ohio, and how God had provided for him each step of the way.

God. Had he even prayed since they'd hit the road? He bowed his head to do so; and then hesitated. Could one pray to obtain stuff if it meant taking it from someone else? No, there had to be a better way! Well, that was it, wasn't it?

A better way. That's what he would pray for.

CHAPTER FIFTEEN

SARAH

As I stared out at the growing plumes of flame and smoke shooting out of the barn, Tex drew me away from the window, his eyes creased with worry. He lowered the metal shade—it still worked on that half of the window—and exclaimed, "That barn is gonna blow! I got all that stuff in there to make explosives! Fertilizer and stump remover and—" An enormous boom interrupted him, followed by shouts, falling debris, and then another, smaller explosion. We heard things hitting the ground, and the thudding of running feet. I tried to take a look—all I could see was smoke and flames.

"I can't believe they got past all the new traps," Richard muttered, his lips tight.

I understood his frustration. He and Tex had laid down leg shackles, which were big animal traps, ready to spring. They'd dug new pits and set two new rope traps, the kind that caught Richard and sent him hanging helplessly upside-down when we'd tried to pass through this property. None of it had prevented this.

Tex, frowning, started issuing orders. "Weapon up! Turn the table over for cover! Richard, come with me."

"Where are you going?" Angel asked.

"Out the back way. We're not going to wait for them to breach this cabin. We can't just resist, like last time. This time, we'll meet them head on."

"You mean you're going out *there*?" Angel frowned.

Tex's expression softened. "Don't worry," he said. "They don't have firearms. We do."

"You don't know that!" Angel cried.

"If they had ammunition, I think we'd be hearing it. And if it's the same crew, they ran out, remember?"

Richard said, "If we're going, let's go! You're giving them time to circle the house." Tex grabbed Kane to accompany them.

"No! Not Kane! They'll kill him like they did Kole!" I cried.

He gave me a sympathetic look. "We need to know if they're in the back, Sarah. If it's clear and we have time, I'll put him back inside." He gave me a hard direct stare. "Follow us to the door and lock it behind us."

"Then you won't be able to let Kane in!"

"I'll put him in the shed."

"They'll burn the shed!"

He grimaced. "Not if we can help it. Look, I don't have time to argue with you. Do as I say! Bar the door behind us. If we need to get back in, we'll let you know."

"How?"

"We'll holler or something," he said, heavily. Both men had stuffed their pockets with extra mags for their rifles. I saw Tex grab a two-way and stuff that in his side pants pocket, too.

Heavy-hearted, I followed them to the back. Angel's face told me she felt just as I did about what was going on. Suddenly she cried, "Wait!"

Tex turned. "I have to do this, darlin'. If we fail out there, you know what to do."

She ran forward and barreled into him, crying. "You don't have to do this! We can stick it out in here together, like last time!" Her wheedling voice broke my heart.

We heard whacks—they were hitting the front door with axes or other tools.

"Now or never!" Richard hissed. I gazed at him and my heart just seemed to stop for a moment. What if he got hurt out there—or killed?

"I love you!" I cried. Richard and I had never once said those words to each other in all our lives. Normally it would have embarrassed me to pieces, but I looked at Tex and said the same thing.

"I love you, too," Richard said, his eyes large and full. He said the same to Angel.

"I do, too," Tex said. "Pray for us!" And they turned and ran towards the door. I had no choice but to follow and bar the door after them as Tex had told me to.

When I turned back around Angel was there behind me, crying.

"He wasn't supposed to do that!" she said, shaking her head and biting her lip. "Tex is supposed to stay with me! All of our plans were to stay put!" Without thinking about it I moved forward right into her arms. We were both crying. We shared a good, heart-felt hug. But then she stepped back and wiped her eyes with her sleeve. She looked up at me.

"C'mon," she said, in a determined tone. "We've got work to do."

CHAPTER SIXTEEN

SARAH

Kool, in true guard dog fashion, hadn't ceased barking or throwing himself at the front door where the awful pounding continued. In fact, the noise at the door increased as if they'd found something larger and heavier to ram it with.

Angel tied Kool to a column. "Don't untie him," she said. "I need him out of the way." Rifle in hand, she approached the door, slowly bringing the firearm higher. I braced myself for the noise, expecting her to take a shot; but from outside we heard two loud *cracks!* Angel hesitated, but the pounding at the door ceased! Only the barking of the dogs, Kane outside and Kool inside, rang out in what seemed like an otherwise eerie silence. And then even Kool got confused and began to whine rather than bark. Angel and I looked at each other. Neither of us was sure what to do.

A barrage of gunfire sounded, making us both jump. Then shouts, thuds, yells, and more shots—but the noise was receding.

"I think our boys are chasing them off!" Angel cried. We clasped hands and she launched into a fervent prayer for the safety of Tex and Richard. I tried to put my faith to work, to really BELIEVE what Angel was praying—only I was still wound up like a coil, feeling ready to pop. The image of the barn in flames was too disturbing for me to quiet my heart in prayer.

I tore apart from her to try and get a peek outside but the slit was too narrow to reveal anything but smoke and dust from the explosions. Soon it would be fully dark and we'd be able to see nothing outside.

Faintly, we heard more shouts and gunfire; and then, Kane! Every bark kept my hope alive that all three of our loved ones—Tex, Richard and my wolf-dog—would return to us sound and whole.

Kane's bark grew louder, and soon I was sure he was right outside, heading to the back. Tex had surely left one gate open, meaning my beloved pet would be able to get in the dog-yard to our back door.

"I'm letting him in!" I cried. I turned towards the hallway leading to the back but Angel grabbed my arm.

"I don't want to lose Kane any more than you do," she said, her eyes large in her face, "but you are NOT opening that back door!"

"But he's out there!" My voice sounded whiny but I couldn't help it. "Tex said he'd put him in the shed!"

"He'll scratch and bark to come in, if he's that close," she said.

We heard more gunfire in the distance. "Okay; I'm just going to listen at the back," I said. "If I hear Kane, I'll let him in."

"Not if he's barking at someone out there," Angel warned. I went to the back and listened for sounds of Kane wanting to come in but all I heard was silence.

The sound of shots continued sporadically, though each burst seemed fainter than the one before. Tex and Richard really were forcing this band away from us! And then I heard Kane's bark—he sounded like he was only feet from the door!

I started unbolting the bars, hurriedly opening locks and shoving the steel bars over. When I was at the last one, I stopped to listen again. Kane gave a small yap as though he was saying, "Yes, it's me. C'mon, open up!" I opened the last lock and cracked open the door.

There was Kane standing tall, his tail flying up at the sight of me. I was overjoyed and opened the door further. But right before my eyes, just as he began moving in, he halted, looking sharply to the left; and then, barking madly, ran off! I stuck my head out just enough to call after him but he'd disappeared towards the side of the house into the gathering darkness.

Gasping, I slammed the door shut and ran for a lantern. I had to know what Kane was doing! When I had the door open again I held out the lantern, calling Kane. He was at the fence with two shadowed figures on the other side of it. They jeered at the dog, swiping at him with a bat.

110

"Get in here, Sarah!" Angel called from far behind me but I couldn't make myself do it. Instead, I hollered, "Kane! Kane!" My cry was desperate. Somehow I think I knew what was bound to happen. They'd been missing his head but he kept jumping at them. Sooner or later they'd hit him, I just knew it!

And then they did.

One man landed a hard swat, timing it to hit Kane full in the skull as he rose above the fence during a jump. Kane made one sharp whimper and dropped to the ground. It was a swift blow, and fatal, I was sure. I screamed. The men were already scrambling to climb the fence but one looked over at me as he did—his eyes held an intense darkness, like pure cold hate. I'd never seen such a look before on anyone.

The next thing I knew Angel was pulling me back inside and she slammed the door and had just managed the first lock when the blows at the door began. Together we pulled all the bars across and locked them in place. But I was shaking—and heartbroken.

"Kane--." I said, tearfully, my throat all tight. "He's--."

"I know," Angel said. "I know." She wiped away tears from her eyes. But leveled a severe look at me. "You shouldn't have opened the door!"

"I was trying to let him in!" I saw she'd dropped her rifle to help bar the door, and asked, "Why didn't you shoot them?"

"I was too late; if I missed, they'd have gotten in."

We're gonna get in there! A man yelled, through the door.

"C'mon," Angel whispered, pulling me away. "There's no way they're getting through that door."

"How are Tex and Richard going to get in?" I asked, worriedly.

"I don't know, yet. They'll have to take *them* out," she said, nodding in the direction of the back.

I sat on the floor in the hall where I could keep an eye on the back door and listen for clues that Tex and Richard might be back. But I kept seeing the image of Kane getting slammed with that bat. Inside I felt more than ever like a coiled spring—tight and tense. Angel was busily moving things from the kitchen and living area to that same spot in the hallway as she had on previous occasions as if planning on taking it somewhere. I watched her wearily. Kool barked, and the men at the back door continued hacking at it.

"Why are you doing this?" I asked her, when she went by me again with her arms full of stuff.

She stopped and surveyed me, wide-eyed. "This cabin isn't safe anymore," she said. "And I can't keep living this way."

"But where can we go? How are you going to carry all that stuff anywhere?" I motioned at the growing pile of totes, bags, pots and pans.

She never answered me. A particularly nasty bang at the door made her look at me worriedly. We heard a crack then, as a piece of wood came loose from the outside. Further hits against the door resulted in a second sickening crack, and another, and then a chunk of wood on *our* side of the door lolled to one side, revealing that the solid metal in the door wasn't solid after all; it was steel mesh! I imagined those hateful eyes glaring in at us through it. Kool's barking went up a notch, and he strained at his leash.

Staring grimly at the opening, Angel whispered, "Shut off the lantern!" I did as she said, happy to recall that even though it wasn't solid metal like Angel thought, there was still rebar and seven steel bars locked into place across the door between us and them.

Without the lantern's light, inky blackness engulfed us. Even if there had been a full moon out, with the cabin in shut-down mode, we'd never know it—except as my eyes adjusted I could actually make out a slightly lighter spot on the door where the wood was gouged out.

The sounds at the door continued, accented by angry foul language as the men encountered the impenetrable bars that blocked their entry.

I heard Angel checking the action on her rifle. "Don't move, Sarah! I don't want to hit you by accident," she whispered.

I almost thought I could make her out in the blackness as she went towards the door. And then I heard *from outside* the menacing snarl of a dog—Kane! He hadn't died! One of the men yelled in pain.

112

Then we heard scuffling and a loud thwack, and Kane's cry of pain—
followed by silence.

Angel pushed me away, because I'd run towards the door when
I heard my dog. Suddenly she took her shot, using the opening they had
made. She took another. Covering my ears with my hands and in tears
over Kane, I ran towards the other end of the house, going by instinct
because I couldn't see a thing. I stumbled around and fell onto the sofa.

Angel joined me shortly carrying the lantern, which she'd turned
back on. She looked no happier than I felt.

I looked up at her tearfully. "Why didn't you shoot them *before*
they did it? Before they killed Kane?"

She sat down beside me with an air of defeat. "I didn't have the
chance. When I heard Kane, I couldn't shoot. I might've hit him if I
did." She looked beseechingly at me. "I didn't have the chance," she
repeated. "But I think I got both those men." Her tone was quiet without
a hint of triumph. We felt none.

"Can I go look at him?" I asked, choking back tears. "To make
sure he's not suffering?"

"The boys will take a look when they get back," she said. "We
are not opening that door again unless it is to welcome Tex and your
brother."

At that moment Kool gave a half-hearted yap which I took to
mean he wanted attention. Or food. I went to him, thankful for our last
remaining canine friend, but I was so angry. Why did people have to be
so cruel?

Angel lit an oil lamp and switched off the other which was
battery powered, since we try to ration precious batteries. We heard no
whacks at the house. No dog, no shots. No shouts or running feet.
Occasionally the sound of crackling and snapping timber from the
burning barn could be heard. The barn. We were losing it and there
wasn't a thing to do about it. I felt so helpless I wanted to explode.

"*What* is going on out there?" I asked, beseechingly.

Angel looked up—she'd been praying. "All we can do is pray.
Why don't you join me? You'll feel better."

"I won't."

"You will."

"I don't think so. I don't see how. Not until they come back."

"You will, because we pray to a God who is *real*. The Holy Spirit will keep our minds and hearts safe. That's a promise in the Bible, you know that."

Angel's calm voice seemed miraculous in itself. She had to be worried. Tex was out there with those crazies just like Richard. I was worried sick. But she continued surveying me calmly and motioned me to join her. We sat at the table and held hands. Angel prayed and I mostly listened though my mind was still racing, still obsessed with what was happening around us—and to my brother and Tex.

Suddenly I lifted my head. "That smoke smell is getting stronger!"

She looked around and sniffed. "It's from the barn burning. And the explosion of all those chemicals."

Outside then, we heard a few sudden thuds and thumps. Probably pieces of the barn falling to the ground. Angel bit her lip. "I guess this is my fault," she said, shaking her head. "If I hadn't hurt that woman—"

"Lots of them got hurt or killed that day! It isn't your fault! They *chose* to attack us!"

"But why would they come back when they know we're armed?" She asked. "It seems to me they're out for blood, like it's personal."

"This could be a different gang," I said. "And they're all out for blood."

"They used the same war cry," she answered, her eyes wide. "It's the same gang!"

"Lots of gangs might use a war cry," I reasoned.

Angel just shook her head, sadly. She put her rifle down by her side and pulled out her Bible. She flipped to her favorite book, *Psalms*.

I picked up her firearm and started examining it.

"You ought to have one," she said. "Go and get one."

I got on my knees to check under the sofa where extra firearms are kept but she said, "I already put the guns in the hallway. Go get you one from there."

I used a flashlight and found one. After I got back with a neat looking rifle, Angel said, "Good choice. It's an AR-15, like mine." She checked that it was loaded and then handed it back, saying, "Keep your finger off the trigger."

I nodded. If there was any gun rule they'd drilled into my head during my few lessons it was to keep my finger off the trigger until I was ready to shoot—and intending to.

Angel sighed, and said, "I'll bet they ruined that squash patch we had near the barn. It's probably all burned up."

I didn't know what to say. Our biggest worry was whether Tex and Richard were okay, but I figured Angel was trying not to think about them. And we *had* put a lot of work into those squash. We'd watered them by hauling water from the well; we'd hand-picked squash bugs off and sprayed soapy water to kill more of them. The squash were part of the survival garden, which meant they required little weeding but watching for bugs was a daily chore. Angel had lost a whole squash patch to those pests once. All that work for nothing. Was our work this time also going to be in vain? On account of these lawless marauders? Why had they come to *our* land?

And then I realized I'd called it "our" land. I was at home here. When you put labor—and love—into making something work, it becomes part of you. And I'd been working at the homestead as much as any of the others. These wandering strangers were ruining it all! They'd killed Kole and Kane! A surge of anger rose up within me, strong and righteous and loud. How dare they!

I fingered the rifle, for the first time fully appreciating the power it could give me to defend our home. I'd practiced shooting this rifle only once but I remembered that it was much easier to shoot than a pistol. I was a better shot with it, too.

As I held it in my hands thinking about this, Kool suddenly came growling to his feet. He stared at the front door.

I was on my feet in a flash. I raised my rifle and advanced towards the door. Every cell in my body was determined to defy the goals of these intruders—they would not get their way and enter our home.

Angel said, "Don't let that rifle go to your head! It doesn't make you safe, you know."

"I know," I said. Then, surprising even myself, I added, "It makes me dangerous."

CHAPTER SEVENTEEN

SARAH

"Sarah!" Angel's rebuke was laced with a gleam of pleasure. She was as surprised as I to find I had some backbone. So I ignored her and continued towards the door. A loud ping hit it, telling me someone had shot at us. I froze, waiting for more shots. Kool had quieted before but this newest assault sent him into full pitch, straining at his leash and barking furiously.

I went to the window, to that one slit, knowing I could get the muzzle of my gun through it.

Behind me Angel said, "You go, girl!" And then, "They finally got you good and mad! Well, I don't blame you."

"Good and mad" was an understatement. My fury at all the injustices these marauders had committed against us was sending adrenaline pumping through my veins. I waited on high alert, listening for movement out there. Purposely—determinedly—I placed my finger on the trigger.

And then I had a flashback of the moment I'd stabbed Mark Steadman when he'd been about to murder my brother. Normally I hated that memory and did my best to suppress it. I didn't like that I might have mortally wounded him—I'll probably never know. But right now, the memory *boosted* my resolve. I didn't have to see myself as a victim—I was a protector! I could help defend us now just as I'd saved my brother then!

With Kool barking behind me, I couldn't hear if anyone was within range. I was about to take a blind shot--what the heck—when Angel stopped me.

"Wait! Your brother and my husband are out there somewhere!"

"So put Kool in the bedroom," I answered "and then I can listen." No sooner did Angel return than I heard voices! I looked at Angel. "Can I shoot?"

"Oh, glory," she murmured, which meant she was perplexed. But she said, "No. Wait. Our men could be out there."

"I wish they were. I wish we knew for sure they're okay."

"Me, too."

And then we heard a beep—from the two-way radio! Angel turned without a word and rushed to the counter where she'd put her unit. We all had our own. If we went any distance from the house we were supposed to take one with us. We'd been good about remembering to do that, especially since the last attack. We hadn't initiated contact because each unit emitted a beep even when turned off, when another tried to connect with it. One beep could give away their location if Richard and Tex happened to be hiding and within earshot of the enemy.

But they'd contacted us. Angel gave a sigh of relief as she surveyed the trusty instrument, grasped it and was about to turn it on.

"Don't!" I shouted.

"Why not?"

"What if they're hiding? What if you turn it on and it crackles and gives them away?"

She hesitated, thinking it over. "I don't think Tex would've beeped us if he couldn't talk."

"But he might just be trying to tell you they're okay."

She stared at me a moment. Slowly, she said, "I guess that could be the case; but it's not. I know my husband!" Before I could say another word she flipped on the unit. I stared at her, at a loss. Had she just endangered our men?

At first we only heard static. To me, Angel said, "We need to know if they're coming so we can be ready." Into the unit she said, "Tex? Honey, you hear me?"

The static grew for a few seconds and then suddenly cleared. We heard Tex's heavy voice. (Later I'd remember this and chuckle because he sounded like they'd just returned from collecting eggs from the hens, not facing an enemy!)

"We're at the back door, sweetheart. Think you could let us in?" Angel didn't even bother to answer but with a gasp of joy nearly threw down the unit and both of us rushed pell-mell to the back.

"Why didn't they just knock?" I asked, as we ran.

"Probably so we wouldn't mistake them for marauders and shoot!"

In seconds we were working on the locks and bars and then we had the door open and there stood Tex and Richard! My exuberance faded because at their feet were the two bodies of the men Angel had shot. And Tex was holding Kane, who was completely limp, in his arms.

Kane is a big Husky. But Tex is a big man. He carried him into the house and it was all I could do to lock up once they'd entered. I wanted to rush to my dog. Kool was let out of the bedroom so he could slobber all over Tex but for once Tex didn't stop to greet him. He put Kane on the sofa, on a blanket which Angel quickly provided, and we all gathered around him.

As we said his name, his tail gave the smallest, feeble wag. He whimpered faintly and blinked. Angel and I were crying.

"It's okay, wolf-dog," I said, wishing I could believe it. I spoke softly beside his head. His tail thumped lightly. I stroked his head and face. Angel handed me gauze which I used to dab at the wound. It broke my heart that Kane's beautiful head now seemed misshapen on one side, where he'd sustained the worst blow.

Richard looked glum, and Tex—for the first time since I'd known him—looked truly despondent.

"What can we do for him?" I asked. Angel brought water. I lifted Kane's head gently but he showed no interest in it.

"Find a piece of meat," Tex said. Meat, of course, was scarce. The dogs had gradually gotten used to a diet of stored dry dog food, occasionally getting scraps of meat if it was available. Angel got a piece of salt pork—it was all we had handy—but Kane wouldn't even sniff it.

Kool had to be held in order not to grab it but when Kane wouldn't so much as open an eye, Angel gave it to him, and he gobbled it up. As I continued to sit with my dog, stroking him softly, Tex and Richard gave a run-down of their exploits outside. "That barn exploding helped us," Tex said. "When we got out there, we took down the two at the front door, but we saw a lot of 'em running away already."

"A couple of them looked injured from the blasts," Richard added.

"It sounded like you were running them off," said Angel. "Except for the two who did this to Kane," she added, ruefully.

"They must have rounded back," Richard said.

"We took down six or seven," Tex added. "The others got off."

"How many were there? Do you have an idea?" Tex and Richard looked at each other. "Looked like at least a dozen," Tex said.

"Daisy?" asked Angel.

"She found us. Walked right through the bushes and poked me with her nose. I almost shot her! They must have tried to take her—but she's as stubborn as a *mule*." They chuckled at that. I don't think I even smiled, because I was too heart-sick about Kane.

Suddenly Kane shuddered. I spoke faster, softly, trying to comfort my poor wolf-dog. Everyone came back around him, and then, as I stroked his side and head, he gave a sudden, wracking shudder that seemed to travel through his whole body—and went still. It took me a few moments to comprehend that Kane—my poor, loyal protector—had died!

Tex turned away. I sobbed against Kane's body, so soft yet. Angel's face, tear-stained and red, must have mirrored my own. I tried not to lose control of myself, but the day's events, the constant danger, losing Kane—I was suddenly sick of it all!

"Listen," Tex said. "We always knew that if things got bad, we'd eventually have to give up the dogs." He was speaking to Angel. She nodded, sniffling.

"What do you mean?" I asked. "Why would you give them up?"

120

He turned to me. "There's no room for the animals in our escape plan."

"So what is that plan?" asked Richard, who had sat down in a side chair wearily.

"It's what we do when we have to vacate the cabin," Tex said.

"Yeah, but what is it? Where do we go from here? And how do you figure on getting away safely?"

Tex looked at Angel for a moment. "Let's get us some grub and then we'll sit down and explain it to you both. But first," he glanced down at me and Kane. I was still holding him with my head against his side, not able to stop stroking his fur.

"We need to bury Kane."

Angel said, "I don't want you going back out there! We can *wait* for daylight!" Tex hesitated, and said, "Okay. But let's move him to the back." He gently nudged my head up and removed my arm from Kane's side. "Sorry, dumplin'."

It normally makes me smile when Tex calls me that because even though we eat well here, I'm still the furthest thing from a dumpling. I was way undernourished when we arrived and I'm still skinny. I think he calls me that *because* I'm so skinny. He says it affectionately. But as I watched him carry off my beloved pet, I had no smile.

"C'mon, Sarah. Help me get some supper out," Angel said. I suspected she was trying to get my mind off my grief. There was no discussion about trying to put out the fire. The barn was destroyed by the blasts, and we did not have enough water readily available to fight fire, anyway.

I thought about our loft going up in smoke and it gave me an all-too-familiar feeling. The loss, the emptiness. It was like a replay of what had happened back at the apartment building right after the pulse. We'd lost everything then; later we'd lost a stash of great food when the soldiers burned up that abandoned home we'd found; and now our barn, the place I'd slept until recently, was gone, destroyed.

When Tex returned, he said, "We did overhear enlightening conversation out there." Angel and I looked up at him curiously. He continued, "I was wondering why they would keep at us when we're not an easy target. I mean, let's face it, most people don't have rebar and steel mesh in their walls. But we heard them saying this was personal, on account of us killing somebody's cousin the last time they were here."

Angel said, "I knew it was personal!"

Richard said, "They also think we're hoarding a lot of good stuff or why else would we be protecting it so well?"

Tex said, "And they would be correct."

Richard and I exchanged impressed glances. We'd searched high and low in the cabin for a secret panel, a sliding door, something that might open to this hidden treasure we'd gradually realized existed. But we'd never found it.

"Richard, tomorrow you and I will go back out and double up on our traps—close to the house this time." He looked at Angel. "But we'd better start emptying this place out. It's only a matter of time. They're determined to get us."

CHAPTER EIGHTEEN

SARAH

Somehow we managed to fall asleep last night and held Kane's burial today. Before we lowered him gently into a hole that Tex and Richard dug, I stared hard at his lifeless form. I dug my hands into his thick fur and stroked his head. I was afraid I would forget my wolf-dog. Angel took pictures of him as a puppy but we had no recent photos. I wished I'd taken the time to sketch him.

Things like that—art and hobbies—there's no such thing these days. Every minute except for the time I spend on my journal is taken up with living.

The smoking remains of the barn is another sad testament of yesterday's attack. Like last time, Tex and Richard took anything we could use from the dead marauders and then placed the bodies onto a pile of simmering embers, which Richard had stirred into flames. I refused to look closely at any of them. The very idea of there being dead people around is creepy enough for me. Since the pulse I've seen more than my fair share of dead bodies—but I'll never get used to it.

While the men did their work, Angel and I took stock of our remaining garden. We actually found a few baby squash hidden among greenery that hadn't burned or been destroyed by the explosions. They need to grow, so we left them. Tex didn't want us venturing far from the house so we didn't get to check on more of the survival crops; instead, Angel and I got busy inside the cabin, boxing up all the food that isn't already boxed up.

"C'mon, Sarah," she said. "Let's get the rest of our stuff into the hallway." I eyed her doubtfully. I still didn't get how piling all our things into the hallway was a good idea, and I realized then that Tex had never explained their backup plan last night.

"Angel, how do you figure on getting any of this out if we're attacked? Tex forgot to tell us what Plan B is." I shook my head, following her from the storage room with our arms full into the hallway. The length of the hall was now lined with plastic tote bins and boxes. There were also a few white buckets like the ones we'd seen at that house before the soldiers burned it.

"We're just making it easier for them to get this stuff," I added, wearily.

"Tex wants to explain it to you and Richard," she said. "Just know—we've got a plan. It's an emergency plan, and I hoped we'd never have to use it—but it's coming to that."

I kept my backpack handy and began squeezing some items into it as we worked. Extra dried beef sticks, small wrapped packages of crackers. One tote held vitamins and minerals and I shoved a bottle of multivites into the pack as well. It was absolutely stuffed, now. But if we were going to be on the run, I wanted to be ready.

When we'd finished boxing up most of our supplies, Angel said, "Well, I guess I could use help moving all this stuff, so you'll get to see Plan B!"

"Cool!"

But at that moment Tex and Richard slammed open the front door and ran inside. Tex was already pulling extra mags from his pants pocket and checking them.

"We've got company!"

Angel and I gasped. "So soon?" Angel asked. "They don't want to give us time to regroup, that's for sure!"

Richard and Tex continued to stuff their pockets with ammunition and extra mags. Angel cried, "Not again! You are not going out there again! If they are back, then they are ready for you this time, or they're fools!"

Tex pulled her into his arms and gave her a kiss. "Richard and I set up a barrier in front of the cabin. Keep the front door unlocked. If we get overrun, we'll get right back inside."

124

Angel nodded but her eyes watered up. I was instantly filled
with fresh indignation at these horrible marauders. Two people
shouldn't have to face that they could lose each other so violently every
single day!

Tex peered out the door, Kool at his heels, rifle ready. Angel
grabbed the dog. "You can't take Kool!"

"Okay," he said. He and Richard disappeared outside.

"I wish I had a view from that window!" I said. "I can get the
muzzle of my rifle through that slit but what kind of back up is that
when I can't see hardly anything?"

"I know it," Angel said, as she leashed Kool, still barking, to a
wooden column. "But we can open up the side window shades and keep
watch from there so they can't come at our men from the back! You
take the storage room, I'll take the bedroom!"

I grabbed an AR and two extra mags, my heart pumping madly,
and ran to the storage room. It was dark in most of the house since we'd
kept the metal shades down but I could see dimly. I'd have to raise the
shade in order to see outside so I got to work. Tex was able to do this in
seconds but it took me longer.

When I finally got the shade up a couple of inches, I had a
decent view, checked the action on the rifle, and flipped off the safety.
Suddenly it felt surreal—and voices in my head accosted me.

*Who are you, Sarah Weaver, to keep guard at a window with a
rifle! Do you really think you can shoot a fellow human being? What
gives you the right? You are a coward! The girl who wouldn't take the
elevator alone if she could help it. If you see someone out there—who
are you kidding? You'll panic and do nothing!*

"No!" I said, out loud. "No! I am *not* that girl!"

Angel came rushing to the room. "What is it?" she asked,
running to the window to peer out.

"I'm sorry—I'm just—talking to myself." I felt my cheeks flush.

Angel surveyed me, her face a mixture of compassion and
curiosity. "I never heard you do that before," she said. But she put a
hand to her heart. "I'm glad that's all it was, though. I thought you were

talking to one of *them*." She looked hard at me. "Can you do this?"

"Yeah! I want to do this! I want our men to be safe!"

"Okay," she said, patting my arm. "Because if you can't, let's close up this window right now."

"No, I'm doing this," I insisted.

We heard shots. Tex and Richard! Angel dashed back towards the other room. "Shoot on sight!" she called.

"I'm doing this," I repeated to myself, grimly. "I can do ALL things through Christ who gives me strength." Suddenly Angel was back and she handed me a shotgun. "This might be better in case there's more than one. Just shoot in their direction!" And she was gone again.

I hadn't ever used the shotgun but I could tell it was ready to go. I got in a position that would allow me to shoot instantly.

Then I smelled smoke, which seemed strong and close. Were they going to burn the house down around us? I heard thumps against the house off to my left.

"You burn the house, you burn their supplies, you idiot!"

"I'd rather burn them than leave them!" came the reply. "They killed my cousin!"

I turned in the direction of the voices but they were still out of sight. Evidently they'd come from the back of the property—if they got past me and Angel, Tex and Richard would be at their mercy!

A third voice joined the others. "Tell me you did not try to burn this place!"

"It was Kyle," said one.

"Look, we're not getting in there," said the man who must have been Kyle. "They got armor or something in these walls. I was just gonna burn the wood away so we know what we're up against."

"Stupid!" said a new voice. Something about that voice bothered me. Had I heard it before? I was dying with fear at this point. There were at least three grown men out there and I was only me!

"Watch out!" Someone yelled. Shots rang out. They weren't from me—I couldn't see anyone! But I heard them running away and then Tex's voice. "They went around back."

I heard Angel cry, "Get inside, now!"

"Go to the back!" I yelled, dropping my firearm, and rushing out of the room to get to the back door. As I ran I yelled to Angel to lock up the front—our men weren't out there any longer. There was gunfire outside as I worked on the bars and locks and I realized that I couldn't see who was getting shot—what if Tex and Richard were down? What if I was unlocking the door for the enemy?

A loud blast shook me to the core. Angel was in the doorway to the storage room—the one I'd just fled from—and had shot at someone. They'd found my window unmanned! Shame filled me. "Did you get them?" I asked.

"I got one," she said. Then, "Let me at the door. You close up that window. We can't keep more than one opening at a time." But the door handle jiggled and I heard Richard's voice. "It's us—me and Tex! Let us in!"

Gasping, I quickly lifted the last bar and opened the door to our men. As they hurried inside we heard a shot. A second later and I think one of them would have taken that bullet. The three of us hurried to get all the bars in place while Angel went and closed up the window. Then I finished the locks while Tex and Richard ran to the front of the house.

"Are we all locked up?" I heard Tex ask.

The walls and door suddenly erupted into a symphony of *plinks*, thuds and cracks from outside as they took the impact of attack. I wondered how the marauders had managed to find such arms, when last time they were clearly lacking them. Anyway, with the door secured, I went to join the others in the front room.

Angel was saying, "That's it! I can't take this anymore! I need us to leave!"

Tex nodded. "Looks like we have no choice."

Kool was whining now, unhappy to be leashed. "What about Kool?" I asked. "You said there was no room for him in the escape plan."

Angel and Tex looked at each other. Angel said, "We have to bring him! We can walk him in the tunnel."

From outside we heard a voice. "Look—why don't we work together? All we want is for you to share your stuff!"

Tex shook his head and put up his hand, signaling us not to answer. After a short silence the voice returned. "We can burn you down, you know! Your house is strong, but not fire proof! All I'm asking is that you work with us. I promise you, we will not kill you—if you work with us!"

Again Tex raised his hand, signaling for silence, but he went towards the door. "Give us time to talk it over!"

Angel gasped. I saw by the look on her face that she did not think talking it over was a good idea.

"You've got fifteen minutes!" the man called.

Tex turned to us. Whispering, he said, "Quick! Let's get our stuff out of here!"

"Mercy!" cried Angel, in a loud whisper. "I thought you really meant to bargain with them!"

He took one of her hands and kissed it. "Not on your life, sweetheart!"

"And where exactly are we supposed to move our stuff to?" Richard asked, sardonically.

"Follow us," Tex replied, motioning us to do so. He turned into the hallway as Angel rushed ahead of him.

Outside the storage room, I thought I heard voices and went towards the shuttered window. "Get every man we have to the front. We're gonna get a wall down. Burn it if we have to."

"What about their stuff? If we burn it, we don't get it."

"We'll start with saws."

"They'll shoot!"

"If they can shoot out, we can shoot in. I think there's a lot more of us than there are of them." He paused. "Where the heck is Walt, anyway?"

My heart constricted unexpectedly. Walter—that was my father's name. His friends and my mother called him Walt. It maddened me that our enemy shared that name. It felt sacrilegious.

"He's in front. Got someone negotiating! As if that's gonna work!"

"Sarah!" Angel hissed, in a loud whisper from the doorway. "What are you doing? C'mon, we need you!"

I told them what I'd overheard but as I reached them, I came to an abrupt stop. Tex and Richard were moving totes and boxes from the hall, taking them through an opening in the wall—an opening! I must have been gaping because Angel looked at me and smiled.

"Welcome to Plan B."

CHAPTER NINETEEN

ANDREA

I never did get to talk to Lexie last night but this morning I am determined to confront her. I could swear I heard her throwing up again this morning! That has GOT to be a sign of pregnancy. She seems perfectly fine otherwise. Well, not perfectly fine. She does look tired these days.

Anyway, I met her in the hall. "Are you sick?" I asked.

Lexie frowned. "I've had an upset stomach."

I stared at her. "You were sick yesterday morning, too."

She nodded. "It's been longer than that; a whole week, I think. But it seems to get better as the day goes along."

This sounded so OBVIOUS as to the reason that I cocked my eyebrows. "I guess you haven't told your mother?"

"It would just worry her."

I blew out a breath and leveled a "look" at her.

"What?" she asked, puzzled.

"C'mon, Lex. It's kinda obvious, don't you think?"

She looked mystified. "What? What is? Do you know what it is?"

I kept staring at her because I couldn't say the words. I finally said, *"Morning. Sickness?"*

Now her eyes widened. *"Are you crazy? No!"*

"That's what it sounds like. Did you—"

"No! Just because the world is crazy doesn't mean we are!" She said, harshly. "We're still Christians, and we're not married yet; that would be sin."

"Well, I know it must be hard to wait," I began, but she cut me off.

"You don't know. Evidently you don't know *me* because I wouldn't do that! Blake wouldn't, either."

"It might be a good thing if you did," I said.

"What?" She looked at me like I was nuts. "What are you talking about?"

"Girls, what are you doing up there?" It was Mrs. Martin calling.

"Be right there, Mom!" Lexie called.

"Lily is crying for you, Andrea," she added.

"We gotta go," Lexie said, but I grabbed her arm.

"It would make them let you get married."

She just shook her head, looking at me like I was incomprehensible. I followed her downstairs and took a crying Lily from Mrs. Wasserman, whose own little girl was sniffling back tears. The Wassermans were one of the first families to join the compound and were good friends with the Martins. Mrs. Wasserman was often working in the kitchen alongside Mrs. Martin. "Sorry," I mumbled.

"No problem," she said.

As I bounced Lily on my knee during breakfast, I kept throwing glances at Lexie and Blake, who sat together as usual. They were nearly inseparable when they weren't off doing different chores around the compound. I caught Lexie's eyes and she glared at me. I just shrugged at her. I still felt she had to be pregnant. Her symptoms proved it!

Looking around, I felt oddly lonely despite the presence of the Martins and the Wassermans and all the children. (Everyone else on the compound eats in their own cabins, now.) With a pang, I realized my loneliness was because Roper was missing—he was still off in harm's way!

Later as I was taking Lily to the play area downstairs, Lexie came beside us and walked along. "I just want you to know that I don't appreciate your suspicions," she said. "Or your so-called advice." We stopped walking.

"I think it's wicked!" she added.

My temper flared. "Look, Lex! Jared said those foreign soldiers could be back any day and with bigger guns; more weapons! Life is precarious! We don't have a guarantee for tomorrow!"

"I've got news for you," she said. *"We never did."*

"I'm just saying—you should take advantage of the time you have together. Because you never know when--." and suddenly my eyes filled with tears and I had trouble continuing. "You never know if you'll have another chance!"

I saw the anger drain from her face and knew she was feeling sorry for me but I swirled and turned away, hurrying down the stairs with Lily. She didn't follow me, probably because she had chores to finish. I was glad. I didn't want to hear any more of her "holier than thou" sermons. I didn't want to hear any of her objections.

And when I think back to Roper and his hesitation about us because of my age, it just makes me sad! I could have loved him with my life. I could have.

CHAPTER TWENTY

ANDREA

So I'm sort of disappointed that Lexie isn't pregnant—I guess I'm dying for some excitement! She's a little miffed at my attitude. I get it. It would be wrong for them to "do it" without being married, I know that. I even agree. But I feel so restless! If only Roper would get back. I feel like everything would be more bearable if he were here.

In the meantime, I need to keep my mind occupied. My hands are busy enough! I thought winter was terrible at our house in the plat, with having to haul in snow to melt for water. But summer isn't any better here. You know what life is like without technology in summer? *Endless chores. And HEAT.*

And water is still a big deal and not easy to get. The Martins have a well, but we still have to haul the water—every day. Even with my injured arm I'm not excused, and Lexie and I have to keep the food crops watered. Which I think is so unfair. Water is heavy! I think men should do the water jobs but they're doing construction at the cabins, or on lookout duty, or working on that infernal, never-ending fence.

Water is like, one of the biggest hassles of life! I heard Mr. Martin say he was drawing up plans for a pump house that would be right outside the back door—he said they could build it and it would work—so my question is, WHEN? The days are getting hotter, the water feels heavier—the bugs are worse, and I don't get to use our camp shower nearly often enough. Every day of hauling water simply *sucks.*

That pump-house should be a priority but it's not. If the adults were hauling the water, I bet things would change! We'd see that plan go into effect. But they don't care because they're not the ones doing it. All they think about is safety issues and getting ready for winter, even though it's only mid-summer. And we're still seeing dark plumes in the sky. They're usually far off in the distance, but what if they get close? What if our woods were to get on fire? It could spread to the cabins and barn—even to the house! (Just one more lovely fear to contemplate!) But that's another reason we should have a pump house for easier access to water.

I try to keep my complaining to a minimum—except for here in my journal. But the reality is that when we're not watering the garden, we're mulching with sawdust from the cabin area, or pulling weeds or killing pests. Ugh. I never knew squash bugs and aphids existed, but Mrs. Martin gave us gardening lessons early in June and explained how we have to pick them off the plants EVERY SINGLE DAY. We even have to check the underside of the leaves for eggs and cut them out. They go into a glass jar of soapy water, where they die. You'd think you could get all the eggs and then relax, right? But no. They lay eggs like you wouldn't *believe!* It's a never-ending battle.

And this is my *life!*

I tried enlisting my little brothers. The children help with the chickens by feeding them, gathering eggs and keeping the water troughs full. I figured they could do a little more. And at first, squishing the bugs was a game for them and they were excited to help. But each day they got less and less enthusiastic.

"It's too hot!" Aiden would say, drawing out the word, *hooooooooot.*

"I'm hot, but I'm still doing it," I told them.

"You have to," said Quentin. "It's not our job." I glared at him but he was right. Lexie and I tried to make them help anyway, but we gave it up. It was more work than just getting it over with ourselves. Thing is, we have tons of squash plants, at least 1/2 acre, because they're good storage foods. It takes the two of us at least an hour to go through that stupid garden checking for pests.

Jared said once that he'd find us pesticides and Mrs. Martin said she liked her garden organic. Even now! When there's so much other work to be done! I hope, when Jared gets back (And Roper! Please,

God, let Roper come back!) that they'll have pesticides. Right now we can't worry about eating organic—we need to worry about eating, period!

Mrs. Buchanan said to spray the leaves with a soap mixture to kill the bugs. We tried it—but it only slowed them down. And then Mrs. Martin said not to waste soap on the plants, anyway. So, despite all our efforts, we lost a few plants to those wretched creatures.

By the time we're done out there, we have shooting practice or raid drills, and then I have childcare, and then I have to help with dinner or cleanup. In the end, I feel like I don't have a life. And that's not including that I have to help in the barn! I wouldn't mind the gardening or animal work too much except we can't skip a *single* day—that gets to me.

I've been asking Mrs. Martin to adjust our chore schedule so I can get a break from some of it—especially cleaning the horse stalls—that is my least favorite task. (I'd rather do milking than mucking out stalls!) Mr. Martin says "cleanliness is the biggest factor to having healthy livestock"—over and over. Mrs. Martin promised to make a new schedule but so far my entire summer has been the same. I said, "Lexie gets to keep the records of which animals produce the most and which might need to be culled—why can't I do that?"

She said, "There's no reason you can't do that. Why don't the two of you work out a schedule so you can switch responsibilities?"

"I already asked her. Lex says she likes record-keeping."

Mrs. Martin frowned. "Alright, I'll get to it, sweetheart." Well—that was two weeks ago. Meanwhile, Mr. Martin plopped a book down between me and Lexie last night and said, "Girls, here's your new school subject." I stared down at the book. It was a field guide to edible wild plants.

"You're kidding, right?" I asked, weakly. I had a sinking feeling he was serious.

"The two of you can make a real contribution to the food around here by using this book."

"We're the gardeners!" I protested. "We're already making a real contribution!"

Lexie seemed okay with it, which baffled me. I said, "Mr. Martin, what if we make a mistake and someone dies of food poisoning? I don't want to be responsible for that."

"That's what the book's for," he replied. "It's got good, clear, pictures. I don't think you'll make a mistake. Just don't touch mushrooms. They pose the biggest danger of being misidentified. You'll be okay."

I groaned. "My arm is sore! I can't do this with one arm."

He grinned. "You haul water with one arm. I think you can pick a few plants, little girl."

Now and then Mr. Martin calls me and Lexie "little girl." I think he says it because we're really NOT little girls, but it's a term of affection, so I don't mind. I started flipping through the pages of the book. "Some of these are roots! Roots are hard to pull! I'll need both arms and I'm sure I'll hurt myself if I try."

He blew out a big breath. "I don't think so. If you need help, you'll be with Lex. She's done this before."

I looked at Lexie. "You have?"

She grabbed the book out of my hands and began leafing through it. "Not recently," she admitted. Then, "Chicory! I thought only horses liked that!"

"Hey, that's a great place to start! Find us chicory--it's bitter unless you cook it right but we can grind the roots for a coffee substitute. You get us a coffee substitute and you'll be everybody's darlings." He smiled, but I just sat there unhappily, resenting this new task while Lexie continued turning pages and making comments.

"Oh, I've seen this plant!... This does NOT look edible... Even *you* can recognize this one, An."

Watching me, Mr. Martin said, "Look, Andrea, Lexie can go after the exotic stuff while you concentrate on ordinary things like dandelions. This farm is full of dandelions. Get the greens and the flowers, even the roots—we'll use it all. You can do that, don't you think?"

"All except the roots," I grumbled.

"I'll help with that," said Lexie. "Even my little sisters could do that."

"Oh, thanks!"

"I didn't mean get the roots; I meant they can recognize dandelions." Lexie touched my arm.

Mr. Martin turned to leave. "Stay out of the pasture. We leave what's there for the horses—except maybe the chicory!" He frowned. "Unless there's too many weeds. Have you looked, Lex?"

"What's wrong with too many weeds?" I asked.

Lexie said, "In summer it's not a problem. But weeds get more sugar and starch in them when nights are cold. Too much of that can give a horse laminitis. We've had it happen."

I groaned. "Great! So we're not just looking for edibles, we'll be weeding—for horses!"

My reaction seemed to amuse Mr. Martin, who was trying not to smile. "Maybe it won't come to that."

Lexie said, "It came to that last year! But we have good tools—it won't be so bad."

I had a thought. "Mr. Martin, when Roper gets back you should have him study this foraging book. He's got a photographic memory. It'll be easy for him to do the foraging!"

He studied me kindly. "I know you don't want to forage, Andrea; but that is precisely what you two are going to do. I read once that when people first went west across the plains and deserts—not the Indians, but pioneers and gold seekers and such—many of them 'starved amidst abundance,' because they couldn't identify what was edible. We can be smarter than that."

"Fine!" I got up with a humph and came up here to write in my journal.

When the Martins first rescued us from starving and brought us here, I thought we'd have a pretty good life. Maybe I'm forgetting how horrible it was to be hungry. And that awful Mr. Herman at the end of the block—he was a big worry. I know I should be grateful. But my parents are gone, and life is drudgery. I can't wait for this season to be done.

Then I remembered how I'd had to forage for wood last winter. It was blisteringly cold, and nothing came easily out of all that snow and ice. Maybe foraging for wild edibles would be much, much easier. At least it isn't freezing cold out there.

TWO DAYS LATER

I was beginning to enjoy foraging—it is surprisingly satisfying to get praise from the adults for finding so many salad greens. And there's something about picking a wild plant and being able to eat it that's like—magic! I thought Lexie was right after all—foraging wasn't too hard.

And then I woke up this morning. My arms were itchy. Really itchy. There were red spots on them. Now they've become bigger reddish blotches, on my hands and arms, and they are itching like mad.

Lexie took one look at me and said, "Oh, no! You DO know what poison ivy looks like, right?"

I just stared at her while my heart sank. I didn't know. I never thought about it. We went outside and I showed her where I'd been poking around the past few days.

She pointed. "There. That's poison ivy. See the leaves? Remember this: Leaves of three, beware of me."

"Would've been nice if you told me this BEFORE we started foraging!"

Lexie looked embarrassed. "I'm sorry. I thought everyone knew what poison ivy looked like."

So now I'm itchy all over, even on my sore arm, which is like adding fuel to a fire. Mrs. Philpot is treating my spots with anti-itch cream but it only helps a little. And she keeps "tsk-tsking" me for not being more careful. I have to wear long sleeves and plastic gloves in order to pick up Lily, and then I'm even hotter and itchier than usual. That itching can be fierce! I never dreamed anything could itch so much! And I have to be careful because if I scratch it I could spread it to other places on my body. I shudder at the thought. I thought life was bad before.

This is sheer misery.

NEXT DAY

This morning I awoke to find a new red blotch—on my face! I cried. The itching is torture and now it's on my face and it's ugly and I feel ugly enough already. If I hadn't been forced to go foraging, this wouldn't have happened! That book should have a warning section on what NOT to touch.

I am not doing any more foraging. What can they do, kick me off the compound?

◆

This afternoon I saw one of our men building something along the side of the barn. I asked what he was building, and guess what? It's cold frames! It means we can grow extra food—but I'll have more gardening to do even after the cold weather sets in! *Just perfect.*

I've been thinking a lot lately of my old life. If I could only have ONE day like it used to be! A hot shower, faucets that worked, internet, cell phones, computers and games. I feel angry that it's all gone. And worst of all? My *parents,* gone!

This poison ivy is sending me into a deep pity party. I cried myself to sleep last night. I ask God *why, why* did he take it all away?

People here say it was judgment for the sins of our nation. But how long do we have to pay? How long do we have to suffer? Won't things ever get back to normal? Mr. Martin says they will. We just have to wait.

Well, I'm waiting.

CHAPTER TWENTY-ONE

LEXIE

So Andrea has poison ivy and is whining a lot. I almost feel like we need an attack—it would remind her we've got bigger things to worry about! But I do feel for her—poison ivy is miserable, I've had it.

I haven't written about Blake in a while. I think about him all the time, though. I'll be seventeen in two weeks, and he's going to ask my dad if we can get married! I've been hoping and praying that we can! I mean, Andrea is right about us not knowing what's gonna happen tomorrow. And what is that famous line? "Better to have loved and lost than never to have loved at all?" I agree!

Despite how busy we are, I manage to see him every day even if he's not at breakfast with us. One of my sneaky methods is to bring him lunch. He gets so involved in the task at hand—no matter what he's doing—that he'll just forget to eat. That's Blake. So I use that as a good excuse to grab lunch for the both of us and then I go off and find him.

He hardly ever does lookout these days, so I don't always know *where* to find him. (It's not that we don't need lookouts; we do, as much as ever. But Blake is scientific, so he's been reassigned to other work to take advantage of his brain.) Right now my dad has him working on a number of projects for the compound, such as the water-power. And he's in charge of irrigation—which I remind him of all the time—and today he finally came up with something!

Andrea and I were dying for him to work out a way for us not to have to haul water to the garden. He wanted to set up a system using hoses and trenches but we don't have the hose. That was enough to stop him from doing anything—Blake's a bit of a perfectionist—but since I complained so much, he came up with another idea.

First, he told me and Andrea to ransack the garbage dump for containers that could hold water—but they had to be safe, not used for anything toxic. (The garbage dump is on the property, because, well, it has to go somewhere! It's far enough not to bother us with an odor but close enough so we can reach it reasonably fast and without needing more than one person to stand guard. If having a dump on the property sounds yucky, consider that some people just throw their garbage all over their lawns, according to Roper! At least we keep ours in one heap, and burn whatever we can. We even bury some, but that takes a lot of manpower.)

Anyway, the containers had to withstand being buried in the ground through the growing season. That meant cardboard was out. We gathered a whole bunch of empty tin cans. Blake said they weren't big enough if we wanted to save labor. So we had to go back to that smelly dump and rummage around until we found a few #10 cans, and a whole bunch of empty 2 liter soda bottles.

Before the pulse we used to clean empty soda bottles and fill them with filtered water. The bottles came in handy when the power went out –I wish we had more of them! But we used them up. So that's why we had lots of empty ones and now we would put them to another good use.

Blake put holes throughout the containers—which was tricky because he wasn't allowed to use our battery-operated drill—and meanwhile we dug holes near the biggest, water-hungry plants. He put the containers in the holes, we filled them with water, and then tamped down the dirt around them. We left enough visible to make refilling easy. It was a lot of work. But it's untold *bliss* to have less watering to do!

Blake is such a whiz. I'm very proud of him.

He's helped us now not only with that irrigation but with creating vertical growers; and he was the one who came up with the recipe for the mortar the men use in building. The vertical growers (my name for them) is what he calls "stepped boxes." My mother took one look and exclaimed in delight that we now had "terraced" gardens. Whatever you call it, I think it was pure genius. I told that to Andrea this afternoon when we both came in for a glass of water. My dad was passing through the dining room at the moment. He broke into a grin.

"Don't you think it was ingenious?" I asked him in surprise. "It's like vertical gardening—space saving."

His eyes twinkled at me. "Honey, people have been building raised beds for thousands of years." The smile left my face.

"But WE haven't. Maybe other people did, but YOU didn't think of it."

He nodded, and his look changed abruptly. "Well, you got me there."

"And Blake is a genius, Dad, you know he is," I added, determined to make him concede defeat and give my future husband his due.

The twinkle was back, as he said, "He is a very bright young man, I agree."

As he walked off, I called, "So does that mean I can marry him?" Andrea clapped a hand over her mouth, trying not to laugh.

Dad didn't even turn around. "In a couple years, sure, honey."

I rolled my eyes and turned to Andrea. "We ARE going to get married sooner than that. Why can't he just accept it?"

Andrea was scratching her arm. "Because he's your father. Fathers don't accept it when their little girls fall in love."

"Don't scratch!" I scolded. "Go get more anti-itch cream. If you scratch you'll only make it worse."

She gave me sad eyes. "That's what everyone says. But I don't think it could possibly get any worse!"

"It can keep spreading."

She frowned. "Look, about your dad. You didn't really expect him to change his mind because of Blake's superior intellect, did you?"

I sighed. "No. But I don't want him to forget that we are ready. Whatever they say, Blake and I are ready."

She studied me. "Did Blake say that? I thought he wanted to wait."

When I didn't answer immediately, Andrea frowned. "I thought so. If he wants to wait, and your folks want you to wait, you just have to wait."

"Blake is ready! And besides, I thought you were all for NOT waiting."

"I am! But it's not up to me."

The next words came tumbling out of my mouth. "You're only saying that because Roper and Jared are gone and you don't know if you'll see them again, and you don't want me to get married while you can't."

Andrea's mouth hardened. "That's not true!" A heavy pause. "You think I'd marry either of them, like they're interchangeable or something?"

"You want to marry Roper; but if he dies, you'll settle for Jared." I should have kept my mouth shut—why was I provoking Andrea, my best friend?

She stood up and slammed her chair against the table. "I'm *thrilled* that you know me so well!" She glared at me. "And thanks a lot!" Then she stalked off, followed by Bach, who had been sitting at her feet.

A pang of guilt assailed me. "I'm sorry!" But she was gone.

I'll apologize later. I don't know why Andrea and I fight so much. Before the pulse we were friends and never fought at all. Now, it's like we're sisters more than friends. I guess it's normal for sisters to fight. But if I want to show my folks I'm ready for marriage, I'd better start acting more mature.

I went outside to see what Blake was up to and met him coming towards the house. He looked sun-browned and swarthy and handsome—in a sandy-haired Clark Kent kind of way. Meaning he seems totally oblivious to the fact that he's a looker. He gave me a little peck of a kiss in greeting but his eyes were somber. "I was just coming to find you. I have to go shopping."

'Shopping' is a euphemism for scavenging. It means they'll be looking for abandoned homes that might have good clothing, tools, hygiene items—anything we'd normally buy at a store if there were any stores to buy from.

I felt my face crumple into a frown. "Who's going with you?"

"Your dad and Mr. Simmons."

"All three of you?" *Shocking.* Seldom would my dad risk the lives of three men who were vital to the running of the compound, all at once. Shopping was avoided unless absolutely necessary because it was risky. But if deemed necessary, then whoever went out was charged with bringing back whatever they could find that would be useful.

At one council meeting Cecily suggested we put an end to such trips. As she spoke, she looked confident and strong. In fact, whenever I see her I admire her tall, brown beauty. Though she wore jeans and a t-shirt, she always struck me as someone who would look more comfortable in an evening gown. "First off," she said, in her calm voice, "it's stealing, isn't it?"

Jared had been here then, and he snorted. "From the dead? They don't need it," he said, heavily.

"But it isn't ours," she insisted.

"Look, you don't have to use anything we bring back." Jared's eyes blazed. My dad broke in and said, "Okay, look folks, Cecily has a tender conscience about this and I can understand that." Jared stared at him warily. "But Jared has a point. We aren't taking anything from anyone who's alive to use it."

"What about when things return to normal?" Cecily asked. "What if a relative comes to these houses and finds them wiped out? Aren't we stealing from them?"

"We're surviving!" Jared cried, with harsh finality. He seldom showed much emotion at council meetings and his outburst surprised me. "If there's relatives who come, it means *they* survived, and we have no idea what they did to do that, or what they took from anyone. We are doing what we have to do. We can't think about a future that we may not live to see. We have to think about today."

Cecily then suggested we label goods with the address where we took them from. My dad said he wasn't about to let Cecily go along on a shopping spree so she could affix labels of ownership onto everything, risking life and limb in the process. The atmosphere felt tense then, until Bach, our German Shepherd, loped into the room, went straight to me and rose on his legs. Tail wagging, he put his great big paws on my lap, but then he looked at Blake and growled, which made everyone laugh.

But still, it is my father and my husband-to-be risking life and limb! Why do they *both* have to go? I asked my dad about it and he insists he needs Blake, and that he has to go also. He won't say why, so I'm thinking he must be on the look-out for something special. And Mr. Simmons, I suppose, being our only ex-cop, is probably there to watch their backs.

I intend to pray hard and keep praying hard. Tonight is Bible study and I'll make sure everyone else is praying for them, too. I guess now I know how Andrea must feel with Roper being gone. We live with the knowledge that we might fall under attack at any time, and I'm sort of used to that. But knowing Blake is OUT THERE—off the compound—fills me with greater dread.

CHAPTER TWENTY-TWO

ANDREA

So today I was helping the children at lunch when Lily looked up and called me "Mama" again. I've told her not to do that. I feel like it's proof that our mother is dead. I said, "No! I'm Andrea! Silly." My little brother Aiden came over and took Lily's hand. She smiled happily at him and then back at me, and stroked the side of my face.

"Mama," she repeated.

"She thinks you're Mom," Aiden said. He turned his big eyes to me. "When IS Mom coming back, Andi?"

Quentin was suddenly there too, which was no surprise since the twins are rarely apart. "Yeah, why isn't Mom back yet?" he asked. And then Laura and Lainie, Lexie's twin sisters, perked up their ears and stared at me. And then I saw that the little Buchanans, all four of them, were also looking at me, staring. All the children were interested.

What could I say? I tried to smile at my brothers. "I don't know. Remember, she can't call us." I wasn't about to say she'd probably never be back. I don't ever want to say that to the kids!

"There's no phones," Quentin intoned, nodding.

Aiden's face lit up. "She could write a letter! Right?"

I frowned, and shook my head. "There's no mail, sweetie. We just have to wait."

"Wait for what?" Aiden asked.

"For Mom to get back," I said. But I was beginning to feel dishonest. Who was I kidding? How long should I try to protect them from the truth? The boys returned to playing, and soon Cecily ushered them away. She often does child-care, thankfully, because she's got amazing patience and genuinely loves the children. Lexie and I do less with the kids now during summer since we have so much more outdoor work.

I sighed and stood up with Lily balanced on my hip. I'd check her diaper—though I hate changing them because we only have cloth diapers now—and then hand her off to Cecily or another child-care worker.

"Mama," she said again, and giggled.

"I'm not Mama!" I scolded, but she just surveyed me with her blue Lars eyes. I don't understand it. She knows my name, so why does she call me that? Lexie said it doesn't mean anything, but it's like an omen to me.

After giving her to Cecily, I had to escape upstairs for a while. I still had chores waiting, but they'd just have to wait. I flopped onto my bed and cried.

I'd been trying hard not to think about my mother, and especially hard not to blame her for being gone. But right now I was mad. Why was she so—*stupid*—to leave the compound? Why hadn't she thought about her children needing her? Why hadn't she realized that meant I was all they had left—and I didn't want to be all! I didn't want to take her place and be Mama.

I used to pretend she was okay somewhere, getting along fine with Mr. Washington. Even when Rhema came back, I convinced myself they'd sent the horse away because they couldn't feed and care for her. That makes sense, right? But when Lily calls me Mama, I can't hold on to those fantasies. I know what it means: My mother really is gone! Forever. And I have to live with it. That makes me—all of us—orphans! Ugh. I hate that word.

Maybe I'm too old to be considered an orphan. I hope so. But nothing can change the fact that I have no parents. And my mother was *stupid!*

CHAPTER TWENTY-THREE

LEXIE

I don't know how to comfort Andrea. What could someone say to me if my mother was presumed dead? Would there be any way to comfort me? I can't even remind her about heaven and the hope we have in Christ because I have no idea if her mother was a believer. Anything I come up with sounds empty to my own ears.

So I'm just not saying anything; giving her space so she can grieve in peace. Besides, we still don't know for *sure*. It doesn't look good that Rhema came back without them, but if they had really fallen into evil hands, how would a horse have escaped? People are not above eating horse meat these days, let me tell you.

Tonight when we should have gone to sleep, it was oppressively hot. The air was heavy and humid. The shutters to our room were open, so I sat at the window and watched the blackness outside through the screen. Nights are truly dark now unless the moon is full. But sometimes, somewhere far off, I'll see a vague light. It reminds me we're not the only survivors, not the only ones using oil lamps and candles, not the only ones getting by! I wish it were safer out there so we could contact these people. If they used amateur radio we might be able to communicate with them. But neither Dad nor Mr. Buchanan have been able to reach anyone really close by.

After a few minutes my eyes could discern between the darkness of the tree line and the slightly less black of the sky, broken up by an amazing number of stars. Some nights we can see the outline of the milky way! What amazes me is the thought that it's always been there, exactly the same, only we couldn't see it because of electricity and all the lights of civilization. It seems ironic that having so much light made us miss this remarkable spectacle of creation.

I heard Andrea moving in bed, and then she was beside me, falling to her knees to join me at the window. "It's hot," I said.

"Yeah. See anything?"

"No." I knew Andrea didn't mean 'anything' when she said 'anything.' What she really meant was did I see any sign of Roper and Jared coming back? Or her mother and Mr. Washington? Many times, I'd found her searching the landscape from this window, hoping to see them. Some days she even goes up to the watchtower for a better view. (That's our attic. Lookouts are up there 24/7—especially Marcus and Bryce—so we dubbed it the watchtower.)

"They've been gone almost a month," Andrea said, wrenching me from my thoughts. "I hope they brought enough food."

I said, "They've got hardtack."

"But how long could that last?"

"They used hardtack on ships for centuries and even during the Civil War. Men carried it for months and it didn't go bad."

"Really?" She seemed impressed. "Why don't we use it? Instead of having to bake every week?"

I glanced at her. "Because it tastes like dust. It'll keep you alive but it's not exactly yummy."

Andrea sighed. We fell silent for a few minutes. Then she said, "I wish we could go back."

I instantly understood what she meant because now and then one of us would utter those same words. Back to the past, to the days before the pulse. "I know." I missed modern comforts, of course, but in truth, Andrea had lost a lot more than we'd ever had on the farm, not to mention losing her parents. The expensive house and fancy clothes were just the start. Life was nightmarish in some ways for everyone now, but for Andrea, it was like, irreversible. We had hope that maybe one day the United States would re-organize, that power would return, and life would be mostly peaceful again. But Andrea's parents weren't going to reappear, ever.

I put my hand on top of one of hers and gave it a squeeze. She didn't say anything, but she sighed again, and I knew she'd understood my sympathy. I tried to think of something we could do, something that might bring her hope.

"Hey," I said. "Why don't we pray for Roper? And Jared?"

"Okay. Let's pray they come back—tomorrow!"

"Good idea," I said. We faced each other and held hands. There in the dark we lifted up the two men before the Lord. We ended up praying for a lot of other things too, like for electricity to return, and for law and order. We both cried. And then we returned to bed.

Sometimes I get really mad at Andrea, but I do love her.

Lord, send Roper back—like, tomorrow!

Chapter Twenty-Four

ROPER

The men waited until dusk to finally approach the barn. Crouching in the tall brush, they'd watched in silence as two head of cattle were brought in for the night—but not, to their surprise, to the barn. The animals were taken inside a walk-out basement.

"S'the only way to keep 'em safe," said Jared. "But that means the barn is open season."

"Look," Roper said, "Open season, it's not. We're only taking stuff if it looks like they're not using it."

Jared's usual look of disdain settled upon Roper. "Sure. Whatever you say, preacher."

I'm not a preacher, Roper thought, *but boy, you sure need one.* As soon as the farmer had disappeared into the basement with the animals, the men went quickly across the road and climbed the fence, carefully because Jared had to stop and use his bolt cutters to clear barbed wire.

"Whoa, you came equipped," Roper murmured.

"What'd you expect?" Jared asked.

They headed to the barn. There was a lock-and-bolt on it, but Jared swung his backpack off and again pulled out the heavy bolt cutter. After he cut the bolt they hurried inside, pulling the door shut behind them. The lantern revealed a medium-sized interior which might have held up to six animals at one time. The stalls were empty now, clean but for a light layer of straw. Jared began rummaging around like a woman at the annual Christmas clearance sale. Meanwhile, Roper took note of the obvious stuff: a few bales of hay against a wall, some dead farm equipment, perhaps a thresher, but it was rusty and ancient looking; a dead 1980s car, dirty buckets, the empty stalls, the still present scent of manure, and an old hand-plow and manual mower. Piles of wires, cabling, ropes, and oil cans. No fertilizer, no stump remover, no saltpeter.

"So this was a wash," Roper said, on their way out.

"Not completely," said Jared, who had tucked something into his backpack. "We'll try another, and then another, and keep on trying, until we hit gold. I am not going back without getting what I came for." Roper considered those words as they crept back to the brush line and their horse. He had visions of having to be out for days and days yet, maybe weeks, if it took that long, and he didn't like the thought.

"Look, dead cars are everywhere. Like I said before, why don't we just pull the airbag initiators—you said that could do it for you." Jared was silent. They started for the road as the hazy dusk of a summer night began to fall. "Maybe we should do that," he said finally, to Roper's surprise.

"Great!" he said. "Let's just check out Andrea's house, first. Once I pull the airbags, we want to get them back as soon as possible, nice and gentle like. The less carting about the better. So let's do that on the way back."

Jared nodded. "Fine. We'll check any barns on the way, just in case. Can't hurt."

The sky was inky black, lit with stars, but dark on the ground when they found Andrea's house. It was in the same condition all the other houses in the plat that they'd passed were in: burned out, windows broken, ghostly looking. Not surprisingly, the door was unlocked. Looters had surely preceded them there.

Both men switched on flashlights as they entered, Roper leading their horse right across the threshold. They came to a halt inside, listening and sweeping their lights across the dark interior. The air was thick with the smell of smoke. Roper brought up his bandana to cover his mouth and nose.

Hearing nothing, they explored further, the flashlights leading the way. "It's a shame, isn't it?" Roper said, softly. Jared didn't bother to reply but the signs of ruined grandeur filled Roper with pity and sadness. Such a waste! The sheer size of the rooms, the granite counters and tiled floor in the kitchen, dirty and blackened except for small areas that had somehow escaped the fire's fury, spoke silently of the luxury that once was. The staircase was blanketed with ash and debris but Roper, for some reason, brushed it away on a step and sighed.

"This is marble," he said, impressed.

"Was," said Jared, moving cautiously past Roper.

"Still is," Roper murmured to himself. He followed Jared, then, mirroring his example by drawing his pistol though he still felt averse to the idea of shooting first and asking questions later. They did a quick reconnaissance of the first floor, locked any doors that led outside or to the garage or basement, and then circled back to the wide staircase. They left the horse tied to the banister with handfuls of hay—that last barn had held plenty of it.

Upstairs they entered a bedroom—it seemed the fire hadn't reached this room but only smoke and ash. Looters *had* reached it. Blankets and sheets were absent from the beds, dresser drawers were opened with items hanging out here and there, dusted with ash.

Roper examined the contents of the drawers, looking for anything Andrea might want. He started stuffing his pack with lingerie and socks.

Jared turned harsh eyes to him. "We're looking for Andrea's mother, not girly stuff. Why are you so eager to waste time on non-essentials?"

Roper didn't flinch or stop but continued adding things to his bag: scarves, belts, hair accessories, dirty as they were. Finally he turned to Jared. "Because," he said, patiently, "Essentials enable us to live; but non-essentials make life worth living." He paused. "Besides, girls love this stuff. Why not get some?"

Jared's eyes didn't soften. He said, "Just don't EVER tell me you don't got room for the essentials because of that garbage."

Just then they heard the sound of distant gunfire.

153

"Get that light out," Jared ordered. "C'mon, let's get near a window and get a look outside."

"I can't see a thing without the light," Roper said, switching his flashlight back on.

"Turn it off!" Jared repeated. "Your eyes will adjust!"

The men waited, listening, exiting the room slowly. It was a south-facing bedroom, and the shots seemed to be coming from the other direction, so they worked their way to another room that faced the front. One of the windows was still intact. They crept up and peered out. The world was black. Faint lights appeared here and there, flickering, distant, coming in and out of view.

They heard no more shots. "Might've been someone hunting," Roper said. "Got himself a raccoon or something."

"Maybe," said Jared. "Just in case something's coming our way, we'll spend the night here. Take turns keeping watch."

CHAPTER TWENTY-FIVE

ROPER

There was no gunfire to be heard the rest of the night. Roper spent his watch time in prayer and thinking about Andrea and this big house. Jared had done a quick sweep of the remaining rooms on the second floor, and together they'd gone down to the basement to check it out. There was no sign of Mrs. Patterson or Mr. Washington, no sign that they'd ever been there. Roper did not relish the moment when he'd have to give Andrea the disappointing news. He'd try to minimize details of the damage to the house—let her remember it as it had been, before the pulse.

They kept watch for an hour after daylight, but when the street remained quiet, they headed out. They didn't bother searching homes adjacent to the Patterson's because most were mere shells, their wooden exteriors nothing more than charred remains. A few other brick edifices were in the plat, but upon closer inspection, they were burned out on the inside, too.

A dead Mercedes was in the driveway, its windows smashed out and tires slashed. "I'll grab the initiators," Roper said. Jared stood nearby, letting the horse graze on the tall grass of the lawn. In twenty minutes, ten of which were spent merely waiting after disconnecting the battery to be sure the juice was cut—he had the items. He wrapped them carefully in a scarf he'd taken from the house and put the package gingerly in his backpack.

As they headed out of the plat, Roper said, "I sure wish we could stop whoever's doing this." He motioned at the sad remains of houses. "Destroying everything—for what?"

"It's foreigners," put in Jared. "Soldiers, like the ones who came against us. They do it to demoralize a population. They know it's easier to control people if they've lost hope."

155

"Why do you say that?"

Jared shrugged. "It's a classic form of guerrilla warfare."

"Man, why isn't the army coming against them? Even if they have tanks, like the reports are saying, all we need is a couple of anti-tank guns. Aren't there anti-tank guns? If only we could get one of those."

"Yeah, they're just sitting around for the taking!" Jared replied, his eyes never leaving the road in front of them.

"Look, I'm trying to be helpful here...you got anything other than sarcasm? Because that's not helpful."

Jared studied him silently for a moment. "What we need is air power. Our military has it...but doesn't look like they've brought it home."

"Brought it home?"

Jared nodded. "From our bases around the globe. That weren't hit by the pulse. We know it wasn't global, the EMP. Our compound has had contact via ham radio with Australia and New Zealand, and they say the EMP only affected our continent, and Greenland and Iceland. So the fact that we haven't seen U.S. air power means they haven't sent it. If it's true what we heard about a mile of foreign army trucks entering the country from Canada, we need that air power. A squadron or two of F-16s would do the job. We need 'em now."

"So how can we get them?"

Jared snorted. "Try becoming the Secretary of Defense. Even generals can't send help unless they get the Secretary's okay, and he needs it from the President. So the President hasn't authorized it. That's the only conclusion you can make."

"But how long are they gonna let these foreign invaders terrorize the country, man? They gotta do something! That's the role of government."

"What is?"

"According to God the primary role of government is to protect its citizenry. That is their *primary* function, their *sole reason* for being. If they're not fulfilling that function they shouldn't be in existence!"

156

Suddenly Roper's eyes flashed. "Government was instituted by God so people can live in peace. In a sinful planet you've gotta have government but if they turn on their own people they forfeit their right to exist. Then it's tyranny, not government! And if our government could be helping us but isn't then they are not doing their job!" He punctuated his words with his free arm by slashing it through the air for emphasis, and kicked a rock out of his way with surprising force.

Jared nodded. "That's about the first thing you've said that makes sense. But who knows what our government is up to right now. Working out some kind of treaty or concessions, no doubt. Giving up our sovereignty as a nation! That's been coming a long time thanks to the U.N.. Now they've probably got us over a barrel." He shook his head. "The globalists are probably loving this! We've had enough chaos to bring the U.S. to its knees—right where they've always wanted us."

"It sure seems that way," Roper agreed. "I don't follow politics closely, but—." His words were cut off by a sudden shot which sent both men running for cover with the horse in tow. They had passed the last house and were on a stretch of road that led to the main road. It was lined with trees on one side—from which the shot had come—and, on the other side, nothing but an overgrown field. They were out in the open and there wasn't a thing they could do about it.

Another shot sounded, frighteningly close, as they dropped to the ground in the field. The horse remained a standing target.

"How do you get a horse to lie down?" hissed Roper.

"I don't think you can," Jared replied.

"Man, if they hurt this horse too--!" seethed Roper. "I'm starting to get really angry."

Jared's face broke into a semblance of a grin. "It's about time! If this junk don't make you angry, I don't know what would."

They had their rifles out, pointing them towards the trees.

"Someone is either a very bad shot," Jared said, his eyes alert and watching the trees, "or they just wanted to scare us."

After waiting for what felt like a long time and seeing no movement, Jared said, "We can't stay here. I'm gonna send a few shots over there, and then you're gonna follow me. Keep low." He paused. "But leave the horse."

"What? Why?"

"They can't see us in this grass. If the horse moves with us, they'll know exactly where we are. Leave her."

"We're gonna need her. And what about our stuff?"

"We'll get her back!"

"You hope so!" Roper took off the saddle bags, sighed, and dropped the reins.

"She's gonna run when I shoot. So let her run."

"Look, if anyone was there, they just had an open shot at me and didn't take it." Ignoring him, Jared peered through the sight on his rifle, took aim and then crossed the tree line spraying shots steadily. Just as he'd expected, the mare whinnied and took off behind them. There was no return fire. Staying well within the tall grasses and brush, they started creeping back toward the houses where there was cover.

The first home was a burned-out brick shell, enough to offer protection. When they got as close as they could in the grass, they stood up and made a run for it.

Minutes crawled past as they kept watch. Half an hour later they saw the horse in the field, her head rising above the brush, munching. Apparently she hadn't run very far, or maybe got slowed by loose reins. Now she was grazing but slowly meandering in their direction.

"Man, we are wasting time," Roper muttered, pulling out a piece of jerky. "I'm almost out of rations, by the way."

"Patience," said Jared. "Sometimes a fight comes down to who is gonna be the most patient."

"They are gone," returned Roper. "We are waiting on—*nothing!*"

"We don't know that," said Jared.

Roper eyed his companion. "So why don't we find out?"

Thirty minutes later Roper and Jared had worked their way down the street all the way back to the Patterson's house, staying behind the houses. At the end of the street they crossed over so that now they were on the same side as the stand of trees from where the shots had come.

Using the same method, staying behind anything that gave cover, they slowly worked their way towards the area. When they reached the last house there was only brush and grass between them and the stand of trees.

"We're gonna have to crawl or we'll be seen," Jared said.

Roper sighed. "Let's do it."

———————◆———————

Within fifteen minutes they stood up in the middle of the trees. And they were alone.

Across the street the mare was visible near the edge of the road, still cropping at the grass. "I'm gonna get her," Roper said, laying down saddle bags and his backpack.

"Good luck with that," Jared replied. "She ain't your horse. Heck, she ain't mine, either. She's not gonna come to us."

"I gotta try."

"We already lost most of the day, so why not?" His voice was tinged with its usual sarcasm. "Fine. I'll cover you."

Roper strode casually across the street. He would've hurried so as not to be out in the open but he didn't want to spook the horse. On the way, he prayed.

When he got within a few feet, the mare raised her head and surveyed him. Her eyes looked alarmed but he spoke softly and slowly crept closer. "Lord, I'm asking you to let me get this horse." Then, "That's a girl! Whoa, nice and easy, girl." The lead-rope was hanging at her side. Just as he made a lunge for it, she whinnied and reared up. Roper got beside her and she came back down and quieted. He stroked her neck and spoke softly to her again.

When he emerged from the brush leading the horse, he heard Jared give a low whistle from the trees. "Good work," he said.

They stayed off-road as much as possible, only venturing onto black-top when they spotted dead cars. Then it became a nerve-wracking business of removing the airbags while Jared kept watch. Even though most cars were pushed to the sides of the road, it still felt vulnerable because many roads were surrounded only by open fields.

"We ought to find a car lot—more places to hide, and lots and lots of airbags we can get at," Roper suggested.

"Yeah, well, car lots are closer to population hubs, and I prefer to stay out here by the farms, thank you," said Jared.

"A repair shop, then. They've usually got cars sitting around."

"And a mechanic who probably figured out he could use the airbags just like we want to."

They'd retrieved six initiators when they came across a farmhouse that looked ransacked and abandoned. It had two small sheds, both with doors hanging open, but worth a look, according to Jared.

It turned out to be their first big break. One shed had two gallons of stump remover, a gallon of fungicide and two empty jerry cans. Jared called it a windfall, grabbing the stuff while Roper packed it on the horse.

The second shed housed a dead tractor. Jared examined it and said, "This thing's got gas in the tank!"

"Are you telling me we can ride that tractor?"

"No. It's got electronic parts. But we can siphon the gas."

Roper coughed lightly. "Did you happen to bring a siphon?" His raised brows and tone of voice intimated that he thought not.

Jared eyed him evenly. "It just so happens, I did."

Roper laughed and said, "Gotta hand it to you, buddy. You do know how to pack for a road-trip after an apocalypse."

Afterwards they munched on jerky and hardtack, taking water from a stream on the property. Both men had portable water straws— miraculous filtering devices, according to Roper, who'd been on the road in the past without a good means of purifying water. He'd used snow to keep from dehydrating but he would only do it when he'd made a fire to melt it—otherwise it would've just froze him faster.

They waited for nightfall, dozing by turns during the afternoon hours. Having supplies not only slowed them down but also made them a bigger target, so Jared figured moving by night was their safest course. Being on the road at any time was dangerous—but being there with useful stuff was courting disaster.

Roper napped first and then stood watch while Jared, who had covered his eyes with Roper's bandana, slept. He'd been watching for an hour when five tough-looking men came over a hill, a few hundred feet from the shed where they were. The horse was tied on the other side of the shed, grazing in the brush, out of their sight—for now. Roper knew they would soon see the horse, even if they didn't look in the barn and discover him and Jared.

If he went out to get the animal, he'd be seen. If he didn't, they'd lose their horse. He scanned them quickly for weapons and his heart sank when he saw two rifles. That meant there were likely more hidden weapons that he could not see. He jabbed at Jared with the butt of his rifle.

"We got company," he whispered. Jared tore off the bandana and sprang to his feet. He joined Roper near the single window where they stayed out of sight. The five men were now close enough to see their features.

"What're you waiting for?" Jared hissed. "This is why I told you—shoot on sight." As he spoke, the men, talking among themselves, turned to follow the downward slope of the property. They weren't interested in the sheds. And if they kept going they'd miss seeing the horse! Jared lifted his rifle, ensuring it was locked and loaded, ready to fire. He flipped off the safety.

"Wait," Roper said. "They turned away."

"Perfect. This is our chance," said Jared. He charged out the door and, right before Roper's horrified eyes, gunned down the five men. There were shouts, cries, and then—silence.

161

Their backs were to the shed—it had been nothing but a slaughter. Shocked, Roper dropped to the floor, his back against the wall. He sat, trying to process what he'd just seen, heart pounding wildly in his throat. When Jared came back, Roper could only stare at him.

"I'm gonna reload," Jared said. "Then let's see what they had on them." He set his rifle down and removed the magazine as if nothing out of the ordinary had just gone down. He drew a new one out of his pocket and shoved it in; and looked expectantly at Roper.

"C'mon, they had guns. We can use them."

Roper stared at Jared. "You had no call to do that. You just killed someone's father, and brother, or cousin, or uncle. You just murdered those guys in cold blood. For no good reason." He spoke in a subdued tone as if still trying to accept that it had really happened.

Jared frowned, shaking his head. "You just don't get it! If we let those guys go, I guarantee you, half a mile down the road, they'd be taking *us* down. They were heading in the same direction we have to follow. I just made our passage home five men safer."

"You don't know that. You don't KNOW that!"

Jared looked like he wanted to spit. "Forget it, I'm not arguing with you. This is war. You ain't a fighter, I get that. But I've been on the front lines. I know how it goes. You eat your enemy or they eat you."

"This is not Iraq!" Roper picked up a stray stone on the floor and threw it at the wall opposite him. "This is not Afghanistan!"

"This is worse than both those places," Jared answered, now wiping down his rifle with a rag. "Over there, we had command; we had officers in charge! Now we got nothing! Just our brains. We gotta do what we gotta do."

"You didn't have to do that."

"Get over it!" Jared snapped. He peered back outdoors. The sky was just beginning to show signs of a coming pink and orange sunset. "We need to check the bodies and get going."

"I'm not checking their bodies, man," Roper said. "You killed 'em, you check 'em."

Jared shook his head in disgust. "You are—like—useless! You know that?" He picked up his pack, slung his rifle over his shoulder and left the shed, still muttering to himself. After he'd gone, Roper suddenly wondered if there might be survivors. Maybe Jared had only wounded some of them! He scrambled to his feet and hurried after Jared. He would not leave if there was a man alive but suffering. He'd give him the gospel and pray with him.

To his dismay, all five men *were* dead.

Jared certainly knew how to kill a man from behind.

---------------------------------◆---------------------------------

Neither man spoke for hours. Roper had nothing to say to Jared and apparently Jared felt the same way, for they trudged on in silence, only breaking it now and then for one to say, "Wait," if they came upon a dead vehicle. Roper would remove the airbag mechanisms and then they'd move on, still in silence.

As the night wore on it began to look like they'd make it back to the compound. They were passing through the outskirts of a small town, only miles from the Martins' farmstead when Jared, looking over at Roper with an unreadable expression, said, "You're still planning on heading back to your home state—California, right?"

Roper glanced over at him but couldn't make out his eyes. There was something about Jared's tone, almost *too* casual, that set him on edge. Then suddenly he saw the gleam from his eyes shine out in the dark like an unholy light.

He decided to ignore the undertone, if in fact there was one. Maybe he was imagining things. "California's a long ways off. I don't know when I'll get back there. I'd like to return but I don't know."

Jared was silent a moment. "You know we don't really need you at the compound, right?"

Roper gave him a wary look. "I get that *you* don't; but the Martins want me and my trumpet. I'm the new alarm system."

Jared snorted contemptuously. "Your trumpet! Do you have any idea how lame that sounds?"

"Look," Roper said. "Car batteries are powering our alarms. When they run out, my trumpet will sound the alarm. Like in the Old Testament, God used trumpets lots of times for *important* things. He had the people blow trumpets to take down the walls of Jericho, man. They circled the city and circled the city and they blew the trumpets—and only then did the city fall."

Jared shook his head. "So you think your trumpet is some kind of weapon?"

Roper smiled, a slight crescent of a smile, though it went unseen by his companion. "No, no, I'm not saying it's a weapon. It's just an alarm system. When there's danger, I blow the trumpet."

"So what's the Jericho story for?"

"I'm just saying—God likes trumpets. Way back in Genesis he saved Isaac with the horn of a ram, right? A horn. That's what early instruments were made from—horns. And later instruments were based on them. Horns are wind instruments—like the *trumpet.*"

Roper knew that Jared's point—that he wasn't needed at the compound, couldn't be leading to anything good. So he kept talking, hoping to stave off a confrontation. He'd keep talking as long as Jared let him. "Jericho falls after the Israelites circle the city and the priests blow the trumpets. Then you have Leviticus where God tells them the trumpet blasts signify liberty throughout the land. In fact, there's a Feast of Trumpets in the Old Testament."

"You gotta be kidding me! You are putting me on!" Jared sounded more annoyed than disbelieving.

"I kid you not." He took a breath. "So this Feast of Trumpets was a memorial of the blowing of trumpets. That's pretty cool! You don't have a Feast of Lyres, or Feast of Harps, as beautiful as those instruments are, but you got a Feast of Trumpets. I like that, man!"

"That's dumb. A Feast of Trumpets!" Jared shook his head in disgust.

"Well, the high priest in Israel would blow the trumpet to signal people to stop working and come worship. It's a way to point to God, see? The trumpet, whether to signify freedom, or worship, or victory— it's always about God and what he's doing for his people. Freedom comes from God, man, and worship is all about God!" Roper spoke lightly but with great conviction. "There's no reason to blow a trumpet if God isn't in it. When Jesus returns—guess what you'll hear?"

Jared's tone was sour and getting sourer by the minute. "Don't tell me. A trumpet?"

"You got it! The 'trumpet shall sound; and the dead shall be raised!'"

Jared sniffed and sent a searing look at Roper. It would have been missed in the dark except a beam of moonlight broke through the clouds and suddenly the men were facing each other, eye to eye. Jared said, "We don't need no trumpet on the compound. We don't need *you* on the compound."

So this was it. Jared wanted a showdown. "I got it; you want me out." He paused. "It's about Andrea, isn't it?"

Jared balked and snapped, "It's about feeding someone who doesn't earn his keep!"

"I don't think so."

"I'm telling you, that's what it is."

"Does your mother earn her keep?"

Jared flushed. "She's a woman. That's different. Leave the women out of this. It's about you—a man, and you ain't pulling your weight."

"I just pulled those initiators. And I seem to recall you saying you couldn't do that."

"Yeah, so you served your purpose!" he shot back.

Roper said, "I think this *is* about a woman. It's about Andrea. You're worried that I'm getting in your way, aren't you?"

165

"You are in my way, okay? You ARE in the way. But I want you out because we can't take in dreamy troubadours; we need soldiers, men who can *fight*." He paused. "You proved to me earlier that you can't hold your own."

"That wasn't fighting, that was *slaughtering.*"

"What do you think fighting comes down to?" Jared's voice was strident.

"For terrorists. I'm not a terrorist! And neither are you!"

"We're all terrorists," Jared said. "We have to be. Like I said, either you take them out, or they take you out. That's what it's about. And you don't get that. You'll never get that. That's why we don't need you." He paused, his eyes blazing at Roper out of the darkness.

"So I'm going to give you a choice. Either you go your own way right now, or I'll have to do something to make you do that. I am *not* bringing you back to the compound with me."

"Who asked you to bring me back?"

"Right," he said, hotly. "So get lost."

Roper slowly nodded. "Fine. How do I know you won't shoot me in the back the minute I turn around?"

"I guess you don't know."

"I'm not turning. I'm not running. If you want to get rid of me, do it. Do it now, while I'm facing you." Both men were sweating, and it wasn't only the heat of the night that caused it.

Jared fingered the gun at his waist, eying Roper steadily. But he dropped his hand and then went to take the reins of the horse from Roper.

Roper tried not to give them up but Jared said, "You don't get to keep our stuff."

Their eyes locked in a contest of wills. Roper finally allowed Jared the reins. "Take it. Build your bombs and protect the compound."

Looking somewhat mollified, Jared took the reins and began leading the horse forward. He tossed his head back to say, "Don't follow me." His words were heavy, final. Roper watched him going off for a moment and then called, "How do you know I won't shoot *you* in the back?" Jared didn't even turn around.

"You won't."

Roper wiped the sweat off his face and brow, watching Jared as he got smaller in the distance. He had to decide on his next move. If he followed Jared, he had no doubt the stoic ex-soldier would shoot him. If he didn't follow, where could he go? They'd seen a refugee camp but there was no way he'd willingly enter one. They reminded him of Nazi prisons despite being fly-by-night ensembles with more canvas and tarps than brick or stone.

Suddenly he heard a muffled voice. He froze, listening. He heard the unmistakable sound of rustling branches and footsteps— approaching from beyond a low rise not far behind him. Roper hurried to get in the shadows of bushes that were lining the nearest sidewalk against a fence that housed a tiny front yard. He went inside the fence and crouched behind the shrubbery. He'd wait for them to pass. The sounds grew louder. Seemed like another small band of survivors –but this one included female voices. He almost wanted to jump up and warn them to change course because they were going in Jared's direction— and that could be deadly.

He knew what Jared would do if he felt the least bit threatened. But he had no way of knowing if these people could be trusted not to treat him the same as Jared treated strangers. As they came alongside the sidewalk where he lay on the other side of the fence and bushes, he huddled there, quiet and still. And waited.

CHAPTER TWENTY-SIX

JARED

Jared followed a main road keeping to the side, and came across no one. He stopped briefly with the idea of resting and grabbing a bite to eat—and then remembered Roper had been carrying the rest of the food. Muttering beneath his breath, he started out again and covered miles as the night wore on. When he was only a few miles from the compound, dawn lightened the sky. He peered steadily down the road but saw only dead cars now and then on one side or the other.

Suddenly he wondered why they hadn't thought to move all these cars to form a great road block? Using the horses or even enough manpower they could line them up, row upon row, and form a serious delay barrier. If they did it both north and south of the compound, it would give them enough time to be good and ready when the enemy broke through. In fact, using the cars' batteries, they could even fill a vehicle with fertilizer and set it up to explode with a pressure plate. *Why hadn't he thought of this sooner?* Jared felt suddenly that he wasn't thinking clearly, or hadn't been. His mind was so full of one method of defense that he'd missed the forest for the trees.

This conviction grew worse. For, continuing on, he realized if they'd simply gone out for airbag initiators to begin with, they could have had all they needed right here within a few miles of home! His mind had been fixed on searching out things like fireworks or gunpowder, or farming chemicals. They'd passed all these vehicles on the way out—how stupid he'd been!

Most air bags worked via sodium perchlorate—it was what made them pop—and, seeing all these vehicles, he suddenly realized what a windfall of an arsenal he could make if they accessed them all. The cars were just sitting here waiting to be picked clean. He saw himself as the future hero of the compound like he was after they deflected that last attack with his grenades.

Except Roper was gone. Because he'd chased him off.

Stupid! I should have waited. He should have let the man hit all these cars before getting rid of him. Suddenly it seemed impossible to move on, while here were airbags for the taking. It was so convenient— so much easier than getting the other stuff—and why not get as many as possible? Roper had pulled a bunch of the things while he'd watched. It was as good as getting lessons on how to do it, wasn't it?

He'd considered getting rid of Roper permanently—and probably should have. Now that wuss would go back and complain about him to the leadership team. But, despite having no qualms about killing an enemy, he couldn't deny Roper wasn't quite that. He disliked him, saw little reason to respect him, and he was jealous of Andrea's obvious preference for the man. But Andrea was still a child-woman. He'd have preferred a real woman if the compound had any that seemed like prospects. Other than Cecily who was older than he liked and way too religious, there were only married women. Anyway, he hadn't been able to do away with Roper.

He began trying doors on the cars he passed. Not surprisingly, they were locked. Breaking windows was a noisy proposition, so he kept going until he found one whose window was smashed in.

Tying his horse to the passenger side door handle, he grabbed the tools he'd seen Roper use, and went around to the driver's side. He also knew from Roper that it'd be easier to extract that airbag than the one on the passenger side since it was right in the steering wheel. Roper would have taken both but Jared would make do with only one from each vehicle. After prying out plastic cover pieces and removing two side bolts, he felt relieved when the whole middle apparatus—which held the airbag—came out easily in his hands. He was right—he could do this!

He lifted it, but it was still wired to the car. Jared suddenly remembered Roper had always disconnected the battery before cutting these wires. In fact, disconnecting the battery was the first thing he did even before entering the car. He'd forgotten that step.

But heck, the batteries were probably dead anyway—even Roper had acknowledged that. Cars don't take nicely to sitting and doing nothing for long periods of time; it drains their power. If he cut this wire without disconnecting it, would it deploy the bag?

He considered his options: If he disconnected the battery, he'd have to wait a minimum of three minutes for residual power to dissipate. (According to Roper who played it safe and opted to wait ten.) If he followed Roper's method, it would mean ten extra minutes per car. But these cars hadn't moved since the pulse! Roper was an absolute *girl* when it came to boldness, and probably way more careful than necessary. Even three minutes seemed needlessly cautious.

Why, Jared remembered a time when a car battery died on him after sitting unused for only four months. These cars had been dead since January, through freezing temperatures—unfriendly to car batteries—and it was now late July. That settled it. He grabbed a wire cutter and snipped a yellow wire connecting the airbag to the car.

———◆———

When Jared awoke some time later—the sun was more to the west—his head was pounding. His whole face ached. Something else was wrong—his left arm and hand. He tried to lift it, to get it in his line of vision, but it was shockingly difficult. He felt strangely heavy and unable to move. His arm and hand throbbed, and when he finally got it lifted and into his line of sight, he wasn't surprised to find it bloody and burned. And fuzzy. Wait-*fuzzy*? That was his vision. He blinked, looking around, and realized he couldn't see anything clearly. Slowly he recognized the whitish material in front of him—the deflated airbag. *The airbag had deployed!* So car batteries *could* hold charges for that long! It was a painful lesson, and he realized he was lucky to be alive.

He took a better look at his left hand, blinking, willing it to come into focus. He tried raising his head. Other sounds were outside—

his horse was scraping the ground with its hoofs and nickering. The explosion would have frightened the animal. She'd be impatient to get moving. Jared had no idea how long he'd been out, but realized he had to get up, go soothe the horse. Then he heard another sound, and it made him curse at himself under his breath. There were people out there, coming his way, no doubt. Had they heard the blast? Perhaps. In any case, he was in poor condition to defend himself. And all of the stuff he'd gathered—it was all in the saddle bags! He had to get out of there—with the horse—pronto.

With his left arm throbbing violently now, he tried to pick himself up with only his right for leverage. He had to get out of the car. He was woozy—unbelievable that an airbag could do so much damage, but then again, he'd been holding it when it blew. How stupid of him! So Roper hadn't been too cautious! That knowledge only added to his fury.

Getting shakily out of the car, he accidentally put weight on his left hand as he slid out. Red hot pain shot up his arm, enveloping him in momentary agony and almost making him cry out. He must have broken it, in addition to the burns and seeping flesh wounds he'd sustained on it.

His rifle—still on the car seat! He bent over to grab it with his right arm while simultaneously peering through the front window to see what was approaching. Looked like four men—at least there were only four. Normally that number wouldn't worry him too much, but he was handicapped. One of them had on a cowboy hat—thought he was in the Wild West. He pulled the rifle out, swung it over the edge of the car door window for support—he'd need that support to shoot with only one hand—and crouched behind the door, resting his bad arm on one leg. It was fortunate the window was smashed in; it put the rifle at a good height, and the door made decent concealment. But would it offer cover? He hoped they'd have to use AK47s to get a bullet through it—either that, or a supremely lucky shot—and so far he hadn't seen any rifles. Not that he could see all that well, but his sight was improving by the minute.

The men had seen him by now and came to a stop.

"I'm armed!" he shouted. "Turn around and keep going!"

"We're armed, too," one man replied, reaching to his waist. At that moment, a shot rang out, a shot that came from the wooded right side of the road. It rang past the head of the man who'd been reaching for his weapon. Jared had no idea who the shot had come from but as the men reacted, ducking and scrambling for cover, he saw a tactical advantage and used it.

He aimed as best he could and took a shot at the men but he couldn't be sure if he hit anyone. "I'm not alone, morons! I got guys in the woods here. Now turn around or you will all be slaughtered!"

The men took cover behind a white Toyota about fifty feet from where Jared was crouched behind his car door. "He's lying!" The cowboy said, looking sharply into the sides of the road where trees and bushes might have hidden any number of men. "I think he made that shot. I think he's all alone."

Jared heard the remarks, marveling that his ears seems to have escaped damage. If one of them stepped out from behind the car, they'd be in range. He struggled to get his wobbly sight on one because they weren't buying his bluff. But then another shot came from the woods, neatly shattering the Toyota's side window facing the thick green brush. Jared wondered fleetingly if the unknown shooter was as much a danger to him as them—but so far he'd only sent shots their way, so he called, "Get moving, or we'll shoot—and this time it will be to kill!"

"Show yourselves!" shouted the cowboy, looking at the woods. He came to his feet and stood with his hands up. He had on jeans and boots and even a western-style holster in addition to the hat—a real cowboy wannabe, Jared thought, with disdain. Jared's finger was on the trigger of his rifle. He bent his head to get the guy in his sight. His vision was still not what it should be but he could get a fuzzy figure in his sight as good as a sharp one.

He could only take down one man at a time in his condition—and there were four of them. He couldn't depend on help from the stranger since he had no idea who it was or what his motives were. So he waited at the ready but did not fire. He was not going to shoot first. This was one battle he'd rather avoid.

The cowboy nodded at his companions, saying, "Don't hit the horse!" —and then everything happened at once. Shots came at Jared, pinging into the car door as the men fired and then scurried behind the Toyota and out of sight. One peered around from the back pointing a pistol at Jared, who quickly sighted him and took a shot. Luck was on his side because the bullet sent the guy backwards, head first. It must have landed square on his forehead. Jared felt no relief for bullets were still landing around him. The front windshield to his right shattered, sending glass pieces flying, and making Jared crouch even lower behind the door. But there he was blind to the scene! Also, he knew his feet and legs were visible.

A momentary silence revealed that the horse was scraping and stamping, whinnying, and attempting to break free. As Jared glanced over, the animal reared against the car. No sooner had he raised his head to get a look when a volley of shots ensued, plunking into the seat and body of the car. He'd be dead if they had AK47s! But he'd seen the horse hadn't been shot—at least, not yet.

As he considered his options a voice cried out—it was the cowboy again—"Leave us the horse and we'll let you go!"

Jared was silent for a moment, thinking. Then he shouted, "Come and get it!" He was weak; his arm was bleeding heavily and his hand felt enormous, grotesque, like it was ten times its normal size due to the immense throbbing pain—though a single glance assured him it wasn't; it only felt that way—but he badly wanted to be able to dress it and get out of there. Yet there was no way he would walk away and leave the horse. They'd shoot him in the back, for one thing; and he'd shoot the horse himself rather than let them get it.

"We're coming out!" The cowboy called. "If you shoot, we'll kill you!"

Jared readied himself to take a shot. He watched as two men, including the cowboy, came out from behind the Toyota. The men held up their arms. "We're not gonna shoot! Don't fire!'

173

"Stop!" Jared called. "Stay where you are!" He wished he could shoot the two of them on the spot but with his injuries he felt he'd only get one quickly; then the second would kill him. They halted, but said, "Look, we only want the animal."

"What for?"

"There's a lot of meat on a horse. We got hungry people to feed."

"So do we," Jared said, tightly. "But we don't eat horse meat. You don't need to, either."

"Oh, yeah? You got another food source you might want to share, stranger?"

Jared thought for a moment. "Farm silos. They got grain, and they're all over this part of Ohio." He knew, as he spoke, that many of the silos were already empty. The pulse had hit in January—not after harvest. Farmers had been going through their grain, either by using it themselves, or selling it, or having it stolen.

The men looked at each other; Jared could see they'd been too stupid to think of that before now. "That's nice," the cowboy said. "But we need meat." He was peering towards Jared as though to see exactly where he was in order to shoot him, no doubt.

"Let's talk about it!" the cowboy called.

"Ain't nothing to talk about," said Jared. "Turn around and get going or you'll end up like your buddies!" He had only taken down one guy but he gathered, since there were only two of them in sight, that the unknown shooter must have taken down another. Whoever it was, he owed him big-time.

The men moved forward a step, but Jared yelled, "Don't come any closer! I WILL shoot!"

"If you're not going to eat that animal," the cowboy said, "you have no right not to let us have it!"

"Yeah? How about ownership? This horse belongs to me, not you."

"Haven't you heard?" the cowboy replied, sardonically. "There ain't no ownership no more."

"Forget it!" Jared called. "You come one step closer and you're dead."

"Fine!" said the cowboy. "But if we can't have him, neither can you!" He swiftly pulled his pistol out, as did his companion. At the same moment, a shot rang out from the woods, and then a second shot. The gun dropped from the cowboy's hand and he turned and ran, holding an injured arm. The second man had been hit in the shoulder and he, too, turned and started running. Even so, a final shot—from the stranger!—blew the hat off the cowboy's head. Jared's rifle had swung to the side and he frantically maneuvered to get it back in position but he was getting weaker by the second. He wanted to finish them off if he could, even as they retreated—but he couldn't.

The stranger in the woods—whoever it was—had saved his neck. The throbbing in his left hand and arm was becoming all consuming. He felt dizzy and nauseous. His vision seemed worse than before.

As he lay back against the car, gasping in deep breaths to try and get stabilized, the world began spinning. He lost his grip on his rifle, and felt himself slipping from consciousness. And then he saw it—the shadow of the stranger from the woods, coming from his right—and he could do *nothing* to defend himself. It was a horrible realization. No doubt he was about to die at the hand of this unknown person. Then he saw something else, something that settled his mind in an unexpected blanket of relief. It came just at the moment when he was slipping away into unconsciousness.

A face appeared in front of him. "Don't say I never gave you anything." To Jared's astonishment, he knew that voice. He knew that face. It was Roper.

CHAPTER TWENTY-SEVEN

LEXIE

The whole compound is in shock! Dad's latest news from the radio—it's crazy! He was in touch with a new contact from Arizona who told him there were nuclear strikes against California, Oregon and Washington State! Why would anyone want to nuke the West Coast instead of the East? New York City, Washington, D.C.—these are the cities we usually think of as nuclear targets. It doesn't make sense. Dad and Mr. Buchanan are taking turns so that one of them is on the radio 24/7 until we get further word. Everyone wants to know, how big were the strikes, will there be more, and who caused them?

The idea of nuclear war has made everything we've done (and are doing) to prepare for the next attack seem pointless. We can't deflect a nuclear strike with barriers or a fence, no matter how strong they are. The cabins would be useless in such an attack. Every cabin family suddenly wants to find a bomb shelter, or at least, a basement, because they know they can't all fit into ours. I've never seen such unrest among our families.

No one feels safe anymore. I mean, it's been a long time since we've felt really safe even here on the compound, but we had confidence in our preparations, in Jared's ideas of building bombs and defenses; we had hope! The idea of a nuclear strike makes all of that seem meaningless. It's like trying to fight a forest fire with a cup of water.

After hearing the terrible news Andrea and I went up to our room. We cried, we held hands and prayed, and we talked about possibilities. I reminded her that our safe room was big enough for not only my family but for her and the twins and Lily.

"How safe *is* the safe room?" she asked.

"We built it in case of nuclear war," I said, "But it depends on whether or not we're in the strike zone. Dad doesn't think we are. Wright-Patt Air Force Base will be, but we're upwind. Being upwind is important."

"So what are you saying?" she asked. "Is it safe—or isn't it?"

"Well, like I said, it's safe if we're not in a direct strike zone—and we're not; not unless their bomb goes off target and hits us by accident. And it's safe from fallout—if you get early warning and get down to the room and stay there for a few *weeks*."

"Haven't we emptied supplies from the safe room to make it a nursery?" she asked.

I nodded. "Somewhat. We have what's left in the storage room, but we've been going through that stuff. I don't think we still have the supplies we'd need to hunker down for a few weeks."

Andrea sat on her bed, heavily. "This is so unfair! Like it wasn't bad enough that we have to be ready to fight for our lives at any moment because of foreign morons!"

I went and sat beside her. "Look. My dad's called a council meeting tonight. We'll probably talk about all this stuff." I took a deep breath. "In the meantime, let's just try to live as if we didn't know about California, or Oregon. There's a chance the information is wrong! It could be rumors."

"Wars and rumors of wars," she said, sadly.

"Right! Jesus said that would happen! Let's try to hope for the best."

She nodded. "Okay." Then she looked at me plaintively. "Would you do me a favor?"

"Sure, what is it?"

"Could you scratch my shoulders?"

I almost laughed but it wasn't funny to Andrea. She was still in the throes of poison ivy which had somehow crawled up her arms to her shoulders and the back of her neck.

"I can't. You know it's not good for you—it only makes it worse!"

"It's driving me crazy!"

"Where's the cream? I'll put more on for you." Using a cotton ball, I dabbed on cream.

She said, "Imagine if this was radiation poisoning—how much worse that would be!"

I nodded, though she couldn't see me behind her. "I know. But don't think like that. We do have the safe room."

Afterward, Andrea and I tried to get back to business as usual, but everywhere I went I saw people talking in groups rather than staying to their usual tasks. I found Blake coming in from the field and walked straight into his arms. He knew how I felt—he understands me so well.

"We don't know for sure, yet," he murmured, and then planted a kiss on my cheek. "My dad says they're waiting to get confirmation from another source." He paused. "There are people who try to learn our frequencies for the sole purpose of spreading fear and lies. So— don't lose hope."

I looked up into his amber-brown eyes. I love Blake's eyes. He has a lot of feeling in them. "Your dad was talking about going back to your house! Because you guys have a safe room. You know it's been totally ransacked—probably burned by now!"

His eyes clouded and he nodded. "Maybe. But a basement is a basement. We can't all fit in yours."

I stared up at him. "But *you* could. You could stay with *us!*"

He let out a breath. "I don't know. I have to see what my parents say. They'll need help with the little ones." Blake's four younger siblings, along with my twin sisters and Andrea's twin brothers, and the Wasserman's young tribe, were collectively called "the little ones." Right now he meant his siblings, and I knew he was right. I couldn't blame him for wanting to be with his family. But I ached at the thought.

"If you go, other people will want to join you. Just like some have been asking my dad if they can stay in our basement room."

He nodded. "I know. I've heard the talk. They really want to find a bomb shelter."

"My dad says they'd be better off digging a cave into our hill, that all you need is a foot of dirt between you and fallout and you'll be okay. Assuming they can close up the opening tight." Blake nodded. "That would work. But it would take a lot of manpower." He paused, and his mouth tightened. "We need to know for sure if those strikes really happened."

"Maybe Dad will know by tonight's meeting," I said. The dinner bell rang. I saw my mom at the door, waving me to the house. Blake and I shared a sweet, short kiss, and then we parted.

As I walked back to the house I had an empty feeling in the pit of my stomach. If we ended up needing to take shelter in our safe rooms, Blake and I would be separated! For weeks! And it hadn't seemed to bother him, not the way it was bothering me, already making my heart ache.

Nuclear bombs were scary enough. Nuclear bombs without Blake? Unthinkable.

LATER

I sat by Blake during the meeting. We held hands and I tried not to worry about him and his family possibly leaving the compound. I was glad when my father stood up to speak for he condemned the idea roundly, saying that to leave was madness. "And for those of you thinking of leaving without a firm destination? That's doubly mad." He looked at the Philpots who had joined us later than most. "You remember what it's like out there—you'd be walking right back into danger, not out of it."

"What's the latest word, Grant?" Mr. Simmons asked my dad, before the Philpots could answer. "Have you heard anything new?"

Mr. Buchanan spoke up. He'd been stationed at his rig for hours, according to Blake. The Buchanan's had brought their AR equipment to their new log home behind ours and built a shack to house it in. AR—that's amateur radio. "We've had one confirmation," he said, loud enough for the room to hear. "But it was from another new contact.

New to us, anyway. We're still waiting to hear from some of our known contacts." After a pause he added, "They've gone quiet."

Mrs. Wasserman, like most all of us, had been listening intently. Her eyes grew large with a thought. "Those known contacts—are they from California?"

Mr. Buchanan pursed his lips. He nodded, "Yes, some are." The room broke into a buzz as everyone talked at once. Blake squeezed my hand as voices rose louder and louder in contention.

"Where are these new contacts from?" someone asked.

"They say they're broadcasting from Idaho," said Mr. Buchanan.

"We *have to* leave," I heard Mrs. Wasserman say to my mom.

"If you leave the compound," my dad's voice broke in louder than the rest, "you could end up in a refugee camp. You know what you'll have for protection there? A tent. A *tent,* people."

"If we get hit by a nuclear strike this compound isn't any safer," said Mr. Prendergast. I don't see Mr. Prendergast often; he lives in a cabin by himself. He helps with lookout duties but not often because he falls asleep on the job. He has the gaunt face of a man who used to be large and has lost too much weight.

"But it can be," said my dad, spreading out his hands. "Out there, you get picked up by one of those trucks, and you're no safer from fallout than if you had no protection at all. At least here we do have a basement. You can't all fit into the safe room but the basement will hold many of you, and it's safer than being on a ground floor anywhere. In the meantime, we'll dig a cave into the hill—caves are used to this day in some parts of the world for shelter. You can use one, too."

Mr. Simmons shook his head. "That sounds Neanderthal! You gotta do better than that for us, Grant."

"There are hundreds of empty houses around," put in Mrs. Wasserman. "Many of them have basements! We can each find a house with a basement and stay there."

"And eat what, exactly?" said my dad. "Here on the compound we've been growing new provisions. You've all been drying produce, smoking meat, storing food. Are you gonna take it all with you? How are you going to keep it safe? You don't even know WHERE you're going, which homes have basements that are fairly air-tight—and a walk-out basement isn't gonna cut it, I hate to tell you." He paused.

"Look, if you want a bomb shelter, build one. Start digging."

After a short silence, Cecily said, "I agree with Grant. Why not build a shelter? With all our manpower and horsepower we should be able to dig one. We can line it with stones and mortar, the way we've been building the wall around the cabins."

"Yeah, that's great—a year from now," said Mr. Prendergast.

Mr. Simmons added, "We need a safe place—now."

My dad said, "I know it's disheartening and frightening, what we've heard. But I don't consider one confirmation from a new contact good enough. Those blasts might not have happened. Fallout may never come." He looked around. "It's daunting to hear that our shores may have been attacked by nuclear strikes—but remember this: Our country is only on its knees on this continent; we still have a global army. We have return fire. Whoever sent those bombs our way—IF they were sent—will be stopped by our government."

"You don't *know* that," said Mrs. Wasserman. Her voice was beginning to sound whiny. "You're just hoping that's true. If our government was still a government—if it had any power—why haven't we seen evidence of it? We haven't seen a sign of our military! Not a single plane!"

"I believe we will see them," said my dad. We just need to survive long enough."

Mr. Simmons said, "But we need a *way* to survive, Grant."

"So let's get that shelter started!" Dad said.

Mr. Prendergast said, "Why should we build a shelter on your property, when it will become yours when this is all over?"

That started off a whole new argument about whether "this" would EVER be over, some saying how stupid it was to worry about ownership, and if we wanted a chance to live through a nuclear war we needed a shelter yesterday.

Suddenly someone said, "Blake, what do you think?" and the whole room fell silent. We all considered Blake our scientist-in-training. My mom used to call him an "encyclopedia of useless information," but she doesn't call him that any longer. Blake's vast knowledge was anything but useless. I tried not to beam with pride when all eyes turned to him. Even my father watched, waiting to see what my smart future husband would say.

Blake was silent for a moment but didn't seem the least surprised to be called on. I got a little nervous for him, wondering if for once he'd have nothing to offer from that amazing mind of his. But he nodded thoughtfully and said, "Actually, it's very conceivable that we can build a shelter here—and quickly. See, the thing is, you don't necessarily have to have mortar and cement and huge stone blocks to keep out fallout. You just need a foot of dirt to shield you from radiation." He paused. "Of course if it's a direct hit, you're outta here, no basement is safe enough. You'd have to be down in Area 51."

Most people in the room were nodding their heads. "I think we can do this, people," said Mr. Simmons.

"Now, I'm not saying you're gonna live like you're in the Hilton," Blake added, "but it'll keep you safe from initial radiation. If you can make it for a few weeks, even two weeks—and there are no more blasts—you can start coming up for air."

Again everyone talked at once. Mrs. Wasserman held up her hand as if she were in a classroom. When Blake nodded at her, she said, "Would we have to worry about radon?"

I saw my dad shaking his head in the negative. Blake said, "No. Radon is only dangerous over long periods of exposure. And even if there is radon down there, it's a whole lot better than gamma rays up here!"

But Mrs. Wasserman frowned. "I still don't understand why we should bother. I thought nuclear war was not survivable."

"That's a common myth," Blake said. "Most people believe that but it's not true. The only time you can't survive nuclear war is if you're in the direct hit zone or a fallout zone without shelter; or if you didn't store food or water. Otherwise, with shelter and supplies—you *can* wait out the worst danger."

Mrs. Wasserman asked, "But wouldn't the air and soil be poisoned for decades?"

Blake shook his head. "The worst fallout happens in hours, and that's when it's most dangerous. There *are* particles small enough to be inhaled by humans that pose a continual threat, but most of them take longer to fall—weeks or months—and by the time they do, they've gone through radioactive decay and are far less dangerous. Now, if there's snow or rain following a blast, that could rain down those smallest particles that otherwise would have time to decay. Aside from that, air and soil get safer by the day."

Mrs. Wasserman nodded as she listened. She had three-year-old Emma, the youngest Wasserman, on her lap asleep. Emma is a cute, chubby-legged toddler when awake, and she has huge dark brown eyes that always make me smile.

Blake continued, "Nuclear weapons are made to do the greatest amount of damage possible, and sent to military targets and maybe huge population centers. And nuclear power plants are targeted because they have their own payload."

"What do you mean, their own payload?" asked Mrs. Buchanan, who, like the rest of us, had been listening intently.

"They've got radioactive elements that will leak out to the surrounding area in a hit, so it magnifies the damage of a strike."

As I sat beside Blake watching him answer questions, my heart swelled with love. I couldn't stop noticing how cute Blake is—it's like he keeps getting more attractive. He's got a great profile, a Roman nose and high cheekbones, and though he shaves often enough to hold back a full-blown beard, he often wears a "five o'clock shadow" (as my mother calls it). It makes him look mature and handsome in an earthy way. So either he's gotten more handsome, or—I'm in love!

Anyway, while I was sitting there admiring Blake, my father said, "Look, folks, we're 35 miles from the nearest air force base—it *is* a target, no doubt about it—but we're upwind. That's the good news."

"Isn't it precarious to think we're safe just because we're upwind?" asked Andrea. She surprised me with that question because normally she didn't speak at council meetings. She was usually cornered up with Roper whispering, and often seemed less interested in the discussion than most of us. She added, "What if the wind shifts? We can't just assume it's always gonna blow the same way, can we?" She turned her gaze to Blake, naturally.

"The high wind movement is very predictable," Blake said. "The mushroom cloud sends particles into the atmosphere really high up, so the trade-winds take them, the prevailing globally predictable winds. The fallout that happens down by the ground, what they call deposition, happens immediately following the blast, but hundreds of thousands of pounds of particles are sent up and out, and they can travel tens of thousands of miles before landing. Those travel pathways are pretty well predictable."

"So yeah," he continued, "to a large degree, being downwind or upwind makes a *huge* difference. These high atmospheric movements are generally the same for any given area of the globe. The trade-winds over the U.S. blow west to east."

Mrs. Wasserman raised her hand. "I don't mean to change the subject, but how could we build a shelter that's big enough for everyone?"

Blake said, "That's not really my department--."

My father broke in and said, "If we do this, we ought to do it as quickly as possible because it's a distraction from everything else we've been trying to accomplish here, which is to build a safe, working compound, with enough food production and water to take care of everyone. If we stop to build an underground shelter, we're still going to need lookouts, we're still going to need people working on the cabins, and garden workers, and kitchen workers, and we're still going to need waste disposal, and washing, and everything else we have to do daily around here."

He looked around, letting his words sink in. "What I'm saying is that we can't hire this out, people. If we do this, WE do it. And not instead of everything else that keeps us busy but in addition to it." Again he paused while everyone listened silently, faces somber. "Be sure you're ready to sacrifice extra hours for this. We can't afford to let our other endeavors lapse."

Mr. Simmons said, "Why don't we stop cabin work? Those who already have a decent roof over their heads can make do. Those who are still waiting for a habitable cabin have been getting by in the Martins' household—they can do that longer."

My mother slowly nodded. "I agree. We can keep our people."

Mr. Simmons frowned. "The thing is," and he paused, his face hard in thought. "What we've been talking about is how to last it out after a blast, maybe two. But we haven't discussed what would happen if there are dozens of them. The last time I heard, Russia had thousands of warheads. Thousands. What if they used them all?"

Mr. Martin said, "They're not gonna empty their armament on us. They'll be getting the same back from us, for one thing, and no one wants to make the earth uninhabitable or spread that much nuclear fallout over the globe."

"But the reports we've heard say there were numerous blasts on the West Coast. That's fallout coming our way; and what if these blasts cross the country?"

"We still have to do what we can," said Mrs. Wasserman, looking sadly at little Emma. She looked up then, with indignant eyes. "Just because that may happen doesn't mean it will. Think of all the guerrilla soldiers around—they wouldn't nuke their own army, would they?"

"We may not be dealing with just one nation's strength, here," Mr. Prendergast returned. "If a number of different nations come against us, we could be in worse trouble."

"So what are you saying, that we do nothing? Just give up?" In a high, wavering voice, Mrs. Wasserman continued, "Blake just told us if there's a blast, maybe even a few, we can survive by waiting it out. I think we need to act on that instead of your worst-case-scenario which might not ever happen. We do what we can and pray that it's enough!"

An immediate murmur went around the room, agreeing with Mrs. Wasserman.

Emboldened by the approving nods of those around her, the young mother added, "If we build a big enough shelter, it can be a place to run in case of a ground attack by those trucks. We should build it so that even if everything up here is destroyed we can still survive!"

My father was shaking his head. "You're talking about something we don't have the tools or the technology to make. We'd have to think about food preparation, waste disposal, clean drinking water—each of these things requires systems, extensive systems and pipes and—heck, more than we can possibly put in place. I think, if we're going to do this, we need to stick to the original idea of a temporary shelter for waiting out the worst fallout."

He looked around and added, "Every family is responsible for its own food. You need to pack jerky and hard tack. No one is going to have good food if something like this happens. We're talking about survival food." He paused. "We will assign areas for each family. We will stock bedding. There will be no washing up except for the smallest ways. There will be one area for bathroom needs." He looked at my mom. "I believe you still have a good number of plastic bags and we have a few makeshift toilets—storage buckets with a seat." Looking back to the rest of us, he added, "We'll put them in one area, along with a bucket of dirt. You who are mothers will have to teach your kids to cover waste with dirt, and tie up those bags real tight—keep down odor as much as possible."

I glanced at Andrea and had to stifle a chuckle. She looked like she was enjoying the current topic about as much as I was. If we'd been alone, we'd have happily announced how grossed out we were.

186

My father must have seen our faces. "Look, girls, we have to talk these issues out. We don't want any surprises or false expectations. And if a lot of us have to survive together underground, this will be just as important as any other issue."

I nodded. Andrea and I shared a smile.

My dad continued, "But first, let's get this thing dug out. If we get it dug and we still haven't been attacked with nuclear, then we can stock the place and get it livable."

Blake said, "I think we should build into the side of the hill as Mr. Martin first suggested. That gives us three walls. All we need then, is a way to close up the opening. Fortify that outside wall, too. Instant nuke shelter."

"We could run into rock, though," said my dad. "We cleared a lot of rock on this farm with a bobcat when we first got here."

"Then we'll clear more if we have to," said Mr. Prendergast.

"With only man and horsepower," cautioned my father.

"There IS equipment that still works," Blake said. "Not all power vehicles use electronics."

My dad nodded. "That's true. If we get more gas, we can use my small tractor." His gaze swept the room. "Okay, folks, we're all tired. Let's wrap this up. We need to go home—well, to your cabin or room— (everyone chuckled)—and pray about this. We'll go out tomorrow and see if there's a good place to dig into the hill."

"Has there been any word from Jared and Roper?" Mr. Simmons asked. Andrea's head went up sharply.

My father shook his head. "They're out of range. But we'll keep trying."

CHAPTER TWENTY-EIGHT

JARED

Sharp bumps thrust Jared awake. His first sensation was—*pain.* His left arm and hand, his head, all were throbbing. He blinked, trying to get his bearings. He was on a horse. Someone held him firmly about the middle. Then it came rushing back. The airbag fiasco, the shootout—and that Roper had saved his neck.

Roper was seated behind him, one hand holding the reins while the other held him fast. "How ya feeling, buddy?" Roper asked.

Jared sniffed. "How do you think?"

"You nauseous?"

"Check."

"Weak?"

"Check." Then, "How long was I out?"

"Not too long; we're almost home. How's the pain?"

Jared hesitated. He was no whining sissy. "What you'd expect." He saw that Roper had bound up his left arm in a cloth and strapped it high against his middle so as not to dangle. The measure stopped the worst bleeding but did nothing to mitigate the explosion of pain that was his arm.

"You could have lost that hand," Roper said calmly. "You were holding the initiator, weren't you? When it went off?"

Jared grimaced. "You've already got that figured out, so why ask?"

A moment's silence passed. "I could'a told you that late model cars use sodium azide, not potassium perchlorate; even if you had disconnected the battery—which you didn't—you gotta handle those babies with care!"

"I thought you didn't know anything about explosives," Jared muttered.

188

"I don't know anything about building bombs," Roper agreed, "but I do know airbags. I've replaced about a hundred of 'em. Every car that isn't totaled after an accident needs a new air bag."

"Did you get us more?" was all Jared grunted back.

"Since you got injured? No. Your arm needs attention."

"That was stupid," Jared said. "We're already out here. Should have taken advantage of being out here and pulled a few!"

Roper shook his head. "With your arm, I was afraid--." he stopped.

"Afraid what?"

Roper hesitated. "I don't know; I'm no doctor."

"Afraid WHAT?" Jared replied. "Tell me what you think."

"I'm not a doctor," Roper objected.

"Just tell me, you d---- sissy!" Jared cried.

Roper shook his head but he had to smirk. "This *sissy* just saved your life, soldier."

That hit its mark and Jared went silent. Finally he said, in a more subdued tone, "Tell me."

"Fine! My ignorant, un-expert opinion is that you may lose that arm or at least your hand. You were bleeding out and your hand was looking blue—what was left of it. You need medical help NOW! I'm surprised you haven't gone into shock."

Jared nodded. If he thought he owed thanks to Roper, he didn't say it. His voice was lazy when he asked, "So, if I'd cut the battery, I would have been okay to pull the bag?"

"Not immediately. If that battery had power, you gotta wait after you cut it. I wait at least ten minutes; some guys wait up to an hour or two; some guys wait up to a day or two." Roper swallowed and added, "Some newer cars have capacitors that can hold a charge for awhile—so you always have to be careful."

"I never saw you wait that long. When you were removing them."

"Like I said, ten to fifteen minutes ought to do it. But it's a moot point, now. We're home—look. I'll come back out with someone else after we get you back, and we'll grab us a bunch more of them for you."

They moved on in silence until Jared suddenly said, "Tell me what else to do. For next time." Roper had to hand it to Jared. If nothing else, the man was determined. He wasn't worrying about losing a limb or planning on letting someone else do the dangerous job of pulling the initiators; he wanted to know how to do it himself. It was the first time Roper felt any admiration for him.

"You used the right tools," he said, "which is good."

"You didn't leave any behind, did you?" Jared snapped.

"No way," Roper said, "Are you kidding? A good T30 Torx bit socket, a ratchet, and a flathead screwdriver? I'm not that stupid."

They came up over a small rise in the road and now could see the compound ahead. The frontage no longer had the tree and bush cover of its former days, thanks to a company of soldiers whose parting gift, after a battle, was to throw Molotovs at the greenery, burning it up. The entrance was barricaded, though, with a mountain of debris, including the two destroyed trucks the soldiers had left, tree limbs, discarded furniture, and just plain garbage. Recently someone had come up with the additional pungent idea of dumping human waste around the frontage, too. It was supposed to be just one more deterrent, they hoped, against any intruders, even an army of them. Roper and Jared would agree it was effective.

"We have to enter up the side, along the ravine. We did a good job of blocking the front—good FARMSEC," Jared said, nodding at the barrier.

Roper pulled a two-way from his pack and turned it on. FARMSEC—that was farmstead security. The compound no longer had the look of a farm but the term had stuck. The sound of crackling air and garbled speech met his ears. Then the voice became clear.

"Who's this?"

"Hey, Prendergast. It's Roper. Roper and Jared. We're back. Hold your fire. We're coming in."

190

"Roger that, Roper."

"Call the D.O.; Jared's been hurt."

"Roger that." Another voice came on the line. It was Mr. Martin. "What happened, son? Was he hurt badly?"

"Let me talk," Jared grumbled, and so Roper gave him the radio which he took with his good hand. "Airbag deployed on me while I was trying to pull it. My arm's been hit."

Mr. Martin and the other lookout, Mr. Prendergast, exchanged grave glances.

"Roger that. Come on in," said Mr. Martin, softly.

CHAPTER TWENTY-NINE

ANDREA

I was in the garden when I heard Lexie calling my name. She approached on Rhema, crying, "AN-DRE-AAH!" My heart sank. I thought it must be bad news. But when I stood up and she saw me, a big smile crossed her face and she spurred Rhema to come alongside where I was, careful to keep the horse off our precious vegetables.

"They're back!" she cried, happily. "Roper's back!"

I'd been hand-picking pests off the squash leaves. I gasped and grabbed my jar of bugs, aware that a huge grin had spread across my face. I picked up the lid and screwed it on rapidly. A second ago I was weary and hot but suddenly I couldn't move fast enough! I hurried towards Lexie, smiling as big as I could.

"C'mon up," she said, patting the saddle behind her. I peeled off my gardening gloves and carefully placed the jar and gloves against the short fence around the squash plot. Using one of the wooden stakes for a precarious lift, I heaved myself up, flopping on my stomach across Rhema's wide back. The mare jostled on her feet.

"Keep her still!" It wasn't until I raised myself up and straddled my legs, putting my arms around Lexie's middle, that I felt safe.

"I can't believe it! He's back!" I cried, as Lexie spurred Rhema gently on.

"I know," said Lexie. *"Thank you, Lord!"*

I saw Mr. Martin heading to the wooded side of the property ahead of us. He turned, saw us, and waved. Only then did I recall that I was hot with sweat, dirt-stained from kneeling in the garden, and wore no makeup. None of the women at the compound wore makeup but before the pulse, I always did. Even after I came here, I tried to wear a little. Especially after my face got cut up during that attack. Now with

Roper back, I wanted to look the best I could, particularly because I still had a smudge of poison ivy on my cheeks.

I nudged Lexie. "Maybe I ought to go wash up, first."

"No way! He's gonna be tired, maybe hungry and thirsty. So the first thing he's gonna see is your pretty face!"

"My pretty *dirty* face," I said.

She turned on her seat, trying to see me. "Haven't you heard? We've had an apocalypse. No one cares if your face is dirty!" She laughed, but I still felt uneasy. A girl likes to be confident at times like this and I wasn't feeling confident. It suddenly struck me that I was possibly far more enamored with Roper than he was with me. What if a dirty face DID matter?

"Lex, I need to wash up!"

"You don't!" she said. "Trust me! You look pretty. You have a pretty face and it's not dirty, and even if it was, it would still be pretty."

"I don't *feel* pretty."

"You will when Roper looks at you and you run into his arms."

I loved the sound of that but wasn't sure I had the nerve to do it. "You think I can do that?"

"Don't you want to?"

"Well. Yes!" We were about to enter the woods and Lex cried, "Whoa," bringing the horse to a stop. She turned enough to see me.

"So when you see him run into his arms. You've been telling me for weeks how much you care for him. And he'll love it."

"What about Jared?"

"Do you care about Jared?"

"No, not romantically."

"Then don't worry about him."

I nodded. "Listen! I think I hear his voice!"

Smiling, Lexie spurred her horse lightly and we went towards the voices.

—————————— ◆ ——————————

A group of men were gathered in an opening in the woods. Lex and I, still astride Rhema, made our way towards them. I saw Mr. Clepps, our D.O., and felt a pang of worry. Was somebody hurt? Was ROPER hurt?

"Let me off!" I gasped. Lexie halted Rhema and I swung my leg over and prepared myself for the drop to the ground. Rhema is sixteen hands, which is quite tall for me--but I landed on my feet and stayed there.

I hurried forward anxiously until I saw Roper and Jared astride a horse. Jared looked terrible, needing Roper to hold him up. Mr. Clepps said, "May as well continue on to the house with him up there, Roper. We've got a stretcher—we'll take him off your hands there."

"Good enough," he said. He looked up and our eyes met. I drew in a breath, feeling his gaze like a thunderclap. Suddenly I was blinking back tears but he smiled that sweet, beautiful smile—though he looked tired and was caked with dust. As he nudged the horse forward, I kept my eyes on his face as he approached. He'd be going right past me to get to the house.

"Hey, young lady," he said, with a wink, as he came abreast of me. His eyes surveyed me with interest, and I felt myself blush.

"Hi!" I could think of nothing more to say though my heart was full, and so I just stared up at him. He pulled on the reins and came to a stop. I swept my gaze over Jared, noting the blood-stained cloth his arm was wrapped in, and felt a pang of unease. But he was nodding as though it was difficult to keep his head up. His eyes were only half-opened.

"I gotta get him to the house," Roper said, motioning at Jared with his head.

"I was worried about you," I offered. He nodded. A familiar look crossed his face. I knew instantly that he was about to tell a joke. I was coming to know him well enough to recognize this! I smiled in anticipation.

"Worrying *works.* 90% of the things I worry about never happen." He grinned and seemed ready to be off but then, looking at me closely, frowned. "What happened to your face?"

"Poison ivy," I said, unhappily.

"Okay. It'll heal." Then he said, "I almost forgot. Check that first pack and take out what's on top." I went and checked the pack. There on top was a beautiful dried flower garland. I gasped and pulled it out, smiling.

He grinned. "Thought you'd like that."

"Thank you!" I called, as he rode off slowly. I took the garland and hung it around my neck like a boa. And then I had to get a hold of myself. I was overjoyed at his return but weirdly I felt like crying.

Lexie was suddenly there with Rhema again. "Hey—pretty!" she said, about the garland. Then, "Get back up. We'll follow them to the house."

"Did you see Jared's arm?" she asked, once I had mounted and we were moving again.

"Yeah. Didn't look good. I wonder what happened."

"My dad said something exploded. I wonder if he was trying to make a bomb out there."

We fell silent for the rest of the short ride. Three men were helping get Jared off the horse. When he was down, they moved him onto a waiting stretcher made from an old wooden door.

"Don't touch the arm!" I heard him bellow despite how weak he looked.

Roper dismounted and Cecily stepped forward to take the reins. She turned and started walking the horse towards water and a meal.

I scrambled off Rhema, leaving the garland, and ran towards Roper, who was already surrounded by a group of people, all asking questions. I noticed, on the outskirts, Mrs. Schuman, our seamstress, with her arms wrapped tightly around a sobbing Evangeline. My heart constricted. I knew then that Roper had brought back no good news regarding my mother and her father. But he looked over and saw me and broke through the ranks, coming out with his arms outstretched.

With a muffled sob, I ran into his warm embrace, throwing my arms around his middle and hanging on for dear life.

He held me, stroked my hair, and then kissed the top of my head. "It's okay," he said, soothingly. "We're back, safe." Then, "Good to know you missed me."

I looked up at him. "You have no idea! What kept you away so long?"

He pursed his lips, thinking. "We had a lot of ground to cover."

I had a million more questions but I wanted to soak up the warmth of his embrace. I shut my eyes and clung to him and didn't want to let go.

Mr. Wasserman came over and began questioning Roper, whose hold around me loosened as he answered. I grew impatient, wanting his full attention. And I, too, wanted to ask a question, even though I dreaded the answer. Evangeline's uncontrollable crying gave me an inkling of what was to come but I had to hear it from Roper. In a shaky voice, I asked, "Did you get to my house?"

He swung his gaze back down at me. Regret filled his eyes. "We did."

"Any sign of my mom? Or Mr. Washington?"

He sighed. "I'm sorry."

I wasn't surprised but I felt a sharp stab of grief. "They might have been next door! Did you remember to look next door?"

"There was nothing next door. A burned out shell of a house. I'm sorry, sweetheart."

Mrs. Martin had been waiting patiently but now she stepped forward. "You must be tired and hungry, Jerusha," she said, in her soft southern drawl. Roper and I shared an understanding look because I knew how he hated the name. Mrs. Martin was the only person who he allowed to use it. She put a hand on my arm. "Let this man come and get some rest and nourishment."

Roper glanced at Mrs. Martin. "One minute." He met my eyes and drew me up close again. He was going to kiss me!

196

It meant the world to me that he kissed me there right in front of so many people. If I hadn't already loved the guy, those moments in his arms would have sealed the deal. There we were, in the middle of a hot summer day and suddenly, tight in his arms, I had the feeling of—*Christmas*! Being held and wanted by Roper was like Christmas morning—the best memory of my childhood, the best present I could ever get. Afterward, he allowed Mrs. Martin to turn him towards the house.

I had more questions about my house and neighborhood but they had to wait. Later I'd find out that our executive, upscale home was burned out like our neighbor's house, a huge shell of brick and stone, with little inside but charred remains. I now have the sad image of our marble staircase covered with dirt and ash and fallen debris, just like the kitchen granite counter-tops.

As I watched Mrs. Martin lead Roper off, I hurried after them. "Wait!" I cried. "I can get him something to eat!" I didn't want to let Roper out of my sight, to be honest. In fact, I hoped not to let him out of my sight for a long, long, time.

Passing Evangeline, who was still crying in Mrs. Schuman's arms, I realized that she and I now had a sad thing in common. We'd each lost both father and mother since the pulse. But she was only eleven. I made a mental note to be kind to her for now on.

CHAPTER THIRTY

ANDREA

Mr. Clepps and Mrs. Philpot spent a long time yesterday taking care of Jared in sickbay—the former women's bedroom. Jared's mother Jolene wanted to assist them but she kept bawling. "Don't amputate his arm! Don't you amputate!"

Mr. Clepps assured her he was not planning on doing that but Jolene hasn't been well for a long time. Even Jared, in a lucid moment, told her to get out of the room. Finally, they had to call Mrs. Martin to remove her. She got even more hysterical and some of the men had to forcefully take her out and back to her cabin.

I went by sickbay briefly but then stayed far away, because there was no anesthetic—I got the last of it when my arm took the bullet— and I couldn't stand to hear a man groaning. It made my legs tingle and go weak. (Lexie says that's the beginning of getting into a faint! Never thought of myself as squeamish but I do feel guilty I used up the anesthetic.)

Roper is still asleep in his room, and I don't dare try to wake him. He looked so exhausted, poor man, when he got back yesterday. But tonight we'll have a council meeting, see what information we can get from Roper about their trip—and find out about Jared's condition. I hope Jolene was really way off the mark about him possibly losing an arm.

LATER

So tonight there was another large gathering at the house. Mr. Clepps reported that Jared may be lucky enough to keep his hand and arm despite what may be an infection. Even so, he said there'll be significant nerve damage. I heard him telling Mr. Martin quietly, though, that if circulation didn't improve, and if we had the means to do it, Jared's arm would warrant an amputation. He urged Mr. Martin to get a posse together to go "shopping" for more medical supplies.

"We just did that," he said. "I took Blake and Mr. Simmons and we found very little—mostly just gauze and tape."

"We should try again," said Mrs. Philpot. Of course that raised a big argument because most people think there are no such supplies out there—whatever *was* available had surely been taken by now. There were lots of questions for Roper, and I was ALL EARS. I wanted details! What was it like out there? Did they see a lot of survivors? Did they see trucks of soldiers like the ones who attacked us?

Everyone had questions. Even Bryce, who hated violence, came to listen. Bryce was trustworthy as a lookout—he had an eagle eye—but we all understood that he'd never shoot anyone. Ever since that day when I'd easily grabbed a rifle right out of his hands to save my little brother, we knew that having PTSD after serving in Iraq meant he'd never again be a fighter.

Anyway, back to questions. My little brother Aiden asked if the world was still there, making everyone chuckle. But I get it! Life on the compound is like being in prison—it's a safe prison unless we get attacked but it's a restricted environment. No variation, day after day after day. I daydream about how we used to take drives, even to the store—at least it was doing something, going somewhere. *Riding in a car!* The monotony here can drive me *crazy* if I don't distract myself. (And boy, do I miss *real* shopping. It's hard to believe all our beautiful department stores must have been looted and destroyed. It makes me sad to think about it.)

Anyway, since Jared was in sick bay, Roper was the star of the show. But he seemed uncomfortable. He wouldn't give us a lot of details but said, "There's bands of people, and you never know who is liable to shoot you in the back if given the chance." I saw a shadow cross his face when he said that. I wished Jared was well instead of in sick bay so he could shed more light on that remark. But I'm thinking they must have had a few close calls out there. People kidded him about being so mysterious but Roper just shook his head and said, "It's a jungle out there, that's all there is to tell."

No one mentioned my mother or Mr. Washington which I knew was because everyone had already got word that Roper and Jared had seen no sign of them. I was glad they didn't talk about it—it would have made me cry all over again. Then the men discussed the new supplies. Roper said it wasn't nearly as much as Jared wanted but we had more than before. All we needed now was for Jared to recover enough to use the stuff and start building those bombs!

There's a tension growing in me day after day. I thought it was that I missed Roper and wanted word of my mother. But it's actually a feeling of impending *doom*. I mean, those soldiers are bound to come back! Or those reports of nuclear strikes could be true, which means fallout could be affecting us. Every day that passes feels to me like one less day between us and *disaster*.

Anyway, everyone was happy to have Roper back and the mood became fairly jolly. And then Mrs. Martin surprised us by bringing in a real cake—with icing! She pulled a cake mix out of food storage (because she didn't have time to make it from scratch) so we could celebrate the return of the men. I thought I'd smelled something really yummy coming from the kitchen but I didn't dare hope! We don't have dessert often except for fruit and cream.

Mr. Buchanan had left the room earlier, saying he had a contact to connect with on his radio. When he returned, he looked serious. Everyone was still around Roper so I watched as Mr. Buchanan went and spoke to Mr. Martin. In a minute Mr. Martin stood up and went to the center of the room.

Without a word his expression silenced everyone. He looked like he had bad news. "Mr. Buchanan has been on the radio," he said, taking in first one side of the room with his eyes and then the other. "We've had word from known and trusted contacts that soldiers like the ones who attacked us are being seen like never before—as well as a few tanks. If ever we've needed to pray for the safety of this compound— and our country—it's now."

L.R. Burkard

A heavy silence fell as the air of festivity vanished. And then, adding to the sudden sobriety of the atmosphere, Jared came into the room, walking slowly and with difficulty. The children gawked at his bandaged arm and hand, not missing the red-stained under-dressing, which was slowly beginning to leak through. Mr. Clepps put down his cake. "Jared—you had an I.V. on! You should not be up and about! Your body needs rest."

Jared glanced at him but otherwise ignored him, moving further into the room. Like a wake after a ship, an aisle widened around him, as people moved their chairs or scrambled out of his way. I cringed at his bruised and swollen face.

He looked at Mr. Martin. "So there's tanks, now? We got us some supplies but I'll need more initiators right away. The amount we brought back isn't enough. We need to destroy the road out there so nothing can come down it—not even a tank."

"How do you propose to do that?" Mr. Martin asked. "And even if we destroy that road—somehow—tanks can roll over most anything."

"There's a culvert about a half mile down the road," Jared said. He paused and winced in pain, bolstering his injured arm with his other hand. "If we blow up the bridge even a tank is gonna think twice before crossing that gully."

My heart rose at that idea! Imagine if we could really make our road inaccessible! I'd feel safer—except for the nuclear threat, but there was still a chance it was only a rumor. I decided right then to cling to that chance.

"If they've got a tank, they don't need a road," said Mr. Buchanan. "I think you ought to prepare for what to use if and when they arrive at our doorstep—just like last time."

Mr. Martin said, "I agree. I like the idea of taking out the bridge, but with our limited resources we need to keep our explosives on the compound to use if and when they're needed."

Jared shook his head. "Look, unless they've got ground-attack aircraft—and we haven't seen any—our best chance of deflecting a hit is by taking out that bridge. The harder you make it for them to reach us, the greater the chance they'll go elsewhere." He seemed to be swaying on his feet. Mr. Clepps hurriedly stood up and moved his chair towards him.

"Sit down, Jared. At least sit down!"

Frowning, Jared did so. Mr. Clepps studied him while Jared returned his look with a scowl. "I think you're burning with fever," said Mr. Clepps. Jared's forehead was red and bruised, so he put a hand on the back of his neck. "This isn't good. If you want to live to build us anything, you have got to return to bed."

Mr. Martin said, "You heard him, son."

Jared nodded. "Give me five minutes." He looked around. "I need you—all of you—to understand. There is no reason why those tanks will seek out this compound. It's not like we got any military secrets stored next to the pinto beans. They're more interested in targets that matter—military, manufacturing, even cultural. But they'll attack us *opportunistically* if they happen to be going by and don't like the looks of us. If we take out the bridge, it makes us a whole lot safer from opportunistic attacks—that's all I'm saying. Chances are, a tank will never come our way. But those army trucks are all over the place. You take out the bridge—no more army trucks."

For once I was totally in agreement with Jared. I longed for the safety of being inaccessible to those soldiers!

Mrs. Wasserman said, bitterly, "You haven't heard, have you? We may be under nuclear threat!"

Mr. Martin said, "Now, we don't know that, Sandra. We still don't know for sure if there have been any strikes--."

"What's up with that?" Jared asked him. Mr. Martin quickly filled him in on the scattered reports that had come via the radio—from unknown contacts. "We're still trying to reach some of the people we've spoken with in the past, to get confirmation."

Jared nodded. "Those reports could be planted by an enemy. Disinformation to destabilize us more than we already are. I say we work with what we know for sure—and we know there are hundreds of trucks and a few tanks out there."

A murmur went around the room. Mrs. Buchanan spoke up. "What if things start getting back to normal and we've ruined that bridge for nothing? What if food and medical supplies become available? If we ruin the bridge, we don't only make our compound difficult for the bad guys to reach us; we make it difficult for anyone to."

"I agree," said Mrs. Martin. "And God forbid, we could even be held accountable by the government for the destruction of public property—when things return to normal!"

Jared was staring at the ceiling as though far removed from the mere sound of voices. He returned a level gaze to us in the room. "We have no idea if or when things may return to normal. Things may *never* return to normal. Or it could be *years* before there's any kind of normal. If we don't do what we have to do to protect this compound, if normal does return, it will do so without us—because we won't live that long."

A louder hum of voices started up, and from the side of the room where all the youngest members of our compound were playing with toys on the floor, Lexie's little sister Lainie stared at Jared in horror. "Mommy, are we gonna die?" Lainie asked. Her high, innocent question got the room's attention. I think we'd all forgotten about the children.

Now my brothers stared at us with fear in their eyes. Quentin's little upper lip began to quiver. "We're gonna die?" asked Aiden. I hurried over to them.

"Nobody's going to die!" said Mrs. Martin. And then, "It's time for the little ones to go to bed." I reassured my brothers, repeating that no one would die, and then joined Lexie as we helped them put away toys so we could take the children upstairs. But my heart felt heavy, even hollow. The children had voiced the question we'd been suppressing all summer since the last attack—heck, since the pulse. *Are we gonna die?*

Mrs. Buchanan got up to gather her brood. Mr. Wasserman handed baby Emma to his wife and proceeded to take the other two Wasserman children from the room.

I hated to leave without a chance to spend time with Roper so I planned on getting the boys to bed and then hurrying back to the living room for the remainder of the meeting. Lexie surprised me by stopping me at the stairs. "I'll put them in," she said. "I'm taking the girls up anyway."

When I went back to my seat, Roper was watching. He came and sat beside me, where Mrs. Buchanan had been before. We shared a smile.

"Jared, I'm taking you back to your bed." Mr. Clepps said. He put his hand on Jared's good arm, but Jared pulled away.

"I'm not done, yet." In a voice that rose above the room (which amazed me considering how weak he looked) he called, "We have the right of self-defense, and if that means taking out the road, then that's what we do. Like I said before, we're not special in a military sense. We're just an opportunity." In a lower tone he added, "I'd like to deprive them of this opportunity, if it's all the same to you."

Many adults around the room nodded in agreement. "I guess it's settled then," said Mr. Martin. "What else do you need, Jared?"

"Unless you know of a good supply of fertilizer, I could use a whole bunch more airbag initiators."

From there it was only a few seconds until Roper—to my horror—volunteered to go back out. I looked at him, aghast, and poked him in the arm. "What? Why *you*?" I hissed, in a whisper.

"Because he wants airbag initiators and I know how to get them," he whispered back.

"You keep risking your life! And breaking my heart!" I was actually on a fast track to getting boiling mad at him.

He stared at me, looking faintly amused, though sympathetic. "I got here to begin with and that was a miracle. I came back after being out there for weeks—and that was a miracle. I can come back again by God's grace."

I shook my head. "Let someone else go! You did your part! *'Thou shalt not tempt the Lord thy God!'*"

He pressed his lips together. "I'm the only one on this compound who has removed a hundred of those things from all types and models of cars. I can do it faster and safer than anyone else." He looked pensively towards Jared as he spoke.

I wanted to voice more objections but other people came around to speak to Roper. I waited, biting my lip, to have his attention again. I wanted our compound to be safe from attack as much as anyone but I did NOT want Roper going out there again!

As soon as I had the chance, I resumed our whispered conversation. "There's gotta be somebody else who knows how to do it."

Roper nodded. "Yup. Jared."

"I thought that's how he got hurt."

"It is. He knows better now."

I wanted to say, "So let Jared go," but I knew that wasn't going to happen. Jared didn't look like he would be doing much of anything for awhile. It was so unfair!

Before the meeting broke up, Mr. Buchanan came over and volunteered to go with Roper. But Mr. Simmons, who is our ex-cop, said, "I ought to be the one. I've done little besides lookout duty and cabin work. I'm ready to do my part out on the road." He paused. "In fact, with my training as a policeman, I'll be more of an asset than a lot of you all."

I'm glad Mr. Simmons will go with him. Better him than Jared! At least I have that small comfort.

EVENING

After thinking about it, I realized Roper was right—he has to be the one to go. He's the best qualified, and look what happened to Jared when he tried to pull an airbag! Would I want that to happen to someone else? No. I can't just think about what *I* want, anymore. I have to think about what's best for the compound.

My sweet, beautiful man has to go!

CHAPTER THIRTY-ONE

ANDREA

I insisted that Roper give me a good hour of his time before leaving the compound again. Mr. Clepps, to my delight, went even further. "He ought to have a few days to recuperate, eat well, and rest," he said. But Roper (who I'm finding out has a stubborn streak) said, "If Jared is in good enough shape to use the things, then I need to get them ASAP."

"Well, he's not in good enough shape," Mr. Clepps returned.

We were at breakfast in the dining room, and Mr. Martin sat listening. Roper asked him, "Is there anyone else here who can build the weapons?"

Mr. Martin looked thoughtful a moment. "I have a lot of printed material about how to make defensive weapons—but I don't recall seeing instructions on how to use airbag initiators." After a pause he said, "You understand them more than anyone. You're our best shot at using them—if Jared can't."

"Why couldn't he?" I asked. "That's what he's been wanting to do." I saw a guarded look cross Mr. Martin's face. Looking around the table, I saw that Mr. Clepps, Mrs. Martin, and even Lexie all had a similar shadowed expression. And then I realized: They weren't sure Jared would recover!

Roper asked, "How bad is he?"

"Raging fever today," said Mr. Clepps. "We've given him pain relievers and antibiotics—but I don't have the right stuff to treat him. We've got amoxicillin—he needs something stronger."

I was filled with pity for Jared. And then it hit me that if he didn't recover, we wouldn't be able to tear up that bridge—at least, I didn't think so. I felt frightened by the thought.

Mr. Clepps said, "If we had a hospital he'd lose that arm but live to talk about it. Here—I don't dare try that."

Lexie said, "Mr. Clepps, during the Civil War didn't doctors do amputations right on the field? Without any hospital? And lots of those men survived."

Mr. Clepps pursed his lips. "Most of them didn't. And I've never done an amputation, Lexie. We don't have the right equipment. I can't even do a blood transfusion."

"But you're giving him an I.V.," said Mrs. Martin. "Can't you do a transfusion with that tubing?"

He shook his head. "No, it's much too narrow and I'd need a bigger gauge needle. And he's already lost a grave amount of blood."

Mr. Martin said, "Okay, we get it. But you think the odds are against him anyway, so what is there to lose?"

Mr. Clepps drew in a deep breath. He shook his head. "I understand where you're coming from, Grant, but—I may just make him suffer more on his way out." He looked around, as if pleading with us to understand. "I don't want to be responsible for giving him that misery—he's suffering enough as it is." Then, when no one said anything he added, "Look, if he comes through this fever, he may be alright."

Mrs. Philpot spoke from the doorway. I didn't know how long she'd been there listening. "Charles," she said, to Mr. Clepps. "You know that the longer you wait, the less chance there is for him to survive. That gangrene will be systemic. I agree with Lexie and Grant— you need to do this."

Gangrene? I shuddered.

Mr. Clepps stood up in agitation. "I am only—*technically* qualified! I have no experience with amputations!"

Mr. Martin said, gently, "Sit down, Charles. Just think about this a moment. You are the best qualified. No one is expecting you to work miracles. But we do have good medical books. My wife and I—and anyone else who wants to—will be by your side to coach and support you."

Mrs. Martin's face blanched. I remembered she didn't like the sight of blood. I had to admire her because she nodded, accepting what her husband had said, despite her dislike of it.

"You're not hearing me," Mr. Clepps said. "I don't have the equipment!" His voice was thinner, no longer as strong. Maybe he realized he'd have to give in.

Mr. Martin said, "Let's pore through the books and see what we need. I think we'll be able to do whatever we have to do."

"He's gonna lose a boatload of blood," said Mr. Clepps. "Like I said, if we attempt an amputation, it'll just usher him out of here faster than he's already going."

Mr. Martin seemed to consider this. "There must be a way to minimize blood loss."

I met Roper's eyes. He looked the way I felt: sorry for Jared. "Can I talk to you?" I asked.

In a few minutes we'd cleaned our dishes and then we headed outdoors. It was a fine, hot day for early August, less humid than it had been of late. The gardens were exploding with growth. I had much labor waiting for me in those beds but for now I would think only of Roper. He took my hand and swung our arms casually as we walked. Passing the empty playground, we went and sat side-by-side on two swings.

He looked at me expectantly.

"I want to know more about what happened out there," I said. "How many close calls did you have?" Roper nodded, but was silent for a few moments.

"I really only had one close call." He paused. "There were a few times shots came close—and you know we lost the horse—but there was only one time when I thought I might be about to die."

I gazed at him with a full heart. Softly, I prodded. "What happened?"

He pursed his lips. "I hate to talk about this--."

"Why? What are you not saying? Are there more enemies out there we don't know about? You have to let us know!"

He smiled gently. "No. Only one enemy—and it's my enemy, not yours."

I groaned. "Don't be so—cryptic! (I pulled that word from an English lesson I remembered from school and felt proud of it.) "What are you talking about?"

He took a deep breath and looked away, and then back at me. "I didn't want to say anything." He stared into my eyes. "You've got enough to worry about."

Now I was really alarmed, and gasped, "You have to tell me!"

He nodded. "I will. But don't let it worry you." He took another breath. "Okay. I thought Jared might do me in. He threatened as much."

Another gasp escaped my lips. All my feelings of sorrow and pity that I'd had for Jared vaporized. "That is *exactly* what I was afraid of!"

"I know. But you have to understand—."

"Everyone needs to know about this! Who Jared really is! He's dangerous!"

"Look, I think the guy was losing it. I don't think he was in his right mind."

"No, he's always been dangerous. We warned you before you left! And you wouldn't listen."

He put his head back, looking up into the sky. When he looked back at me, his eyes were somber. "He was okay for most of the trip. But he killed a bunch of guys—shot them from behind. Just like that, with no warning—they didn't have a chance." His face creased in a frown. "That's when I first suspected he was losing it."

As we continued to talk, I got the whole story little by little. I was horrified that Jared might want to get rid of Roper because of me! I wanted everyone to know about it. "You have to tell Mr. Martin, you know that, right?"

Roper didn't look convinced. "I think, now we're on the compound—I hope, anyway—that if he recovers, he'll back off. He'll build his bombs and be satisfied with that. He'll leave me alone."

"You don't know that. I think he's always gonna be a threat for you! Not to mention anyone else he doesn't like the looks of! Remember those men he shot!"

Roper said, softly, "We'll see."

"If you don't tell the Martins, I will."

He eyed me with a gleam of amusement. "Let's wait and see if Jared's gonna recover. No sense bringing him shame if he don't come through this."

I didn't like it but said, "Okay." In my heart of hearts, I was torn. I wanted Jared to get well and make those bombs—I wanted that road to be destroyed!—but I didn't want him well enough to hurt Roper.

He came to his feet and then took my hand, pulling me off the swing. We stood facing each other. I felt a jolt of excitement go through me. Staring into Roper's beautiful, long-lashed eyes, I hoped he would kiss me.

"I appreciate your concern," he said, looking deeply into my eyes.

I drew in a breath. "Oh yeah? How *much* do you appreciate it?" With a little smile he lowered his head towards me—just as the sound of boisterous children, laughing and chattering as they burst from the house—came at us.

I sighed and took his arm. "C'mon. If they reach us here we'll be conscripted into playtime." He allowed me to turn him away and we walked quickly towards the barn. The children adored Roper and his gentle, fun ways, but I wanted him to myself, at least a little longer. Plus, he'd been about to kiss me—no way did I want to miss that!

Inside the barn we dropped into a pile of clean hay. Roper put an arm around me. "Looks like we're gonna roll in the hay," he said. I started to laugh but then he kissed me. My whole world melted away, all my worries, all my fears, the chores, the tedium of life, the heat, and dirt and sweat that was my existence. All I knew was the feel of his mouth on mine, warm and sweet; and his arms holding me tight, and my arms wrapped around him. I felt such happiness! When he kissed me the second time, I realized it was the first true happiness I've had since the pulse. In some ways, it felt like the first real happiness I've *ever* known.

Weird. No, *wonderful!*

After we'd kissed, we sat holding each other. A lovely thought occurred to me. "If Jared doesn't recover, there's no reason for you to go out there for more airbags!"

He sniffed and pursed his lips. "Maybe not. But Grant—Mr. Martin—is hoping I'll learn what to do with them."

"You mean build bombs? That has its own dangers!"

He nodded. "Can't be helped."

I pressed my head into him. "I can't stand the thought of ever losing you."

He kissed my head. "It's a scary world right now."

I pulled away from him again and looked up into his deep blue-grey eyes. "But less scary when I'm with you. I wish we could stay like this for a long time."

He smiled, looking around the barn. "In the hay? Why not."

I poked him gently. "You know what I mean. I want to be with you."

When he was silent, I added, "Do you still think I'm too young?"

Another smile. "Well, you've grown by what—a few weeks since we last talked about it?" His eyes sparkled at me. But suddenly the sadness of my life returned, hitting me like a flood. The loss of my home, my parents, Roper's long absence, my loneliness and weariness. The constant feeling of impending doom.

I shook my head. "No," I said softly. "Maybe you haven't noticed. I've grown *years* since then."

He nuzzled his face against mine. "Hardship does that to you. But you're still a young lady."

"I'll be seventeen in September."

"That's better than sixteen but still *only* seventeen."

"I'm older than my age."

He pulled away to study me. Slowly he shook his head. "We have to wait until you're at least eighteen. Before we can get serious."

I stared up at him in dismay. "I'm serious now! I hoped you were, too."

He winced. "What I mean is, before we can...you know, tie the knot." My heart surged with hope at his words. He stared into my eyes. "Or do other things that go along with that." He kissed my forehead.

"Lexie and Blake want to get married and she's not eighteen yet," I told him.

"And they're not married, yet," he said, firmly.

"But they will be. Sooner than you think."

He studied me. "Are they gonna do something foolish?"

"No!"

"Okay, look. I don't know what Lexie and Blake are planning on doing, but I know me, and I'm getting to know you, and for right now, we're gonna wait. We're gonna do it right. Just because the world ended doesn't mean we don't know what's right anymore."

I stared up at him plaintively a moment. "If Mr. Martin said it's okay--would you marry me?"

He chuckled. I realized I'd just proposed to him—instead of waiting for him to do it. He drew me close and, putting his mouth against my ear, whispered, "How about, you wait for me to propose, and to get permission, and most of all, for you to turn eighteen?"

I pushed him away. "Eighteen? That's more than a year away! You don't know if we'll still be alive!"

His face creased into a frown. "Don't think like that." Again he pulled me up close. I could have stayed like that for hours but I had chores waiting. We kissed again and then went our separate ways.

I loved our time together but I'm disappointed. I don't want just a little bit of Roper. I want all of him. I want to be his wife.

CHAPTER THIRTY-TWO

ANDREA

Later on I saw Lexie heading to the barn. I was knee-deep in green beans, picking away. I put my basket down and hurried to join her.

She was brushing down Rhema, which didn't surprise me. She'd showered her horse with extra attention since the mare returned.

"Any word on Jared?" I asked. I was on pins and needles waiting to find out if Roper would have to go out on the road for more airbag thingies. If Jared got well, he'd have to go. If not, he might not have to—not unless we were sure he'd be able to use the things for building weapons, and so far we weren't sure. I wasn't exactly hoping Jared wouldn't recover but after learning how he'd threatened my man, I wasn't exactly praying for him, either.

"He's still got a high fever," Lex said. She paused and met my eyes. "I think they're going to attempt an amputation today."

I shuddered. "Mr. Clepps said he'd lose too much blood if they amputate."

Lexie nodded. "I know. My mom says they have no choice. He'll die from gangrene poisoning if they don't." She patted Rhema and came out of the stall. She hung up the brush and turned to me, wiping her hands off on her shorts. "We should pray for him."

"You can pray for him," I said. "I can't."

She studied me. "Why not?"

I sniffed, wondering if I ought to tell her. Roper had said there was no sense shaming Jared if he was about to die. So I said, "I don't want to talk about it. I'll pray for him, I guess."

Lexie's brows went up. "So what did you come in here to talk about?"

213

Then I remembered I had good news. "Roper. We had special time together! And we kissed more than once."

Lexie's eyes lit up. "Tell me what happened!"

Smiling, we flopped onto the hay. It was almost exactly where I'd been with Roper earlier. I told her about our time together. Lexie was delighted. Sitting there chatting, we were suddenly just two girls, not soldiers or laborers or survivors. Just girlfriends talking about guys —and we had more fun than we'd had in ages.

"I'm in love," I said, finally.

She giggled. "I could have told you that!"

"No really. I love him, Lex." I paused. "I love him so much it hurts."

She nodded. "I know. Love brings worries. You could lose the one you love."

"Or lose his love!" I said, with a forlorn note in my voice. The thought of having Roper's love—and then losing it—was horrible.

"That's what marriage is for," Lexie said, musing. "My mom says that during the length of a marriage at times you don't FEEL like you're in love anymore. But the marriage is there to keep you together. It's bigger than the both of you. It's God's framework for when feelings aren't enough; it catches you and holds you in place until the feelings return. And if you work at it, she says, they WILL return."

Her words sounded amazing to me—I'd never thought of marriage in such a way. But I frowned. "Marriage wasn't enough for my parents."

Lexie was silent a minute. "Your mom didn't honor her vows. That's the one thing that even the Bible says is good enough reason for divorce—being unfaithful to a spouse." Quickly she added, "Your mom didn't get that marriage isn't about feelings, primarily. It's about *commitment*."

"I like that," I said, nodding. Then, "Roper says I'm too young for us to marry." Lexie turned to me, smiling slyly. "No doubt AFTER kissing you, first!"

I grinned. "Yeah. But I told him I was older than my age."

214

We sat back, staring at the roof of the barn. Lexie picked up a piece of hay and played with it, turning it in her fingers. She said, softly, "Doesn't it feel like we're so much older than we used to be? Doesn't it feel like we've lived for *decades* since the pulse?"

I took a deep breath and sighed. "It does. It's hard to believe it hasn't been a full year, yet." I turned to her. "But you *are* older. You're seventeen, now. Which reminds me—speaking of *marriage*—when is Blake going to ask your father if you two can get married?" We'd had a little party for Lexie and I even decorated her birthday cake. (The Martins were so *supremely* thoughtful to store things like cake mixes— it made life feel almost normal to bake a cake—even though we had to do it in a sun oven.)

She frowned. "He did. My dad told Blake I'm still too young."

Surprised, I sat up. "You mean, Blake asked your father for permission?"

She turned over to lean on an elbow and surveyed me, frowning. "Yeah. But he said no."

"How could you not tell me this?"

"I'm sorry! If he'd said yes, I'd have told you!"

"I told Roper you and Blake were ready to get married."

"We are! It's just my dad isn't ready."

"I still can't believe you didn't tell me Blake asked."

"I was depressed about it, I guess." She smiled. "So you and Roper are talking marriage!"

I laughed. "I sort of proposed to him."

Lexie eyed me with amazement.

"I thought, why not? What have I got to lose?"

She was still grinning. "What did he say?"

"That we have to wait until I'm eighteen."

She'd flopped back down to face the barn roof. "So we both have to wait." She turned to look at me. "Your birthday is coming up. How can we make it special?"

My birthday was in early September, less than a month away. I smiled. "Just give me chocolate cake. All I need is cake and I'll be totally cool."

"I think we can manage that," she said. "That's it?"

"Cake and Roper." We both chuckled. "I mean it," I said. "Your father isn't my father. There's no reason Roper and I can't get married." I drew a stray piece of hay from Lexie's hair.

She said, "Well, my dad feels responsible for you. You're like his daughter, now."

"But I'm not really his daughter."

"But he's old-fashioned. I don't think he'll let you. And you haven't even convinced Roper."

"He's just hung up on the age thing. We live in a brave new world, right?"

"You mean a crazy new world."

"Exactly! We can't afford to wait, like in the *old* days."

"I agree!"

Studying Lex's cowgirl blonde hair and pretty profile, I had an idea. "You know, Lex, even though we can't convince your folks to let us get married, I wonder if Blake could?"

She turned, her face alight. "I'll bet he could! When he asked my dad, he wasn't thinking about HOW to get permission. He just wanted to know if it was okay. My dad said no, and to Blake, that was that. But if we ask him to *work* on my father, I'll bet he could!"

"I think so, too! He has a way of putting things so people understand...like it's a scientific fact and you can't disagree with facts."

Lexie nodded. "Uh-huh. And it's a scientific fact that this girl wants to marry him before things get even crazier and we lose our chance."

"Go for it!' I said, coming to my feet. "Speaking of which, I have to go." I'd left a basket of green beans sitting out in the sun and needed to finish picking. But I was also slightly jealous—Blake probably COULD convince the Martins to let him and Lexie get

216

married. But then I realized that if he did, it would pave the way for me and Roper to follow suit!

Outside, the sun was beating hot but for once I didn't care. I was on cloud nine at the thought of my future marriage.

After getting as many beans as I could find, I stopped in the bed of acorn squash to check that the watering containers still had water. To my relief, they did. Finally I went back in the house where I dropped off the beans in the kitchen.

Mrs. Martin peered in my basket. "Good picking," she murmured. Then, "We're going to can these. Would you mind fetching me some buckets of water? Put them in the outdoor kettle. I've already got a fire going."

So I had to fetch water, anyway! I might've made a smart remark about it but then I thought of Jared. "Is Jared's arm—?" I couldn't finish the question. Mrs. Martin leveled her gaze at me.

"They're operating right now. Cecily and Mrs. Philpot are assisting as well as Mr. Prendergast." She paused, her eyes deep, troubled pools. "Pray for that boy."

At that exact moment we heard a deep, groaning cry coming from upstairs. It was a cry of agony and sent horror shuddering through my bones. I knew immediately that it was Jared. Stoic Jared, in so much pain he couldn't contain it!

Gasping, I hurried out of the house while tears stung my eyes. Even Jared shouldn't have to suffer that much, I thought. Nobody should have to!

LATER

I tried to keep my mind off Jared by thinking about things I could do for Lexie's wedding. Like, make her a veil. Or help her mom bake a big, beautiful cake. I wracked my brain trying to think of something I could give as a wedding present. I was that confident that Blake would certainly convince Mr. Martin to give his consent. But suddenly I heard shouting, children screaming and crying, and then

Lexie went running past me like the wind. I put down the bucket I'd been filling for Mrs. Martin and hurried after her. My heart was in my throat. I was sure one of the kids had been hurt.

That wasn't the case. But what happened is just as bad. Lexie and Blake may not soon get married. Maybe not ever! Blake is unconscious and may die! He was intending to rig up a hose system to drain manure runoff into a fallow field, but he got overcome by fumes—we think it must have been methane!

The manure pit was designed for the Martins' animals but wasn't big enough for all the animals that are now on the compound. (The Martins used to have three horses and one cow. Now there's eight horses, a cow and a mule.) The pit filled up before summer started so since then, we've just piled up the animals' waste in a large heap on a concrete slab.

According to Lexie, manure is needed around the farm and it never used to build up too high. But the amount of gardening we can do by hand is nothing next to what used to happen on this farm using power equipment. We just aren't using the old stuff—the manure that's had time to ferment and rot—nearly as fast as the animals produce the new stuff. So Mr. Martin asked Blake to set up a hose system whereby the decaying manure could be vented into our gardens or fallow land.

Lexie explained that it shouldn't have been a dangerous task because the pit was never enclosed; any gases that built up would have dispersed into the air. But during early summer rains, the manure started to leak out in rivulets and was running into the cabin area. To stop the runoff, someone put up a rudimentary wooden wall on one side and then covered the heap with a tarp—because if manure stays dry, it won't leak out.

Anyway—Blake apparently didn't think about it (he knows better, we know he does!) and he pulled aside the tarp and moved into the enclosure—alone—and he was immediately overcome by fumes. If Mrs. Wasserman hadn't been taking the kids out to the playground—or happened to look over at just the right moment—no one would have seen Blake go down and we figure he'd have died!

As it was, little Mrs. Wasserman ran and dragged him by the arms after taking a deep breath and holding it in. It's a miracle she got them both out—but she fell down herself afterward. The children's shouting alerted the rest of us.

I hurried with a few other people to the Buchanan's cabin where Blake is on a sofa in the big living area, surrounded by his family and Lexie and Mrs. Martin. (Mrs. Wasserman was helped, on shaky legs, to her own cabin, but it looks like she'll be fine.) Blake, however, is terribly groggy. Hardly responding to anyone.

Mr. Clepps and Mrs. Philpot—just when we need them—are still with Jared! We have no oxygen to administer; no medicine to give that will help! All we can do is monitor his pulse and wait for him to wake up fully—and pray.

I found our encyclopedia and looked up methane poisoning—all it talks about is how methane is formed on farms mostly by cattle, not only in their waste, but primarily in their digestive gases. It didn't help. I guess I need a medical book on methane poisoning. I sure wish we could call an ambulance.

I've never seen Lexie so distraught. Roper came in from lookout duty and put an arm around me. We gathered in a circle around Blake and prayed and prayed.

And now all we can do is wait.

Wait to see if Jared's amputation will save his life.

Wait to see if Blake will be himself again.

I keep wondering, *Oh Lord, how long? How long!*

CHAPTER THIRTY-THREE

SARAH

So this was Plan B! An opening in the wall! But where would it lead?

In the dimness of the hallway, Tex's hand nudged my arm.

"C'mon, dumplin'. Grab a tote and follow us." Angel hung on to Kool's collar as he snarled and barked, straining to free himself.

Pound! Something rammed the door from outside. We heard scuffling.

"Hurry!" Angel whispered tensely. And then Kool wrangled loose and tore towards the door. He jumped at it, barking furiously—and, before Angel even got close enough to grab his collar again, a shot came through the door—and Kool, without a sound, flopped to the floor.

"Noooooo!" I yelled. Angel stood there frozen, staring down the hall at the animal.

Tex had to take her arm. "C'mon, hon. Just leave him." Tex adored the dogs as much as any of us. Kool's loss would be keenly felt by him but he issued directions, keeping us on task, making us move despite the numb grief creeping over our minds.

"Lower your head," he said, nudging me back towards the portal. It was a sliding door but it felt like a portal to me, as though I was in a science fiction world where magical doorways appeared just when you needed one. If only we'd taken Kool through this doorway before he could run off! I held onto Angel ahead of me and, crouching slightly, passed through the opening from the murky darkness of the house into a deeper, thicker, darkness. I could see nothing. I felt a blast of cooler air hit me but I might as well have been blind.

Hands took my arms, moving me gently back against the wall. Tex said, "Stay right here. Do NOT move." Something in his voice told me he meant business, so I stayed put. But was this their idea of safety? Staying crammed behind a wall like sardines in a can?

He and Richard, from what I could tell, were going back and forth from the hallway to this dark recess, bringing all the supply totes that were stacked there.

"Angel? Are you in here?" I asked.

"I'm here, Sarah." She sniffed. She was crying for Kool. "I'm keeping the door open for the men." Her voice was sad. I listened while Tex and Richard brought all the boxes and totes from the hallway into this dark domain. I could understand why they wanted the stuff: We had essential things in those totes but what I didn't understand was how we'd use any of it if we were stuck here. Sure, we were on the other side of the wall but how long could we hide here? Even Anne Frank had a whole apartment to live in when she and her fellow Jews went into hiding during World War II.

I could still hear pounding at the door. My heart was in my throat. The image of Kool on the floor was fresh in my mind and I wasn't feeling a whole lot safer just because we'd entered a hidden recess.

"Keep this door open," Angel said.

Tex said, sharply, "Where you going, hon?" I heard Angel's voice come wafting as she went further away. "I'm grabbing our chickens!" Tex gave an exasperated snort.

I stayed huddled there, wondering what good any of this would do—it seemed impossible to me that we'd survive once those marauders gained entry to the house. Noisy chickens seemed like the last thing we needed!

When Angel was back with her chicken (only one, it turned out, because the others went squawking off in all directions) Tex said, "Richard, you in here?"

"Yup," came the answer.

"Okay, we got our stuff, I'm gonna close us in," Tex said.

"What are we doing?" I whispered. "How can we stay here?"

"Shhh!" Angel said. "Hold onto me and follow."

Behind me I heard a *whoosh* and a *whump* as the door in the wall shut. The darkness was complete.

Tex struck a light using a cigarette lighter—and relief flooded over me. Until I realized we were on a wide ledge of dirt and rock. Looking around Angel's short frame, I saw it ended a few feet ahead. She put out a hand to stop us. "Don't move, Sarah. I want you to watch what I do—and then do exactly what you see." I peered ahead of her to see what came after the end of the passageway. It was a sharp drop—into nothing.

"C'mon, do what I do, Sarah," Angel said again. She turned around to face me, slung a burlap bag holding the chicken over one shoulder, and got on her knees. Moving slowly, she inched backwards towards the drop.

"What are you doing?" I hissed. "You're gonna fall!"

"There's a ladder there," she said, calmly. "You just need to find it with your feet." And then she began descending. She put her legs over and then soon was disappearing until finally her head went out of sight. The last thing she said before vanishing was, "Turn around and get on your knees!"

"Go on, girl," Tex's deep voice came from behind me.

I swallowed, turned around and got slowly onto my knees. My hands were on hard, packed dirt and my backpack felt suddenly heavy. What if its weight pulled me over before I'd found my footing on the ladder?

"I need to take off my pack!" I said, and stopped to do so. Then I started backing toward the edge just as Angel had. My foot went over the side and I felt—nothing. Air! Frightened, I pulled it back up. "There's no ladder!" I gasped.

"Shhh," Tex said. "It's there, just put your foot down lower, you'll find it. It's very straight—built into the dirt."

"Here," Richard said, taking my hand. "I've got you. You won't fall. Find the top rung."

Again I dangled my foot over the side, and reaching down, swung my leg around to find the first step. I've heard of taking a leap of faith but this felt like suicide. I was nearing panic level when my leg brushed something protruding slightly—I'd found it! I planted my foot on the rung.

Tex had gotten to his knees and now he held the cigarette lighter out over the edge. Peering down, clinging to Richard's hand for dear life, I could see the next step. The ladder was vertical, not angled, which made it harder to descend and I didn't relish going down further. Beyond the next step, I saw only darkness.

Angel's voice came up from the dark: "C'mon, Sarah, you can do this. It isn't that bad," she chided.

"What do I hold onto?" I fretted.

"I've got you," Richard said, firmly. "Just get on the ladder with both feet and then you'll be able to hang on."

Tex squeezed in next to Richard and grabbed my other hand. Between the two of them (and since I had no choice) I got both feet on the ladder. "Okay," I said. "Don't let go! Now what?"

Richard let out a breath of impatience. "You keep going."

"Don't let go, yet!"

"We won't. Don't worry!"

I realized I'd have to let go of their strong hands in order to proceed. Gingerly, I released Richard's hand but told Tex not to let me go, yet.

Clinging to him with one hand, I felt around with my other for something to grasp. When I felt the wood of the ladder, relief shot up my spine. Slowly I felt around for the next step—but it didn't materialize.

"The next step is too far!" I cried.

"If I can climb up and down this ladder," chided Angel, who was at least three inches shorter than I, "then you can, too!" That seemed reasonable. I slowly dropped one foot—it felt like a long drop—until I found the next rung. Finally I had to let go of Tex's reassuring hold, and I went down the next step. Almost immediately I saw Richard's feet coming over the edge above me. I had no choice but to keep going. Each step felt like a shot in the dark. When I finally reached bottom it was with immeasurable relief.

Angel lit a battery-operated lantern, and its glow revealed we were now in a small circular area, a cave, I guessed. There were two red children's wagons in one corner, and a single passageway leading out—where it led I was yet to discover. Angel put a hand on my arm. "I didn't know you were afraid of heights."

I was embarrassed but shaken. "If I could have seen where I was going, I would have been fine."

"Watch out," she said, "Give your brother room." I stepped aside just in time for Richard to hop off the ladder beside me. He handed me my pack. He had taken both our packs, which made me feel more embarrassed.

"Heads up!" Angel cried. Suddenly I saw a huge wooden crate coming down from the ledge to the right of the ladder. It was on a pulley system and inside it were a couple of the totes we'd taken from the cabin. When it landed with a thud on the ground, Angel said, "C'mon, get these totes out so Tex can fill it again. Move them onto the wagons."

I was beginning to see there was a method to their madness. The wooden crate came down five times and each time, we emptied it and sent it back up to Tex. Richard loaded the red wagons until they could hold no more.

Angel picked up a tote bag filled with kitchen stuff. "Take whatever you can carry," she said, to me. "Then, come, follow me. The men will pull the wagons."

I grabbed a box that was very heavy but Tex stopped me and took it. "Here, this one's more your size, dumplin'."

I would have argued with him but I was still feeling shaky. I took the lighter box. Besides, I had no idea how far I'd have to carry it.

I turned and followed Angel, feeling awed by what was happening. Angel and Tex really did have a Plan B! They'd been prepared for something like this—for when they'd have to abandon the cabin. I still had questions, though. How long could we survive underground? What would we eat, beyond what we were bringing with us? What if that gang liked the cabin and decided to stay? Would our presence be detected if we made noise?

I swallowed my questions and concentrated on following Angel. The passageway had many turns, each one just big enough by a hair for the wagon to maneuver. After a few minutes we went by a passage that went off to the right. "Where does that lead, Angel?"

"It's a dead end."

Tex added from behind us, "It's a decoy tunnel. Gives an intruder something else to do before finding us, hopefully."

I don't know how long we walked but we passed two more decoy tunnels. Somehow it was hard to track time underground—I had to fight claustrophobia, and minutes ticked on like hours. And then Angel came to a stop. In front of her was a large, narrow steel door. It reminded me of the hatches that submarines use.

Angel took out a heavy key chain and only then did I notice all the locks on the door—seven of them. She opened each one methodically. I had the distinct feeling she was very familiar with the procedure. Then it hit me: this was where all those supplies had disappeared to! She'd been bringing stuff here all along without our ever knowing it.

Finally, with the locks open, Angel used her whole body to shove against the door. It began to open with a slight creak, revealing that it was thick and insulated. It even had the wheel on the inside to open and close it like a submarine door! It was evidently waterproof—and probably fire proof, too. Angel and Tex never ceased to amaze me. We were just about to go inside but Tex said, "Shh!" Angel froze, leaving the heavy door ajar. Above us, but as though far away, I could hear thudding steps like people running, pounding the floor.

"They're in," Tex said, in a grim voice.

Angel pushed against the door again and it opened all the way. I followed her in, feeling like Alice in Wonderland. The interior was dark except for where her little lantern shed a circle of light. All I could tell was that we had entered a room. The men left the wagons outside, and started carrying in the contents. Angel moved farther in and a motion-detector light came on. I blinked, looking around me in astonishment. We were in an apartment!

CHAPTER THIRTY-FOUR

SARAH

I set down the box and let the pack slide off my back. The place was so homey I felt immediately relaxed but hurried to explore. There was a living room and kitchen area, much more modern than what was upstairs. Above, we lived like colonials—heating and cooking with a wood stove or over an outdoor open flame. Here there was a glass-top stove, a microwave, even a toaster! I caught myself gaping and then shook my head. What was I thinking? We had all this stuff too, back at the apartment. The pulse had rendered it all useless. Even down here, there couldn't be any electricity. All the huge transformers in the country had been fried by the pulse—Richard had explained it to me more than once.

Richard let out a low, admiring whistle as he carried a tote full of kitchen supplies past me. Tex said, "We're fairly soundproof but to be safe let's keep the noise down."

I continued exploring, going further along the underground home, which seemed to be long and narrow—it really was like a submarine—only much prettier. Tight hallways led to a bedroom and, all the way at the end, a bathroom with a shower! We'd been using an outhouse. I had an insane desire to sit right down and try the system for the sheer joy of flushing. But I figured it probably didn't work and so I headed back towards the others, retracing my steps along the narrow passageway until it widened into the main living area.

"It's like a long submarine," I whispered admiringly to Richard.

Angel smiled. "Yup. Something like that."

Richard sighed and fell onto a sofa—he seemed no more impervious to the homey atmosphere than I was. "I gotta hand it to you," he said, putting his hands behind his head and leaning back. "This is really…impressive. I can hardly believe it!"

Angel smiled. "We figured if we had to resort to living here, we ought to make it as comfortable as possible!"

Richard said, "You sure did that."

Tex crossed his arms, looking at Richard on the sofa. "Don't get too comfortable," he said. "We still have to take these wagons back for more supplies."

While the men left to get the rest of the totes and boxes, Angel and I unpacked. As I did, looking around at the cozy furniture and pretty décor, I had a feeling of euphoria—this apartment seemed even better than the cabin!

When the men had returned and brought in the rest of the boxes, Richard turned to Tex and Angel. "So you really did have a Plan B! I was beginning to wonder."

Angel smiled. "We even have a Plan C," she said, grinning. "Sort of."

Richard's brows went up. Curious, we followed her as she motioned us to a closet. Two doors opened outwards. When we peered inside, there was a row of four fat backpacks hanging on hooks, each labeled with a name.

"These are our fail-safe packs—Call them Plan C—in case we ever have to vacate in a hurry."

"You made one for me and Richard?" I asked, surprised.

"I've been filling them for weeks," she said, proudly.

I was deeply touched by this thoughtfulness. Tex had come up behind us. "Now, don't touch these except to familiarize yourself with what's in them. They are strictly last resort. They have enough food and supplies for four days or so."

"Can I take a peek?" Richard asked.

Angel nodded. "Sure."

Richard took down the pack with his name and began rummaging through it. I was content to watch him, leaving mine on its hook.

"Wow!" Richard said. "This is good. It beats the pack I've been using."

"Over here's body armor," Tex said, moving to an adjacent cabinet. He opened it to reveal a neat row of firearms. There were rifles, pistols, boxes and boxes of bullets, ammo cans, and other things. The body armor was folded on a shelf.

Richard reached for an armored vest. "Cool! Why didn't we use this upstairs?"

Tex looked sheepish. "In all the excitement, I never thought of it."

"Can I try this on?" Richard asked.

Tex looked amused. "You shouldn't need it down here but go on. Let's see you wear it." Richard removed his shirt, put on the body armor, and was about to replace his shirt, but Tex stopped and handed him a different one from the closet in camouflage green.

"Here. We'll do a dry run. See how geared up we can get you." Richard allowed Tex to help him strap a Glock to his ankle with an ankle holster, and accepted other gear, including a knife, a second pistol, and a rifle, which he said was an AK. Richard slipped on the heavy pack that Angel had prepared. Afterwards he stood there, undeniably pleased, knowing he looked like a fully equipped soldier—ready for battle.

"Well, son, you look like a force to be reckoned with."

I stifled a smile, hoping Richard had noticed that Tex had called him *son*. I'd never heard him do that before! It was proof that Tex really cared for my brother. After Angel and I oohed and aahed over him, Richard put everything away, and we got busy unpacking more supplies. We only made a dent in all that had yet to be put in cabinets or in the storage room but it was a start.

Tex then began moving from one area to another, pressing small panels that opened to the touch. They held controls of some sort. At one he stopped and did something. "Let's see what's going on up there," he said. Suddenly we could hear voices clearly…Tex had some sort of system rigged so he could eavesdrop!

"Another walkie-talkie?" Richard whispered. He jumped to his feet and headed to the speaker, just like Angel and I. We congregated around it, staring up at this little black speaker built into the ceiling as though it were a television screen.

Tex shook his head. "Oh, this is higher tech than a two-way," he said. "This cost me a bundle."

"Let's listen!" Angel cried.

Silence fell as we focused on hearing what was being said above. A man's voice came across louder than the rest: "There's no one here. I told you, they ran."

Tex had thoughtfully opened up the front metal shade and unlocked the front door before we closed the secret panel that led to our new refuge. It helped give the illusion that we had escaped from the house.

A new voice came through the speaker: "I want you three—" A pause. He was probably pointing out the three. "To hightail it after them."

Another pause.

"What are you waiting for? Go after them now!"

"And do what, if we find them?" A voice asked.

"Make sure they're not coming back," the man said.

Listening to his voice, numbness came over me. No, it was worse than that. I felt suddenly sick as a dog. My head reeled. I stumbled back, making Angel cry, "Sarah! What is it? Are you okay?"

I stared at her in mute horror. I recognized that man's voice. I glanced at Richard and saw that he'd recognized it, too! He wore a stupefied look on his face that mirrored my feelings.

That man upstairs, the one who seemed to be in charge of this gang? He must have been the one called Walt, which was my father's name. Because I knew, now.

He *was* my father.

CHAPTER THIRTY-FIVE

SARAH

Angel led me to the couch where I lay back, gasping. The wave of nausea receded but my feeling of dismay did not. I took a deep breath, searching Richard's face. Angel looked from me to Richard and back. "What is going on?"

Richard frowned. "That man up there sounds like our dad."

Tex's brows went up. "Your DAD?" He shook his head and gave a low whistle. "The one who just ordered his men to go after us and get rid of us?"

I began to cry. Richard nodded. "We both think so."

Tex and Angel looked at each other. They seemed at a loss."

Richard said, "I'm going up to confront him."

"No, you're not!" Tex said. "He may be your father or he may just sound like him. If you go up there, you give away our location, and that is not an option."

"I know my dad's voice," Richard retorted. "It's him, it's definitely him."

Tex looked at me. "I think it's him, too," I said.

"You think."

"No, I'm sure."

He sniffed, looking around, thinking. "Here's the deal, Richard. Sarah." He motioned for Angel to join him. When she was beside him, he circled her waist with one arm, and she turned into him so they were close. I understood he was speaking for both of them. Leveling serious eyes upon us, Tex continued, "Maybe it is your dad. But he's with marauders. He's in *charge* of them. They have been terrorizing us, stealing from us, destroying our property—and they're trying to kill us.

DEFIANCE

They're probably gonna wipe us out of anything and everything that's left up there. Your dad is behind that."

Richard and I listened in silence. Everything Tex had said was true. "Whatever he used to be—." He fanned out his hands as he spoke—"he is no longer. The pulse changed people. Look at those old folks you stayed with," he said, turning to Richard. "They put mines outside their home. Mines that'll tear a man limb from limb, leave him in agony! They probably used to be your average old couple, working their garden and flower beds." He paused and took a deep breath. He came and sat beside me. With regret in his eyes, he took my hand. In a softer voice, he said, "Your father is no longer the loving dad you once knew. He's responsible for a gang, now. The fact is you just don't know him any longer; or what he's capable of."

Richard shook his head. "Look, we know our dad. He isn't a monster."

"You mean, he wasn't." Tex said. "Did you hear him charge those men with finding us and getting rid of us? For all he knows, we high-tailed it out of there. We posed no threat to him or his gang, but he ordered our deaths."

Richard crossed his arms, then uncrossed them and strode towards the speaker. "Which is why I want to confront him!" he hissed. He raked a hand through his hair. "He's probably doing what he thinks he needs to do. We've been out there—it's a cutthroat world. He's just going with the flow."

"Richard—I know this must be hard, for both of you," he added, including me in his gaze for a moment. "But we are not giving ourselves up--."

"Not you, just me. Not even Sarah. I'll go alone."

"You'll just pop up inside the house? With no explanation? How long do you think our escape route will stay hidden if they find you in there?" He paused. "And if the wrong person sees you first, you could be dead before you get a chance to lay eyes on your father. It's too dangerous, the outcome is uncertain, and I don't like it. You're not going, and that's final."

232

Richard looked around, frustration emanating from him in waves. "So what is your plan? To hide down here like rats? What are we going to do? How long can we stay down here without going out of our minds?"

Tex took a deep breath and said, "Richard, come sit down. I want to speak to both of you." I moved aside so Richard could fit on the couch. Angel came and sat on the arm, and stroked my head reassuringly. I tried to give her a smile but inside I was feeling torn. I should have been overjoyed to know my dad was alive but it was like discovering he was Mr. Hyde. Like Tex said, my father was a stranger—a scary, dangerous stranger. I wished I hadn't heard his voice. I'd have preferred to think of him as I long had been—as having died somewhere tragically, rather than becoming a monster gang leader!

"I'll explain this to you once," Tex said. "We built this bunker a long time ago; but we added to it, in time putting up the cabin above us."

"You built this first?" I asked, surprised.

He nodded. "That's right. I worked for the government and we saw the writing on the wall. The media down-played the dangers of any kind of Armageddon—whether it be a pandemic, an EMP, or a nuclear holocaust. But we believed something was coming and knew it could have dire consequences."

"What did you do for the government?" Richard asked.

Tex eyed him gravely. "I'll tell you about that another time."

Angel piped in, "Tex has a double PhD!" Richard and I must have gawked, because she giggled.

Tex said, "Right now, this here's the point: "We made this place to be nuke proof—that makes it bullet proof and pretty much impenetrable. We have enough power, thanks to hidden solar panels on the property, to generate electricity—more electricity than anyone above ground has seen since before the pulse. We have food, running water from an underground spring, and can send waste into a septic tank just for that purpose. We have enough of everything we need to live here for six months or more."

"Hon," put in Angel, "that was if it was just the two of us. We didn't plan on having four people."

He nodded. "That's true, but we've been adding to our provisions steadily, so my estimate should be good."

"People need sunlight to live," Richard breathed. "I could never stay down here that long."

"We got that covered!" piped in Angel. "We have sun lamps. We just need to spend twenty minutes a day in front of one. That's enough to manufacture vitamin D and ward off the winter blues."

"We also got nutrition covered," said Tex.

"Storage buckets, right? Richard asked. We both were probably picturing the shelves of white storage buckets we'd had brief access to before the guerrilla army torched them.

"Oh, we did better than that. We got special stuff--."

"MREs?" Richard said.

Tex shook his head. "What we got is even better than that. We got space food! NASA certified. It packs better nutrition than MREs, including what they call 'sunlight nutrition.' It has more vitamins like D3 than you could get in anything except IV drips of the stuff."

Richard nodded his head, looking duly impressed but I suspected he was not a happy camper. He said, "Look, I get it. We can get by. But even if they found the route down here, you got that heavy steel door at the entrance, right? If I go up and they find the tunnel, that door will keep them out."

"Richard, I don't want them at my door. That's what happened upstairs and it did not go well. Those doors were reinforced, too. You are not going up there, do you understand?"

Richard stared at Tex and Tex stared at Richard. I did not like the tension in the room.

"Richard," I said, nervously. "It might not have been Dad."

"You know it was!"

"I'm not really sure!"

"It doesn't matter!" Tex barked. "No one is going up there until these people clear out. Hopefully they will go through what is left up

234

there in a week or two and we'll be able to return. We can add a room to the cabin for you two—if they don't burn it down."

"You said it's reinforced with steel," I said. "They can't burn steel down, can they?"

"They can burn the wood around it. It'd be a skeleton of steel, angle iron, and rebar, but a skeleton just the same."

That seemed to end the discussion for the time being. We spent the rest of the day getting settled. For dinner, we enjoyed ready-to-eat dehydrated food—each of us getting to select what we wanted from a big box of packaged meals. All Angel had to do was heat up water, which she did in the microwave. What a joy to have electricity! Tex cautioned that it wouldn't last forever—even solar panels run out of juice—so we had to know from day one that using electricity was a privilege and only to be done with permission.

If we weren't underground, I could almost have believed we had a chance for a normal life again. I felt at home with Tex and Angel. They were my new family. Whoever that man was upstairs, Tex was right. He was no longer my father.

CHAPTER THIRTY-SIX

SARAH

The next morning I awoke on the sofa to find Tex, Angel and Richard congregated around the speaker. Richard saw me getting up and said, "Something's happening up there." Tex turned up the volume and I immediately heard shouting, rapid gunfire, and muffled explosions. It was pandemonium.

Tex whistled under his breath. "Man, that is the sound of warfare."

A great deal of scuffling and pounding, interspersed with more rapid fire, continued for the next fifteen minutes. I pulled my legs up, wrapped my arms around them, and rocked nervously on the couch. I was hearing a real battle going on. People were probably getting killed! I wondered if a second band of marauders had come. Would they kill my father?

Richard said, "I think it's soldiers, like the ones Sarah and I saw. They come by truckloads."

Tex said, "Maybe it's a good thing we got chased out of the house when we did. Maybe it was a God-thing."

And then faintly, very faintly, we heard something amazing: THIS IS THE UNITED STATES ARMY. COME OUT WITH YOUR HANDS UP.

The gunfire ceased and for the next fifteen minutes we heard footsteps, low voices, furniture being moved here and there, along with someone saying, "C'mon, c'mon, Give me that weapon. Let's go. Out of there." And then, at long last—nothing.

"Do you think it's really our army?" I asked. "You think they're here to help?"

"Remember what we saw out there," Richard said quickly. "No U.S. Army. Just foreign troops claiming to offer help—and taking people prisoner to their camps."

"They also burn everything down," I muttered. I thought of our cozy cabin upstairs and felt a deep sadness. Tex was just reaching up to turn off the speaker when we heard a man's voice. "They're still out there. And that is NOT our army, I'm telling you!"

"That's him!" Richard said. "That's my father."

I closed my eyes and covered my mouth, wishing away the tears that filled my eyes. As much as I believed he was no longer my loving father, I still cared for him.

"I'm going out," another voice said. "Look, they aren't killing us—they're putting everyone in a truck. So what if they go to a refugee camp? I'm a refugee. I'm ready."

My father let loose a string of expletives that sent a wave of shame through me. I'd heard him swear on occasion as I was growing up but never in such a way as this. It didn't make me feel like he was strong or brave—just the opposite. And it underscored the fact that he was no longer the man I once knew.

"If you go out with your hands up, they *will* slaughter you."

"They didn't slaughter the others!" A man's angry voice.

"Fine! You go if you want! You go crawl to the enemy! See where that gets you." And then the sound of a terrific blast, something exploding, made us jump—and resulted in footsteps running, doors slamming...and then silence. Richard's eyes met mine. Despite everything, I felt heartsick at the thought of someone brutally killing my father. Richard's expression told me he felt the same.

Angel reached over and took my hand. She was often attuned to how I felt when I hadn't said a word. Tex had joked once that they could read me like an open book. "You couldn't hide your heart if you tried," he'd said.

"Let's pray, y'all," she said. Angel wasn't a blue-blood southerner but she liked to say "y'all," now and then. It had a homey sound to it. I tried to smile as I clasped her hand.

We closed our eyes to pray. But a barrage of shots, louder now, came through the speaker and silenced us. Once more, we sat listening. My father's voice: "Quick, get under there again!" A few seconds passed and we heard a foreign language.

"Sounds like an Arab," said Tex.

Angel nodded.

Richard jumped up. "I'm getting my dad."

Tex faced him. "You will do no such thing! You don't know that he'll even be alive when you get up there, for one thing. And you may *not* bring him here."

"I have to do this," Richard said. "They'll take him to a refugee camp and let him starve!"

"And what's to stop them from taking you, too?" Tex asked. "If your father's band couldn't keep these guys off, you can't, either."

Richard nodded. "I need to face my dad. I don't think you'll ever understand this, okay? But I have to. I have to see him, man to man."

"I can't let you do that, Richard. You may not understand this— but you left once before and brought back trouble. That may be your dad, it may not; you are not going up there to find out. And that's *final.*"

Richard stared at Tex. Slowly he looked away. His face was stony.

"Richard!" My voice broke. "Tex is right! Dad abandoned us, and you heard what he said up there. He's not the man we knew."

"He did what he had to do to survive," my brother said. "To stay alive."

"Yeah, but why didn't he come back? To help his family? Why didn't he come back to us?" I took a shuddering breath, trying not to cry. "He could have come back, he could have—but he didn't! He let Jesse die! He let Mom die!"

"It's not his fault they died!" Richard said.

"They'd be alive if he came back," I said, shaking my head and staring at my brother accusingly. "You know they would!" I paused.

238

"Instead of saving his family he chose to lead this—gang!" I stared hard at my brother. His face was like flint, unmoving.

"I gotta know what happened. I gotta face him, like I said."

"If it was just you and me, Richard, I'd let you do it. But I can't let you put Angel and Sarah in harm's way. Listen, after the battle's over we can look for survivors, and maybe your dad will be one of them." Tex said. "After this force moves out."

Richard said nothing.

Tex shook his head with pursed lips. "We brought you down here with us, Richard, because we care for you. And we trust you." He paused. "Don't make us regret it."

Angel, with sympathetic eyes, sat next to Richard. Her voice was sweet and caring. "Richard, you do not want to go up there. There's just no good reason for you to risk your life."

"And ours," Tex added.

"If you went up," I said. "We'd never see you again! Don't do that to me, Richard!"

"Look, nobody's going up," Tex said, in his heavy voice. "This discussion is over."

We spent the next hour unloading the last of the supplies, stacking canned goods, and putting everything away. Richard still looked unhappy. He came beside me as I transferred supplies to a storage cabinet and said, keeping his voice low, "I need to see him."

"Richard, please!" I whispered. "You can't!"

"Don't you want to know what kept him away? I want to know. I need to talk to him."

I placed a hand on his arm. "So because you're curious you're going to risk everything?"

"I'm only putting myself at risk."

"Even so, that's enough! You don't owe him anything! He abandoned us!"

He gently removed my hold on my arm. He sniffed. "You can pray for me, okay? Pray for me."

"Wait. You are going to tell Tex and Angel, right?"

He shook his head. "I think Tex would tie me up, if I did!"

I looked pleadingly at him. "I wish you wouldn't do this." The sound of gunfire from upstairs coming through the speaker made me desperate. "You hear that? That's what you're going up to! You're going to—a war zone!"

Richard frowned. "I'm sorry. I have to do this." He turned away but stopped, looking halfway back. "I'll come back. I promise."

"Don't make promises you can't keep." He turned back to me then and gave me a quick hug. "When are you leaving?" I whispered.

"Tonight, when they're asleep."

I stared at him, deeply troubled. He met my gaze lingeringly, his eyes full—but also hard. "I'll come back for you," he said, softly.

"I won't leave Tex and Angel," I said. "No matter what Dad says."

He nodded but made no reply.

I finished my work, planning what I would say to Tex. I had no choice but to tell him what Richard was going to do. It would save his life. I loved my brother—I couldn't let him carry out his stubborn, stupid plan!

———————◆———————

Richard must have known that I would tell. When I finished unloading the supplies that were my responsibility, I found Angel preparing dinner. She looked over at me with a strange expression.

"Your brother's gone."

"Gone?" I asked, dumbfounded.

"We found the door unlocked," Angel said ruefully. "Which means someone went out—you can't lock it from the outside without keys." With a sudden suspicion, I ran to the closet and saw that two of the packs were gone—Richard's and Tex's.

Angel said, "We hid Richard's pack, hoping it would discourage him from his foolishness—but he took Tex's."

"Where is Tex?"

"He went after him," she said, but she'd turned around and wouldn't meet my eyes.

"I'm sorry," I told her. "I was coming out here to tell you that he was planning on leaving. But he told me he'd be going tonight! When you and Tex were sleeping!"

She shook her head. "I sure wish I hadn't shown him all that stuff. I think it encouraged him to go. I should have guessed he'd defy Tex."

"He's so stubborn!" I said.

Angel sighed. "He's a strong-willed boy, that's for sure. But I don't think he wanted to go. I think he had to. I can imagine if it was my father up there. I'd want to do the same thing."

I started pulling out dishes to set the table. "Do you think Tex will be able to bring him back?"

Again, Angel's eyes were veiled. "I sure hope so, Sarah." Suddenly she looked tearful. "I sure hope so."

———————————— ◆ ————————————

Tex returned before we'd finished making the meal. Alone.

Angel gasped when he came in and said, fearfully, "What happened? Did you--?"

"He was already in the cabin," Tex said. "I wasn't gonna follow him in there." For some reason, Angel seemed relieved.

Then, as we ate, they gave each other strange looks and nods and I finally threw my fork down. "What is going on? What aren't you telling me? Did something happen to Richard?"

Angel just looked at Tex. He took a deep breath and turned to me. "I have no idea what's happening to your brother," he said. "But I'll tell you what might have happened. If I had caught him before he got back up there, I would have stopped him. I would have done whatever I had to, to make sure he doesn't compromise our position."

I remembered that Tex had come back with his rifle slung over his shoulder. Suddenly I realized he was telling me he would have shot Richard if he had to, in order to stop him!

Somehow, the knowledge didn't shock me. The truth was, I couldn't blame Tex.

He saw my face and said, "The rifle was backup, Sarah. I was counting on being a whole lot stronger than your brother."

Angel said, "Well—I am really glad it didn't come to you having to hurt him. Richard left in defiance because he felt it was necessary."

"Sometimes it is necessary," Tex said, leaning back in his chair. "Sometimes it's the only way to get justice or righteousness. But this time, it was plain stupid."

I gave a big sigh and stared down at my plate. And then I had a thought: "Shouldn't we be listening?" I asked.

Tex made a face. "Yes, we should." He stood up and turned on the speaker. We heard some muffled sounds but nothing distinct. After some minutes of continuing to hear only muffled sounds, Angel said, "Let's pray for him."

And so we did.

While we prayed, I kept thinking about how stubborn Richard was to disobey Tex. I asked God to forgive him and watch over him. I pictured Richard sneaking into the cabinets—stealing supplies like a criminal! Then I pictured him undoing the locks and turning the wheel on the great, heavy door. I could almost hear it whoosh open. And I saw Richard step through it into the waiting darkness like going into the jaws of death.

My heart brimmed with worry and sadness. Would he really find our father? Even more I wanted to know: Would I ever see him again?

CHAPTER THIRTY-SEVEN

RICHARD

Richard hurried through the tunnel using only a small penlight to navigate the multiple twists and turns.. He couldn't help but feel like a rat in a maze, and so was glad to know the tunnel wasn't endless. He stopped once to shine his beam at the ceiling, curious as to what held it up. He was both surprised and impressed that wooden beams like railroad ties crossed the dirt ceiling at regular intervals. Tex hadn't said what he did for the government but it must have brought in a pretty penny. This tunnel and the bunker had to have cost a great deal.

As he continued on, he noticed the profound silence. He hadn't noticed it on their first walk through but he'd been with the others, then. Now on his own, he was acutely conscious of the isolation. He was traversing ground between the house and the bunker. There was nothing overhead but maybe fifteen feet of dirt. He was insulated from the fighting, the desperation, the madness. But he had to find his father. For reasons he couldn't fully explain himself, he had a need to lay eyes on his father's face, confront him with what he'd become. He would do it if it was the last thing he did; and he understood it might well be. Underneath, too, he wanted to let his father know that he and Sarah were still alive.

He hoped it wasn't too late. What if the soldiers killed their father? Or had taken him prisoner? Should he try to follow them? How far should he go to find the man? In the back of his mind, he half expected to find his dad badly injured, left to die. If so, it would comfort a dying man to know two of his children lived.

He reached a dead end and kicked himself for taking one of the decoy tunnels! Backtracking, he began to recall memories of growing up, memories he hadn't allowed himself to think of for a long time. His father had been rough, stern, not too affectionate, but Richard's memories were mostly good. The man might not have showered praise upon Richard but he had showed up for ball games and helped with homework. He'd always been a figure of strength.

He reflected how that strength must have come in good stead after the pulse, making his father a leader of a gang. But he had to believe his dad had no choice. He wasn't a monster. He was still Dad, the man he'd grown up with. The man he had differences of opinion with, to be sure; sometimes strong differences, but he was the father Richard loved.

A sudden sound from behind him made him stop, listening. Was that someone running? In a flash he knew: Tex was coming after him! He'd try to stop him! He doubled his speed, feeling like the tunnel was endless but then he rounded a bend and finally saw the ladder in the dim beam of his light. There was no sound of the staccato blasts of sporadic gunfire coming from the cabin—he hoped that meant the soldiers had left.

He crawled up the ladder and came to his feet and then, staring at the wall, realized he didn't know how to open the door. There had to be a mechanism—he'd seen Tex at the wall before the door had whooshed shut on them.

He heard muffled shots, but none were loud and close—that reassured him the fighting was outdoors. He pinned the pen-light to his shirt and gingerly began to feel around with his hands, looking for something, anything, a lever perhaps, that might be the means of opening the door. It had to be there somewhere!

He felt his first sense of caution. What if Tex was right and his father was dead already? What if he was on a fool's errand and would accomplish nothing but getting himself killed? Why was he risking his safety—when he and the others were truly safe for now—when he had no guarantees?

There was only one good reason to keep going and a thousand reasons why he shouldn't. But that one reason—and maybe it was crazy—was that he believed his father had not fundamentally changed. When he saw Richard he'd break down, be his old self, and immediately want to abandon the gang in favor of his kids. Richard believed this—but he needed to give the man a chance to prove it.

After feeling around the door and finding nothing, he shone his slim light up and down, back and forth. Nothing. He started again, going around it, then spread out to the dirt walls on either side. He slipped off the cumbersome backpack and shoved it towards a corner. He could search better without it.

From the tunnel, he heard Tex hiss at him. "Richard! Don't do it! Wait a minute!" He was trying not to raise his voice.

In despair, Richard did a last search around the door, forcing his hands to move slowly, slowly, despite his thudding heart. He couldn't let Tex stop him!

Then, there! Near the ground, on the left, was a hole in the rock, angled so that you couldn't see the opening—only feel it, if you knew where to feel. It was just wide enough for a large hand to slip inside—Tex's large hand, he figured—but it reminded him of a snake hole, and he half expected to get bitten as he slid his hand into it.

Tex had reached the clearing. His voice, getting louder, insistent, said, "Richard! Don't be foolish!"

Richard's hand found only a metal box—an empty one. His heart sank. Then, at the back end of the box there was, not a switch as he expected, but a square, flat panel.

"Clever," he murmured, "but I gotcha now." A single press from his hand would cause the door to slide open and reveal the hallway of the cabin. This is what he came for, what he wanted. Nevertheless, he couldn't help but feel that a single second lay between him and eternity. He stood waiting, listening intently. Tex had reached the ladder!

"Hold on, Richard!"

Weariness washed over him, and with it, doubts returned, stronger than before. What if he'd been wrong and it hadn't been his dad's voice? Even Sarah said she was no longer sure. If Tex was right, Richard might be rushing headlong to his death. And what if Angel was right about eternal damnation waiting? Was he about to jump into hell?

He didn't want to think about that. Heck, he wasn't sure he believed it. But the thought persisted...*What if?*

He lay his head against the cool metal of the door with one hand still poised on the panel. All he had to do was press it and he'd be back in the cabin. *All he had to do was press it.* Seconds ticked by.

Tex's head appeared over the ledge. "Richard!"

Fear ran through him. Without another moment to weigh his actions, his hand hit the panel.

◆

The wall whooshed open, sending Richard sprawling to the floor in the hallway. Hurriedly, he pulled his feet clear—just in time for the door to whoosh shut again. He looked around frantically, saw no one and came to his feet. He went cautiously up to the nearest door—Tex and Angel's bedroom.

The wood was riddled with bullet holes. He put his ear to it and listened but heard nothing. After trying the handle, some instinct made him jump to the side—a good thing, because a barrage of shots came from inside. Standing back against the wall and out of range, he heard a voice—his dad's! "See if you got him."

"What if I didn't? I'm not opening that door."

"Did I *ask* you to open it?" Silence. "I TOLD you to see if you got him. Now open that door and check."

Richard's mind raced. If his father knew who it was, he'd be safe. And suddenly he was calling, "Dad! It's me, Richard! Richard Weaver. It's *me!*"

Hurried footsteps, the sound of something being pulled away from the door, and then it opened. A bearded man stared out at Richard, his face frozen in shock.

"My God!" he said. Richard blinked, taking in the sight of a man who looked nothing like the businessman his father had been. He wore fatigues and combat boots, had long hair and a scraggly beard. A shadow crossed his father's features, a darkening of the eyes, as though

246

something was wrong. Richard felt a check in his heart but there was no time to examine or dissect it.

"Get in here!" his father cried, pulling him roughly into the room. He stopped to look up and down the hallway, then shut the door behind them and locked it. He motioned with his head to another man, an individual who, rising from where he sat on the floor in the corner, looked wilder and more unkempt than his father. The man proceeded to push a heavy dresser in front of the door. Afterward he returned to the corner where he sank to the floor, rifle in front of him, and stared at Richard with open hostility.

Meanwhile his dad shook his head, still staring in shock at Richard. "I can't—I can't believe my eyes!" he exclaimed. Slowly he broke into a smile. "It's really you? It's really you!"

"He's really *who*?" the other man demanded. He picked up his rifle and pointed it at Richard. "You trust him?"

"He's my son, you idiot! Put down that weapon!"

The man didn't seem impressed. Didn't seem as if he believed what he'd heard. He looked Richard up and down. "You with that outfit?" he nodded his head towards the outside.

"No."

"Then how'd you get in here? Who are you with?" he asked, suspiciously.

"If you don't mind," his father said, "I'll do the questioning." The man sniffed and sat back but kept his rifle in his hands between raised knees. He continued to regard Richard with deep distrust.

"Son," said the older man, now faintly smiling. "I can't believe it! I can't believe you're alive!" He stepped forward, arms out, as if to give Richard a hug. The younger man instinctively stepped back.

"Son, son!" His father said, searching his face. Once again he opened his arms and Richard allowed the embrace, but his face was hard, the gesture on his part, half-hearted. *What was wrong with him?* He'd been adamant about seeing his father, wanted to see him with every fiber of his being. Risked his life to do so. But now in his presence he felt none of the affection that had fueled his search. All the nostalgic warmth he'd had in the tunnel now abandoned him and he felt, in its place, anger.

"I just can't believe you're alive!" His father said, again.

"I could say the same thing. I can't believe *you're* alive. Because the father I knew wouldn't have abandoned his family if he was alive. He'd have done everything in his power to get back to them."

His father's expression sobered. "Don't you think I did that?" But then his face softened. "How are they? Your mother—."

"Tell me why you didn't come back," Richard replied, coldly.

"I will tell you," said his dad. "I'll tell you everything but first you need to tell me a few things. Like, where is my family? How did you get here? How did you know I was in this room?"

"I heard your voice," Richard said. "I was hiding in this cabin, and I heard your voice."

"Hiding here? We went through this place with a fine-toothed comb," he returned. "You weren't hiding here, before."

"I was. You missed me." He stared at his father belligerently.

"Where were you hiding? Is it big enough for all of us?" Suddenly the man's eyes gleamed with interest. "Is that where your mom and the others are?" When Richard stayed silent, the older man grasped him by the shoulders. "Richard! Speak to me, son! What is wrong with you?"

Richard shook himself free and said, pointedly, "Why—didn't you—come back?"

Suddenly there were sounds in the hallway. His father rounded the bed quickly and motioned Richard to follow suit. They crouched on the floor, listening. The man in the corner lifted his rifle, pointing it at the door with the dresser in front of it.

Minutes went by. The only sound was the far-off fighting Richard had heard earlier.

"This place is really something," his father murmured admiringly, as they crouched between the bed and the wall. "The walls are reinforced with steel or something. Is that how you survived this long?"

"Maybe."

The other man said, "Walt, if this is your son, he ain't actin' like it. Tell him to cooperate, man! He's holding out on us!" He stared at Richard. "Answer the d---- questions!"

"Lay off!" Walt said, curtly. He looked back at Richard. "Where *are* the others? I want to see my family, Richard."

Richard weighed his options. He would not reveal the bunker—he'd promised not to.

"Somewhere safe," he said.

"Oh, man, are you gonna make him talk, or do I have to?" the other guy cried. He stared at Richard's father. "He ain't talking. He needs encouragement. Like we gave that last son of a—."

"Shut up!" Walt cried. He turned back to Richard. "I need to know they're alive. I need to see them with my own eyes."

This was the first argument that struck a chord with Richard. Hadn't he felt the same way? "That's how I felt about seeing you. Until now." Sadly, he was filled with only a deep distrust for the man he once knew and loved.

"What does that mean, until now?" He stared hard at Richard. "I'm glad to see you're alive, son! But I need to see your mother and sister and cousin."

"I understand," he said. He let his eyes roam over to the other guy. Without a word, he'd conveyed to his dad that he would not disclose their whereabouts while that man might hear it.

His father looked over at the companion. "Oh, you don't want Axis here to know?" The man turned hate-filled eyes on Richard, and pointed his rifle at him again. "Put that gun down, stupid!" Walt cried. "My son doesn't know you from Adam. He's just being cautious, is all."

"Well, I don't know him from Adam," Axis said, his words dripping with hate. "And if he don't want me to hear, I don't trust him, either." He put his rifle aside and sat back against the wall as if to watch Richard better. "If I had my say," he sneered, looking straight at Richard, "we'd kill you right now."

Richard's father had drawn a pistol out while Axis spoke. Richard wondered why. "You mean like this?" his father asked. He pointed the weapon at the man.

Axis eyed him with surprise, but decided it was a joke. He snorted. "Yeah. Something like that."

And then, *bam*! Richard jumped, while Axis slumped back, his head slowly falling to the side. A spatter of blood on the wall where his head had been was the only sign of the execution.

Richard felt the blood drain from his face. He turned to his dad. "You shot your friend!"

"He wasn't my friend, son. And he threatened you." He didn't seem the least bothered by having just shot a person in cold blood. Calmly, he said, "Now; where are your mother and sister and cousin?"

CHAPTER THIRTY-EIGHT

RICHARD

Richard stared at his father but said nothing. He could no longer deny the man was cold-blooded and dangerous.

"C'mon, Richie! It's safe now, you can tell me where the family is."

Still Richard was silent.

"Your mother!" He said, urgently. "Where—."

"She's dead."

His father stared. "You're lying to me."

"I'm not lying!" Their eyes held for long seconds during which the older man saw Richard was in earnest.

"Sarah?"

"She's alive."

"Jesse?"

"No."

His father swallowed and looked away. It was the first time Richard caught a glimpse of the man he used to know; his heart softened.

His father lay the pistol upon the bed, removed the magazine and checked it. "What happened to your mother?" His voice was low.

Richard's face hardened. He swallowed. "She needed you."

His father let out a breath, sighing heavily. "I know that….I tried...I couldn't get back. It was the snow. And the cold—."

"Yeah, I don't want to hear about it, okay? We had our own troubles."

"I'm sorry, son. I'm sorry." A tense silence fell for a few seconds. "How did she die?"

Richard's eyes blazed. "You really want to hear? You really want to know about that?"

251

When his father just stared but made no answer, he said, "Fine! She starved to death, Dad. Slowly, and painfully. Just like Jesse."

"Why couldn't you—." His father turned on him but caught himself.

"I did what I could! We ate mice. MICE! Think about that."

Their eyes locked, each filled with resentment. His father said, "You think I wanted that? You think I wanted—this? To leave my family alone? To lose my wife? A child?"

"I don't know what you wanted but I do know what you did. Nothing. You never came home. We waited. We got stuck living in the library—."

"The library?"

"There was a fire. Days after the pulse. Some idiot on the third floor tried to heat his apartment with a wood fire or something. We had to leave. We lost everything."

"Everyone lost everything."

"Some of them," Richard returned slowly, "lost it *together*." At that moment gunshot sent them both instinctively ducking for cover. The walls were reinforced but the wooden door wasn't and had only the dresser in front of it.

"How'd you get here? Where's your sister?" his father asked.

Richard didn't speak right away and his father said, "Richard! You said you were hiding and we missed you. Where? Take us there now, son."

"I can't do that."

The older man looked startled. "You can trust me, Richie! I'm your father!"

When Richard remained silent, he hissed, "How did you get to this cabin, anyhow? Of all the places in the world for you to show up….how is it that you are here?"

"I live here," Richard said, heavily. His father almost choked. "*What?*"

"You heard me, Dad, I live here. Or did, until you came along and ruined it all. I lived here with wonderful people who took me in. Me and Sarah. You attacked us for no reason—and *ruined* it!"

The man had that stunned look on his face again as he slowly sank back against the wall. His lank hands loosely held his rifle.

"I didn't know," he murmured. "How could I have known?"

"What have you become?" Richard asked. "What kind of man comes and attacks peaceful people?"

"They weren't so peaceful last time we were here!" he retorted. "One of you shot Tiffany—one of us. After we indicated that we were leaving."

Richard stared at him. "We should have shot all of you. After what you did!" His voice lapsed off, and then he spoke again, sounding troubled. "Why didn't you just keep going? Why didn't you look for somewhere easier to attack?" When his father didn't answer right away, he added, "I don't know you, anymore. I've done things I'm not proud of since the pulse but I never went around attacking and terrorizing people in their homes. If you hadn't come against us the first time, no one would have been shot. You are to blame for that, not us. You are a man I don't recognize."

The older man nodded his head, accepting Richard's words. Finally, he said softly, "Sarah. Where is she?"

"She's safe."

"Where?"

"Somewhere. I'm not telling you."

His father leaned his head back, tiredly. But again, he said, "She'd want to see me. You know that. Where is she, Richard? Take me to her." Richard stared at him but made no response.

"Look, you came out here to see me. I know you must still care." He spread his hands out as he emphasized the next words, "I'm *still your father.*"

"My father wouldn't go around leading a gang of marauders."

"Your father would!" He whispered loudly and sat up in anger. "Your father would do whatever he needed to do to survive!" He stared hard at Richard. "It was lead, or be led. It was lead, or be slaughtered."

"Yeah, I think you mean lead and slaughter others," Richard said.

The man's eyes blazed but they both fell silent as the sound of running feet went past in the hallway. "Walt! Walt! You here?"

Walt put up a hand, motioning Richard to silence. The voice stopped outside the door. "Walt! You in there?"

He made no response and soon the person walked off. They heard the sound of the back door slam. After another minute passed, his father said, "You know, I'm proud of you."

"Don't start, Dad!"

"But I am. I'm proud of you. You lost your mother and Jesse but you've managed to keep yourself and Sarah alive."

"YOU lost mom and Jesse!"

"Okay. I lost mom and Jesse. But you kept yourself and your sister alive." After another silence, he added, softly. "Please. I want to see my daughter."

"Well, forget it, because I can't take you to her. If you showed your face there, they'd want to kill you for what you did to their house and property. Which reminds me, why'd you do it? Why'd you have to destroy the doors and walls? Burn the barn? That was where we slept, Sarah and I!" His voice rose as his anger grew.

The older man shook his head. "They've got blood-thirst, son. Hungry people are desperate people; out of control. They're not happy unless they're causing destruction. If I tried to stop it, they would've turned on me."

"That sounds real good, Dad. You're just an innocent bystander. Except not all hungry people turn into killers, and I heard *you* order them to go after us and—quote—'make sure they're not coming back.' You're a killer, now. Admit it! I don't dare take you to the rest of us."

After a moment's silence during which his father just studied Richard, still keeping his head back, he said hopefully, "You probably need a leader. I don't have to be cold-blooded. I'm telling you, you don't understand what it's like out there--."

"I've been out there! I DO understand! Sarah and I both have been out there. We didn't become cold-blooded. We only fought back, we never started it."

"Are you telling me you haven't done bad things? Haven't stolen anything? I don't believe it."

"I've stolen. From the dead. But I didn't kill anyone. The first time I shot to kill was when your gang descended upon us and almost found me and—a."

Suddenly from outside they heard shouting and gunfire— foreigners speaking excitedly—and then staccato blasts of bullets.

"Take me to your sister." He sounded desperate now. "You can have all my guns. I'll go unarmed. Just take me to see her!"

"I couldn't do that if I wanted to. She's not here any longer."

His father's face hardened.

"But you know a place to hide," he persisted. "You can get us out of here, Richie." Suddenly the smell of fire entered the room.

"Something's burning," his father said.

Richard gave a grim nod. "This is their calling card. They burn up everything before they leave." Now curls of smoke began to pour in the room from beneath and above the door, and were even coming through the bullet holes.

"Look, Richard! You have to get us out. If we walk out of this cabin, they'll shoot or take us. Is your hiding place safe from fire?"

Richard had to make a decision. If he waited, they'd both die from smoke inhalation. He nodded. "I can take you to a temporary safe spot. It's just a ledge, not a place to *stay*, but good enough to sit out until the fire dies down and they're gone."

"That's good enough for me!" He rose to his feet. "C'mon, boy, lead the way!" His father opened a dresser drawer and pulled out a few of Tex's white t-shirts. He threw one at Richard. "Put it over your mouth and nose." Together they moved the dresser aside and then cautiously opened the door to the hallway. Immediately smoke stung their eyes as it billowed around them into the room. The hallway was dark and oppressive.

The older man cried, "It's now or never, son!"

Richard frowned. He didn't want to take his dad to the ledge. But what choice did he have? If he hesitated, they'd die from smoke inhalation or burn alive. If he tried to escape alone, his father would only follow him and they'd both get captured by the soldiers. Coughing, he motioned to his father and led the way, thankful they had only to cross the hallway. Flames were shooting into the hall from other rooms. The walls were already hot to the touch. He crouched down and felt around the bottom of the wall for the hidden lever—and prayed that he was doing the right thing.

CHAPTER THIRTY-NINE

ANDREA

We spent a tense hour praying and waiting for Blake to show signs of recovery. He nodded at a few questions but didn't speak! When he remained groggy like that, his mother said we should let him sleep.

Mr. Martin feels responsible for what happened. I heard him say more than once, "I just assumed Blake knew to remove that tarp first and let any gases out—I just thought he'd know to do that."

Mr. Buchanan, Blake's father, has been kind. He's a compact, muscular man with thinning hair. He shook his head, saying, "Blake *should* have known better; we've discussed this in the past, how manure pits can be death traps; he knows they build up methane, hydrogen sulfide, ammonia, carbon dioxide. He's not new to this stuff."

Lexie stood near the bed, her arms crossed tightly, and with a tear-stained face. "Why wasn't he more careful, then?" she asked, plaintively.

Mr. Buchanan shook his head again. "He must have figured that lifting the tarp would give enough ventilation. Or maybe he wasn't planning on doing more than taking a peek but was overcome so quickly he couldn't back out."

Mr. Clepps finally arrived after finishing up with Jared. He didn't look too well with blood spattered on his shirt sleeves and he seemed stressed out—probably because he'd just performed his first amputation. He checked Blake's vital signs and forced an eyelid open. Then, turning to Mrs. Buchanan and Lexie, he said, "Well, his blood pressure's low but not dangerously low; his pulse and respirations are slightly elevated but that's not concerning; what concerns me is that he's sleeping so soundly and hasn't spoken, yet." He frowned. "We need to wake him up."

He began talking loudly to Blake, moving his head with his hands and lightly slapping his cheeks. He said, "Until we hear him speak, we can't be certain there hasn't been brain damage."

What horror his words sent through me! Our brilliant boy wonder! I can't stand to think that Blake could have brain damage! While everyone talked at once, Mrs. Buchanan said, "Please, everyone, just keep praying." She seems brave, but like Lexie her face and eyes are swollen with tears. We all want to trust God and believe Blake will be fine but I can see the struggle in everyone's eyes.

Marcus came in and said that Mrs. Wasserman was thoroughly revived—she rescued Blake but is back to her normal self. If only Blake would come to and be his normal self!

Cecily got word of what happened. She came in and asked if she could pray over Blake. I *love* how Cecily prays. She makes us all feel stronger because she has such strong faith. She has a smooth, silky voice, and she comes before the Lord as comfortably as breathing. We circled the bed and laid our hands on Blake or whoever was closest. I had one hand on Mrs. Buchanan's arm and the other on Lexie's.

Cecily prayed, "Father, in the mighty name of Jesus, we come before you on behalf of our brother Blake. He is my brother but he is also a son, and a big brother, and a-a-boyfriend," she said. "Lord, you are the God who heals us; according to Isaiah 9, you take away all our diseases; according to Malachi 4, you have healing in your wings!"

"We ask, in your mighty Name, to touch Blake with that healing power; bring restoration to every cell in his body, Lord; we bless him right now in the powerful Name of Jesus. And Lord, we ask you to restore him to complete wellness. *Thank you* for your power. *Thank you* that you accept us before your throne because of Jesus and what he did on the cross. *Thank you* that nothing is impossible for you. That no illness, no sickness, no poison, is stronger than your healing power!"

She said a lot more but that's the best I can do at remembering it all. Lexie prayed also, but cried, and I think it tore us all up.

Mr. Clepps had stood aside respectfully during the prayers but now he came forward and continued trying to wake Blake—and then, miracle of miracles! Blake came to!

Everyone tried to talk to him at once but Mr. Clepps raised a hand and said, "C'mon, now, stay back, please." He turned to the patient. "Blake," he said, in a strong voice, "How're you feeling, son?"

The young man blinked. "Not good."

"Do you know what happened to you?"

He nodded. "I think so." His voice was weak. Lexie couldn't stand it and went and sat on the bed and took Blake's hand. His seemed limp, but then he gave hers a light squeeze.

Mr. Clepps nodded at us as though to say, "This is good." He then asked, "What's two plus two?"

"Four," Blake said, and tried to smile. We all chuckled because Blake is such a brain.

He asked a few other questions, such as, "Where'd you get hurt? Can you remember?" When Blake answered correctly, though weakly, Mr. Clepps asked, "Can you sit up, son?" Blake tried to sit up but fell back exhausted, closing his eyes.

"Should we help him sit up?" Mr. Buchanan asked.

Mr. Clepps turned with a frown. "No. Let him rest. I think he'll be okay. I wish I could administer oxygen but all we can do is let him rest. He's not bouncing back the way I'd expect him to but I'll come and check him in another hour."

Mrs. Buchanan, like Lexie, seemed glued in place, and was staring steadily at Blake as if wishing him back to health. I saw her reach for Lexie's free hand. It looked right, somehow. Mother and future daughter-in-law in mutual concern for Blake, were uniting like family should.

◆

I am so relieved that it looks like Blake has escaped serious damage—at least, no brain damage! I couldn't imagine Blake not being his usual science-geeky self. And he's been such a help to this

259

compound! All I can say is, *Thank you, Lord, for sparing his life. And now please, bring him back to full health! We need Blake.*

CHAPTER FORTY

ANDREA

At breakfast this morning Mr. Clepps said Blake had slept for fifteen hours and was still groggy. *Not good.* Then, motioning to Roper, he came over to us.

"Jared's awake and asking to see you."

"Me?" Roper was surprised.

"Yes. Look, he's not doing well. He was delirious last night. And he's weak from blood loss."

Roper nodded. "Okay." He pushed away his bowl of oatmeal and blueberries.

"If you're going, I'm going with you," I said. I looked at Mrs. Martin. "Would you mind feeding Lily? She's almost finished." She nodded and came and took my seat.

Lily wailed and raised her arms and stared at me, saying, "Ma-ma! Want Ma-ma!"

"I'm not Mama!" I cried, gritting my teeth. "I'll be right back!"

Roper gave me a look of sympathy as I took his hand. He knows I dislike that Lily thinks I'm Mom. It still creeps me out.

As we approached sickbay, Mr. Clepps said, "Andrea, you'll have to wait outside the room." I was okay with that because I wasn't sure I wanted to see Jared after he'd lost an arm. But I felt protective of Roper and needed to know what Jared would say to him, so I hoped I'd be able to listen.

At the doorway Roper lifted my hand and kissed it. "Be right out."

I stayed in the hall out of sight but listening with every fiber of my being.

Mr. Clepps said, "Jared? Jared, look, Roper's here."

After a moment I heard Jared's weak voice. "Are you going out for more?"

"Oh—more airbags? Yes."

"Good. Listen. All we need is a simple high-explosive package. You can make that. No one's asking you to make a smart bomb or a PGM."

Roper must have looked the question because Mr. Clepps said, "Precision-guided munitions, I believe."

"Right," Jared said. "We don't need something high-tech. All you gotta do is cause a big blast."

"Okay," said Roper.

There were silences between words, making me think that Jared must have been struggling to speak.

"Don't worry," Roper said. "We'll take care of it. You rest."

"Listen." (Pause) "Get a whole bunch of 'em, empty 'em out and dump everything in a couple of containers, metal cans, whatever you got." His voice sounded labored. I found myself biting my lip out there in the hall. He continued, "Bind 'em together. Plant it beneath the culvert." He stopped to take a deep breath. "Make a fuse; light it, hightail it out of there, and blow the thing up." He went into a spasm of coughing.

"Got it," Roper said. "Don't worry. I'll get it done." He spoke firmly, doing his best to reassure Jared. I loved him for it.

Jared coughed again. "Don't—."

When he didn't finish the sentence, I couldn't help myself and turned to peek into the room. Mr. Clepps and Roper were beside the bed where Jared, wincing in pain, was laboring to speak. His chest rose and fell heavily. The stump of his arm was bound up in thick layers of cloth, making a garish, rounded bump. I forced my eyes away.

"That's enough," Mr. Clepps said to Roper, who nodded and would have turned to leave but Jared said, again. "Don't!" Roper turned back to face the injured man. He'd hear what he was trying so hard to say.

"Fail. Don't fail!"

"I won't," he said, looking down at Jared with somber eyes.

"And take this." Jared stretched himself out and stuck his good hand into a pants pocket. He pulled out a chain of some kind—or was it a necklace? "Give it," he said, and then took a labored breath. "To Andrea."

My heart jumped into my throat. I turned back into the hallway. Jared had something for *me*? I felt terrible. I didn't want something from him. I didn't *deserve* anything from him. I heard Mr. Clepps say, "Okay, that's enough. He needs to rest."

Roper said, "Wait. I gotta pray for him."

I waited a few minutes longer and then Roper came out. He took my hand. He opened it, facing my palm up, and laid something in it. When I looked down, I saw the chain I'd seen Jared take from his pocket. It was a necklace. And on it was my bullet. So this was what he'd done with it: he'd made it into a necklace for me!

Roper said, "You okay?"

I said, "I shouldn't keep this. I didn't think well of Jared."

"He made it for you. He wants you to have it." He touched my arm. "Besides, you earned it. If he didn't make it into a necklace, I would have."

"You would have?" I smiled.

"Definitely. This is your badge of honor. A soldier's souvenir."

He took the necklace from me and lowered it over my head.

I held the bullet wonderingly in my hand. I couldn't get over that Jared had kept it all this time for me. I looked up at Roper. "I need to say thank you."

He met my eyes and slowly nodded. "Good idea."

While Roper went on downstairs, I returned to Jared's room. Seeing me, Mr. Clepps said, "He needs to rest."

"I just need a minute," I said.

I went over to Jared, whose eyes were closed. He must have heard me though, because he cracked open an eye and watched me. I held out the bullet. Unexpectedly I had to blink back tears. Jared's eyes were sunken and his skin grey, giving him a pale, deathly look.

"Thank you!" I said. "I'll wear it every day!"

He nodded. "Good." His voice was raspy.

I sat down on the bed beside him and took his good hand. It was hot—I'd forgotten he still had a fever. His fingers lacked strength when he tried to return my grasp.

"I'm sorry," I murmured. "I'm sorry you got hurt." I think I meant that in more ways than one. We both knew my interest in him had vanished after I'd met Roper. I felt guilty about it.

He nodded with eyes half open. "Goes with the territory." Soon his eyes closed, as though it took too much effort to keep them open. I leaned over and softly kissed his hot cheek. He moved his head to look at me and then, because somehow I knew I would not see him alive again, I kissed him once more, this time on the mouth. I gave him a good kiss. As I came to my feet, he whispered, "Thank you."

It was all I could do to run out of the room before sobbing against the wall in the hallway. *Why was I upset?* I loved Roper, there was no question of that. But I felt terrible about Jared. He might have had his bad side but he'd helped our compound, and it seemed he'd really cared for me.

Please God, I prayed, *spare his life!*

As I tried to get a hold of myself, Mr. Clepps stepped out of the room. I hurried to dry my eyes while he said, "Tell Mr. Martin it's time for goodbyes." We were out of Jared's hearing but he kept his voice low anyway. "He'll know what I mean."

I nodded. Sadly, I knew what he meant, too.

Downstairs I was directed to Mr. Martin's "rig"—the room where he keeps his AR equipment. When he saw me, he removed his headphones and I delivered the message.

Throughout the day Mr. Martin quietly went around telling people when to visit Jared. Jolene, I'm told, remained by her son's side, holding his good hand. One by one the members of the compound, from the oldest to the youngest in their mothers' arms, filed in and thanked Jared for all he'd done for us.

Lexie told me later that Mr. Martin went in last with his Bible in hand. He prayed over Jared, and then slowly walked him through the gospel. He read Scripture to him about the life, death, burial and resurrection of Jesus, explaining that God the Father sent his Son to die for our sins. For Jared's sins. So that we can be forgiven and live eternally in heaven with the Lord.

Lexie said, "He could hardly speak, but he asked God to forgive his sins and he received Jesus as his Lord!"

That is the ONLY thing which comforts me right now. Knowing Jared accepted Jesus gives me hope. Even if the worst happens and he dies, it helps immensely to know he'll not suffer hell's agony. We'll see him again one day. On the other side. *Thank You, Lord!*

Earlier, after I'd delivered my message, I found Roper getting a cup of coffee in the kitchen. I appreciated that he'd given me time to be alone with Jared. He came towards me, his eyes searching mine, and met me with a short kiss. He put an arm around my shoulder. "You okay?"

"Yeah. Thanks." I remembered that he'd be leaving soon, going back out to get more of those initiators. We sat down on a sofa in the living room. "When do you have to leave?" I asked, my voice laced with reluctant acknowledgment that his going was inevitable.

"Later today," he said, lightly. But his eyes were anything but light.

"Don't go far this time," I said.

"I'll use every vehicle we come across that we haven't hit already. And come back as soon as possible."

──────◆──────

An hour and a half later it was time to say goodbye.

"Please be careful," I said. Roper and I were standing near the back door in the kitchen while Mrs. Martin and Mrs. Buchanan finished loading the men's packs with homemade "road food." They got hardtack, jerky, chia seed trail mix, and granola bars. They also had water filters, tools, guns and extra mags. I felt forlorn—and he hadn't even gone, yet. I took his arm and pulled him outside where, standing beside the door, we could have a few minutes alone.

I gazed up into his beautiful face. Roper's clear blue-grey eyes studied me in return and everything else fell away. I'd planned numerous things to say before he left but I forgot them all. Standing so close to his masculine beauty—there's no other word for it, because Roper is just so handsome—my mind went blank of everything except the sweet nearness of him. Studying my face, he sighed, and took me in his arms. "Don't worry."

I clung to him and blinked away tears.

He pulled apart enough to meet my eyes. "What did the French chef give his wife for Valentine's Day?"

I had to smile, even though it seemed distancing—he was making a joke when I was feeling so serious. "What?"

"A hug and a quiche." He lowered his face towards mine and my annoyance vanished. "Here's my quiche." Time felt suspended when his lips found mine. I wrapped my arms around him as tightly as I could and he tightened his hold on me, pulling me up against him. Warmth and sweetness and comfort filled me. It was soooooo nice. He ended the kiss—and then I kissed him for an encore.

From inside, I heard Mr. Simmons ask, "Where'd Roper go?"

He gently closed our kiss, and then glanced at the house. "It's time," he said, apologetically.

"One more?" I asked, raising my face to his. Smiling gently, he kissed me again, and it was our longest kiss yet. When I followed him back inside, knowing he was about to venture out into that crazy world again, my heart filled with longing and regret.

As I write this, I realize there is only one thing that will keep me from ceaseless worry and heartbreak—and that is, faith. I'm determined to pray like mad for Roper and trust the Lord to keep him safe.

It's the only way I won't lose my mind with worry.

CHAPTER FORTY-ONE

ROPER

Roper and Mr. Simmons were in somber moods when they got out to the road. They'd chosen to go on foot. Horses were highly visible and it would be a lot easier to hide from army trucks or other people without them.

They'd only walked a quarter mile before spotting a vehicle. It was a Ford Focus, tilted to one side, with the driver's side door facing the road. They circled the vehicle and decided it was stable where it sat, which meant Roper could climb in and get what they needed.

The battery was missing—someone at the compound had probably removed it long ago, which meant Roper didn't have to wait to make sure there was no juice going to the initiator.

He climbed in while Simmons kept watch. Ten minutes later he was wrapping the device in cloth and he tucked it gingerly in his back pack. If they could keep going at this pace he felt they might be done in less than 12 hours. It would be great, he thought, if this road-trip was that short.

As they walked from one vehicle to the next, the men chatted. Roper had known only that Simmons was an ex-cop. Now he learned the man was divorced and that his wife and two kids had moved to Oregon—her parents' home—a year before the pulse. Since the pulse, he'd not had a single word as to their fate. He'd enlisted both Grant and Gerard (Mr. Buchanan) to try to find out about them via amateur radio contacts, but he'd never gotten any news. The recent report that Oregon had been hit with a nuclear weapon had him almost crazy with worry—another reason he needed to get off the compound and do something different. He needed distractions to keep him from imagining the worst.

Roper was sympathetic. He himself had parents and siblings in California—and no way of knowing their fate. When Mr. Simmons apologized for being uptight and touchy on account of his worries, Roper shook his head. "Nothing to apologize for. I couldn't tell you're uptight or touchy."

He mused inwardly that compared to Jared's uptight, Simmons's was a barrel of laughs. If he fell into a dark mood, it would be understandable. Jared's dark moods, by contrast, were mysterious and downright dangerous.

———◆———

It was late afternoon when they stopped by a Dodge van which had somehow landed completely on its side in a gully off the road. If they'd been driving by, they wouldn't have seen it. They'd managed to get ten initiators so far but Roper wanted closer to two dozen before going back. They descended the ditch and circled the vehicle, as they did every car or truck they found.

"You sure you want to try this?" Mr. Simmons asked. "You've done cars that were sitting at odd angles, but this one's on its side. You're gonna have to work in there—."

"I can do it," Roper replied.

Finding the doors locked, Mr. Simmons suggested they smash in the windshield.

"No," Roper said. "Too noisy. Just in case there's anyone within earshot." So Mr. Simmons went to work with his tool kit—and experience from years on the force—and got the passenger door open. The driver side door was flat against the ground.

"Something smells foul in here," he said, in disgust.

"Pull the hood lock," Roper said, unconcernedly. Foul smells were part of life now more than ever. It took Simmons a minute to climb in, swing his legs ahead of him, and then slide down to the driver's side. He found the hood lock and opened it.

But the hood was stuck closed, probably because the vehicle was on its side. So Mr. Simmons had to climb back out—not nearly as easy as climbing in—to help budge it open. Finally, Roper was ready to get what they'd come for. He handed Simmons his pack.

"Don't let this drop."

"Not on your life," Simmons answered.

Roper was about to hoist himself up and climb in—when they heard something. He stared at Simmons in amazement.

"That sounds like a baby!"

Mr. Simmons, alarmed, dropped Roper's pack.

"Careful! Careful!" cried Roper, horrified that he'd just dropped it. When nothing exploded, he saw that Simmons had drawn a pistol and was cautiously peering in the van.

"What are you doing? That is a baby, I'm telling you!" cried Roper.

"That must be a toy!" Mr. Simmons said. "How could anything be alive in there?"

Roper yanked on his companion's arm. "Let me look in there, move aside."

Mr. Simmons said, "I am the police officer, if you don't mind. And this could be a trap. If there is a baby, it ain't alone!"

Roper, ignoring him, stuck his head in the van. "Hello? Anyone in here?" For response, an infant whimpered. Then silence.

"I'm going in."

"Let me get by. I'll go in," was Simmons's response, but Roper heaved himself up and climbed into the vehicle, carefully lowering himself so that his feet landed on the driver's door.

He tried to peer into the shrouded interior, and then, working his way between the front bucket seats and over the console, almost falling over in the process, he got into the second row of seats, planting his feet against the side for support. The infant's cry! Louder than before.

His eyes were adjusting to the dim interior. He saw a heap of clothing on the floor of the third row. Or was it a pile of blankets? Reaching his hands out, Roper pushed at the blankets—and felt something. A *body*.

"So what's there?" Mr. Simmons called. "Is it a baby?" With a terrible feeling of foreboding, Roper pawed at the heap, trying to find the opening, and then, *there*. Moving the blanket aside, he saw the white, lifeless face and staring eyes of a young woman, probably in her twenties. The whimper came again. Moving more of the blanket, he found the baby beside the woman's breast. She must have fed that child with the last of her strength. He shut the eyes of the mother but just in case, checked the side of her neck and then one wrist, hoping to find a pulse. Her skin was cold but not stiff. He covered her mouth lightly with one hand, feeling for breath—but it was no use—she was gone.

Simmons had been keeping up a chorus of "Well, what is it? What'd you find?"

In a flat voice, Roper said, "One dead girl." And then, with a slight lift in his tone, "and one living baby." The child let out a louder wail and Roper, his eyes filled with tenderness and concern, lifted the newborn carefully. The cord was still attached. Roper laid the baby back down to grab the blanket, but discovered it was mostly soaked with blood and body fluids. "Get the first aid kit and hand me some gauze–and—antibiotic ointment—and—something warm!"

"What?"

"You heard me! Gauze! Antibiotic goop! And a space blanket! Get them from the first aid kit."

In a few minutes, Simmons dangled the items behind Roper who turned and grabbed them. He cut the cord with his army knife, quickly doused the end with ointment and wrapped it in gauze. He hurried to open the space blanket and, pulling his bandana off, wrapped the baby in it, and then in the blanket. The child, eyes shut tight, whimpered louder.

He turned, baby in his arms, and saw Mr. Simmons gawking at him in astonishment. "What are you doing?"

"What does it look like? I'm saving this baby."

Mr. Simmons shook his head. "For what? Life after the apocalypse? You're gonna bring another mouth to feed to the compound? We don't know this child from Adam. We don't owe this woman anything."

"You were a cop!" Roper replied, hotly. "Weren't you trained to *save* lives?" He looked at him reprovingly. "You should have waited outside. Now we both have to climb out."

Mr. Simmons began hoisting himself up, pushing against the console for leverage. He grabbed onto the door frame and started pulling himself out, head first. Just as his head emerged, he cried, "Wait! Hear that?"

Both men listened. There was a moving vehicle on the road, getting closer. Mr. Simmons lowered himself, landing again with his feet upon the driver side door. So far the only vehicles they'd seen since the pulse were either horse-drawn, or foreign army trucks. Now and then some intrepid souls on bikes were seen but surprisingly few—and this was no bicycle approaching.

"We're in a gully well off the road," Roper said. "They ought to go right on by and never know we're here."

Waiting, hearts thudding, they listened. The ceiling of the van faced the road so they couldn't see what was coming but they heard it. Seconds stretched out, taut as a high-tension wire, while the noise grew—and then suddenly, it was past, the rumbling getting fainter.

"Sounded like one of those trucks," Simmons said. "We'd better wait in case there's more." After a pause he added, "And hope they're not on their way to attack the compound."

Roper eyed him gravely. "We'll see," he said.

As they sat in silence, the baby whimpered again. Roper rocked the child in his arms. Mr. Simmons stared. "You ought to put that thing back where you found it. Leave it with its mother."

Roper shook his head. "This is a child, not a thing; not an 'it.' And I'm not leaving it, so forget that idea."

Simmons grinned. "You just called it, *it*."

Roper made a face. "Fine." He unwrapped the baby, took a look and then wrapped it up again. "It's a she. I'm not leaving *her*." But that brief unveiling had not been to the infant's liking, and she now let out a much louder cry which led to prolonged crying. Roper went into fast-action rocking but he was bewildered. He shifted the baby first one way and then another, up and down, back and forth, but the crying continued.

"Now look what you did!" cried Mr. Simmons.

"It's your fault!" Roper returned. "Calling her an it!"

"What is *wrong* with her?" Simmons demanded, in agitation.

"There's nothing wrong with her lungs," Roper said. But suddenly both men were as disturbed as if they were under attack. The wailing of a newborn was about as alarming for them as a battle cry.

"Quiet her down! What if another truck comes by?" They were hissing at each other, trying to keep their voices down, though the baby had no such inhibition.

"She must be hungry!" Roper hissed.

"Should we give her some hard tack?"

"No!" Roper thought frantically. "Get my water! I'll give her that."

"Good! At least I'll get out of here!" cried Simmons. With a grunt he got himself up, and then, after shouldering the heavy door of the van, got it to swing open. Then, using the door frame for leverage, he pulled himself out and dropped to the ground. The van door swung shut with a bang. Suddenly, with unmistakable clarity, they heard the grinding sound of another truck.

"Great!" Simmons muttered. He took cover behind the van. The truck's approaching noise grew louder. Inside, Roper tried frantically to quiet the baby—to no avail.

Chapter Forty-two

ROPER

With the sound of the vehicle getting closer and a bawling baby in his arms, Roper got an idea. Seconds later, the baby's wailing ceased suddenly.

The truck's approaching noise grew louder—went by—and moved on. Simmons poked his head in the door. "How'd you shut her up?"

Roper lifted the bundle in his arms, revealing a little baby sucking contentedly—on his pinky finger.

Simmons was impressed. "Good idea."

Roper climbed carefully into the front and gingerly reclaimed his finger, hoping the infant wouldn't cry. To his relief, she yawned and went back to sleep.

"Get the airbag while you're in there," Simmons said.

"I'm not pulling an airbag with an infant in this vehicle," Roper returned. Checking now, he was surprised the bags weren't already deployed, for the van must have landed violently when it fell to its present position. But no, there wasn't a spent bag in sight. Simmons was watching, and his outstretched hands appeared in the door opening.

"Take Hope," Roper, said, as he deposited the baby into them. "And be careful."

"Take *hope*? What're you talking about?"

Roper stuck his face out the door, and grinned. "That's her name. Hope!"

As Simmons looked down at the baby who was starting to fuss, Roper added, "And give her your pinky finger if she cries." He gave Roper a look of perplexity before returning a gaze of distaste to the infant.

Sheesh, thought Roper. Hadn't the man ever held his own children? "Move away from the van!" he called, now. "Get at least ten feet out!"

Mr. Simmons did so, watching the little bundle in his arms. After staring down at the baby, he gingerly raised a finger and pushed down the material around her face. In a high, soft voice, he said, "Hey, little one, it's okay. Mr. Simmons gotcha."

Meanwhile, Roper started working the bolts around the steering wheel. In two minutes he'd removed the device, which was, like the others, round, and the size of a small salad bowl. He eyed the passenger side dashboard and called to Simmons. "I'll pull the passenger bag, too."

Passenger airbags were trickier, since there wasn't a single standard installation method. But he knew what to look for. He had to pull the CD player first, and then the glove-box. In a few minutes he had the device, and motioned for Simmons to come take both of them.

"Gentle!" he ordered. "Just put them down gently until I get out of here. Keep them away from the baby!"

He pulled himself up and out with some difficulty, deciding as he landed heavily on his feet not to bother with overturned vehicles any more.

Simmons was holding the baby awkwardly, looking worried. It would have been comical except Roper was worried, too. He was still trying to wipe out the image of the dead girl in the van, but he didn't want to let her down by failing to save her baby.

Simmons said, "What if those trucks are attacking the compound?" He held out the infant. "Here. She's all yours."

Roper blinked, thinking. "If they were attacking, we'd be hearing gunfire." He added, "Keep her until I stow these things. And then you're gonna have to carry my pack."

"What if the soldiers are just removing the obstacles we put out front? That would take some time."

"Jared put mines in that obstacle field" Roper said. "If they hit one, we'll know about it."

"I didn't hear about any mines! I think you're wrong—he *wants* to put mines there. But first we need to get enough of these things to blow out the bridge."

Roper zipped up his pack. It held twelve initiators. Putting it back down, he held out his hands for the baby.

"Put your pack on, first," Simmons said.

Roper shook his head. "Not if I'm carrying an infant. If you carry her, I'll take the pack. Otherwise, you get the pack."

Simmons handed over infant Hope. He picked up Roper's pack and would have swung it across his back, but Roper cried, "Easy! Don't swing the airbags, man! These babies are volatile! How many times do I have to warn you? Did you even *see* Jared's arm?"

Simmons nodded. "Yeah. Sorry."

◆

They kept to the side of the road or off-road where they could, as they hurried back towards the compound. The baby slept against Roper's chest, held up by one hand.

When they reached the culvert, they stopped to check it out. Roper wished now he'd stopped on the way out but he'd been anxious to get what they needed and figured they'd stop later. He hadn't counted on having a baby in tow while doing so. Carefully picking their way down the slope, they stood at the edge of the running stream that was there, peering around beneath the bridge to find the perfect spot to place the package that Roper was yet to prepare.

"There's plenty of room to hide an explosive," Simmons said. "C'mon. We're done, here. Let's get us some more initiators. I'd say we have two hours yet before it gets dark."

Roper said, "We have all we're getting. This baby's going home to get looked after." He looked down at the infant, who gave a soft whimper. Worriedly, he said, "She must be weak. We haven't fed her anything. I think she oughta be squalling."

"She was squalling loud enough before," Simmons returned. "Besides, newborns are supposed to sleep a lot. We can let her sleep while we finish what we came out here for."

"Life first," said Roper. "Baby goes back to the compound. Then we get more if we need to."

CHAPTER FORTY-THREE

ANDREA

I was taking down laundry from the line when I saw Mr. Martin hurrying down the hill from the lookout shack. His face looked serious. My heart skipped a beat. I thought it might have to do with Blake.

"Mr. Martin! What's up?"

He met my eyes, looking as if he was trying to decide whether or not to tell me. "Roper and Simmons are back."

I gathered up the clothes and tore to the house. Inside, I dropped them in a heap on the sofa. Mrs. Martin would chew me out for doing so but I didn't care. Roper was back!

Last time the men had been out, they'd returned through the woods on the side, so I ran back outside and made a beeline in that direction. I couldn't believe my luck! Roper was good at getting the gadgets we needed but his speed this time was really impressive! I was smiling with anticipation when I saw Lexie running out of the Buchanan's cabin. I came to an anxious halt. Was there bad news about Blake? But as she got close, I saw she was grinning!

"He's awake and okay!" she cried, coming up to me. Tears were brimming in her eyes—tears of joy. "I'm going back but I just wanted to let everyone know! Blake's awake and he seems fine! Tell the others, okay?"

"I will! And Roper and Mr. Simmons are back!"

She gasped in surprise and we smiled at each other and then hugged. "Praise God!" I whispered, as we embraced.

As Lexie ran back towards the Buchanan's cabin, I saw Mr. Wasserman coming. "So they're back?" he asked, rubbing his chin. He didn't look happy.

"Yes! Isn't it great?"

"I hope so."

"What do you mean?"

"Well; we saw two army trucks go by before, and I don't think there's any way those two could have collected enough initiators that fast. Let's hope they're not back with bad news." This dampened my enthusiasm but I was still secretly glad to have Roper back whether we had the gadgets we needed or not.

And then, coming off the horse trail, was Roper, Mr. Simmons, Mr. Martin, and Mr. Prendergast. Roper was carrying something— holding it carefully against his chest, but I had no clue what it could be. I ran up to him, a big smile on my face—and then halted in shock when I saw what he carried.

"Is that—?"

"A baby," he said, smiling gently.

Mrs. Martin was suddenly there. "Oh, my! Oh, my!" she said, taking the infant from Roper. "Where—How?" she asked, hardly knowing what to ask, first.

"Meet Hope," Roper said, proudly. But then he frowned. "I think she needs medical care. And food. Pronto."

"Tell me later, then," Mrs. Martin said. "I'll take care of her." And she whirled off with the baby towards the house while I stared after her in amazement. A *baby!*

Roper and I shared a hug, and then he kissed me with a quick touch on my lips. "I'm so glad you're back," I said. "But where's the mother?" I actually felt a tinge of jealousy towards this woman, whoever she was, because she'd allowed Roper to take her baby. She must have trusted him. Had he witnessed the birth? Did he know this woman? What if he'd known her since before the pulse? It was astonishing, all the jealous questions and thoughts that flew through my head at light-speed. I don't know what all I was thinking in that few seconds when I was trying to grasp the situation but he said, "She didn't make it."

"Oh." That changed everything. I went from feeling jealous to feeling ashamed.

Mr. Simmons spoke to Mr. Martin as we went towards the house and Roper told me how they'd found the child. "It was a miracle, if you think about it," he said. "If we hadn't come along when we did, the baby would have died with her mother."

In the house we found Mrs. Philpot and Mrs. Martin feeding the infant from a bottle. Someone had put away the clothing I'd left—probably Cecily—so I went to get a better look at the baby. Her face was so tiny! I can't remember Lily being that small, and now that I see a newborn, I realize Lily is actually large at nine months!

"So her name is Hope?" asked Mrs. Philpot. "Did the mother tell you that?"

"No. She was gone before we got there," Roper said.

Mr. Martin entered the room and said, "Good news." Smiling, he added, "Blake is going to be just fine!"

I'd forgotten to spread the word about Blake! After we cheered and the "Praise the Lord's" had all been said, Roper asked, "How's Jared doing?"

"Not much change there," said Mr. Martin. "We're still waiting."

Mr. Simmons had washed up and grabbed something to eat. Still chewing, he came into the room. "Listen folks, I know you're all baby happy. But we cut short our mission on account of that child."

Mr. Martin said, "I don't blame Roper for stopping to save an infant's life."

"We heard two trucks go by," said Mr. Simmons. "They were probably the same outfit that attacked us in the spring."

"We saw them," said Mr. Prendergast. "They went right on by."

"Look, I'm gonna play devil's advocate in Jared's place." He made a face. "It's a dirty job but someone's gotta do it." He swung his gaze at Mr. Prendergast. "So those trucks didn't stop. That's great! But they could have! We need to get our supplies and take that bridge out! Once we get what we need, then Roper can indulge his tender little feelings for a baby! But he interrupted our mission!"

Mr. Buchanan had come in at some point and was standing, listening. "We just got good word today," he said, "that Washington is back in business. From what I understand, they are mobilizing our forces. We should see help soon from our military!"

"*Sweeet* dreams!" said Mr. Simmons. "Who are they gonna mobilize? The National Guard? It's the Guard's job to defend home soil—have you seen any of 'em? They were just as unprepared as most folks when the pulse hit. Even if they survived this long, and even IF Washington is back up, how are they gonna mobilize a force they can't contact? They can't call up the Guard, when the Guard don't have phones!"

"They can pull men from around the globe," said Mr. Buchanan. "We've got bases all over this planet and there are people manning those bases. They can be pulled back to our shores."

"If they could be," he asked, spreading out his hands, "then where are they?" He looked around. "Let me tell you something about our global army." He paused, surveying the room as though to be sure he had everyone's attention. (I couldn't believe my ears. It was like Mr. Simmons was channeling Jared—except I don't believe in channeling, of course! But it was eerie how much he sounded like the ex-soldier.)

"One," he continued, "You don't know for a fact that the pulse wasn't global."

"We do know," said Mr. Buchanan. "We've got contacts in places that weren't affected."

"So they say," he retorted. "But regardless—most of the people the army has around the world aren't infantrymen—ground fighters. You got tech guys, and pilots—you got administration and commanders and navy. You got nuclear subs—they aren't gonna be a lot of help to us here in the heart of the country. You following me? We haven't seen any F-16s going by or F-15s or any aircraft capable of taking down an enemy target. We haven't seen any aircraft at all—or ANY sign of U.S. military, let's face it. We're on our own. And so we have got to think like the military and set up our own protection." He looked at Roper. "We should'a stuck to the mission and got the job done."

"We do have mines out front now," said Mr. Martin. "Soon as they hit one, they'll think twice about taking us on; and as for the bridge, we'll use what we do have and go out there tomorrow and take care of it."

"But see, this is what I'm saying—we still don't have enough of what we need. Take those mines out front—a few mines is not gonna stop the bad guys from demolishing this compound. If they've got the numbers, and if they got Miclicks—um, Jared said Miclicks are 'rocket projected explosive line charges,' and they clear an area of mines—then they'll get through. That's just plain battle facts."

"How do you know so much about battle facts?" asked Roper. "I thought you were a cop."

Mr. Simmons said, "I was. But I've spent a lot of time picking Jared's brain about these things."

Now I understood why he sounded so much like Jared—he was probably quoting him!

"You know," my father said. "Everything you're saying makes sense, Simmons, but here's something you left out. This little baby that Roper saved is no less important than any one of us."

"Saving one life is stupid when you do it by endangering forty." He looked down, and scuffed his shoe on the floor. "I'm just being Jared, remember."

"I think one Jared is enough for this compound," said Mrs. Martin, drily.

"Roper did not endanger us," my father asserted, calmly. "We've made it this far by God's grace and we'll make it longer by that same grace. God doesn't need mines and trenches and blown-up bridges to protect us—He did it in the past when we had none of those things and He can do it again."

"No weapon formed against me shall prosper," quoted Roper, softly.

"Right," said Mr. Martin. "It comes down to a matter of faith. So try having some."

Mr. Simmons nodded but looked sullen. "I'll have faith when Roper gets out there again at daybreak and comes back here with another dozen initiators."

"Why does Roper have to keep going for them?" I asked, before I could stop myself. My face grew hot so I knew I was blushing. But Mr. Martin said, "Roper, why don't you teach a few of us men how to do what you're doing? Andrea's right. You shouldn't be the only one responsible for collecting these things."

"Sure," said Roper.

Before the gathering broke up Mrs. Martin came over to us carrying little Hope and a small glass baby bottle. "Here you go, sir," she said to Roper, in a jocular tone. "This is sugar water. Just give it to her whenever she'll take it." She held out the baby but Roper just stared at her, dumbfounded. "You want *me* to feed her?"

Mrs. Philpot joined us. "She was a bit dehydrated but I think she's perfectly healthy otherwise; if you keep getting fluids into her, she'll be fine."

Roper swallowed.

"You need to learn how to do this," added Mrs. Martin. "She's your little girl, now."

Roper held his hands up. "Wait a minute. I only *found* her. I'm not the daddy!"

Suddenly Cecily was there. Smiling, she said, "Oh, that makes you the honorary daddy. Even Jesus was adopted by Joseph, so adoption is a God-approved idea."

Little Hope started to whimper. Roper stared down at her.

"Better feed her," I said, smiling.

"Would *you* want to do it?" he asked, hopefully. "I've seen you with Lily, you're good at this." I almost said yes, instinctively wanting to rescue him. But something made me hesitate.

"No. I want to see you feed her." He gave me a look of defeat and then proceeded to place the little nipple gently into baby Hope's mouth. She took it with gusto and started sucking. I led Roper to the sofa where he could sit with her. There, I almost couldn't see the baby through Roper's thick blond hair, long and curly, hiding her as he bent over her in concentration.

"She's good at this!" he said, in a moment.

"Sucking is a God-given instinct," I said. I watched him affectionately for a minute. "You look good with a baby." He pulled his eyes away and up to mine.

"Something tells me you'd look even better. Here." He tried handing her over but I laughed and said, "Oh, no. She's yours." I swallowed, found my courage, and added, "Of course, if I was yours too, that might change things."

He gazed at me with interest. "Are you proposing to me again?" He'd lowered his voice though most everyone had cleared out of the room. Only Cecily and Mrs. Martin were in a little pow-wow together, on their way out.

"I am."

His blue eyes probed deeply into mine. "I may accept that offer. Once you turn eighteen. If you still want to."

"Oh, I'll want to. But remember, I'll be seventeen in two weeks. Lots of women get married at seventeen."

"Not in this country."

"Yes, in this country."

"I don't know about that."

"Well, they used to. When life got hard—they did it to form a team. Think of the pioneers. We're just like them, now. Life is about survival."

"The thing is," he said, inching closer to me, baby and all, "if we got married, it could really complicate things. Give baby Hope a sister or brother and then you're talking real complications."

I blushed, frantically trying to think of the right thing to reply but my mind was coming up blank. After all, he had a point.

In a low voice, I finally said, "We can be careful."

He gave me an amused look. "Careful? Sweetheart, my mother always told me not to get married until I was ready to support a wife and kids. She never said, wait until you can support a wife. It was always a wife and KIDS. And now, more than ever, we have to expect kids to come."

"Why more than ever?"

He put his head back and gave me a mysterious look. "See, this is why you need to wait. You're not ready."

"Just tell me why!"

He lowered his head next to mine. "Because you can't exactly run out to the doctor for birth control, okay?" I laughed, first because my question had been stupid—the answer was obvious. But I also wanted Roper to think I wasn't embarrassed (even though I was).

"Okay, stupid question," I said. "But it's a risk I'm willing to take." I looked at him hopefully.

He was silent, thinking. "I'm not sure I am."

I stood up. "Okay. Whatever. Think about it. But this is a limited time offer." I grinned, and turned to go.

"Andrea!"

I turned back, smiling sweetly, my brows raised. "Yes?"

He looked down at the baby and then back at me. "You're not really gonna leave me here to take care of her on my own, are you?"

Again I smiled my sweetest smile. "I certainly am."

◆

That night I was called downstairs into Mr. Martin's study. He sat behind his desk with Mrs. Martin standing beside him. Someone was in a chair facing the desk—Roper! They all looked at me expectantly. Mr. Martin invited me to sit. I took the chair next to Roper.

"Where's Hope?" I asked.

"Cecily has her for the night," he said.

Mr. Martin got right to the quick. "Andrea, we've been discussing the matter of baby Hope; we all think she rightly belongs to Roper." He paused, waiting to see if I had a reaction, I supposed, so I nodded.

"And because of that, we've agreed—now, this is important, so listen up. We've agreed that IF you are READY, the two of you may tie the knot."

I gasped. Roper stretched out a hand and I grasped and squeezed it so tight he chuckled.

"Oh, my gosh!" I said. "I've been praying for this."

Mr. Martin smiled gently. "Hold on—I'm requiring marriage counseling first, and—."

"Wait a minute," said Roper. "Before we get to that." He turned to me, eyes large in his face. "I can't be responsible for the life of a child on my own. And I can't think of anyone else I want to be responsible for her with, than you."

I smiled happily. I thought he was done with his say. But he continued, "So—will you, Andrea Patterson, marry me, Jerusha Roper?"

I let out a breathy, "Yes!" His grip on my hand tightened, but I was so excited I got up and dropped myself on his lap and planted a big kiss on his smiling lips.

I turned around to see Mr. and Mrs. Martin grinning. Mr. Martin cleared his throat. "Now, as I was saying..."

We stayed for another half hour while the Martins gave us what amounted to a lesson—our first marriage counsel. We even had homework. We each had to write down ten things we believed to be true about the other person. Then we'd compare notes when we met back in the study with the Martins in two days.

For once in my life I didn't mind having homework. I'd be getting to know Roper better! And I'd do whatever it took to become his wife!

We left holding hands. Roper walked me upstairs where we stopped in the hallway outside my and Lexie's bedroom. Leaning against the wall, I looked up at him in the dim light that came from a small oil lamp he'd placed on the floor. I marveled that soon I'd be marrying this handsome man. It filled me with joy.

"Ready for sweet dreams?" he asked. He pulled me close and nuzzled his cheek against mine.

"They will be sweet, thanks to you." I tightened my arms around him. But he pulled his head back and looked at me funny. "Uh-oh, joke time," I said.

He grinned. "Nah. Listen: Never give up on your dreams. Keep sleeping."

"Hah."

He lowered his head and we shared a sweet, slow kiss. I didn't want it to stop but too soon it did. When I thought about the dangerous stuff he'd be doing with the airbag chemicals, I wished I could keep him with me forever.

"So tomorrow you're going to make the explosive?" I asked. "To blow the bridge?"

He nodded. "I'm gonna try."

"What if you don't have enough of the chemicals?"

"Then the bridge won't blow and we'll have to get more."

"I'll be praying we have enough. And for your safety!"

"So will I."

"Promise me you'll be careful!"

"I will."

"Andrea, is that you?" It was Lexie's voice, coming from the bedroom.

"Be right in!" I called.

"Good night, sweetheart," Roper said. He kissed me one more time. And then he picked up the oil lamp and was gone.

Excitedly, I told Lexie the news—Roper and I would be getting married! I expected her to be happy for me though also envious because she wants to marry Blake. She *was* happy, majorly happy—but there was no need for envy. Blake's close call with methane poisoning seems to have shaken things up, so now he and Lexie are allowed to marry also! We had so much to discuss, we stayed awake for ages planning our double wedding, and chatting about our guys and how much we love them.

"So how did he propose?" I asked.

Lexie said, "Well, we already knew we want to get married. Blake just decided to ask my dad again. So when Dad came to see how he was feeling—Blake asked him!"

Blake, I knew, had remained on bed-rest for the day. She paused. "Dad didn't seem surprised—not like I thought he would be. And he gave his consent—really fast!"

We figured the adults had realized that what I told Roper today is true. We are like modern pioneers. Our lives are hard, and may be short.

Before I fell asleep, I kept thinking about it. We *are* like pioneers but our frontier has post-apocalyptic dangers that the original pioneers never had to worry about, like foreign guerrillas or nuclear bombs. Then I remembered reading, *The Last of the Mohicans,* and how brutal some Indian tribes had been, not only to the Colonists, but to other Indians.

Humanity, I decided, has never had it easy.

CHAPTER FORTY-FOUR

RICHARD

With flames beginning to lick along the floor of the hallway, Richard continued to search for the panel to make the hidden door swing open. Fear—and heat—made him move fast, maybe too fast, for he made two passes along the floorboard and still hadn't found it.

"What are you doing?" His father screamed at him.

"Just leave!" Richard cried. "Get out if you want to!"

Tex had shown him how to open the door from the hallway, so he hadn't anticipated having trouble locating the panel. Behind him, his father started coughing. "Richie! What're you doing! We're gonna suffocate in here!"

"Get out!" Richard gasped. He hoped his father would go, abandon him to the fire, but he stayed. Richard's nostrils burned and his throat began to close—and his hand found the baseboard panel! His father grabbed his arm just as he pushed the panel, hard. When the wall slid open, he fell inside, just as hard and stupidly as he'd fallen into the hallway earlier. Only this time the landing was even worse, for his father was right on top of him.

Richard's first thought was to shove him off, remove the weight, but his father screamed, "My leg's caught! My leg! Open this thing!"

The door had automatically closed! Richard hadn't expected that. He distinctly remembered moving totes from the hallway through an open doorway which meant there was a way to keep it from closing—but he didn't know what it was.

"Get off me!" Richard cried. "I'll open it!"

"I-I can't move! I'm stuck!"

With a grunt, Richard pushed himself out from underneath the older man, but smoke was pouring in through the narrow opening where his father's ankle was caught. Unable to see in the smoky darkness,

288

Richard felt his way to the wall and searched again for the hidden panel on this side. His father kept crying, "My leg! My foot! It's caught! Help me, Richie!"

The ledge was dark to begin with. The thick smoke stung Richard's eyes, so that he had to use only his hands to find the rock that held the panel. As he searched, his father's cries made him realize that the door, being solid steel, might cut his ankle clean in half if he didn't get it free soon. Richard groped the floor around the door blindly, his hands spread wide—he couldn't miss that recess this time! And then he found it, stuck his hand in and pressed on the panel. His father gasped and drew in his leg with a shuddering breath, and a wider torrent of smoke and fumes poured in as well when the door slid open. In seconds it whooshed shut.

"Is your leg in?" Richard coughed and fell to his knees.

"Yes."

They remained there in the dark, taking in deep breaths, letting the toxic air move on into the tunnel and dissipate. He heard his father pulling himself around and into a sitting position.

After they'd sat in silence, drinking in deep breaths of air, his father said, "I think my ankle's broken. Is there a light in here?" Richard fumbled in his pocket, drew out his penlight and turned it on. His father, blinking, surveyed their position, taking in the walls of rock and dirt, and the wall behind them, which now appeared solid. He didn't even look at his ankle but searched the darkness in the other direction. "Where does this lead?" he asked.

"Nowhere. It's a ledge—drops to an underground spring. It's just a temporary hiding spot; something we hoped never to have to use." Richard felt as though his voice would somehow betray the fact that he was lying; so he added, "If it led somewhere, I wouldn't have come back into the house, that's for sure."

"Why did you come back?"

After a moment's silence Richard answered. "I heard your voice. I thought I wanted to see you." He paused. "I wanted to see my father. Not you."

"I'm still your father, Richard." A short silence ensued. "I know I've let you down..."

"Let's not talk about it, okay?"

A silence fell while Richard shifted his position, trying to sit back against the door. It was warm, but not hot—yet. If the fire burned away the wood paneling in the hallway, the steel door would be revealed. Hopefully, those soldiers wouldn't stick around to search the embers—and find them.

"So, what do we do now, son?"

The question pulled Richard from his thoughts. "Wait for the blaze to die down. When it's safe, we'll get out of here and then it's back to what life's been like since the pulse. Trying to survive; looking for a way to eat and stay alive."

"That's right," said his dad, strongly. "That's exactly right. You know what it's like, so you ought to understand I've only been doing what I had to do." Richard made no reply. He didn't understand. He saw a man who'd become ruthless, maybe even heartless. The world did require toughness, but not heartlessness.

His dad had been sitting with his two legs stretched in front of him. He slowly drew up the injured leg.

"You're bleeding!" Richard said.

"I am. Help me get my shirt off," he said, grimacing with pain.

"Wait, I've got some gauze." Richard retrieved his backpack, thankful that Tex hadn't taken it. He opened his first aid kit and took out some supplies. He examined the gash across the ankle—it was deep, ugly, and bleeding. He cleaned away dirt and some torn pants fabric using alcohol wipes—while his father sucked in his breath and tried not to groan. He sprayed the wound with antibiotic spray, causing another muffled gasp from his father.

Then, as he bound up the gash, his father asked softly, "So, where's your sister? Where's Sarah? You said she's safe. Why can't we go to her?"

"We can't. I don't know for sure where they are. We got separated after your attack," Richard lied. He paused. "You wouldn't be welcome anyway, like I told you. So just forget that idea."

"What about you? Don't you want to find them? Sarah, and those people you were with? Aren't *you* welcome?"

Richard didn't answer. He'd never go back if it meant leading his father to the others. He was already responsible for bringing the gang to the property; responsible, perhaps, for the fire that even now was destroying their wonderful cabin. He would not be responsible for leading anyone to the bunker.

"How far in does this go? What is it, a cave?" His father tried to peer past the area lit by the weak beam of the penlight.

Richard shone the light to the edge of the ledge. "It leads there—to a long drop. We don't know how far down it goes, but it's deep. And there's water at the bottom." He had to think of lies, talk fast, as if he was relaying facts; speak smoothly, and not as though his heart was pounding in fear that his father might discover the truth. He could not, must not know that they were a mere hundred or so yards from the bunker. As he finished the gauze dressing he added, hoping to bolster his story, "If you drop something from the ledge, it takes ten seconds to land, so it's far, and that water is likely hundreds of feet deep. This is all we've got. This little spot right here."

"Is that your drinking water?"

"We used a well. But it's probably the same water, yeah."

"You got any water we can drink right now, by any chance?" His sardonic tone conveyed that he didn't really hope as much, but Richard did have some in his pack. He found a bottle and handed it to his father.

He took it, saying, "A water bottle! Well, well. Just like the old days. Where'd you get this?"

"We refill them," he said heavily, remembering as he did that the seal on that bottle hadn't been broken, yet. His father would realize that in a second.

He grabbed it back, saying, "Me first, if you don't mind." He gave a loud, fake cough as he broke the seal—and hoped his father wasn't paying close attention.

"Thought I'd taught you better manners than that," his dad murmured. "Making your poor old man wait."

Richard said roughly, "You shot a man in cold blood and then talk to me about manners?" He handed him the now opened bottle. His father hungrily grabbed it and guzzled down a large amount.

Richard heard a muffled sound coming from the tunnel, from the direction of the bunker. He shifted uncomfortably. He hoped Tex wasn't venturing out for his sake. He knew Tex's first concern was to keep Angel and Sarah safe—so why would he leave the bunker? But who else could it be?

His father heard the noise. "I think we got company in here!" he whispered, sharply. "You figure there's any wildlife?"

"Yeah, they're called rats," Richard retorted. He hadn't actually seen a single rodent in his coming or going through the tunnel but he wouldn't have been surprised if he had. After a short silence, his father said, "Rats don't live in hundreds of feet of water."

"I'm sure they've got their tunnels," Richard said.

Grunting, his father started working his way towards the ledge, dragging his bad leg. In a soft voice, he asked, "Is she here, son? Is Sarah in here?"

Richard said, "Stay back! The ledge is dangerous. And she's not in here, there's nothing in here, I told you." His voice was harsh. "If you want to take a trip down the ledge to see what's down there, be my guest. Be sure to send me a postcard from hell."

His dad sighed. "Fine, fine." He groaned, softly. "Can you shine that thing on my leg again? You bound it too tight. It hurts bad, son."

Richard shone the light back to his father's injured ankle. It was swelling, and the gauze was saturated with blood.

"I didn't wrap it too tight. You're still bleeding!"

He wondered if the gash had gone clear to the bone. Even distrustful as he was of his father, Richard felt a pang of sympathy—and worry. "We need to rewrap it," he said.

"You got more of that stuff?"

"No. But I got an extra t-shirt."

Richard pulled the shirt from the pack. He had to hand it to Tex and Angel. They certainly knew how to fill a backpack. They'd thought of everything. He made cuts in the shirt with his army knife, and then tore it into strips. After unwinding the bloodied gauze, he quickly dabbed the blood and doused the wound again with the spray—making his father curse at the pain. Then, still moving fast, he wound strips of the shirt around the ankle, and taped it up with surgical tape. The area felt swollen and hot to the touch, but there was nothing he could do about that.

Another sound came from the tunnel, this time closer than before. "Can I borrow that light?" His dad asked. "I want to look over the ledge."

"Why? You can't see anything. You think we haven't tried to look down there?" He was afraid his father would spot the ladder, though it was so close up against the wall of dirt that it was unlikely; still, he didn't want to risk it.

"You know how it is, son," he said, nonchalantly. "Sometimes we just need to see things for ourselves."

"I'm not giving up my only light."

"What?" He feigned surprise. "You mean you don't have something better in that mighty pack of yours? Seems like you got a whole lot of provisions in there—you sure there isn't a real flashlight or battery lantern?" The tone was almost jeering, reminding Richard that he was right to distrust the man. His memories said this was his dad; his gut said it was a cold-blooded killer.

"No."

His father sighed but once again began to maneuver himself forward, moving with his hands, still dragging his bad leg.

293

"If you fall off that ledge," Richard warned, "Don't expect me to save you. I'm not risking my life to save your sorry neck."

His father stopped. Richard heard him heave himself back, still on his haunches. He worked his way back until he was again near Richard. He seemed to be breathing hard. "Look, Richard—if you don't want to take me to Sarah, okay, okay, I can understand that. But bring her to me. You can do that, can't you?"

He studied his father in the narrow beam of light. His eyes, almost slits, revealed nothing.

"I don't know. I'd have to find her, first."

"You said you knew she was safe! You can only know that if you know where she is!"

Here was the real man coming through, his anger so near the surface he couldn't keep it down. After a minute—when Richard didn't answer—his father added, softly, "They're close, aren't they?" He leaned his head back against the wall, but quickly yanked it away. "The wall's hot!"

Richard felt helpless and angry. The hallway paneling must have burned away by now. Would the secret door be revealed?

In a lower voice, as if he understood Richard's feelings, his father said, "I'm sorry, son."

Richard didn't believe for a moment he was sorry. He kept his light towards the man, somehow feeling he needed to keep an eye on him. His father scooted forward enough to lay flat on the ground; he closed his eyes. Richard suspected he wasn't feeling well. The gash might lead to an infection...but that probably wouldn't develop for hours, yet. In any case, the injury was taking its toll.

"I get the feeling they're close....*realllllll* close." He cocked open one eye and studied his son. "They're probably down here somewhere, huh? You say there's water down there—I don't hear any water. I say there's a tunnel or something." He nodded his head towards the drop. "If I could walk, I'd go exploring."

"You'd take a nice fall," Richard said. "I'd think you'd want to put that off."

His father peered at him. "What d'you mean?"

"Taking that fall. It'll lead ya to hell. You're heading that way anyhow, but why take the express?" His voice held all the studied nonchalance that his father used.

"Well, I didn't raise a fool, anyway." His dad closed his eyes. "I'm glad to know you're no fool, Richie." His father was the only one to call Richard by the shortened name. Somehow, it made Richard angrier.

"Don't call me Richie," he ground out.

His father cocked an eye open. "I've always called you that—."

"Yeah, when you were Dad. Stop calling me that."

Now both eyes were opened. "Richard, I'm your father. And I'm telling you, I will not rest until I see my daughter. Take me to her."

"Not an option."

"I know they're close!" he said, almost yelling, now.

"Keep it down! What if those guys are waiting in hearing distance? You want to lead the soldiers right to us?"

"They aren't coming back. They're long gone..." His dad looked away, but his face was hardened, his mouth set in a thin, tight line. "Listen. You will show me where my daughter is. I have the right to see her. I'm not asking you, Richard, I'm telling you. Show me where she is. You have to."

"I don't have to do anything," Richard said. "I don't even know you."

His father stared at Richard. After a tense silence that lasted seconds but felt much longer to Richard, he blew out a breath and shook his head.

"Okay, I get it." Loudly, he said, "You're a man, now! Your own man. You don't take orders, right?"

Richard said nothing. Grim-faced, he listened. He was sorry he'd shown himself to his father. This man, this conniving, manipulative man was a stranger to him. He wished he hadn't discovered the change in him, that he could remember him the way he used to be. It was better not to know what had happened to him than to discover the reality.

It was his own fault. He'd gone against Tex and insisted on seeing his father. One thing was sure: he would never reveal Sarah, or the McAllisters. It might come to a battle between him and his father but he wouldn't drag the others into it.

Another sound came from the tunnel, this one right below them. A timid voice, just loud enough for them both to hear: "Dad? Is that you?"

Richard's heart sank.

It was Sarah.

CHAPTER FORTY-FIVE

RICHARD

"Sarah! Sarah, baby!" cried his father, coming sharply to attention. "Where are you, baby?"

"I'm coming, Dad!" she cried.

Richard scrambled to the ledge and crouched at the top, peering over. He saw a glimmer of light below, rising higher. "Don't!" he cried. "Why did you come?"

The light wavered. "I want to see Dad, too!"

"It's not Dad!"

"Don't listen to Richard!" cried their dad, who was now on his hands and knees, dragging his bad leg. He reached the edge and peered over. Seeing the faint light, he called, encouragingly, "C'mon, baby! It's Daddy!"

The light began rising again and Richard hissed, "It's a trap, Sarah! We can't trust him!" He hoped that would stop her from coming up, but as he watched, a sudden sharp blow to his arm almost sent him reeling over the ledge.

"Shut up! You're scaring her! I want to see my daughter!"

Grimacing, Richard yelled, "Did you hear that? He punched me! This man claiming to be our father! He's a cutthroat—." His father shoved him so hard that his upper body appeared over the edge.

Sarah screamed. "Richard!"

"Don't make me do this, son, to my own flesh and blood—."

"Run, Sarah!" Richard cried.

"Leave him alone!" she screamed. She'd switched off her light, but her voice, clear and distraught, was now close.

"Don't worry about me!" Richard growled. "Just get out of here. Set the traps as you go. He's injured but if he tries to follow, they'll get him!"

"The traps?" Sarah asked, in a troubled tone. Richard sighed inwardly. *Oh, Sarah!* He'd made that up about there being traps to deter his father from following her if he somehow managed to get down the ladder.

"How is he injured?" she asked.

"I need you, baby! Richard hurt my leg! Almost cut off my foot!"

"It wasn't me!" Richard cried. "His foot got stuck in the door!"

"Come on up here," crooned their father. "Richard's been on the road too long. He's skewed in his thinking, sweetheart. I want to tell you, I am so happy that you're alive!" Sarah said nothing, so he continued, "I'm sorry about your mother. About Jesse. I wish I could have done something— "

"Why didn't you?" she asked.

"Sarah, go back!" Richard repeated, through gritted teeth.

His father threw his weight across him, pinning him down. "I gotcha, Richie."

When he felt ready, he'd fight his way off but not until the man was good and distracted. He didn't want to find himself head first at the bottom of the pit. He'd wait for the right moment. But if Sarah came up—he tried not to contemplate it.

"Why didn't you come back?" Sarah asked.

"Let me see you. Let me see your face, baby. I'll explain everything."

"Don't call me baby," she said, petulantly. "You never used to, so don't do it, now."

"Alright, alright; I see you two have grown up on me. I'm proud of you—."

"Don't believe him!" Richard cried. His father raised a hand to strike him but thought better of it. Sarah switched her tiny flash light back on—and caught the movement. Just as her father turned and saw her alarmed face—in that same split-second—she turned off the light and began descending back the way she'd come.

"I'm sorry, baby! I mean—Sarah! I just want to see you so badly! Richard's got some crazy ideas in his head—I don't know why."

"He shot his friend right in front of me!" Richard called, and this time Sarah heard the sound of an unmistakable blow and Richard's helpless grunt as he took it.

"Leave him alone!" she screamed, stopping on the ladder.

"You come on up here," returned her father, in a calm, cold voice. "And I'll leave him alone. But I can't let him keep me from seeing you. Can you understand that? I need you to see me, honey. I need you to know I'm still your father. I'm sorry for everything that's happened! Wish I could take it back, do things over."

"Like, starting with that punch to your son?" Sarah's voice was strident.

"Honey—this boy is deranged or something. I am still your father—and his—he needs to understand that."

"You never hit us before," she said, sadly. "He's right. You've changed."

"Maybe I have! Changed. But I'm still your father--I love you! I love the both of you. I can't understand why I have to argue this point!"

Sarah sniffed. Richard called, "Go back, Sarah! Tell Tex to set the traps if you forgot how!" He hoped that would convince his father that the traps were real; it would not be unlike Sarah, especially the old Sarah, to not know how to do such a thing; or even remember how if she'd been told.

"Richard, you keep quiet, now. I'm warning you—."

"Or what, Dad?" asked Sarah.

"Sarah—I'm waiting for you. I'm waiting."

There was no response, but Richard knew his sister was still on the ladder. She'd been fool enough to come, so she wasn't likely to turn back unless she got what she came for. But there wasn't a chance of her getting that, because she'd come to see Dad and he no longer existed.

He hoped Sarah would accept that. He said, in her direction, "Keep going! Tell Tex to set the traps! I'm not coming back, so it's okay."

"Don't be foolish!" Their dad cried. "Don't lock Richard out, whatever you do. I don't have to go with you—I just want to see you!"

"You did see me." Sarah's voice was still close—too close for Richard's liking. What was she waiting for? Why was she holding out?

"I want to really see you," continued the man. "I want to hold my daughter in my arms."

"Don't listen to him, Sarah! He will not let you go back if you come up here. *Unh*!"

"Leave him alone!" she screamed.

"Don't listen to *him!*" their father's voice rang out. "I miss you. Please, come on. Come to me!"

When there was nothing but silence their father said, "I know you're still there."

He inched towards the ledge. "If you don't show yourself, I'm coming down!"

Richard braced himself to seize the right moment to get free. He thought he heard Sarah climbing down the ladder; he sighed with relief.

"Richard, give me that penlight."

Richard grabbed his father's injured leg and squeezed. The man cried in pain, then cursed, then made a wild grab to hold onto Richard, but the boy was fast and strong and had escaped his hold. He moved away on hands and knees into the blackness. He knew there wasn't a lot of room but enough for him to outmaneuver an injured man.

Grunting, his father struggled to his feet. As he did, Richard quickly grabbed his pack and swung it on.

His father was coming towards him, dragging his leg. "It's alright, son. I know I've changed, but I'm not trying to hurt you, Richie."

Using his father's voice as a guide, Richard crouched on the balls of his feet, staying low but circling around his father. As the man continued in one direction, Richard crept around him. At the ledge, he felt for the ladder, found it and swung his legs over the side, landing his feet on the second rung.

He heard movement in the tunnel—Sarah was going back to the bunker. Good. He'd go with her, leaving their father—and then it struck him that he couldn't just abandon the man, could he? Leaving him on a ledge in the dark? What if he fell off and broke his neck? He couldn't be responsible for his father's death—no matter how bad the man had become.

"Don't play games with me, son! I'll do whatever you say, okay? If Sarah doesn't want to see her dad, fine. I'll leave her alone. I'll leave you alone. All I ask is that you get me out of here."

Richard had climbed down four rungs but he hung on, listening. He needed time to think. He didn't believe that their father would leave them alone. No, he'd get healed up and then find another gang—or meet up with the survivors of his old one—and he'd be back. He'd be back with one objective: To find their hiding place and use it for himself. Richard never should have brought the man this far. He knew too much. But what could he do? He had to think of something, come up with a plan.

"Rich. C'mon, Richie. You know I'd never hurt you."

"I'll be back for you," he said. That was all he was going to say.

"Oh, son!" His voice was pained. "You're not really gonna leave me here, are you? You're gonna leave an injured man alone in the dark? On a dangerous ledge?" He heard his father scrambling towards the edge. "What if I run a fever and start hallucinating? I might—I might just—throw myself off."

"Go to sleep until I come back," Richard said. "You're safe here. You'll be fine."

"Don't do this to me, son. You'll forget about me. Leave me to starve to death. I know you're angry about your mother. But you don't want to do that, son. You don't want that on your conscience."

"I won't forget about you. I'll come back to let you out."

"What if I come after you?"

"You wouldn't make it down here in one piece," he answered. "And I'm setting traps behind me. I wouldn't advise you to follow."

"Oh, son, you don't want that on your conscience, either." After a pause, during which Richard resumed his climb down, he added, "What kind of traps? What kind of traps, huh?"

"Animal traps. For animals—." In a lower tone, he added, "like you." When he reached the ground he lowered his pack, rummaged inside and took out some of the granola bars Angel had sent with him. For a moment he considered leaving his entire backpack to his father but it had tools in it, and he didn't want to give the man anything he could use against them later. Besides, he'd promised to come back for him and so he would. He'd have to. He'd have to show him how to get out, for one thing.

He climbed swiftly high enough on the ladder to get within throwing distance of the top, and stopped to shine his penlight. His father reacted immediately. "Rich! Rich! You're coming back to me? I knew you wouldn't leave your old man here to die!"

"Just take these," Richard called, and heaved the bars, one by one, over the top of the ledge. He heard movement and started back down.

"Wait a minute, son, wait a minute! Just give me a light. Don't leave me in the dark, Richie."

Richard hesitated. He needed the light to get back to the bunker himself unless he wanted to make the whole trip with his arms outstretched in the dark, tight tunnel. The thought of it made him uneasy. Without answering he hurried to descend the ladder. No sooner did he reach the bottom and was readjusting his backpack when he heard someone in the tunnel. A faint light revealed who it was. For some reason, she'd come back. Sarah!

CHAPTER FORTY-SIX

SARAH

I saw Richard at the bottom of the ladder and breathed a sigh of relief. Thank God my mini-flashlight still had power.

Richard held a finger to his lips, so I said nothing. But I was ready to cry! When I'd returned to the bunker, Tex and Angel never answered or came to the door! They hadn't let me back in! I'd had no choice but to return to Richard.

"Don't leave me here!" I heard my father's stern voice.

Richard came towards me, so I waited.

"Why are you back?" he whispered.

"I heard that!" yelled their father, from up on the ledge. "Who you talking to, Richie? Is that you, Sarah? You still here, baby girl?"

"Ignore him," Richard said, turning me back towards the tunnel.

"Wait," I whispered. "I couldn't get in. The door's locked, and Angel and Tex wouldn't answer when I knocked!" I could hardly keep from crying.

Dad's voice, louder now, accosted us. "You two having a pow-wow? How about having some pity on your old man? Sarah, Richard's planning on leaving me here to die!"

"What?" I said.

"Ignore him!" Richard no longer bothered to whisper. "He's exaggerating."

He took my elbow and urged me into the tunnel but I pulled away and stopped. "What *are* you gonna do about him? Did you tell him you'd leave him there to die?"

"No! Look," Richard said. "I'll think of something, but he can't stay here. He just wants to know where we're staying."

"But what'll he do?" I asked.

"He'll go back to his gang or find a new one," he answered "It's the life he chose." We fell into silence, concentrating on taking the twists and turns of the tunnel and moving faster along it than I'd ever done, before. I think we both felt there was a demon at our heels—our dad!

"Problem is, now he knows we've got something down here," Richard said. He turned to me. "Why did you come? Why'd you leave the bunker? I had him convinced there was nothing but water down here!"

I shook my head. "I don't know. We could hear the fire raging through the speaker. We heard you in the hallway. I knew you'd brought dad out of the cabin...and I wanted to see him, too."

"It's too bad you didn't hear when he killed his friend in cold blood—."

"We heard shots a few times...I was so scared that you got hurt." I sniffed. "I guess I thought I might be able to save you if you were hurt up there."

"Well, that was foolish!" he cried. Suddenly he stopped walking. "I have to think of what to do about Dad. You go on. I can't go with you until I know there's no possibility of him following us."

"But they wouldn't let me in!"

"Did you tell them you were leaving?"

I was silent a moment. "No."

"Sarah!"

"YOU left without telling them!"

"That was me! But why did YOU do it? They trusted you!"

"They trusted you, too!" I sniffed. "I didn't want them to talk me out of it. I couldn't tell them. I was worried about you and I wanted to see Dad."

We fell silent. I could *feel* Richard fuming at me, though.

"You shouldn't have done it," he repeated. "You shouldn't have left." He sighed. "Go back. Tell them I will make sure no one can follow."

"What if they still won't let me in?" The very idea filled me with aching regret. *Why, why, had I risked my new life—my new family—for the illusion of my old one?*

"If they won't, we'll be back where we started from—on our own. But try. Go back. I can't see them locking you out." I started crying in earnest. I'd really blown it! We both had. Tex and Angel had brought us to a place of safety and we'd gotten ourselves kicked out.

"Go on," Richard said, pushing me gently forward.

"What are you gonna do with Dad?

"I'll get him out of here and stay with him. I'll get him far away if I can."

"Come with me. Ask Tex what to do. He'll know."

Richard studied me for a moment. "I gave him my word that I wouldn't bring anyone to the bunker."

"But you haven't! He's injured, right? He can't reach us!"

Richard took a breath. "If you hadn't come, I could've gotten him out of here without his ever knowing about you or the bunker."

"I said I was sorry!"

"That's all? *I'm sorry?* How about, *I was stupid.* Or, *I wasn't thinking—as usual.*"

I bit my lip. "Like you were so smart to leave? If you hadn't insisted on going out for Dad, then I wouldn't have left, either!"

"So it's my fault that you were stupid?"

"Why are you so angry? I just wanted to see him, too! Why is it okay for you to see him but not for me?"

"Because I can take care of myself." But he took a breath and said, "I'm sorry. I just wish you'd stayed home."

Home! The bunker was new to us but I realized that for both of us, Tex and Angel *were* home. It didn't matter where we lived, whether a cabin, in a barn, or in a bunker. Somehow, we now belonged to them, and they to us. *If we hadn't totally blown it!*

He nudged me to start moving again. "Since you won't go by yourself, I'm gonna walk you back and then I'll take care of Dad."

I felt relieved he was going back with me. We could apologize to Tex and Angel and beg their forgiveness. Then, we could ask Tex what to do about our father.

The tunnel seemed endless. The air was thick and heavy. I felt tired, and scared, and inside I was mourning because at heart I suspected Tex and Angel were done with us and would never allow us another chance no matter how much we begged them for it.

And the truth was, I couldn't blame them.

As we neared the end, I said, "You know, he might just leave us to live in peace. We ARE his children."

"He won't. I've seen what he's capable of..." In a softer tone, he added, "He's a stranger now, Sarah. We have to accept that."

I felt suddenly breathless. Panic rose in my chest. "What if they won't let me in?" Tears filled my voice. "They took us in and their cabin got destroyed. And now, because of us, there's a threat to their bunker!" I felt a deep hopelessness. "If not for us, they could have lived in safety for months and months!"

Richard nodded. "That's why I have to take care of Dad. I have to make sure he can't come back."

"What does that mean, Richard? What are you gonna do?"

He shook his head. A look of determination filled his eyes. "Whatever I have to."

CHAPTER FORTY-SEVEN

SARAH

I touched Richard's arm. "Why don't we pray?"

From the dimness of Richard's penlight he stared at me and then nodded. "Why not?"

It wasn't a faith-filled response but it was far better than the way my brother used to scoff at my belief in Jesus. I closed my eyes, concentrating. We faced a daunting challenge. No, two challenges; we had to keep our dad from finding the bunker, and we needed Tex and Angel to soften their hearts and let us back in!

"Lord—." I began. Richard nudged me.

"Wait. Listen!" No sooner had the words left his mouth when I heard it. A distant sound, like something else was in the tunnel and it hadn't come from the direction of the bunker.

"What was that?" I asked.

Then, from a long way off, probably from the very beginning of the tunnel, we heard a faint echo. "I made it! I'm down!"

Richard and I froze, staring at each other. Our father had made it to the bottom of the ladder? With an injured leg? It seemed ludicrous. I had to huddle tightly against that ladder when climbing up or down. I couldn't imagine an injured man doing that successfully.

"You think it's a bluff?" I asked. "How could he have climbed down with his hurt leg?"

"It's no bluff," Richard said. "I'll bet he used upper arm strength. And a demon's determination."

Don't set your traps! I'm your father! And I'm coming!

Richard blew out a breath. "This proves he's crazy! He's injured, he's moving in complete darkness; and he thinks there's traps. He's gotta be nuts to do this!"

"He's desperate," I said. "And what traps, by the way? What were you talking about?" I'd been puzzled about that ever since Richard first mentioned them.

He frowned at me. "There *are* no traps! That was a bluff! I wanted him to think he'd never make it if he came after us."

He peered behind us into the blackness. "Go on, get out of here. Get back to the bunker. You're almost there. I'll take care of Dad."

"No, come with me," I said, flicking on my light. I wasn't about to keep going on my own in the dark. Ahead of us was one of the many sharp twists in the tunnel. "Dad's injured; and he's just one man! If we can't get in the bunker, he won't be able to, either!"

"I can't let him try," Richard said. "I promised Tex I wouldn't lead anyone there. I'm keeping my promise."

"But what will you do to stop him?"

Richard held up his pistol. "I'll make him turn around."

I stared at him in consternation. "Are you really willing to use that? On Dad?" It wasn't a question as much as an accusation.

Richard drew in a breath. "Look, it's not your concern! Go back to safety and don't worry about me—or Dad."

Faintly but louder than before, we heard him. *Richie! Sarah! I need your help!*

"He's moving too fast," Richard said. "With his injury, he shouldn't be moving that fast. And all the turns down here—you'd think that would slow him down."

"Why did they put so many twists and turns down here, anyway?" I asked.

"To make it slower going for anyone not familiar with it. And, if you do happen to have a pursuer, they can't shoot you from far away." After a pause he added. "Like right now. I'm glad I didn't give him my penlight."

I hated the idea that Richard was turning back to face our father. I *really* hated the idea that it might end with one of them getting hurt! God forbid!

"Be careful!" On an impulse I gave him a hug. It felt easier and easier for me to show affection to my brother. That was one thing the pulse taught us—how to love one another. He hugged me back and murmured, "Tell them you're sorry. Tex and Angel love you—they'll let you back in."

"I don't know," I said. "I don't know if they will." He gently pushed us apart.

"They will." He flicked off his light. "I'll go back a little ways and wait for him to reach me. IF he can." As I went ahead, I turned to look back at him. His outline was already swallowed up in blackness.

"God protect you!" I whispered, loudly.

"You, too." His words came floating from the darkness. I continued on towards the bunker but my heart was crushed. I'd been so stubborn and ungrateful to Angel and Tex. Why hadn't I just prayed for Richard and my father—and waited? I'd heard my dad's voice and I couldn't erase the desire to see him. Now I'd seen him, alright—and wished I hadn't!

I'd wanted him to be my *good* father, the one who'd take care of us, just like the old days. I wanted him to say it would be alright and that the pulse hadn't ruined life forever.

I guess what I really wanted was a chance to go back into the past. If I had a caring dad, it would remind me of life before, when we weren't worried about where our next meal would come from, when life wasn't so black.

Even more, in my heart I longed to live in a normal world again. Go to school, watch TV, and talk to my friends on a cellphone. It was a reckless impossible longing that made me leave the bunker. I saw that now. Even if my dad was his old self, he couldn't erase what happened to the world!

I'd hoped he would make everything okay. And somehow all he'd done was make everything worse. Now he and Richard and I were stuck in this subterranean limbo-land—not as dangerous as life on the road, but not a life at all!

DEFIANCE

I rounded a final bend and came face to face with the outer steel of the thick door of the bunker. Unless Tex and Angel opened that door, Richard and I were on our own again—only this time with a madman on our heels.

Chapter Forty-eight

ANDREA

As I write, Roper is in an open shed building the "package" (as Mr. Simmons calls it). We hope it will destroy the bridge over the culvert. I am fasting and praying for him. Why? Jared is dying—from just ONE of those initiators! Roper is mixing them all together—I can't stand to think about it! If *one* could kill a man? I can just imagine my sweet, beautiful guy getting blown to bits by what he's doing!

He is such a peace-loving, easy-going person. Why does HE have to be the one to do the dirty work? This morning I was getting ready to mop the kitchen floor and I asked Mr. Martin that question when he was going past. All he would say is that Roper had the most experience handling the explosives than anyone else except Jared.

"He's a worship leader!" I said. "He was an intern for children's ministry! Not a-a—."

"A munitions expert?" he prodded.

"Right! He's not a munitions expert!"

"He's the closest thing we've got." Mr. Martin touched my arm. "We're all praying for him. Try not to worry." As he walked away he turned back to look at me. "Council meeting tonight. Don't miss it."

LATER

Glory to God! Roper and Mr. Simmons went back out today and planted the "package" beneath the culvert—and it worked! We all heard a giant boom when the bridge blew. Everyone stopped what they were doing and gave a great big cheer! The men returned and said it worked like a charm, breaking the bridge abruptly in the middle. They're confident it's impassable! We went, in a long procession—all except Jolene, Jared's mom, who is sitting with her son in sickbay—to view the damage. Even the children were allowed to come because we surrounded them and were armed to the teeth. That is, the men, the lookouts, and we women. (Blake seemed to move a little slower than in the past but I wouldn't mention that to Lexie for the world. Besides, I could be wrong about that.)

Anyway—what a beautiful sight! There was still dust and smoke settling on the fallen blocks of asphalt and concrete which had landed in various places in the stream and the surrounding banks. The road itself ended in a jagged edge, like a scar after an injury.

It looked wonderful. Mrs. Wasserman pointed out the destruction to her children like she was showing them an ice cream truck. "We can't be attacked from this direction now, children," she said.

But Mrs. Philpot shook her head. "We just made our world a little bit uglier than it already was."

Roper replied, "And a whole lot safer."

She stared at him. "Maybe."

Anyway, today Roper is everyone's hero. (Of course, he's my hero *every* day.)

EVENING

So we had a council meeting. I dread these meetings because scary stuff always comes up but at least Roper and I got to sit together with baby Hope—like we're a family.

Mr. Simmons was so annoying. Honestly, he seemed to be channeling Jared again.

"Little good it's gonna do to have that bridge out on our east," he said, "when we still got a perfectly good road on the west. Any army truck—or tank—can just go around to the other side to come at us."

"One thing at a time," said Mr. Martin. "Taking that bridge out was necessary. Now we can focus on taking further measures."

"We *must* get more chemicals to tear up the road to the west," said Mr. Simmons. "It won't be enough to stop a tank, but it should deter those army trucks."

"How are you suggesting we 'tear up' the road?" asked Mr. Buchanan.

Mr. Simmons spread out his hands. "Jared explained it to me; all we have to do is burn out a few holes and then plant a package in the holes. We cover the holes up again, put a pressure plate on there and then all you need is the right pressure—say, an army truck—and *boom!*"

"You said, 'burn' a few holes," said Mr. Philpot. "How do you burn holes in blacktop?"

"It'll melt with enough heat," said Mr. Simmons. "Just need some fire."

"If it won't stop tanks, why bother?" asked Mrs. Wasserman. "They're the new threat, right? It sounds like a lot of dangerous work, and if they have tanks—."

"And mortars," put in her husband. "We don't stand a chance. Those tanks'll roll over a busted up road like ice skates in a rink; and if they have mortars—."

"Wait," said Mr. Martin, holding up his hands. "Most of the sightings are of army trucks—not tanks. Just standard army trucks. So we're talking about men, artillery—."

"RPG's," added Blake.

"Yup, RPGs." Mr. Simmons nodded. "And maybe grenades, maybe even some mortars."

"But mostly it's men, rifles and machine guns we have to worry about," insisted Mr. Martin. "And these are things a busted up road CAN deter. I don't think they'll come at us on foot. As Jared said in our last meeting, we're not an important target in a military sense." He swept his gaze across the room. "And we *do* have obstacles and mines out front. I don't think they'll want to bother with us."

"Okay, we've got obstacles out front but not on the sides of the property, and no barbed wire—and how *many* mines?" Mr. Simmons asked.

"Three," said Mr. Martin.

"We need more!" he snapped. "Rest assured they will have us out-numbered when it comes to artillery AND manpower. And we need fortifications on the sides—mines, at least—so that if the enemy does advance, they'll stay in a kill zone—right in front of us. If we can ensure that they enter there and be ready to hit 'em with everything we've got when they do, we should be able to deflect an attack."

Lexie spoke up. "You mean putting mines by the woods line?"

"That's how we come and go," Roper said. "You can't cut off all access."

"If we leave the sides unprotected and they come at us from the woods on foot—and they can do that in a mile-long formation—we wouldn't have a chance," said Mr. Simmons.

That brought up the old argument about why hadn't we finished building a fence yet. Marcus said, "Fences won't keep out foreign guerrillas—not even marauders. People can climb, you know."

"We can put barbed wire on top, and motor oil over it all," said Mr. Simmons.

"Motor oil?" asked Mr. Prendergast.

"Sure. We'll siphon it. Makes the fence a stronger deterrent." He looked at Mr. Prendergast. "Ever try to climb a fence doused in oil? It ain't easy. Plenty of time to pick off the ones trying."

"Look, we're already building a stone wall," said Mr. Martin. "We don't have fencing. Let's focus our efforts elsewhere."

"What about civilians?" asked Cecily. "When I came here, if there had been mines in front, I'd have been blown up, I guess."

The Philpots nodded. "We would have, too. If we're going to plant explosives in the road, we have to post warnings. And have you thought about this? Since we have no word that the United States is officially at war, then putting out landmines—or bombs that work like mines—is probably a felony."

Simmons took a deep breath and ran a hand through his hair. "Look, people, are you gonna worry about the law when there is no rule of law? Let me tell you what to worry about right now—staying alive. Staying alive long enough to see a return of law and order. But until that happens, we can't just play nice. Our enemy will not play nice."

"If one innocent person gets blown up by a mine, it will be blood on our hands," said Cecily.

Mr. Simmons didn't blink. "Innocent people die in war. We can't *fail* to raise deterrents because it might put someone at risk. If we don't do this, WE are at risk!"

Mr. Martin looked at Cecily. He said, almost apologetically, "When armies move trucks around, they're moving supplies and building arsenals. I hate to say it, but we have no choice but to do what will keep us safe."

Mr. Simmons added, "You can't worry about a few civilian casualties. Heck, some countries count on killing civilians as part of their war plan. Iraq and Iran sent hundreds of scud missiles into each other's capital cities during the Gulf War just to terrorize the populace. In 1986, witnesses said the Iranians tied children together and SENT them across Iraqi minefields—a human wave—to clear the way for their military machine. They did the same thing with foot soldiers, with old men and boys. Those kids, and those men, were sacrifices for what Iran called, 'the greater good.'"

"WE are not Islamists!" Cecily cried.

"No, and I'm not saying I approve of that method," Mr. Simmons continued. "It was brutal; I'm just saying we have to accept that sometimes there is collateral damage; and it can't be helped."

Mr. Martin said, "We can pray for protection for civilians. But I agree that the best defense is a good offense. A good offense is defiance to tyranny."

When silence fell, Mr. Simmons said, "For all we know, these are Iraqi or Iranian soldiers we're up against; and their track record shows they will use anything, even chemical warfare, to subdue an enemy."

"Chemical warfare was banned during the Geneva Convention," said Blake.

"Not fully," piped in Marcus. "It was just a first step. And Iraq is known to have used chemical weapons in this century against Iran." He looked around, "A ban wouldn't stop them, anyway."

"Any more objections?" Mr. Simmons asked, looking around the room.

"What kind of chemical weapons?" asked Mr. Prendergast.

"Mustard gas and nerve agents," Marcus said.

"What about biological weapons?" Mr. Prendergast added. "Do we need to worry about those?"

I had no idea what that meant but the very sound of it—*biological* weapons—filled me with dread. Looking around the room, it seemed that everyone felt that way, for a deep silence fell and faces were grim.

Mr. Simmons said, "Jared wasn't worried about biological weapons. They're the least dependable and therefore the least useful in a military sense. They're hard to control—they strike friends and foe; so I don't think we have to worry about that. Or chemical agents, unless we see the enemy wearing gas masks." He looked at Mr. Martin. "I'm thinking we don't have a lot of gas masks, do we?"

"That would be correct."

"Do we have *any?*" Mrs. Wasserman asked, in a frightened tone.

Mr. Martin seemed reluctant to answer but he said, after hesitating a few seconds, "I have enough for only my family and two extra. And they would go to Andrea and Blake—they're part of our family. They're all taken."

I sat there with mixed feelings. I was honored that Mr. Martin considered me family but what about Roper? He would soon be family, too.

Mr. Buchanan said, "We have enough for our family including Blake, so that leaves one extra."

"That should go to baby Hope," Roper said loudly.

"She'd have to grow up really fast for it to work for her," Mr. Buchanan said. People began talking around the room. I thought I heard tones of indignation because there weren't enough gas masks to go around. "The extra one should go to you," I told Roper.

He gave me a funny look. "I would never accept a mask if every woman and child didn't already have one." My heart swelled with pride. Roper is such a noble soul!

"We don't have any good options if we want to survive, do we?" I asked, sadly. "Either kill or be killed."

Roper said, softly. "That is war." He took my hand. "*Next to a battle lost, the greatest misery is a battle gained.* The Duke of Wellington said that."

"Look, folks, we still have the safe room," Mr. Martin called, loud enough to get everyone's attention. "And it's well sealed; we also have no indication that biological or chemical warfare has been or will be used against us. So calm down—and let's get back to order here."

Mr. Simmons said, "I'll go along with that. So, let's focus on what we DO know and continue building our strength until we can rest secure that our stockpile is going to equal theirs."

Marcus shook his head. "That is not gonna happen. We can't ever hope to equal what they may have."

Mrs. Wasserman said, sadly, "If they are trying to take over our country, I don't think anything will really stop them."

Mr. Martin said, "The forces we've seen aren't the kind to take over a country. For a full take-over, you need armored forces; they require huge amounts of airlift and sea-lift and ground transport—all we've seen is standard army trucks. And maybe a few tanks."

He went to the center of the room and held up his hands for order. "Listen up. I've read that in past wars what decided the outcome of many campaigns wasn't size or might—it was superior strategy, and tactics. Even *audacity*. You see, the fight is about leadership and discipline, not just artillery and manpower."

"Well, there you have it," said Mr. Simmons. "We're sunk. We don't have superior strategy. Our side isn't outfitted like the foreign army and with Jared down, we even lack leadership."

"That is not true," said Mr. Martin, strongly. His face was stern as he looked from Mr. Simmons to the rest of us in the room. In a firm clear voice, he said, "We have demonstrated a strong resistance to the enemies that have come against us in the past; we have resisted their attempts to destroy us. We have resisted marauders and gangs. And now, if we follow through with our plans—." He looked at Roper. "And get these additional explosives built, we can do more than just resist. We can do more than just fight back. We can make pre-emptive strikes and stop them in their tracks before they get anywhere near this compound. We CAN use superior strategy. We've already begun to do this by taking out that bridge. When we tear up the road, we will show that we've got more than resistance. We will show that we've got *defiance*! We've got audacity! And," (to Mr. Simmons) "I beg to differ with you, but, if I may say so"—he bowed his head slightly—"We've even got leadership." As an afterthought he added, "And I don't mean just my leadership. We've got *God.*"

Approving murmurs went around the room, and for the first time since the discussion began, I saw looks of relief on people's faces. Mrs. Martin beamed with pride. Then Mr. Buchanan stood and started clapping. One by one we came to our feet and clapped. Roper had baby Hope on his chest and remained seated but he let her balance there while he clapped, too.

As the applause died down Mrs. Martin spoke up. "I want to thank Roper for saving Hope," she said, in her soft southern accent.

I was happy to hear her say that. Roper is the sweetest guy in the world but Mr. Simmons certainly didn't appreciate him. She looked pointedly at Mr. Simmons. "Even if we do need more initiators. That little baby's life," and she stopped, searching for words. "Gives *me* hope." To Roper, she said, "You gave her the perfect name! She is a reminder that we do have hope. Life will go on."

Roper nodded.

"And to that end," said Lexie's dad, "I want to stress again, we can't just think in terms of defenses only. Not anymore. We have to think offensively."

"I've always been offensive," whispered Roper to me, with a wink.

Mr. Martin's eyes glimmered at Roper. "We need to get more offensive. No more resistance only, folks. Resistance will get us dead or captured. Defiance will keep us free."

CHAPTER FORTY-NINE

LEXIE

Blake and I sat near Andrea and Roper at last night's meeting. I got to watch how cute they were with baby Hope! She was the only child in the room this time besides Emma Wasserman. I wish that watching the baby might have kept me from hearing all the bad news Mr. Simmons kept throwing at us but it didn't. (Like, we don't have enough mines, and taking out the bridge wasn't enough, and we need to blow up the road, etc. etc.) But when my dad talked, I actually felt hopeful. He thinks we can be defiant, not just resistant—I like that idea. Because injustice and tyranny has always needed to be defied!

We are the new American patriots, modern pioneers—and it is upon us to defy the foreign soldiers and keep our nation intact!

Blake told me not to worry before we went our separate ways last night but I kept thinking about things Mr. Simmons mentioned, like "biological warfare," or "mustard gas and nerve agents." They echoed in my mind as I went up to bed. I was sure I'd have bad dreams.

But when I got to our room, Andrea had baby Hope with her. She was just sitting on the bed staring at her. Smiling, I sat down next to Andrea and stared at Hope, too.

"Isn't it funny how everyone loves to stare at a baby?" I asked.

Andrea didn't even look at me but kept staring as she smiled gently and said, "Yeah." After a pause she added, "She's so tiny, but everything about her is perfect. Perfect little fingers and toes, her little mouth and nose and eyes—a perfect tiny human! I just want to memorize every contour of her face, every little yawn." She looked up at me. "If I'm not careful, I won't only be in love with Roper! But maybe that's perfect, too."

"You've got an instant family," I said.

I don't know how long we would have sat there staring at Hope but Cecily and Mrs. Philpot came in carrying a big wicker basket lined with cloths.

"Are you taking her?" Andrea asked.

Cecily smiled. "No. We're giving you and Lexie a baby pep talk."

Andrea laughed. "We don't need a pep talk. We already love her!"

Mrs. Philpot smiled. "We're going to teach the two of you how to care for a newborn."

Cecily added. "You're both getting married, right? Even if you didn't have Hope here, this lesson will come in handy."

"I've been helping take care of Lily since she was born," said Andrea. "I don't need a lesson."

"We'll see," said Cecily, with her warm smile. It was after eleven o'clock, but the ladies sat and talked to us for nearly 40 minutes. We learned not to sleep beside Hope so we wouldn't suffocate her (which is why they brought the basket). Andrea could keep the basket beside her on the bed for now but when Hope got bigger, she'd have to have her own bed. We were told exactly how to make baby formula using storage food (the recipe was taped to a kitchen cabinet) and that we should always use a freshly cleaned glass bottle.

"Where did we get baby bottles?" Andrea asked.

"From Mrs. Wasserman. She still had them from when Emma was little. Thankfully, she included them when they brought supplies from home." They gave us two pacifiers which were used but sterilized. They moved aside things in Andrea's top dresser drawer and put baby clothes in—hand-me-downs, of course. Ruefully, I realized that Hope would only know hand-me-downs for her whole life unless things turned around or if Mrs. Schuman decided to sew her a bunch of clothes.

They gave Andrea a handful of alcohol wipes and showed her how to clean the umbilical cord. They gave us piles of rags, calling them "diapers," and safety pins, and showed me how to pin up a diaper so it would stay in place—Andrea already knew how to do this. They said to try and give the baby plenty of time to be without a diaper while the weather's warm. "It's good for her skin," Cecily said.

"And will help avoid diaper rash," Mrs. Philpot added. They warned us strongly, in fact, that we had to do everything in our power to keep Hope's little bottom clean and dry or diaper rash would result. They said they'll demonstrate how to bathe her in a few days.

Cecily put a hand on baby Hope and one on Andrea before they left, and prayed over them. She prayed for "mighty blessings," and said "God didn't bring us this child by accident; but with HOPE for a future, and in HOPE of her salvation." She prayed, "God, keep this baby—and this whole compound—safe. Protect our little Hope, Lord, because You are our mighty hope. You alone are true hope. And we trust You. Amen!"

Cecily's prayers always feel so fitting, so right. It's like that scripture about good words being like apples of gold in settings of silver. (That's from Proverbs, I think.)

I asked God to help me pray like Cecily—so people listening will be blessed by my words—and because God answers prayers of faith!

Anyway, right after they left the baby woke up! All of the handling the ladies did, unwrapping her blanket and showing us the cord, changing her diaper—did not wake that child. But now she was up and fussing. I volunteered to get a bottle.

Down in the kitchen I found the stash of clean glass bottles and nipples. I used the recipe to give the right amount of water with a little bit of sweetened, condensed milk. Mrs. Philpot says the baby will need more nutrition eventually but since she's so little, this would do for now.

She also said it was a blessing we still have a cow and that raw milk is full of nutrition. Andrea asked, "Isn't it dangerous if the milk isn't pasteurized?"

I smiled, because Andrea now drank raw milk herself but she'd been resistant to it when she first came to the compound. Mrs. Philpot said, "Pasteurization actually destroys all the beneficial bacteria and microbes that God put in milk. Raw milk is truly healthier than pasteurized."

"I told you!" I said.

"But even for an infant?" she asked, ignoring me.

"Especially for an infant," Mrs. Philpot said. "Like mother's milk, it will help stimulate her little immune system and make it stronger. One study," she said, looking thoughtful, "found that infants who were fed raw milk had 30% less chance of developing respiratory infections."

As I was making the bottle and thinking about this, I heard low murmurs coming from the living room. I recognized my dad's voice and went to listen. I figured my mom would be there, too. I wanted to tell her about our baby education and how Andrea and I had officially been given the care of Hope.

But when I got to the doorway I heard Mr. Simmons's voice. Then my dad said, "Okay, I understand. You don't think we have a good chance of deflecting the next enemy attack."

"We may be up against way more than we can handle. We need machine guns and mortars, or antitank missiles, and some *real* artillery." My heart sank at his words. I thought Mr. Simmons agreed we could come through a confrontation if we followed his suggestions. I thought there was real hope!

My dad held up a hand. "You need a little faith, Simmons. If we take out the road and make our peripheral defenses to include offensives like the mines, it's a whole lot better than what we had before, and we beat the last attacks. The Lord will protect and help us again."

Those words made me feel better. I continued listening as my dad asked, "What do you think they've really got in those trucks?"

"Like I said before," Mr. Simmons replied. "Guns, gear and men...."

I slunk away after that, not wanting to hear any more. It shook my confidence that Mr. Simmons still felt we were so vulnerable—but my dad was right. We needed to put our faith in God not guns, or mines, or anything of our own.

I let Andrea feed the baby, ignoring her when she asked, "What took you so long? She's been crying for ages!" I grabbed my Bible and climbed up to my bunk. I turned to Psalm 91, my favorite psalm. Slowly, the Word sank into my soul. I determined that like the Psalmist, I *will* say of the LORD, "He is my refuge and fortress; my God; in Him I will trust." Worries about chemical or biological weapons fell away. Concern about Mr. Simmons's pessimism fell away. I gave my worries to the Lord.

And I didn't have a bad dream.

But sometime in the middle of the night a loud wailing, which turned to screaming, woke us. I heard a lot of commotion from the first floor and jumped down from my bunk. "Stay with the baby," I told Andrea. "I'll find out what it is."

Mrs. Philpot flew past our door holding a lantern. In another moment while I hurried to throw on a robe, she came past again in the opposite direction, this time with Cecily. "What's going on?" I called, after rushing into the hall after them. My heart pounded with the thought that we were under attack before we'd had a chance to destroy the road out front!

Cecily skidded to a halt and turned. "It's Jolene. She's beside herself. Her son is dead."

CHAPTER FIFTY

LEXIE

Mr. Clepps says Jared died quietly in his sleep. He's taking the loss hard as though he is to blame. He says it was probably massive blood loss more than anything else that caused his death. We all know there was no means of giving Jared a transfusion. (And get this—when Mr. Clepps arrived, he introduced himself as "Mr." Clepps—not Dr. Clepps—making us think a D.O. was a step down from a medical doctor. But now we've learned the truth—a D.O. is a licensed physician, a doctor of osteopathic medicine. My dad says Mr. Clepps wanted to give up medicine due to a tragedy that happened a long time ago with a young person under his care. That's why he goes by mister and not doctor. And that's why this is so hard for him.)

I wish we had more details about what happened with that young person in the past but now I understand why he was reluctant to operate on Jared (though D.O.s are licensed to perform surgery). Poor Mr. Clepps!

LATER

My mom told us to pray hard for the doctor so he'll stop blaming himself for Jared's death. And to call him *Doctor* Clepps because, "He deserves the title, and we should show proper respect, especially now with Jared's loss."

Jared wasn't my favorite person on the compound—not by a long shot—but I'm sad he's gone. Andrea told me how he threatened Roper when they were out on the road—that was truly evil! But I'm still sorry we've lost him. He was the brain behind our defense strategies. He was the reason we blew up the bridge. He was the reason we repelled that last attack by the soldiers, and he's the reason we may beat the next one.

Even Andrea is sad. "I ought to be relieved because of how he threatened my fiancé," she said. (She smiled. "I love using that word, don't you? We are engaged women!") But then her face grew serious. "But I am sorry. We needed him here." In yet a quieter tone, she added, "I think I'll even miss him."

I will too. We both felt badly that we distrusted Jared—even if he earned that distrust.

Jolene is being kept under house arrest in her cabin. She was so hysterical last night that she woke the whole household and then went screaming through the cabin area, yelling that we'd killed her son! Mrs. Philpot says she can't be reasoned with and until she comes to her senses, she'll have to stay in her cabin. We'll have a viewing of Jared today (no embalming of course, so it all has to be done quickly). My dad will give a brief word about Jared's contributions to the compound; we'll pay our respects, and then he'll be buried.

I hope Jolene pulls it together. My mom says funerals—and especially open casket funerals—provide "very important psychological closure. As painful as they are," she told me, "they serve a function for the mind."

This will be the third grave on our hilltop. Jared's passing makes me think of Mrs. Preston, our elderly neighbor, who is buried up there; and I know Andrea can't help but think about her dad, the second person we had to bury there.

I am heavyhearted and strangely worn out. I hope this day passes quickly. In my "past life" (before the pulse) that hilltop was a great place. I often rode Rhema up there and then dismounted to sit under a tree and enjoy the view of our surrounding countryside. Now, it holds a lookout shed.

And graves.

CHAPTER FIFTY-ONE

SARAH

As I stared at the steel door of the bunker I felt torn. I wanted to be inside, safe and sound with Tex and Angel. But suddenly I realized I couldn't go back yet—even if Tex and Angel opened that door. Why hadn't I thought of this? I could reason with Dad in a way that Richard couldn't! Fathers had soft spots for daughters—didn't they? And Dad really *wanted* to see me. I felt sure I could talk him into leaving us alone. Besides, what alternative did we have?

The only way to be certain Dad wouldn't return is if he couldn't—if he died! I couldn't let Richard be responsible for that! What had he said? That he'd deal with him and I shouldn't worry? Well, I was worried! How else could Richard "take care" of Dad—unless he meant to be violent? It was suddenly so obvious! I was still afraid that Tex and Angel might not let me in the bunker but I couldn't find out, not yet. I had to get to Richard before he did something he'd regret forever!

◆

My flashlight must have warned Richard I was coming. When I turned the bend and saw him waiting for Dad just like he said, he was glaring at me.

"Why are you back?" His whisper was tense and impatient.

I hurried to his side. "Because I don't want you or Dad to get hurt."

Richard sighed. "Sarah—!"

"I might be able to reason with Dad better than you!"

"You won't!"

327

"You don't know that. I can *make* him listen. I'll tell him he has to forget about us and leave us alone."

Hey! Dad's voice, loud and menacing, came through the tunnel.

I looked at Richard and gulped. "He's getting closer!"

Richard grabbed both my arms. "Not a word! Not a single word!" He snatched my flashlight from me and moved me towards the dirt wall. "Stay back. Don't let him know you're here. *Don't trust him.*"

"Maybe if we trusted him, he'd be trustworthy!" I shot back.

"You're dreaming. He's cold-blooded. You heard him order our deaths!"

"He didn't know it was us!"

He took my arm again. "Don't get weak on me! You've already made this a lot more complicated than it needed to be!"

"He's desperate. He's not thinking straight. We need to remind him that he is our FATHER. He HAS to care about us."

I'm coming! I hear you!

Richard flicked off my flashlight plunging us into blackness. I reached for the wall to get my bearings.

"I'm armed!" Richard yelled.

That's okay. I hear you—I'm coming!

Even though I felt sure I could remind my father of his duty as a dad, my skin began to crawl at the sound of his raspy voice. As he got close, I could hear labored breathing and that he was dragging his injured leg. I couldn't see him but I felt the weight of his presence. He stopped, as if to catch his breath.

"I know you're close!"

Richard tugged me to follow him so I did, holding onto him, shadowing his every step in silence. I knew when my father moved by the sound of his leg dragging. We circled around to get behind him, and so we began a cat and mouse game, moving along the dirt walls, staying in the wake of Dad's movements. We followed the sound of his heavy steps and dragging leg—and kept out of his reach.

"Hey." He came to a stop. "You're my own flesh and blood—I can feel you." He sniffed. "You gotta help me. Help your old man."

I felt terrible—I *wanted* to help him—that's why I'd come back. But Richard gripped my arm like a vise, letting me know he did not want me to speak.

"Richard, I heard you talking to someone," Dad said. "Sarah? You're here, aren't you, honey?" He paused, still laboring to catch his breath. "Remember how you used to make me tea at night?" He took a deep breath. "You'd make it just the way I liked, and we'd sit at the table and play a game of rummy. Remember that?"

Richard's grip tightened yet again. Dad's voice got further, so I knew he was on the move. He seemed to be groping against the wall, searching, shuffling and scraping towards the bunker. Without meaning to, I shifted on my feet and dislodged a pebble. His voice turned to us, sharply.

"Is that you, sweetie? Sarah? Don't be afraid, honey! I'd never hurt my own flesh and blood." I would have gone to him but Richard grabbed me the second I moved.

"I don't want to leave without seeing your face. My little girl." Dad's voice was suddenly tender. Richard's grip grew painful. I tried to loosen his fingers but he held tight.

"Just let me see you, baby. Just once." Dad's wheedling tone broke my heart. And then suddenly a hand went over my mouth, and I knew Richard was afraid I'd speak and give us away.

"I can't leave without seeing you. Why do you think I came this far? In my condition? I know you're close—I've already lost Mom and Jesse—and Richard's gone *crazy,* or something. I need to see my little girl. Take pity on your old man!"

Tears trickled down my face, over Richard's hand. I sniffed.

"There you are, baby!" My father's voice moved towards us, and Richard pushed me ahead of him, which meant we were now leading away from the bunker.

"Move!" he said.

"Wait!" my father cried. "Just wait up a sec." Richard steered me against the wall so that my back was against it. I tried to flatten myself there while our father approached heavily, breathing laboriously.

"Look," he gasped. "I'm dying! It took everything I've got to get this far." I heard a thud, and realized he'd slumped to the ground.

Immediately Richard tugged me to follow. We moved away from Dad. After we'd turned a sharp bend, he turned on the flashlight and led us farther along the path back towards the ledge. I felt a rush of relief with the light, although now I could see the darkness ahead, the dank walls of earth at our sides. The air was stagnant. I wiped my eyes, stifling the sob I wanted to let loose. I heard Dad's voice again, still calling me. After we'd turned another corner, Richard whispered, "He's working you! Can't you see that? He wants us to take him in. He's not dying. You *can't* trust him."

"Sarah!" came my father's voice, fainter now, but pleading. "I want to explain! Tell you what happened. It was never my intention to leave my family on their own. I tried to get back..."

This was what I'd wanted to know all along—why hadn't he come back? I whispered, "I want to hear this. What happened to him."

Richard held my arm. "He's playing you," he said, now wearily. "He didn't give me any spiel about trying to get back. He just kept insisting he's innocent. You have to accept the truth—he doesn't care about us."

Tears kept coming. "So what'll we do? We can't go to the cabin because it's burning. And Dad's between us and the bunker. We're stuck here!"

"We wait." Richard said.

"Wait for *what*?"

"To see what he does. Maybe he'll turn down that last decoy tunnel. Maybe he'll give up and head back this way."

"He's in complete darkness!" I said. "He might just stay lost in these tunnels!"

"He found his way to us earlier," Richard said. "I think he'll find his way back."

That gave me an idea. "We can make noise and draw him back."

He rubbed his chin, thinking. "Yeah, I like that."

Just then we heard pounding; and my father's voice. "I know you're in there! I knew you had a shelter down here! Now, c'mon and open this door!"

Richard slammed the flashlight into my hands. "Here. He found the bunker! Dying, my foot! He's banging on the door! C'mon!" I ran after him but fear filled my heart. What was Richard going to do when we reached Dad?

Ahead, Dad's voice chilled me: "If you don't let me in, I'll have to go back up there. The soldiers will find me. If they find me, they'll find you, too, because *I know where you are.*"

My heart skipped a beat. His words doused all my secret hopes that he was the loving father of my past. Richard was right! Dad should have felt protective of us, maybe even happy that we'd found shelter. Instead, he was willing to expose us to the soldiers! What kind of man would give away the location of his own children—out of spite? Only a sick, selfish man.

Richard stopped and drew his pistol. He checked that it was loaded and cocked it. Holding it out and ahead of him with both hands, he slowed his steps as we crept towards the last bend. When we turned it, we'd be face to face with our father.

CHAPTER FIFTY-TWO

SARAH

I couldn't believe Richard had drawn his gun. I grabbed his arm. "You can't shoot him! He's your father!"

"I just want to get him away from the bunker!"

"Now that he's found it, he won't leave," I said. "Not willingly."

"That's why I need my pistol," Richard said.

"He'll force you to shoot him," I said, crying again. "*Think, Richard! You'll be torn by guilt for the rest of your life.*"

Richard sighed. "Sit down, Sarah. Wait here while I go talk to him."

"Give me your gun, first."

"No way! He's armed, too!" We hissed at each other, trying to keep our voices low, but my father had no such concern.

I hear you two! C'mon, you can return to your shelter! I just want to rest up and get well, and then I'll leave you, never to return!

Richard said, "That's bull. He'll say anything to get in the bunker."

Sarah, don't close your heart to me, honey! I am your father!
Fresh tears came.

"Don't fall for it," Richard said.

My mouth was parched, my palms sweaty. "Oh, man! Do you have any water?"

"I gave it to him."

"Oh—that was nice." It was the first indication I had that Richard still cared for our father. "Look, I think you're over-reacting. It's DAD, Richard. He's not going to hurt you. Give me your pistol."

"I'm not over-reacting! He's crazy! Remember that guy in *The Shining?* Lost his mind and tried to kill his wife and his little boy?"

"He didn't try to kill you!"

"He almost knocked me off the ledge. That would have done it."

I shut my eyes and prayed. "Lord, please protect us! Please make my dad safe again! Let Richard be wrong about him!" When I opened my eyes, Richard was gone.

"Move away from the door!" I heard his voice from around the bend.

"Rich! C'mon, son, show me how to open this thing! We can survive together—be a family, again."

"Not gonna happen. Move away from the door!"

◆

Inside the bunker, Tex and Angel watched an infrared security monitor, grimly.

"He did it again—led an enemy right to us."

"It's his father," Angel said. "You can't blame them for loving their father."

"That don't sound like love to me," Tex said. "And I do blame him."

Angel touched Tex's arm, indicating she wanted a hug. He pulled her up against him. "We'll be fine, sweetheart," he said. "They will not get in."

Angel nodded. "I know. But listen—I want you to get them back." Tex pulled away to stare at her in consternation.

"I want Richard and I want Sarah," she continued. "I love them, hon! And so do you! It'll be lonely here with just the two of us. We've let them into our hearts and—."

"Darlin', how do you expect me to get them back while their father's out there? I am NOT letting that man step a foot inside this bunker."

She shook her head. "I know. We'll have to shut him out." She stared plaintively up into Tex's eyes. "We'll go out armed—he'll be outgunned."

"YOU are not going out there," he corrected.

Angel sniffed. "I can help—."

"YOU are not going out there," he repeated. Richard's voice made them look up at the monitor.

———————◆———————

"Dad, I'm telling you—if I were to let you in there, you'd be shot the moment your foot crossed the threshold. There's a man in there—like *you!*" Richard lied. "He won't take any chances with a stranger! I'm telling you—leave now, while you can!"

"Oh, son, I can't get out of here," he answered. "I'm too weak….my leg..."

I stepped around the bend. "I'll help you get out!" I said.

Richard had hooked his penlight to his belt. Its weak halo revealed my father, his back to the door of the bunker, leaning against it. His eyes fastened on mine.

"Sarah! I knew you'd help your old man!" He smiled at me and my heart fluttered. It was the first time I'd actually been this close, face-to-face with my father in eight months. Everything Richard told me, all the bad stuff about Dad fled from my mind, and all I felt was a powerful sad longing for my father to love me. I ran to him and fell into his arms, while Richard, sighing, stood to the side.

"It's all right," my father said, softly, circling me with one arm. "That's my little girl. Thank you. Thank you for letting me see you." He stroked my hair and then I looked up at him.

"I've missed you, Dad!"

"I know it, honey. I've missed you, too!" He stared at me for a long moment and then kissed my cheek. I felt a surge of joy. I wanted to hug him for a long time but he shifted away and we drew apart, though he kept one arm about my middle. He turned me around to face Richard and then pulled me back against him.

"Okay, Rich. Here's the deal," he said. "If you value the life of your sister, you are going to open this door behind me."

"Dad!" My heart lurched in my throat. I tried to struggle away from him but his hold tightened.

"Don't worry, sweetheart," he said. "Your brother needs a little wake up call, is all. He's not thinking clearly, here. We're family and we need to stick together."

"Move away from the door," Richard said, in a cold voice.

"Are you gonna open that door?" Dad asked, calmly.

"I can't open it until you give me space."

My father, holding me close, moved us away from the door. He was limping.

"Don't try anything," he said. "If you go in there without us, you will not see Sarah alive again."

"Dad!" I was crying uncontrollably. I felt as though my father had just died—like I'd lost him for the second time, and it reminded me how we'd lost Mom and Jesse. And now Angel and Tex would never let us back, either. I'd lost everyone and everything I loved except Richard! And he would never forgive me for how stupid I'd been to trust this man.

I was overwhelmed with sorrow—and anger. I couldn't believe my own father was using me as bait!

"Keep going," Richard said. "And turn around. I can't let you see how I get in."

"If you sneak in there without us—."

"I won't!"

I wondered what Richard was going to do. He didn't know a secret way of opening that door! My father and I were about three feet away from it now. And then suddenly we heard sounds from the inside. Richard and I froze in amazement, knowing it was the sound of the locks being opened. My father flung me away to hold out his gun with two unsteady hands.

As the door began to swing open, I screamed, "Don't come out! He has a GUN!"

But the door swung wider and Tex's tall frame appeared. I lunged at my father to prevent him from shooting Tex but a shot rang out, and then another. I was too late! We fell to the ground, and I huddled there in confusion and horror, sobbing—and too afraid to look at Tex, who must be dead.

And then Tex's voice, same as ever, said, "C'mon, Sarah. Angel's waiting for you." I gasped and looked up at him. He reached out a strong arm and drew me to my feet.

"I thought—!" I couldn't finish the sentence.

Tex gave me a rueful grin and moved aside the nape of his shirt. "Body armor. I didn't forget it this time. Thanks for your help, though. I don't think he would've missed me, if you hadn't done something." I threw myself into Tex's arms, crying pathetically.

Only then did I understand that the first shot must have been Tex's.

And that my father was dead.

CHAPTER FIFTY-THREE

SARAH

I felt less grief over my father's death than I expected. Maybe because I'd been grieving his loss since the pulse. Or perhaps due to his treachery—using me as bait! Either way, my sorrow about the man in the tunnel paled next to my joy and relief to be with Tex and Angel again.

The McAllisters are the most wonderful people I've ever known. Angel took us back without a word of recrimination. I'd expected anger but she gave me a firm hug, and then Richard. She shushed me when I tried to apologize. She was so, so, sorry, she said, about our dad. She fed us and told me to take a shower—a shower!! A trip to the past. She had tea and dessert waiting when I was done and in clean clothing.

"Where's Tex and Richard?" I asked, as we ate a slice of cake together. (It was NASA food—tasted great!)

"They're cleaning up outside," she said, gently. I understood what she meant: they were taking care of my father's body. Tears welled up in my eyes. Sitting there in the clean, orderly bunker, bright with electric lights, I felt a world away from the nightmare in the tunnel. But deep inside I was haunted, as though the nightmare would never leave me. The nightmare was my father! And he'd been willing to let me die, if need be, to get into the bunker. I reminded myself that he hadn't been in his right mind.

"That wasn't my father," I said. Angel looked at me with sympathetic eyes. "The man out there was crazy—he wasn't our dad. He was like, a shell of the man we used to know."

She put one hand over one of mine. "I know, I know that," she said. "I'm sorry."

"No—I'm sorry. I'm really sorry I ever went out there! I needed to stop Richard from being responsible for— "

"I know," she said again. "But I want you to hear this, Sarah. We're going to move on and put the past behind us. No apologies, and no regrets. Tex believes it's only a matter of time now, until our military from around the globe gets organized and will reclaim this country. Life will one day return to where we can live up there like we used to."

"But the cabin's all burned up!"

She nodded. "I know it. We have another home where we lived before the pulse. It may have been looted, of course, but maybe we can fix it up. Otherwise, we'll rebuild."

"You can do that?" I asked, wiping my eyes. "Won't that take a lot of money?"

Angel sipped her tea with a thoughtful expression. "We have an overseas account." Suddenly, she smiled. "Unless Switzerland was taken out too, we should have more than enough!"

It might take me a long time to recover from what had happened with my father in the tunnel, but I could tell Angel was doing better. Her old optimism, that I'd always so enjoyed, had returned.

LATER

Richard and Tex came back all hot and dirty. Said they'd buried Dad in one of the decoy tunnels—but evened out the dirt so as not to leave a mound.

Richard has been silent but less troubled than I expected. He and Tex seem to have made their peace. Like I said, Tex and Angel are the two most wonderful people I've ever met. If there's anyone to live in an underground bunker with, it's them!

Angel said when the cabin is safe, that is, when the fire's all died out and it's not too hot to enter, Tex and Richard will go up and make sure the hidden door in the wall is still hidden. Once that's done, they may take a look among the survival garden for produce but then it's back down here to the bunker. And we'll stay here until we no longer can. We're family.

CHAPTER FIFTY-FOUR

ANDREA

With Jared gone, the compound seems to have lost the feeling of relative safety we try so hard to maintain. It's like we've gone from yellow alert to red. The council agreed Roper has to get more airbag initiators so we can tear up the road like Mr. Simmons said. (It was Jared's idea originally, and so it may as well have been written in stone. Jared's ideas for defense—and offense—are now like law!)

Even so, I've hardly had time to worry about our threat level— I'm too busy taking care of Hope and Lily. But I asked Mr. Martin to let me and Roper get married before they send him out again. He said, no! He wouldn't explain why but later Roper did, gently. I found him outdoors, where he'd been helping mix mortar for the stone wall. Hope was sleeping and Lily was with the rest of the children, so we got to be alone for a few minutes.

He stopped and wiped his hands off, and then we strolled, holding hands, towards the playground. When I told him that Mr. Martin had turned down my request to hurry the wedding, he said, "I won't be gone long, for one thing, so there's no point in rushing it." But he smiled and leaned over and kissed my cheek. "If the worst happened, and I didn't come back—you're better off without us being married."

It dawned on me that what he meant is that if we got married, I could get pregnant right on our wedding night—theoretically. And I wouldn't want to be left with a baby coming. Since I do have the care of Lily and Hope already, I figure he's right.

But—babies or no babies—I still want to get married, and the sooner the better. I just love Roper so much! And I can always find a woman to help with Hope. No matter how busy they are, it's a rare woman who won't drop everything to hold an infant. They're eager to get her and even take turns sometimes. Mrs. Wasserman, whose youngest, Emma, is only three, vies to hold baby Hope, too.

Right now she sleeps most of the day. And changing her isn't bad since she's so little. But when she gets bigger? Let me tell you, Hope is going to be one of the youngest people on this planet to get potty-trained. Without disposable diapers, it is not negotiable!

LATER

Cecily held the baby during dinner. Afterwards, she came over to me and Roper who were sitting together in the living room. She deposited the baby into Roper's arms.

"You need to stay in touch with your daughter," she said. Her eyes sparkled at us. Roper took the infant and fussed over her a little, but Hope wanted to go back to sleep. When she was settled snugly against his chest, I asked, "So, why *did* you name her Hope?"

He put his head back. "I didn't even think about it," he said. "Her name just came to me, because there she was, alive in that van— what were the odds of that? We might have passed that van and gone to a hundred other ones. But she was there, and she was alive. Hope was alive."

He met my eyes. "Life seems fragile right now—but the Lord brought her to us for a reason, to remind us that with Him there is always hope."

I craned my head over and kissed him lightly on the cheek. He gave me a sweet look. I thought he might be having a romantic thought, and I waited with anticipation for him to whisper a sweet nothing. He said, "So. Do you want to hold her, now?"

CHAPTER FIFTY-FIVE

LEXIE

Andrea and I will both be married ladies in two weeks! It's hard to believe. Blake, my wonderful Blake, will be my husband! He's been his usual self for weeks now, though he was easily fatigued after the methane poisoning. Slowly he has regained all his strength.

Our chores haven't changed, but Andrea and I are "walking on air." Days just seem to fly by while we wait to become wives to the men we love.

I don't think anyone is sad to see summer behind us. Our garden work through all those awful hot days has paid off with lots of dried food which is stored away for the coming winter. But it's also a milestone—a whole season gone by during which we suffered no attacks! Not once did we have to rush to arms at the heart-pounding blare of an alarm! Life feels almost—normal. The new normal, of course, with no electricity. But I'll take life without electricity any day over life under attack—even with electricity. And now, since the bridge over the culvert is destroyed (and with plans to make the road on our west side impassable) we feel fairly safe.

What better time to hold weddings?

LATER

I can hardly contain myself. So much good news! Dad heard on his rig that U.S. military planes have been sighted over a number of mid-western states! We even heard that our nearest air force base, which is Wright-Patterson, is re-opening! There are reports that some of those army trucks have been blown to bits by our planes, and even that supply drops for civilians are happening! This could be the beginning

342

of a turn-around for our country—the best thing to happen since the pulse.

And there's more—Dad finally heard from an old contact from California. There weren't any nuclear strikes! There *were* attacks by terrorists, who blew up oil rigs all along the coast. They sent plumes into the sky which people mistook for nuclear mushrooms! The rigs are still burning and there's been a lot of environmental damage. But no nuclear hits!

The compound had a party this evening to celebrate all the good reports, including a time of thanksgiving to God. Afterward, Blake and I talked while he helped me tidy up the kitchen. "What I don't get," I said. "Is what took them so long? I mean, they're here—so where have they been all these months?"

Blake nodded. "I read a book about the war in Iraq; it took our military months and months to mobilize enough air power to take on the Iraqi air force. It takes months just to get stuff where you need it. I mean, the big stuff. Armored vehicles. Missiles. And authorization— every movement, every flight, every ship—the military does nothing without written authorization. The grid going down probably slowed them down tremendously—just like everyone else."

"They should have a protocol to follow when communications are down!"

Blake said, "I know. But in the Iraqi war, there was literally *tons* of paperwork just due to the authorizations needed for every pilot, every pilot's flight, every missile they armed for; *every little thing.* The military, remember, is government. And government is never efficient."

"But when we've needed them so desperately? Don't you think they could've been efficient just this once?"

Blake held the dustpan for me as I swept up dirt but he shook his head. "If they couldn't be efficient when we had everything working, all systems go, why would they be more efficient now with communications down?"

"But my dad said this wasn't a global event. Our military around the world could still communicate. And why haven't we had help from other countries? Our allies?"

Blake emptied the dust pan and took the broom to put both into the closet. "The military depends on chain of command, and chain of command means you've got to have that paperwork. And as for allies? I think we have way more enemies than allies. And even if our allies— say, Great Britain, or Israel—wanted to help, they'd have to be cautious, keeping most of their resources available for threats to their own borders while this mess is going on."

"They could have sent food and supplies!"

Blake came over and took my hands. Gently he pulled me towards him and then gave me a hug. "We don't know that they didn't." He spoke softly into my ear, while I rested my head on his shoulder. "They would have dropped shipments over population centers, the cities. We'd never know about it unless we got word on the radio."

"I think we would have got word if they were doing that."

Blake drew us apart. "Let's sit outside." As we went out, he said, "Our country has always given a lot more than it's ever gotten back from the worldwide community. And I'll bet our military has been busy keeping its eyes on the rest of the world so that we don't get an opportunistic large scale attack. I mean, if they're keeping all their big guns aimed at Russia, for instance, or China, then they aren't focusing on home soil. Much as we'd like to believe otherwise, even our military is limited in what it can handle at one time. They can't keep other nations in check and still carry out rescue missions, or food delivery, or searching out the enemy on our soil. I think they've been more worried about the big guys who are capable of doing even greater damage—like taking over the country."

"But these guerrilla soldiers seem to want to do that, too!"

Blake replied, "They're trying to demoralize us. But they aren't dropping A bombs."

I frowned at Blake, though he probably couldn't see my face. "Not yet."

344

Outside, Roper and Andrea called to us. They were sitting on the hill path where the grass was worn and flat, star-gazing.

"Hey, you guys tired?" Roper asked, when we'd joined them. We sat down ahead of them so we were a little lower on the hill.

I asked, "Why?"

"Because you gotta be tired to appreciate my bad jokes."

Andrea laughed. "I always enjoy your jokes!"

"Well, tonight's jokes are exceptionally poor."

"Try us," I said. Blake threw an arm around me. I felt so comfortable and happy. Blake and I were close, and Roper and Andrea, my best friends, were right there, too. It was a beautiful, starry night and the air was warm for late September.

"Don't say I didn't warn you," Roper said. "Okay, did you hear about the yoga expert who refused Novocain during a root canal? He wanted to transcend dental medication."

Andrea chuckled appreciatively. Roper continued, "Plan to be spontaneous. Tomorrow."

"Ha!" I said.

"I'd kill for a Nobel peace prize!"

Blake turned and shook his hand for that one.

Roper continued, "Did you hear that photons have mass?" He waited a beat. "I didn't even know they were Catholic."

"What day of the year is a command? March 4th."

Roper continued to entertain us with bad jokes that made us chuckle or groan until it started getting chilly, sometime around ten.

"Whose got Hope?" I asked Andrea, when we were finally upstairs in our room.

"Your mom!" She smiled at my surprised expression.

"Justin is still a handful," I said, picturing my little brother. "I wouldn't think she'd want Hope for a whole night after dealing with Justin all day."

"Newborns are special," Andrea said. Then we talked about how the news that morning of U.S. airplane sightings was reassuring. For the first time, I really did have hope for the future.

EPILOGUE

ANDREA

We had a beautiful October day for the weddings with a deep blue sky and a warm sun. Lexie and I were now both seventeen and feeling quite mature.

Lexie wore her mother's wedding dress, a lovely gown of tulle and lace that needed only the smallest tailoring at the shoulders to fit perfectly. Thanks to Mrs. Schuman, our skilled seamstress, it was no problem. She hand-sewed my wedding gown out of a pair of white charmeuse curtains that Mrs. Martin found in her attic, and gave it an overlay of batiste from cloth Mrs. Wasserman provided. Mrs. Schuman amazed me with her skill. The gown was fashioned in the Empire style. (Like the ones worn in Jane Austen's day, with the high waist.) I loved it! The skirt fell in a graceful straight line, which made me look taller than I am; and the overlay gave it a flirty, frilly feel—it suited me perfectly.

The bust (the "décolletage," according to Mrs. Schuman) was daringly low, if you ask me. But when I voiced that thought, she said, "That's the Empire style!" And, "If there's any day where it's okay to be daring, it's your wedding day." Later on, she produced a book with pictures of Dolley Madison, and I saw that yes, it really was the style!

Roper and Blake somehow managed to borrow three-piece suits. Both men looked handsome and ruddy—and nervous. Roper's hair was held back off his face and his eyes sparkled at me as I came down the aisle. I know women are considered the fairer sex, but Roper is a gorgeous man. As I took in the sight of him in his suit, smiling at me, I could not believe that he was going to really truly be mine!

Mr. Martin walked between me and Lexie, giving each of us an arm. The "aisle" was a makeshift center beneath the golden-leaved trees, around which folding chairs held all of our compound members.

And though we gave up the idea of having music by opting to hold the ceremony outdoors (instead of inside by the piano) Mrs. Buchanan surprised us by producing an old-fashioned tape player with batteries. They'd been in their storage, she explained, as she started a tape of Bach's "Jesu, Joy of Man's Desiring." "It's not 'The Wedding March,'" she said, apologetically. But Lexie and I were almost in tears just because we had music—beautiful, classical music—at our wedding.

Because Mr. Martin is the head of the compound, after giving each of us a chaste kiss on the cheek, he switched roles and became the officiator. He did the honors of marrying us! He took the words for the ceremony from an old hymnal. At the end, he concluded, "By the authority invested in me from God Almighty—I pronounce you, Jerusha and Andrea, man and wife; and I pronounce you, Blake and Lexie, man and wife."

He stood back. "You may kiss your brides."

Note from the Author:

If this book had been a movie and I could choose the song to play while the ending credits roll, it would be this:

"UBI CARITAS" by Audrey Assad
https://www.youtube.com/watch?v=Z_Pp0jKn1zQ

Also--Don't miss the **short bonus scene ahead,** as well as how to get a **free extra chapter** revealing the fate of Mrs. Patterson (Andrea's mother) and Mr. Washington!

L.R. Burkard

BONUS SCENE

ANDREA

Shortly after we were married, I couldn't resist teasing Roper. "I should call you Jerusha, now. First, because my name is *Mrs. Roper*, which sounds strange since we've been calling you by our last name."

"And second?" he asked, with his blue-grey eyes sparkling at me in amusement.

"Second, because now Jerusha fits! You told me yourself the name means 'taken possession of,' as in, 'married'—and that's what you are." I smiled.

He pulled me close and kissed me. "First, no, don't call me Jerusha because it's still a woman's name. Second, if anything, it fits you more than me, because you are a woman and—much to my delight—you've been taken possession of, as in married." He kissed me again.

"But how can I call you Roper when my name is Mrs. Roper?"

He grinned. "Maybe you should have thought about that before we tied the knot. Or should I say, *rope*?"

Before you go: *Did you enjoy this story?*

A nice way to thank an author is to leave a positive review of a book. People like to know what other readers think before purchasing a copy. Please share your impressions on AMAZON.COM or other online retailers. Also, don't forget to tell your friends on **Goodreads, Facebook or Instagram**!

Thank you!

Read on to get the bonus chapter!

Acknowledgments

I give deepest thanks to the Lord for inspiring me to write *The Pulse Effex Series.* For this third installment, he provided the perfect critique partners. I had writer Dana McNeely who, among other nifty helps, caught me using the present perfect tense far too often and helped tighten my verbs—and thereby the action. (For example, I might have written, "She had seen that book earlier." Dana would change it to, "She saw that book earlier.") Dana has been with me since Book One, *Pulse,* and faithfully gone over every scene I've written.

I had avid reader Deborha Mitchell (and no, that is not a misspelling!) who never failed to cheer me along with her encouraging remarks ("Wow! This chapter was great!") Even better, letting me know the day she caught herself praying for one of the characters as though she were a real person. (To me, they *are* real!) Deb was also the eagle-eye for things such as skipped spaces, missing quotation marks, or other manuscript gaffes.

Then I had Travis Glaze, my acting content editor. His close reading flagged me on continuity issues and kept me on my toes down to the smallest details. Also, his male perspective offered feedback that strengthened the work in ways I could never have orchestrated. Each of these three—Dana, Deb and Travis—spoke into the work and added to its polish.

Finally my husband Mike read each chapter as I churned them out. His firearms expertise (which is certainly superior to mine) added details and helped me avoid errors. While Mike isn't a writer, his general email reply of "Good," after I'd sent a chapter (which at first amused me) became a welcome nod of approval.

Author Kathy Rouser critiqued a portion of the book, challenging me with her thoughtful writerly suggestions. Horsewoman Annalee Adkins proof-read scenes to ensure equine accuracy; Sharon Greene, R.N., kindly advised me on the medical scenes, and last but *definitely not least,* retired U.S.A.F, E.O.D, Mary Kokoszka, gave me generously of her time to explain the ways and means of "IEDs" for the purposes of the book.

(I did one Google search for that information but decided I didn't want the FBI's attention. I read an account where an author's home office was invaded and computers and files confiscated—yikes!—all because she researched her stories dealing with explosives and homeland security on the internet.)

Deepest thanks to Clarissa Bogan, who did the final proof-read of the manuscript. And to my launch team of beta readers who were the first to set eyes on the finished book and provided early reviews—*deepest appreciation!* Your support and encouraging notes meant so much.

Linore Rose Burkard

Linore Rose Burkard wrote a trilogy of regency romances for the Christian market before there were any regencies for the Christian market. Published with Harvest House, her books opened the genre for the CBA. She writes YA/ Suspense as **L.R. Burkard.** Raised in NY, Linore graduated *magna cum laude* from City University. Married with five children, Linore is a homeschooling mother and enjoys swimming, hiking, gardening, and painting. Linore teaches writing workshops and is developing a coaching program for writers who are as yet unpublished.

YOU'VE FINISHED THE BOOK

But you're still wondering: What happened to Andrea's mother (Tiffany Patterson) and Mr. Washington? Download a free bonus chapter to find out! (For best results, copy the link directly into your browser rather than a search engine.)

http://www.LinoreBurkard.com/BonusChapter_Defiance.html

Or, use the shortened link:

http://bit.ly/2qnQWKf

This chapter will not be published in *DEFIANCE*, ever. It is a bonus chapter that you can *only* access through the link. When you do, you'll be automatically entered into a drawing for a free book. Winners announced each month in Linore's newsletter—check your inbox!

KEEP UP WITH BOOK NEWS FROM LINORE

Don't want the free chapter? You can still get book news, articles, writing tips and more from Linore. Join thousands of other readers and writers by adding your email at http://www.LinoreBurkard.com, or at http://www.LRBurkard.com.

MORE BY THIS AUTHOR

Read L.R.Burkard's Regency romances written as Linore Rose Burkard.

Before the Season Ends – The first installment of the Regency Series sparkles with heartwarming and humorous romance in the vein of Georgette Heyer.

The House in Grosvenor Square -- Mystery, perils and adventure—as well as romance—beset Miss Ariana Forsythe, our lovable heroine from ***Before the Season Ends***.

The Country House Courtship—The third installment of the Regency Series finds Beatrice Forsythe, younger sister of Ariana, poised for romance. Two eligible men, one country estate, and one feisty heroine make for a country house courtship like no other!

DEFIANCE

DEFIANCE

Made in the USA
Lexington, KY
07 March 2018